BLOODY PARADISE

Jennifer Wells

ISBN: 979-8869374349

INDEX

* * *

PART 1

BLOODY FELALAKAS

CHAPTER 1

The Dream Land

After parting ways, Cora embarked on her journey to Felalakas.

"Are you sad?" Onyx asked.

"What?" Cora responded.

Onyx observed Cora's expression and asked again, "Are you sad?"

Cora shook her head. She had been prepared to separate from Ray and Flame from the very beginning.

Onyx chuckled knowingly. "I see... he seems pretty sad, though."

The "he" he referred to was obviously Ray.

Cora furrowed her brow, appearing perplexed.

"He is an Aberrant. He can take care of himself. No need to be sad."

The two of them were clearly talking about different things.

Onyx found it amusing and warned Cora, "Corara, I warn you, we only have one wheelchair!"

Cora retorted, "Don't call me Corara!"

Upon returning to their base, they saw two military trucks parked at the entrance.

Jeremy had given them ten minutes to pack up before their scheduled departure.

Cora had nothing but a backpack as her belongings, keeping it light.

As they left, she noticed the logistics personnel moving several large and small suitcases.

What caught her attention was that the members of Azure, like herself, were traveling light.

They seemed to have nothing to carry.

Cora remembered the powerful mobile artillery she had seen near the formation's eyes, which could obliterate zombies.

She turned to Onyx for answers.

Onyx simply replied, "Anopower with spatial containers."

The military possessed spatial containers.

Cora would eventually learn about them.

Cora eagerly inquired about the containers, causing Onyx to eventually hand her an amulet he had got from Yara.

After a brief period of introspection, she learned to use her psychic abilities to open and close it at will. She became engrossed in experimenting with it, even walking clumsily as she played with it until she got on the second truck.

The back of the second truck was spacious, and someone had turned on the radio.

The melodious song wafted through the air from the speakers.

Cora noticed that Maeda, who sat across from her, had a rare and pleasant smile on his face.

It was the first time she had seen him smile, and her curiosity blazed within her.

She slyly tugged on Onyx's sleeve to get him to notice, as well.

As the catchy melody gradually ended, the person by the radio attempted to change the song, but a junior team member named Patrick Shawn stopped him.

"Hey! Don't change it. The deputy commander loves this song; it's his goddess!"

"Whose goddess?" Payne asked.

"Yuui Hayashi, you guys know her? She's Felalakas' number one sweet songstress, a big star in District C."

"Oh! I've heard of her!" William chimed in.

The three of them huddled together and discussed the song's lyrics, humorously butchering them.

Maeda had a displeased look.

Suddenly, Maeda punched the truck's wall, scowling. He muttered something in his local dialect at a rapid pace.

The others' faces turned red, and Payne and Patrick struggled to contain their laughter.

Apart from this slightly discordant moment, the atmosphere in the truck was relaxed.

Cora saw several members of Azure bringing damaged uniforms to a middle-aged man in the corner.

Vincent had once exclaimed in disbelief, "What? A grown man's Anopower is sewing?"

This man, Florian Richter, was an E-rank Aberrant.

His Anopower, similar to "sewing," could mend two different things together.

Florian had a slender figure, sparse eyebrows, and frequently darting eyes, giving him a shifty appearance.

As Onyx aptly put it, Florian had "shifty eyes."

Although Onyx was known for his sharp tongue, this description was spot-on.

After meeting Florian, Cora was forced to accept that a person's awakened Anopower was indeed entirely random.

As the sun rose on the horizon, the two trucks raced forward, as if chasing the morning light.

It was the most relaxing morning Cora had experienced since doomsday.

There were no zombies, no insect swarms, and no endless slaughter.

Bathed in sunlight, Cora quietly whispered to herself, "Onward to C83 District!"

After three days and two nights of traveling, Jeremy and his team safely reached the outskirts of Felalakas.

Cora eagerly stuck her head out of the car window, and the cool breeze ruffled her shoulder-length black hair.

In the distance, they could glimpse Felalakas.

Huge neon signs floated in the sky, a dazzling Ferris wheel sparkled like a diamond ring; high-frequency searchlights mixed with balloons and streamers; and futuristic holographic billboards continually displayed changing images; steam-powered airships weaved between many skyscrapers.

Felalakas truly lived up to its reputation as a C-grade city, significantly ahead of Flower City in terms of technological advancements.

As their trucks entered the city's main road, they were met with empty roads and no hindrance.

A wandering musician playing the guitar by the city gates spotted them and greeted them with a brilliant smile.

He circled the vehicles while singing, accompanied by lively dance moves, "Felalakas, the free Felalakas, it's the dream you never want to leave!"

Their extravagant performance startled Cora and withdrew her head silently.

After a while, she asked Onyx softly, "Aren't there any safety checks here? This is a C-district, after all. Even F District has checkpoints!"

Onyx was also looking outside, the hazy lights casting intriguing shadows on his face.

"Felalakas prides itself on freedom and art, welcoming travelers from all walks of life."

"However, the welcome is one thing, but being allowed to stay is another."

Indeed, Felalakas had excellent security, and the city was bustling with people.

There wasn't a zombie in sight, making it seem like the apocalyptic events they had experienced in Flower City were just an illusion.

The two trucks finally stopped on the outskirts of the square.

Further into the city, the streets were narrow and teeming with people, making it impossible for them to proceed.

When Cora got off the truck, dozens of flashy motorcycles raced by her, creating a cacophony.

Even after the convoy had pulled away a few meters, the energetic music still resonated in her ears.

Cora looked up and saw the streets adorned with colorful neon signs that continually flashed, almost blinding her.

Gazing higher, she saw towering skyscrapers, their steel and concrete exteriors imposing an invisible weight on the city in the night's dim purple haze.

As Jeremy and his team disembarked and walked a few steps, the clock in Felalakas's skyline struck eight o'clock.

"Dang—dang—dang—"

After three chimes, everyone on the streets and in the skyscrapers stopped what they were doing, gazing upward.

Amidst the multitude of airships, a massive spotlight projected a holographic image between two tall towers.

A slender figure gradually materialized, becoming clearer.

With resplendent, golden hair, a flawless face, and dressed in a pristine white suit, the person's appearance was so beautiful and ethereal that it was difficult to determine their gender at first glance.

The individual extended a hand over their chest in an exquisitely graceful gesture and said, "I am delighted that new travelers have arrived in Felalakas."

Their sapphire eyes swept over the crowd, a faint smile playing at the corner of their lips.

"Let us welcome them to the true paradise!"

"Mmm... how about we sing 'Paradise'?"

The crowd erupted in cheers, whistles, and thunderous applause.

The atmosphere in the square was extremely lively.

The person extended their right hand and made a casual motion, causing the surroundings to take on a hazy appearance.

Cora suddenly saw thousands of blossoms blooming, heard an enchanting siren-like song, and a three-dimensional sound enveloped everyone's ears.

The entire city was immersed in a tidal wave of music.

The crowd went wild, their eyes filled with fascination. They treated the person as the supreme idol, shouting at the top of their lungs.

"Ilia! Ilia! Ilia!"

"All right. The celebration is over. Before I go, let me share a little secret: The Throne Tournament (T.T.T.) is currently open to registration. Ilia has prepared generous prizes. Please remember to participate!"

Ilia playfully winked, causing another wave of enthusiastic cheers.

When the spotlight faded, the holographic projection disappeared, along with Ilia.

However, the impact Ilia had brought continued to linger.

The citizens of Felalakas gazed longingly toward the towers, lamenting how quickly the time had passed.

Cora was astonished. Was this person some kind of superstar?

"Captain Wolf, who is that?" someone from the logistics team couldn't help but ask.

Jeremy gazed in the direction where the person had disappeared for a few seconds before speaking solemnly, "Ilia, the governor of C83 District and the lord of Felalakas."

"Is he... impressive?" Why were so many people going crazy for him?

"It's not 'him'. it's 'it'."

Onyx corrected and used a gender-neutral term in the Alliance's common language.

"Ilia is artificial intelligence."

Felalakas, C83 District, the city of music and art, was also the only city in the Alliance completely governed by artificial intelligence.

The citizens elected the city's mayor.

Ilia originally started as the most popular virtual idol in Felalakas.

In one city mayoral election, Ilia's name somehow appeared in the last list of five candidates, alongside a group of hypocritical and politically astute politicians, making them seem out of place.

It was just a heap of data making up trash, so even if they had some popularity, did they really think they could replace humans so arrogantly?

At first, the competing politicians found it unbelievable.

Then they cursed, "Damn it, have all these artists in Felalakas gone mad?"

Ridiculous! It's child's play!

But the reality was quite the opposite.

After Ilia was elected, Felalakas thrived, and even the crime rate steadily decreased.

In Felalakas, everyone had heard one saying.

"Ilia knows everything."

Whatever you did, it was under the watchful eye of artificial intelligence.

CHAPTER 2

Registration Woes

Jeremy had a mission at hand. After giving some simple instructions, he was ready to lead Azure's people away.

He left with a sense of ease, while the members of the logistics team had tears in their eyes, deeply reluctant to see him go. Jeremy had rescued them from a dire situation, guided them to safety, and delivered them to the peaceful District C. He went above and beyond his duty.

Once separated from Azure's group, Cora and Onyx opted for independent action.

Felalakas was an open and inclusive city, with capsule sleep pods scattered throughout the streets for the convenience of wandering travelers.

Not only were they free to use, but they were also easy to access, requiring only a facial scan.

With the late hour, Cora and Onyx booked separate rooms for a night's rest.

In the following morning, after a quick freshening up, they headed straight for the Aberrants Registration Center. The center was tucked away in a discreet alley on the west side of the square, its architectural style matching the city's vibrant theme. The only thing that seemed aged was its sign.

Upon entering, they encountered a spacious mezzanine, with a few individuals moving about.

Spiral staircases extended to the elevated central desk, where a bespectacled female staff member was sitting there.

As Cora approached, she couldn't help but hear some delightful melodies. She looked down to find a familiar holographic display on a small transparent screen.

It was none other than Ilia, who had been performing earlier. The receptionist watched it with rapt attention, a gleeful smile on her face.

"Hello, I'd like to register as an Aberrant."

The young woman promptly turned off the holographic display and handed Cora a booklet.

"Start by filling out this form. You'll need to complete every item on the first three pages, but the rest is optional. After that, head to the first room on the left for a photo, the second room on the right for genetic testing. Proceed to the second floor for an on-site Anopower check. Once you've completed all these steps, return to me. Oh, and bring all the receipts."

The rapid instructions left Cora somewhat disoriented.

She could only remember half of what was said.

Thankfully, Onyx had an excellent memory and kept track of the instructions.

Cora followed the staff's directions, first meticulously filling out the form and then heading for her photograph.

She felt nervous during the photo session and sat awkwardly, her posture stiff and her lips barely curving, emanating an air of distress.

Luckily, there was no human photographer present, only a robotic arm operating the camera.

The unfeeling electronic voice repeatedly sounded errors.

"Beep—Tilt your head to the right, please."

"Beep—We've detected excessive stiffness in your expression. Relax and tilt your head to the right, please."

"Beep—The system couldn't detect the subject. Return to the center of the frame, please."

Cora's attempts at cooperation left her feeling dizzy, and Onyx couldn't stop laughing for a good two minutes.

After the photo session, Cora proceeded to the second room for blood sampling and genetic testing.

Felalakas had a specialized Anopower measurement device,

significantly superior to the faulty one Jeremy possessed.

It not only assessed Anopower levels but also calculated the potential upper limit Anopower could reach in the future.

Next was the Anopower verification room on the second floor.

Here, the primary purpose was to create a local record for future reference.

Cora finally encountered some individuals in this room, where three assessors, two men and one woman, sat in a row.

The person in front would exit, and shortly afterward, a "Next" call could be heard.

Cora entered the room and found herself inside a four-walled isolation chamber, with a glass window in front.

The green light on the wall-mounted speaker signaled they could see and hear her.

One assessor began speaking.

"Please show your Anopower. We have top-level security measures. Release your Anopower to the fullest extent of our assessment."

Cora's hand touched the table, and after a couple of seconds, the table vanished, revealing a long spear in her hand. She stood obediently in her place.

The assessors were momentarily taken aback. "Is that it?"

Cora nodded.

If displaying her Anopower was the requirement, she had successfully fulfilled it.

"Is there a way to change an object's shape? Could this be considered a support-type Anopower? Perhaps it could help the engineering department with debris cleanup?"

"I have a lot of unused furniture at home; I was just thinking I couldn't find anyone to clean it up."

"If you put it that way, this Anopower seems quite practical, right?"

"Practical garbage collector, isn't that a great idea!"

"Seriously, if she's an E-rank, I might consider hiring an Aberrant to take out my trash every day. That doesn't sound too bad."

Two assessors exchanged glances, finding their own humor quite irresistible, and burst into laughter.

All these individuals seemed oblivious to Onyx's exceptional abilities.

At least Onyx could determine Cora's Anopower category correctly with just one glance.

Cora, growing bored, began playing with the object in her hand.

The long spear emitted a faint blue light as it moved around.

The other assessor seemed to notice something and raised her head, surveying Cora's Ethereal gun.

"The weapon you have, it looks like an old-world melee weapon, right? Does it have any offensive capabilities, or is it more of a decorative piece?"

With one hand, Cora held the weapon but had no intention of using it. She just directed it forward for a simple thrust.

"Swish."

Supposedly with top-notch security, the wall cracked deeply, and a powerful shockwave passed through, knocking over the assessors' papers and rating sheets.

Cora regretted her display of force as the three assessors sat in silence.

"Ahem... Alright, it's good. Confirmed as a highly offensive Anopower. We'll need the results from the genetic test to determine the specific rank."

"Um, can I... get out now?" Cora cautiously took a step forward, intending to cross over the broken glass to retrieve her registration form.

"Don't come out!!"

"The door is in the back!"

The two assessors shouted in fear, and their chairs quickly rolled backward. They scribbled something on Cora's form and promptly handed it to a mechanical arm to transport it back inside the isolation chamber.

"S-submit it at the main desk."

When Cora returned, the young woman was once again immersed in her own world, sneakily watching precious recordings of Ilia's past performances.

Cora placed the registration form on the table, scanned it briefly, and continued in a somewhat formal tone, "The results of the genetic test will be ready in three working days. You can come back to collect your Anopower card then. For now, please make the payment. The total fee is 10,000 NPA credits."

"Huh?" Cora asked, baffled. "10,000 for what?"

"Onetime registration fee, 10,000 NPA credits," the young woman replied with a hint of impatience.

Cora was taken aback.

Oh no! Why didn't anyone tell her that registering as an Aberrant costs money?

The young woman probably hadn't encountered someone so clueless before.

She appeared somewhat bewildered herself.

"Of course, there's a fee. We need to cover the costs of the Anopower testing machine, the AI algorithms, and daily maintenance. We aren't a charity organization."

Cora was in a bind. She didn't have the money. She looked at Onyx with a perplexed expression, as if asking him if he had any money.

For the first time, Onyx couldn't provide an answer to Cora's question. He didn't have any money either.

However, he couldn't be blamed for it.

First, he had never needed to consider money because of his upbringing. And second, he had encountered no one as financially challenged as Cora among the people he knew.

Two broke individuals found themselves in the same predicament. They were both deep in thought.

Perhaps feeling sorry for her, the young woman offered a suggestion, "Well, since you're an Aberrant, you can take on some assignments. Start with any random task to earn some money first and then come back for registration."

"Assignments?"

"Yes, take a left when you exit, walk 100 meters straight, and you'll find the Special Affairs Assignment Center."

Felalakas, the Special Affairs Assignment Center.

This was an impressive building, and it was quite clear that the people coming and going from it exuded a powerful aura, with the majority being Aberrants.

A muscular man with a bald head, whose arm was as thick as Cora's waist, was sitting on a sculpture at the entrance.

His legs were spread wide, his arms were folded, and his beady little eyes looked Cora and Onyx up and down with disdain and contempt.

"Babies and a cripple, are you brave enough to enter any place? Do you think this is a daycare?"

The bald man was robust, seemingly a physical-type Aberrant. He had a loud voice and spoke intentionally for them to hear.

Onyx gave him an icy smile, looking at him with a calm expression.

Cora felt a chill run down her spine

Whenever Onyx showed this kind of supervillain smile, someone was about to face trouble.

But they didn't have time to act because, suddenly, several thick vines flew.

"Smack, smack, smack." They struck the bald man's face multiple times, and then one vine coiled around him and flung him headfirst into a fountain, creating a loud splash.

A striking red-haired woman burst out of the building in anger. "Hey! You idiot, how dare you sit your dirty butt on my idol's head!!!"

The muscular man had lost two teeth because of the surprise attack, and his mouth was filled with blood. Furious, he charged at the woman.

The two of them unleashed their Anopower, and their psychic abilities clashed, leading to a public brawl in front of the Special Affairs Assignment Center. Others didn't find this surprising at all. Some individuals came out specifically to watch the excitement.

"What's wrong with that bald guy? He provoked Chiho Sato, that baffling lady."

"Do you not know about Sato? The only thing that can provoke her is saying bad words about River Locke, one of Felalakas' top ten supernovas. Apparently, he has a massive fan club. And his rich fans sponsor this lifelike-1:1 statue of him. Sitting on that statue is like crapping on Sato's head. She'll probably tear him apart."

"Fan clubs are terrifying."

Sato and the bald man kept fighting, and the situation escalated, with leaves flying, dust swirling, and even the stone walls of the fountain were damaged.

Soon, another man in a uniform came out of the building. With an exasperated look, he took out a computer and started typing furiously.

"Repair cost. 124,000 NPA credits. Would you like to pay at the terminal, or shall I deduct it from your assignment points?"

"Why should I pay? He hit me!" The bald man not only got a beating but also had to pay for damages. He was disheveled, and his eyes were as big as saucers.

As the scene outside the building quieted down, Cora finally squeezed into the lobby.

As expected of the Special Affairs Assignment Center for District C's Aberrants, it was high-tech and modern.

An enormous floating screen displayed various assignments, and above it, holographic projections occasionally flashed with colorful announcements like, "Congratulations to 'The Boss and His Three Goons' Team for completing B-rank Assignment xxxx!"

"The Boss and His Three Goons"? What kind of weird team name was that?

The lobby was equipped with hundreds of self-service terminals where people could check, accept, or submit assignments by swiping their Aberrant IDs.

Notably, the assignments here were not exclusive to Aberrants.

If regular people met the strength requirements and had the courage, they could team up with Aberrants for the tasks.

Cora sighed. "No one's asking for my help. No one wants to team up with me."

Onyx suggested she write her advantages and raise a sign, trying to attract potential teammates.

Cora, with her straightforward and simple language, wrote four words.

"I can really fight."

"Alright, as long as you're happy."

Regrettably, this tactic had little effect.

Most Aberrants ignored her, not even sparing a glance.

Occasionally, someone who had too much free time would pass by, look at the sign, and burst into laughter.

Cora was frustrated.

If only she could speak clearly, she would probably question them.

"What are you laughing at? I can really fight. Don't believe me? Let's have a see."

After spending the whole day squatting in a corner, no one approached her.

Cora realized that most of the people who frequented the center already had fixed team members and established methods of sharing rewards.

They were very cautious about letting strangers join, and even if they wanted to find new members, they preferred strong, physically capable men.

At a glance, Cora, who appeared thin and was accompanied by a limping sidekick, didn't seem competitive.

Cora was not giving up.

If nobody wanted her, she would create her own team, right?

Tearing down the "I can really fight" sign, she confidently walked to the service window, ready to apply to form a team.

That's when she learned about another unfortunate obstacle—forming a team required at least two Aberrants.

Now, Cora was trapped in a never-ending loop.

She needed money to register as an Aberrant. She needed to work to earn money. She needed a team to work, but she needed to register as an Aberrant first. In order to form a team, she needed at least two Aberrants.

This perfectly created a Mobius loop, a never-ending cycle with no way out.

After an entire day of futile efforts, Cora sat on the ground, feeling defeated. She would remain in the shadows, unregistered.

Onyx, who had accompanied her through all of this, tried to comfort her.

"Don't be so disheartened; it's just about forming a team."

Cora looked despondent. "No one wants to form a team with me."

"Why not? You already have a potential teammate, don't you?"

Cora looked up and her eyes lit up. "Who?"

Onyx smirked mysteriously. "This person, he's not dazzling, has a temper, and is worthless more than filling up the numbers."

CHAPTER 3

Little Trickster

The person Onyx mentioned as someone to "make do with" was Damian.

Before parting ways, Damian secretly slipped a note to Cora, with an address where he was staying temporarily, suggesting that Cora could come to visit him whenever she had the time.

Cora and Onyx visited Damian at the provided location, only to find out that it was a seven-star hotel!

The place was luxurious, with a grand white dome, a year-round blooming garden, and stunning high-altitude views.

It looked expensive, and tight security prevented external visitors from entering.

So, they had no choice but to contact a robotic butler and waited for a chilling twenty minutes.

Finally, Damian descended gracefully to greet them, wearing a colorful coat that looked like a fluttering butterfly.

"Sis Cora!" he exclaimed.

Damian promptly hugged Cora, with his eyes twinkling and a sweet smile on his face.

But suddenly, he noticed Onyx standing beside them.

Damian's expression twisted.

He held back his words for a moment, his smile froze on his lips, and frustration crept into his tone.

"Why is he here?"

Cora was puzzled. "What's the matter?"

After Cora explained the situation, Damian understood Onyx had been accompanying her for some time.

He reluctantly said, "Oh," and led both of them upstairs.

Upon entering the room, Cora was left in awe.

Damian was staying in a suite with all the amenities one could dream of: 24-hour hot water, round-the-clock dining services, access to the latest holographic entertainment, and even entertainment rooms, a swimming pool, and a gym.

Cora, dumbfounded, sank onto the couch, feeling like she had landed in a soft cloud.

Damian brought a bunch of snacks and drinks as if he was offering treasures.

Cora asked with astonishment, "Why are you staying here?"

Damian innocently blinked his eyes, "My dad had a lot of money in Aban Bank."

Aban Bank was a well-known commercial bank in NPA with branches in various cities and regions.

With Victor Blackwood gone, Damian was the legal heir to his inheritance. This is something everyone seemed to understand. But that a ten-year-old child possessed such astonishing wealth was bound to attract envious eyes.

Damian had kept this secret when he was part of the logistics team.

He had always seemed like a timid little rabbit, happily munching on whatever snacks he had without giving away any hints. Everyone assumed that he, like Cora, had come from the underprivileged F district and had never seen the world.

"How did you know about this hotel?" Cora was still puzzled.

"I came here with my dad to watch a concert before," Damian replied nonchalantly.

So, it turned out that the truly impoverished person was herself.

Cora munched on the delicious snacks, her mood even more melancholic.

"Sis Cora, why did you come to find me?"

Damian snuggled up beside Cora, leaning against her thigh, asking in a soft voice.

He felt close to Cora. Perhaps a child's intuition was naturally accurate, or perhaps it was because they both hailed from the F district.

Cora was strong and gentle, and Damian had faith that she wouldn't harm him.

Stumbling over her words, Cora explained she needed his help to form a team to meet the required number of members.

She quickly added, "But you don't need to do the tasks; I can do them on my own."

After hearing Cora's request, Damian thought for a moment and readily agreed, "Sure, Cora, sis, I'll team up with you. This way, we'll have two Aberrants, and two... two...?"

He jumped up with a "whew!", pointing at Onyx.

"Two Aberrants?! He's not just..."

Onyx, leaning elegantly by the window, sipped his tea gracefully, looking completely composed.

Cora turned her head to look at him, confused. "What about him?"

Damian looked at Onyx, then at Cora, his speech interrupted and an expression that said "I get it," appearing on his face.

"Sis, are you hungry? I'm hungry. Can you please order some food? There's a service machine in the living room."

Cora found herself inexplicably assigned to place the food order.

The room was now empty, leaving just the two of them.

Damian paced back and forth, hands behind his back, a self-satisfied air about him. He seemed like a little adult who had just found something incredible to hold over Onyx.

"You never told my Cora you're an Aberrant."

Onyx responded calmly, "That's right. She didn't ask, so I didn't have any chance to tell her."

Damian, of course, didn't believe it. He stuck his tongue out contemptuously, his little face scrunched up.

"You're lying to kids!"

"Clearly, you're an Aberrant yourself, pretending to be all helpless and confined to a wheelchair."

"You're afraid that if you tell her, she won't want you anymore, and I'll have to fend for myself. You're shameless!"

Onyx placed his teacup on the table, making a crisp "clink" sound with an unwavering expression. "Saying you're brainless would be a grave insult."

He interlocked his fingers over his stomach, a smug smile as he threatened Damian, "I bet that even if I tell Cora that I'm an Aberrant, given the bond we share, she'll still take me along. But you? You've been acting so innocent all this time. Now that she knows you're a scheming little mastermind at such a young age, well, let me think... she probably won't run to your rescue in time, will she?"

Damian was taken aback. "You!"

"You! You, you, you!" He rambled, making no coherent point, and ended up stomping his feet in frustration.

"You're a bad guy!"

When Cora returned, Damian glared at Onyx, still catching his breath, as if he had been in a heated argument.

"I'm back."

Damian twisted his head, changing his expression even faster than flipping through a book, putting on a smile as sweet as honey.

"Sis, why don't you stay here? There are so many vacant rooms, and I get scared all by myself."

A luxury hotel was certainly more comfortable than a capsule warehouse, so Cora didn't hesitate to thank Damian.

Damian jumped up with delight, eager to show Cora around the rooms. But when he turned, he noticed Onyx had followed them.

He immediately opened his arms, guarding the doorway like a protective little chick.

"What are you still doing here?"

"You can stay outside. You're not welcome here."

Cora felt torn. She had promised to take care of Onyx's leg. She couldn't just leave him alone in a comfortable room.

If Damian really didn't want to keep Onyx, then she... she might have to sleep in the capsule warehouse with him.

She was about to speak, but Onyx casually adjusted the blanket on his lap.

"Little trickster."

"Wha-Ha-wha!"

Damian protested in a fit of frustration, completely under Onyx's control.

In the end, the two of them successfully stayed.

Yet Cora couldn't shake the feeling that something was amiss.

In just a few days, Damian's personality seemed to have undergone some changes, and she wondered when Damian and Onyx had become so close.

The next day, the three of them set off again to the Commission Center.

Damian skipped and hopped like he was going shopping.

"Sis, once we're done forming our team, let's go eat something delicious! My dad took me to a place..."

A person rushed towards them, accidentally bumping into Damian, who almost fell.

Cora reached out to support him.

The person mumbled, "Sorry," and quickly dashed past them in another direction.

"What happened?" Curious heads poked out from the shops along the road.

"There are zombies up ahead!" The excited man yelled.

Cora was taken aback. She was almost certain she had heard, "There's something delicious up ahead," not "zombies."

Were people in Felalakas so thrilled about zombies?

"Should we see?" Cora asked for her companions' opinions.

Onyx and Damian nodded in agreement.

The three followed the crowd and soon arrived at the scene.

In the center of the crowd, a large zombie was tied up with ropes, struggling and growling like a trapped beast.

It had visible knife wounds, carvings, and bruises from the ropes.

Different people held the ends of the ropes, their faces filled with excitement, cruelty, and an indescribable desire to act.

A burly man stepped forward, planted his foot on the zombie's head, spat on its face, and then raised his arms to cheer.

The others cheered as well, as if he were some kind of legendary hero.

Cora couldn't help but frown.

Damian held her hand, whispering in a small voice, scared, and hiding behind her.

Soon, a mechanized forklift with a special identification number emblazoned on its side roared in. A massive iron cage descended from the sky, trapping the zombie, and then it soared away.

"Why didn't they kill it?" Cora whispered.

The people nearby, overhearing her question, gave her a sideways glance. "Newcomer, huh?"

"Kill it? That's so crude, and completely lacking in artistry."

"This is T.T.T., exceptional nutrition!"

CHAPTER 4

T.T.T.

T.T.T.?

The day they entered the city, Ilia mentioned this term.

But they were too stunned by the artificial intelligence's identity to pay much attention.

What's the deal with "nutrition"?

The citizens of Felalakas had a completely different attitude toward zombies compared to the people Cora encountered in F and D districts.

It exuded an almost fanatical hunting enthusiasm.

Onyx leaned down from his wheelchair, his long fingers picking up a poster covered in countless footprints.

He stared at the text and slowly read aloud, "A smooth road only makes you mediocre. Only fire and thorns can temper the true crown of a king."

"The Throne Tournament, accepting registrations, there's an address on the back!"

Damian chimed in with his little head.

"If you're curious, you can check it out," Onyx suggested.

Cora nodded.

Once she sorted out her Aberrants Certificate and resolved the identity issue, she'd go check out this T.T.T.

But for now, they needed to form their team in the Commission Hall.

The three of them returned to the Special Affairs Commission Center once more.

It was only a day, but the damaged fountain outside was already repaired, its surface as good as new.

The efficiency was astonishing. The compensation from the bald guy and Sato were not in vain.

As Cora stepped into the hall, she noticed a crowd gathered in front of the screen.

Excited remarks came one after the other.

"It's 'The Boss and His Three Goons' again. How many B-level missions have they completed now? They're advancing so quickly; they must have over a thousand points soon."

Cora paused for a moment.

The odd team name seemed vaguely familiar.

She glanced at the holographic screen in front of her, and sure enough, as if replaying yesterday, a new announcement flashed on the screen. "Congratulations to 'The Boss and His Three Goons' team for completing B-level mission xxxx!"

They were also leading the overall points with a score of 966.

The ranking of commission tasks had corresponding NPA coin rewards, as well as different point values.

The simplest E-level mission was worth 2 points, and the point value increased as you went up in ranks, with D-level at 10 points, C-level at 50 points, B-level at 200 points, and even an A-level mission was worth 1000 points.

As for the legendary S-level missions, none had appeared, and it was rumored that their point values had no limits.

Given "The Boss and His Three Goons" team's climbing speed, reaching 966 points so quickly showed they had completed at least three or more B-level missions. Their strength was undeniable, and their momentum was unmatched.

Their goal was also quite clear: Aiming straight for access to the B district.

Cities above the NPA C-grade had strict access restrictions.

Regular folks wanting to enter a non-residential C district had to apply for short-term entry permits for reasons like sightseeing, visiting family, or official business.

If the permit expired or you entered without one illegally, you'd become a "straggler," wanted by the NPA's Civil Registry Division.

Out of the 50 C districts, only C83, the art-loving and free-spirited Felalakas, welcomed all travelers from afar.

Even residents of C districts found it challenging to change their residency.

The entry reviews between different cities were very strict. C district residents trying to enter B districts was even more challenging, like trying to reach the heavens.

Before Doomsday, joining Azures might have been a shortcut.

But with the chaos of society breaking down, more and more people were awakening Anopower.

New rules had been established, and the NPA had recently issued an official announcement.

Aberrants could be naturalized into B districts based on points. However, the required number was quite daunting, with a whole 500,000 points needed to move from C to B districts.

Cora had an unspoken wish. She wanted to get out of here.

From childhood to adulthood, she had barely left F199 district. The farthest she had been was to Mount Yue (E104 district) and Flower City (D56 district).

After forming a team this time, she wanted to try her hand at B-level missions.

Even if they weren't as remarkable as "The Boss and His Three Goons," she could slowly accumulate points. Perhaps one day, she'd have the chance to go to the B district.

With dreams of a brighter future, Cora approached the service window.

"Hello, I'd like to... start a team."

Inside, a middle-aged woman in uniform pushed her glasses up, briefly casting a glance at Cora.

Her gaze quickly shifted to Damian's fluffy head for a second, then to Onyx's legs for another, lingered on his face for two seconds, and finally settled back on Cora.

A girl of seventeen or eighteen, a well-behaved little boy, and a... wheelchair-bound individual?

She had been working here for five or six years and considered herself keen-eyed, but this was the first time she couldn't tell which of these three was an Aberrants.

"Who's the team captain?"

"Huh?"

"Regardless of who the captain is, the captain needs to show their AC."

"Huh?"

Cora stood there, dumbfounded.

Weren't they supposed to let regular people form teams for missions? Why were they asking for her Aberrants Certificate?

The staff member looked skeptical.

"Anyone can be a team member, but the captain has to be an Aberrants. How else will you accept and complete missions? You need to present your certificate; all terminals require it."

"Huh?"

The staff member thought she was a rebellious, wayward teenager who had strayed. She attempted to counsel her with a sad expression.

"Honey, you don't seem like an Aberrants, do you? Look at the three of you... sigh. Commission missions are very dangerous. You should go home with your little brothers and enjoy a concert or buy some pretty dresses instead. A peaceful life would be so much better."

"If my daughter ever acted like you, oh my, I'd be furious."

Cora was confused.

What can I do? How else can I do this? I just want to form a team. Why is it so difficult?!

Cora was left speechless. She felt like her thoughts were in disarray.

Her entire world darkened.

Next to the fountain, Cora sat down dejectedly.

Her fair chin rested on the back of Onyx's wheelchair, and she had a look of despair.

Onyx, not used to seeing her like this, patted her head gently and said, "Don't lose heart. There might be another way, and maybe some 'kind-hearted people' will help us?"

Damian crouched nearby, playing with the water. He reached his fingers into the pool, and the surface immediately froze. He pulled out an icicle the size of a finger and was ecstatic, playing with it happily.

Soon, all ten of his fingers were solidly frozen.

"Sis, why don't you just register for an Aberrants Certificate?" Damian asked.

"Because I don't have the money," Cora replied weakly.

"Is it a lot of money?" Damian inquired.

Cora nodded firmly. "Yeah, it's 10,000 NPA coins."

Damian waved his hand, and the icicle fell with a rustle, revealing ten pale fingers.

"Sis, let me just transfer the money to you."

"Why don't you register for the Aberrants Certificate first? Then we can form a team."

"It's your money." Cora refused.

She couldn't just spend someone else's money, especially since Damian was just a child.

"It's okay, sis, look, I have lots and lots of money." Damian handed her his new terminal.

Cora spotted a long string of zeros that seemed endless.

All right, let's correct that.

Damian was a "very wealthy" child.

Cora still shook her head.

However, Damian thought his idea was brilliant. He pleaded softly, "Sis, just consider it a loan. After you finish that... commission, you can give it back to me, okay?"

"I want to register as an Aberrants too, sis. Will you take me?"

Cora was cornered by his coaxing. "Then I'll, um, borrow it from you."

She reached into her bag, lifted her chin off Onyx's wheelchair, found a piece of paper, and wrote a formal IOU.

"Sure, sure," Damian said happily. "Shall we go now?"

Saying this, he discreetly glanced at Onyx, like a proud little peacock, chin held high. "Hmph!"

Onyx, amused, didn't say a word.

Like a little fish, Damian was caught, hook, line, and sinker.

He was kind-hearted, so he didn't want to burst Damian's bubble.

With Damian's support as a young millionaire, things suddenly became much easier.

Soon enough, Cora went through the process again and got her AC-a small, official badge-shaped terminal that could circulate in C districts, with the Felalakas Special Affairs Agency engraved on it.

Compared to Yara's silvery B district terminal, it was less advanced in terms of both appearance and functionality.

It was like the difference between a basic civilian model and a luxury limited edition.

But Cora cherished it; it was her official identification, and she was no longer living in the shadows.

The staff member who had lazily assumed Cora was a "delinquent girl" checked her AC repeatedly. Finally, she pursed her lips and submitted the team formation request in the system.

"Input your team name."

Cora looked back to consult her teammates.

"You're the team captain; you decide," Onyx said, with an attitude that suggested he'd follow her lead.

"Sis, I can't think of one." Damian scratched his head.

Cora was speechless again: I can't think of one, either.

Suddenly, she understood why "The Boss and His Three Goons" had that name. Naming was genuinely challenging.

The staff member saw Cora struggling and said casually, "If you can't think of one, you can use a number. Let me see. You're the 777th registered Aberrants team in Felalakas."

The digits on the screen scrolled to '00777,' right next to the full name of Felalakas Special Affairs Agency.

"So, uh, F777."

On the 2nd of October, New Calendar Year 46, on an ordinary day, that Aberrants team, who would later awe the entire NPA, F777, was founded in the most ordinary manner.

The initial team had three members: Cora (Metal-type Aberrants, level unknown); Damian (Ice-type Aberrants, level unknown); and the "normal" human, Onyx.

The first thing F777 did after its formation was to tackle the B-class mission that had caught Cora's eye.

Cora swiped her AC card at the self-service terminal, sifted through the long list of tasks, and was relieved to find that anyone else had n't claimed it.

The Municipal Hall in Glass Port (D139 district) posted this mission and offered a reward of 2,000 NPA coins and 200 team points.

The earliest posting date was September 25th.

"Help us clear out the zombies on the first floor; we're trapped in the office and can't get out."

September 27th, the mission was updated.

"Is there anyone to rescue us? We're running low on food!"

September 30th, the mission updated again.

"Urgent!!! Zombies are right outside the door; we can't hold on much longer. Anyone, please help!!!"

Today was already October 2nd, and the mission hadn't been updated since then.

Cora checked the system and found that Glass Port had many mission requests, most of which were related to zombies.

The situation there was quite dire.

She turned to Onyx. "D139 district, do you know about it?"

In her mind, there was nothing Onyx didn't know.

Sure enough, Onyx pondered for a moment and said, "Glass Port? Well, it's a resort city in D district known for its maze-like architectural style. It has a complex, labyrinthine interior, and it's easy to get lost inside. It's like Flower City, both of which have won the city planning competition's gold award."

"A maze?" Cora's eyes were bewildered.

She couldn't even distinguish north from south.

No wonder this mission was so urgent, yet no one had taken it.

Onyx smiled. "If it's just a replica of a maze, even if it's a veritable maze, it would be a little difficult to trap me."

With that assurance, Cora confidently selected "Accept Mission," and clicked "Confirm."

Suddenly, the terminal screen projected a message.

"It's detected that your current location is in C83 district. The mission's format has changed. Please refresh and complete it according to local requirements; otherwise, the mission will be marked as a failure. Thank you for your understanding and cooperation."

What did this mean?

Cora refreshed the screen, and a new message appeared.

"To support T.T.T.'s event, please attempt to capture zombies and bring them back to Felalakas. For this mission, you can apply for a free transport vehicle :)"

Capture... zombies?

And what was that :) all about?

Onyx and Damian both noticed this message.

Damian was relatively calm about it, but Onyx let out a mocking laugh.

"Interesting."

What was initially a straightforward mission had instantly taken on a mystical turn.

Cora couldn't help but recall the scene she witnessed earlier that morning on the streets and the passerby's comment about it being "excellent nourishment."

The situation was becoming increasingly enigmatic.

After completing the mission, it seemed necessary to find out what T.T.T. was all about.

As they exited the hall, Cora pondered where to pick up the "free transport vehicle."

Suddenly, the roar of engines reached her ears.

From the high-spanning tracks that crisscrossed Felalakas's skies, a numbered transport vehicle approached and parked right in front of Cora and her group.

This transport vehicle was silver gray all over.

It had a cramped cockpit, but the striking part was the eight compartments in the rear, each filled with iron cages adorned with barbed hooks.

These cages were crisscrossed with dried bloodstains, looking ominous from the outside. It was impossible to tell how many zombies they had captured.

With a "ding," the vehicle information popped up on the terminal. This car was equipped with automatic driving and had set routes.

In theory, Cora just needed to capture the zombies and toss them into the vehicle.

It would automatically return.

Cora and Onyx climbed into the cockpit, and just as the doors were about to close, Damian grabbed her sleeve.

"Sis, I... I want to go too."

"Are you sure? You fear zombies, right?"

Damian was terrified of zombies, and his Anopower had gone haywire twice because of them.

His hand trembled for a moment, then loosened before gripping her sleeve tightly again.

Inside the cockpit, Onyx watched him with a smile that wasn't quite a smile.

Although he hadn't said a word, Damian could discern the disdain in his eyes, as if saying, "Oh? Is that all?"

While Damian hesitated, the spark of courage flared up within the young boy. He stiffened his neck, his voice full of passion.

"I'm not afraid! I want to help you, and I won't cause any trouble!"

After thinking for a moment, Cora agreed.

While Damian was an unstable factor, it didn't matter.

She'd just have to keep a closer eye on him. "Come up."

Steam engines powered the transport vehicle dispatched by Felalakas and didn't rely on "Sora Wings" energy, making it slower than a starship, but it could use the aerial tracks.

After about 10 hours of traveling, Cora and her team arrived at Glass Port.

It was nearing midnight, and they were less than three kilometers away from the Glass Port Municipal Hall.

The area surrounding it was teeming with hordes of zombies. Without clearing a path, they couldn't proceed.

Cora rolled down the window, reached out, and agilely flipped onto the roof of the transport vehicle.

In her hand, she held a rapid-fire crossbow, the same as Onyx's.

"I'll take care of the zombies on the left. Damian, freeze the ones on the right."

Damian clenched his fists, nodding nervously.

"Okay."

Cora shouldered the crossbow, squinted her eyes, aimed, and lightly squeezed the trigger.

Ten arrows shot out accurately and pierced into a small group of isolated zombies, drawing the attention of the undead.

The zombies noticed and rushed towards them.

Damian stood up as well, with his Anopower joining in.

A blizzard erupted, blanketing the area.

The zombies caught in the snowstorm instantly turned into ice sculptures.

The transport vehicle's rooftop surveillance detected the zombies' movements.

A long mechanical arm extended from the rear compartment, similar to sweeping up trash. And it collected these frozen zombies into iron cages. Then it delivered them back into the vehicle.

Once a section was full, the compartment door closed silently and automatically shifted to the front. The second-to-last section was pushed out right after it.

"Keep going," Cora said, changing her aim to attract more zombies' attention.

"Got it!" Damian responded, now full of enthusiasm.

As the first compartment of zombies was passing the cockpit, dripping water fell, and one of the thawed zombies seemed to wake up gradually.

Suddenly, it roared in agitation. Its sharp claws extended through the iron bars of the cage, almost grazing Damian's nose through the window glass.

The sudden attack startled Damian, who was focused on the front.

His pupils quivered, and the blizzard turned into ice shards.

"Crack, crack, crack..."

Zombies that should have been frozen now had several skulls pierced by ice shards. The remaining ones continued to push forward.

With Damian's rhythm disrupted, Cora was also affected.

Her crossbow couldn't attract the attention of so many zombies, and a small portion of them were already charging towards their location.

Cora put down her crossbow, reached back, and slowly drew two short swords from her backpack. She jumped off the roof of the vehicle and headed straight for the oncoming zombie horde. As she landed, she made a horizontal slash, cutting down the zombies charging towards them.

Onyx frowned and shouted quietly, "Cora, capture them alive."

Cora's silhouette stiffened, and her movements momentarily hesitated, as if she were pondering how to capture them alive.

Then, disaster struck.

Everything descended into chaos.

Damian cried out, and Anopower alternated between ice and ice shards.

Cora darted and jumped among the zombie horde, knocking down one and chasing away another.

After finally capturing a group of zombies, she was about to toss them into the transport vehicle when Damian's ice shards came flying and killed them all.

Cora... "She couldn't even find the words."

During endless pandemonium, Onyx buried his face in his hands.

F777's first operation was a big failure!

CHAPTER 5

Teamwork and Competition

In such a critical moment, Onyx remained cool-headed. He surveyed the chaotic scene and quickly decided.

"Damian, stop and use the ice in the direction I show."

Damian, feeling rebellious, retorted, "Why should I listen to you?"

Onyx's icy gaze lingered on his collar for a moment, a steely resolve in his eyes, and he said, "If you don't listen, I'll toss you out right now."

Damian's expression contorted, remembering the pain of being controlled.

Onyx no longer paid attention to him.

His long fingers danced over the complex control panel in the cockpit, and his gaze focused on Cora in the distance.

Just as he was about to speak, he hesitated for a moment.

Suddenly, long-forgotten memories flooded back.

As a precaution, he turned back to Damian to confirm, "Can you distinguish between north, south, east, and west?"

Damian, now irate, shouted, "Of course! Who do you think I am?"

"Very well," Onyx said with a wry smile. "You're brighter than your sis, Cora, after all."

With a slight movement of his fingers, Onyx retrieved a collapsible cane from Anopower space. He extended it with a few clicks, and then, with both hands, pushed himself up from his wheelchair. After steadying himself, he reached out and grabbed the control lever of the mechanical arm on the side of the vehicle.

Damian, in utter disbelief, realized that Onyx was quite tall and nothing like the emaciated figure he had expected from someone in a wheelchair.

He was tall and elegant, with a well-proportioned physique, a lean and muscular build, and powerful forearms.

In his daze, Onyx had already opened the car window and called out from a distance, "Cora, head to 11 o'clock!"

Cora, brandishing her dual blades, responded with a swift cut and with a leap. She jumped ahead of the approaching horde of zombies, luring them towards the northwest.

"Damian, twenty zombies at six o'clock. Freeze them all!"

Although Damian was initially resentful, the thought of being tossed out by Onyx was too intimidating.

He couldn't afford to provoke him any further. He marveled at Onyx's height and reluctantly followed his instructions.

At eleven o'clock in the northwest, where Cora was leading the zombies, they collided with the carriages parked nearby, leaving no way out.

"Six o'clock!"

Almost simultaneously, Onyx shouted the next command.

Cora slammed on the brakes and swiftly turned the car, making the zombies, like rabbits chasing a carrot, change direction and head straight for them.

Damian, anxious, exclaimed, "They're all coming this way!"

Onyx coldly warned, "Watch your ice. If I see one more ice shard, you'll be the first to feed the zombies."

The mass of monsters grew increasingly closer.

The initial zombies Damian had frozen were thawing, and in their disoriented state, they continued forward.

Cora was caught between the approaching hordes, about to be overwhelmed.

Damian's heart was in his throat.

But just then, Cora executed a swift maneuver. She used her blades to anchor herself in a gap filled with hooked bars inside the iron cage, then leaped onto the roof in a flash. She nimbly somersaulted, flipping twice in quick succession, leaving her foes stumbling in confusion.

The mechanical arm attached to the side of the carriage extended and swept up all the approaching zombies.

The iron cage slammed shut behind them, securing their exit.

In an instant, the threat was eliminated.

In the driver's seat, Onyx gave Cora instructions while manually operating the transport vehicle and the mechanical arm simultaneously.

Damian, who was left dumbfounded by the whole situation, couldn't believe how a human brain could handle so many tasks at once.

Thanks to Onyx's guidance, they regained control of the situation.

The zombies were directed into Cora's striking range, or into Damian's storm of snow and ice.

After approximately half an hour, they had cleared a path to safety.

With the crisis averted, Cora swiftly finished the remaining zombies. She wiped her dual blades clean and slid them back into their sheaths, her confidence restored.

Onyx propped himself up on his cane, pushed open the car door, and leaned against it in a relaxed posture.

The night breeze rustled his clothes, accentuating his chiseled features.

Onyx looked at Cora, with his expression resigned.

"What did you say before we left?"

Cora and Damian were both high-powered Aberrants.

But if they didn't cooperate effectively in battle, they could cause chaos and attract unwanted attention.

He had instructed them to work together to lure the zombies. Onyx himself had discussed and showed the method.

Cora had promised to follow the plan diligently, but in the heat of the moment, she had reverted to her usual headstrong approach.

Cora, feeling ashamed, lowered her head, her expression sheepish.

"I... I didn't do it on purpose. I just... forgot."

Cora glanced at Onyx's stern expression.

Her eyes twinkled with a mischievous idea.

She suddenly hopped onto the driver's seat and offered her help in a flattering tone.

"I, I can push you."

Onyx paused for a moment, not shaking her hand away.

Cora signaled Damian to follow her subtle plan.

"Damian!"

The boy, who had just learned to behave like a human under Onyx's tutelage, dared not roll his eyes. He obediently brought the wheelchair out from the cockpit.

In the end, it was all about who had the strength.

Damian was determined to win back his dignity next time.

After a brief inspection, the transport vehicle was roughly filled with four sections of carriages.

The interior was well soundproofed, and they couldn't hear any sounds coming from inside, even if they pressed their ears against the carriage walls.

They were now very close to the Glass Port City Hall. In the distance, they could make out the blurry silhouette of the building.

Onyx folded his cane and returned to his wheelchair, saying, "It's near to here. Let's head over."

Cora hesitated for a moment and was about to ask what to do with the extra carriages in the vehicle.

Unexpectedly, the two remaining empty sections detached from the vehicle.

Small wheels popped out from the bottom and transformed into the type of small shopping carts people used to stock up on groceries, following them like obedient assistants.

Onyx didn't seem surprised. He had discovered it when he was manipulating the control panel.

"The vehicle has a small artificial intelligence system with some degree of autonomous judgment. Just leave it. Let's go."

Cora took a few steps forward and glanced back.

The two carriages were following closely behind them, and the mechanical arms were swinging and swaying in a bizarre and eerie manner.

They looked like supervisors, and the sight was getting stranger the more she watched.

Glass Port City Hall.

Unlike the local naturalistic charm, this was an architectural marvel in a forest steel style.

Its industrial façade was covered in lush vegetation, and a dazzling parade of walkways and platforms floated in the air.

These platforms, large and small, stretched out rampantly, hinting at the complexity and diversity of the interior.

The entrance wasn't tall enough to accommodate the two carriages.

The mechanical arms retracted automatically, entering energy-saving mode.

Two small boxy compartments waited at the entrance, no longer following them.

Cora paid them no mind and entered the entire building alongside Onyx and Damian.

According to the mission briefing, the first floor of the City Hall should have been filled with zombies since September 25th.

However, the reality was quite different.

Upon entering through the grand doors, the vast lobby only had a few zombies wandering around.

Unusual situations raised suspicions.

Cora's guard went up automatically.

She looked up, following the dual spiral staircase that spiraled to the top.

The entire six floors of the building had been removed, creating a unique design with slanted walls and a twisted, eerie environment. The atmosphere was eerily quiet.

"Something's not right. Be careful," Onyx warned in a low voice.

"Okay," Cora said, focusing intently. "D, stay close. Let's proceed."

Onyx took the lead, guiding the two of them up through the seemingly identical corridors.

They twisted and turned, never doubling back.

It didn't take long before his wheelchair came to a halt. "There are people, Aberrants."

Cora was puzzled.

The building had many rooms, and the layout was confusing, making telepathic exploration difficult.

She had heard no sounds or detected any Anopower.

How did Onyx know there were Aberrants?

"Go this way," Onyx instructed, changing direction and leading them up to the top floor. He chose a secluded small platform and peered down.

Sure enough, there were people down there.

On the fourth floor's central courtyard, several groups were facing off from a distance.

Compared to the mysteriously vanished zombies inside the building, the number of creatures here appeared more typical.

They were like cornered beasts, forced to gather.

Cora's keen eyes spotted one zombie with noticeably different symptoms.

Its skin had a unique shade of blue, less decayed than the standard zombies. Its metallic claws were exceptionally sharp, and the most peculiar feature was the completely black, ink-like pupils.

Onyx's expression grew increasingly serious.

"Anopower zombies."

Cora was shocked.

Anopower zombies were Aberrants who had fallen to become zombies.

Onyx had mentioned that the NPA's only approach to dealing with Anopower zombies was execution.

Amidst the tense atmosphere, a man with half of his body composed of machinery took a bold step forward.

His native and mechanical eyes simultaneously scanned the scene, giving him a peculiar appearance.

"I say, Stormrider, your family is in a league of their own. You might not be interested in these low-level Anopower zombies. How about you let us have them?"

Leaning against the staircase, a suave man dressed in a vintage robe smiled.

His voice was gentle, but his words held no trace of compromise.

"Battur, there's no need for such hypocritical words. It's rather nauseating. Our team is climbing the points chart, and I thought everyone knew that."

"Zephyrion Stormrider, don't get too greedy!"

"Exactly! You've already monopolized the B-level tasks. The rest are dirty and exhausting chores. Don't be too unreasonable!"

"Are you not already number one? Isn't 966 points enough?"

On the fourth floor, Cora, who had just accepted a "B-level" task, couldn't help but exclaim, "Wait, is this the top-ranked team 'The Boss and His Three Goons'?"

Cora looked intently and indeed saw a man named Zephyrion Stormrider standing with three others, all hidden in the shadows, sporting stern expressions that warned against any provocation.

"Zephyrion, it wasn't you who found this Anopower zombie first, and A-level missions aren't something you can take on as you please," a white-haired old man spoke with his hands behind his back, descending the stairs with authority.

"Aberrants don't deal in sentiment. Success matters. If you want to claim these 1000 points, you'll have to ask if we agree."

Zephyrion laughed, "I see. Even Master Stark has joined the fray. Very well, let's do it your way. The victor takes it all, and you're all welcome to take these 1000 points from me!"

"This is too audacious! I can't stand it!"

"Let's go together. I don't believe we can't beat him!"

"A-level mission?" Cora had overheard the heated debate below, and her eyes suddenly lit up."D, come here."

"The system has received a sudden red alert mission."

Damian said as he approached, holding the terminal.

Five hours ago, on their way to Glass Port, the Felalakas Commission Center issued an emergency A-level mission.

It read: "Original Glass Port (D139 District), D-level Aberrant, Johnson Stone, Anopower 'Medusa's Eye,' has mutated and at large; This individual is extremely dangerous and is now wanted throughout the entire district. Any sighting should cause immediate execution!"

This was Felalakas' first A-level mission, and it offered a full 1000 points. No wonder it had attracted so many Aberrant teams.

The atmosphere on the fourth floor grew increasingly tense, on the verge of an eruption.

"Since that's the case, let's compete fairly."

Battur, the one-eyed man with a half-machine body who had pretended to suggest a fair competition earlier, suddenly sneered and attacked Stone while the other Aberrants weren't prepared.

"Battur! Are you playing dirty?"

All the Aberrants sprang into action, and shadows rushed towards Stone.

Right as they approached, Zephyrion's robe billowed.

Countless thorns emerged from the ground, binding the lower legs of the Aberrants charging forward.

Plop, plop. One by one, they tumbled back to the ground like dumplings.

Incredible control!

Zephyrion was a formidable Wood-element Aberrant!

After suppressing the situation, Zephyrion and his three comrades dashed from various directions towards Stone, coming within striking distance.

But then something peculiar happened.

Stone disappeared from his spot, reappearing in a corner in the opposite direction.

There was a Space-element Aberrant on the scene!

This unseen Space-element Aberrant was adept at hiding.

He or she was manipulating Stone's position, making it change frequently and preventing anyone from tracking his exact location.

Soon, Cora and her companions were beneath the reappeared the zombie Stone.

The Space-element Aberrant hidden in the shadows seemed to think this location had excellent cover and might have been a good place to take cover or recharge since he wasn't moving.

It was an excellent opportunity.

The praying mantis hunted the cicada, unaware of the oriole behind.

"Shall we... shall we go for it?" Cora asked her companions for their opinion.

Onyx, focused on the chaos below, chuckled lightly. "Of course, why not? An A-level mission will bring in more cash, won't it?"

Cora's eyes lit up. She had a goal now—a reward in the NPA point. If she secured the 1000 points, would it be enough to pay Damian back?

"Go for it, but monitor the 3 o'clock direction," Onyx pointed towards a corner. "That's where the Space-element Aberrant is hiding."

"Okay," Cora nodded.

"Big sister, good luck!" Damian pumped his fist to encourage her.

"D, take care of him," Cora told Damian seriously.

Damian's spirit drooped.

"Okay."

Is there a chance I'm the one who needs protecting? Damian murmured.

Cora locked onto her target's location, drew her twin blades, and leaped from the sixth-floor top platform, charging straight at the zombie Stone.

Almost simultaneously, a nimble shadow jumped down from the opposite rooftop!

There was more than one oriole hidden in the shadows.

CHAPTER 6

Enemies and Rewards

Cora leaped from the sixth-floor platform.

Almost simultaneously, a shadow emerged from the opposite side.

Both of them met unexpectedly in mid-air, their faces showing surprise.

Quickly, they both realized each other's intentions.

Well, it seemed they were both here to seize that A-level mission!

Cora somersaulted in mid-air, her longsword in hand, slashing down toward the shadow's head.

Her sharp blade created a furious whirlwind, pressuring the shadow to make way.

This person was up for a direct confrontation!

"Clang!" The sword struck the arm, hitting what seemed like an armored surface.

The shadow took a heavy blow.

The arm twisted inward, and it charged forward, its speed even surpassing Cora's by a full body length.

Cora wasn't about to let him have his way.

Her short knife immediately followed, slicing quickly and fiercely upwards.

"Clang!" The screeching sound of metal on metal echoed again as the shadow narrowly evaded, leaving a momentary vulnerability.

In an instant, Cora blocked the way, and this time, the shadow was the one who felt annoyed.

The shadow twisted, attempting to choke her and kick her knee pit with the left leg bent.

The move was sneaky, designed to take her out in one hit.

Cora raised her twin blades to block and dodged nimbly.

However, the shadow was clearly skilled in close combat, making elusive moves.

When it struck, it was with a deadly intent. In terms of combat skills alone, this was the most formidable opponent Cora had faced.

But it wasn't enough to outmatch her.

Cora bent at the waist, flipped her body backward 360 degrees, and delivered a powerful kick to the shadow's chest, forcing it to retreat. Taking advantage of the counterforce, she grabbed the collar of the undead Stone.

The fight raged on, but Cora hadn't forgotten her true target.

Just then, an enchanting melody unexpectedly reached Cora's ears.

"Let me... accompany you to sleep... gently pulling my hand away..."

What was even more bizarre was that every time the song continued, Cora felt her spirit grow a little more fatigued, and her desire to fight waned.

Why am I so tired? Why am I crying?

As she was caught up in the intense battle and affected by this inexplicable song, Cora didn't notice the poison-tipped dagger moving swiftly toward her throat.

Cora raised her blades for defense, but her movements were slightly sluggish. She felt unusually lethargic, yearning for a good night's sleep.

Where was this thought coming from?

Her distraction allowed the shadow to shear a few strands of her hair.

In just half a minute, they exchanged dozens of moves.

On the fourth-floor platform, the Aberrants fighting together finally noticed the two interlopers.

"Oh man, they're joining in mid-fight!"

"How sneaky! Hiding until now!"

"Stop! Let's finish them first!"

Seeing victory almost within their grasp, the Aberrants were consumed with anger, unleashing their most powerful moves.

The shadow with the spatial powers once again teleported the undead Stone. It moved from one spot to another like a rubber ball, and then, suddenly, it reappeared right beneath Cora.

Cora and the shadow were surprised, surrounded.

"Sis!" Damian clung to the railing, peering over the edge, with his hands dripping with sweat.

On the opposite side, in the empty hallway, Onyx's wheelchair glided forward.

Half of his handsome face was bathed in the bright light coming from above.

He chuckled.

"What kind of cooperation do you have in mind?"

"Hehe," the female voice giggled sweetly, "Of course, if you all stop right now, I'll let you go."

In the battle's chaos, Cora was under attack from all sides and affected by the strange song, clearly at a disadvantage.

Their situation wasn't favorable.

Onyx tapped his wheelchair armrest rhythmically, creating an eerie, resonating melody.

He looked calm, and the silence seemed to stretch for an excruciatingly long time, making the waiting more unnerving.

The female voice couldn't help but urge, "Aren't you making up your minds? Your companion seems to be on her last legs."

Onyx raised an eyebrow and casually replied, "Is that so? Perhaps you should take a closer look."

The haunting song was everywhere, its lingering notes like hooks inescapably burrowing into Cora's ears, draining her spirit.

Attacks from the Aberrants rained down on her, and her feet were paralyzed. She felt like she couldn't move; she was helpless.

No, this couldn't go on.

Cora closed her eyes and focused her mental energy rapidly coursing through her body. Then, she decisively blocked her own hearing.

The world fell silent.

She opened her eyes abruptly.

Her twin blades emitted a brilliant blue light as they flew from her grasp, cutting through the thorny vines.

These tough vines, when touched by the bluish sword winds, withered and shattered into pieces.

Far away on the staircase, Zephyrion took a sudden step back, shock and disbelief on his face as he clutched his chest. Blood trickled from his mouth.

"Z!" His teammates, now free from their opponents, rushed to his side.

"How are you?"

Zephyrion swallowed a mouthful of blood, and his veins throbbed painfully.

His Anopower was raging, and his life force continued to churn.

He stared incredulously, "What kind of weapon does she have? It's suppressing my Anopower!"

Cora's twin blades flew out, clearing the area with swift sweeps before returning to her grasp. She collided with the hilts together, merging them into a serrated and elegant saw.

With a single hand, she lifted the large blade and unleashed a sweeping strike, using a technique she dubbed "The Grass Cutter."

The shadow was forced back, unable to get close, and any previous advantage had vanished.

In contrast, Cora pressed her advantage, and her serrated saw had a broad and menacing attack range. She swung her blade towards her opponent's back.

"Crack, crack," the body armor couldn't withstand such violence. Pieces shattered, and shards of metal scattered.

Just a mundane "shield" against a "spear" that could pierce anything?

Metal Anopower had that kind of overwhelming superiority, no debate.

The situation downstairs dramatically reversed, and the negotiations on the sixth floor also took a subtle turn.

The mellifluous female voice had been silent for a while.

With her black-armored companion now unprotected, it seemed he couldn't withstand Cora's assault.

Onyx nonchalantly leaned against his wheelchair.

"It appears we should discuss our terms of cooperation once more."

The mellifluous female voice, with a hint of frustration, asked, "What do you have in mind?"

"Cooperation is built on mutual benefit. I need to make sure that our goals align with no conflicts," Onyx said composedly, showing no signs of haste.

However, under Cora's relentless attacks, the injured shadow couldn't hold on much longer.

The mellifluous female voice couldn't endure any longer.

She disclosed her last card, "The zombies can be yours... we only want the crystals."

Onyx's eyes flickered, and he smiled gently, "Deal."

In Cora's world of silence, she remained focused only on her opponent, her strikes growing even fiercer.

Amid the heat of battle, a familiar ice shard appeared in her vision. It circled her before hovering right in front of her.

Cora sensed something and looked towards the platform where Onyx was located.

Perhaps aware that she couldn't hear at the moment, Onyx signaled her with two gestures.

It was a code they had agreed upon earlier.

"Prioritize capturing the target," and "Retreat quickly."

Cora understood and stopped attacking the shadow.

Her gaze wandered for a moment and quickly found the position of the undead Stone.

The shadow's movements also ceased, and it turned its ear as if hearing something. It redirected its dagger, following Cora into the crowd.

Battur caught the undead Stone during the chaos.

He was ecstatic, and his cold mechanical arm spiraled forward, stabbing through Stone's left chest. Then, he stood with his hand on his hip, roaring, "Haha, A-level mission, it's mine!"

Stone, who had been moving like a puppet all along, suddenly sprang to life.

His expression turned fierce as he tilted his head backward.

The black patterns on his neck rose, and he let out a loud, furious roar!

From the center of his pitch-black pupils, invisible ripples spread out.

All Aberrants within reach who couldn't escape were instantly petrified, frozen in place like stone.

This was Johnson Stone's Anopower, the "Medusa's Gaze."

Its original effect could briefly paralyze enemies who met his gaze directly.

After he turned into a zombie, the Anopower mutated into a more terrifying petrification ability, with an even larger and more frightening attack range.

Two Aberrants, who were entwined, took the brunt of the attack. Their bodies turned as hard as stone, and one of them was on the edge of the railing.

His footing gave way, and he fell heavily from the spiral staircase, instantly shattering into pieces.

Master Stark, who had been overseeing the situation, urgently ordered, "Where are the people? Bring Stone back!"

The spatial distortion behind him gradually revealed a blurry-faced Aberrants.

In a hoarse voice, he said, "The target disappeared. My psychic powers can't detect them."

"Hmph," Stark snorted, "Then block all the exits; they can't escape."

A slender Aberrants hurriedly approached and reported, "Master Stark, Zephyrion's team retreated."

"They retreated? At this time?" Stark was puzzled.

Zephyrion had been boasting just a while ago, showing no intention of giving up the A-level mission.

Now, he was strangely silent? Something was amiss; there had to be a problem.

With the keen eyes of an eagle, Master Stark meticulously toyed with his jade finger guard and issued a command in a low voice. "Investigate what happened."

"Yes, sir."

Master Stark took two steps forward, and Battur's severed head rolled by, clunking on the ground. He kicked it away with his foot.

"Useless!"

With Onyx, the living navigator, leading the way, Cora and her group navigated the complex labyrinth of corridors swiftly.

Sometimes they'd approach what seemed like a dead-end.

But magically, Onyx would change direction, revealing another path.

Their pursuers in the rear couldn't keep up, quickly becoming disoriented within the maze-like structure.

They lost their way, and soon, the annoying flies were shaken off.

Finally, on the third floor, the group discovered a locked office. They forcefully entered.

Cora dropped the half-dead zombie, Stone, on the ground. Then she finally had time to inspect the two people who had come along with them.

First was the shadow that she had been dueling with.

He was a young man, slightly taller than Onyx, with dark skin and a rugged physique. He was dressed entirely in black combat gear, his eyes wild and untamed, like a lone wolf.

Noticing Cora's gaze, he looked back at her coldly.

The knife in his hand had a faint greenish glimmer.

This person's Anopower probably had something to do with poison, assassination, or something of the sort.

The other person, the mastermind behind the disruption of Cora's singing during the battle, now revealed her true self.

She was a strikingly beautiful woman, appearing to be around twenty-five or twenty-six years old. She had chestnut brown, loose, wavy hair tied in a loose ponytail, smooth and fair skin, luscious and vibrant cherry lips.

Her natural beauty was breathtaking. As she getting up close, she seemed to have a radiant aura.

Cora was completely awestruck by her unparalleled beauty.

The beautiful woman's lips curled into a gentle smile, and she spoke to Cora in a friendly tone, "Hurry, let's divide the loot."

Cora was bewildered, "Divide... the loot?"

"Hey, we agreed. You get the zombies, we get the crystals. No cheating!" The beautiful woman reminded her.

"Sis," Damian whispered to Cora as he leaned in, behaving like a tattletale.

He quickly spilled the beans about the deal Onyx had made with her while pretending to trade her.

Cora listened and then glanced at Onyx.

He seemed to have noticed something in a corner of the office. When he caught her looking, he smiled as if he had nothing to hide, not showing a hint of guilt about using her as bait for the trade with someone else.

Cora didn't really mind. After all, their only aim was the A-level mission.

She did not know what this "crystal" was, and would someone like Onyx allow her to be taken advantage of?

She thought it was fine and had no objections.

Cora turned her attention back to the two people before her. "No, we won't cheat."

"In that case, go ahead, kill it." The beautiful woman pointed to the ground where Stone lay.

As soon as Damian heard that, he hurriedly ducked behind Cora, desperately trying to make himself less noticeable. He clearly didn't want to get involved in this dirty work.

As for Onyx, he wasn't much of a help, either. Although he had killed Yara and Bob without hesitation, he showed no inclination to get involved at the moment.

It seemed Cora was the only one who would do the dirty work.

She gripped her icy saw, hesitated for a moment, and then remembered something. "I still have to... complete the mission."

She nearly forgot; the mission hadn't been submitted yet!

But how were they supposed to submit this kind of mission? Did they need to carry the zombie Stone back to Felalakas and do it in front of everyone at the commission hall terminal? Just thinking about that scene seemed bizarre.

The beautiful woman chuckled and pointed to her badge. "You don't need to go through all that trouble. You can submit it at the terminal."

Cora glanced down at her badge. Indeed, special assignments could be submitted remotely.

However, the process was strict: it required recording a video and scanning the target's biological data.

She wasn't very proficient with the terminal, fumbling for several attempts but not getting it right. Flustered, she finally removed her badge and handed it to Onyx, asking him to do it.

"You're taking forever," the beautiful woman grew impatient.

She pouted and said, "Suchat."

The young man, Suchat, walked up and swiftly slit Stone's throat.

The zombie didn't even grunt; his head fell off.

"All right, submit the mission now," Cora finally figured out the process.

She aimed her terminal at Stone, which automatically scanned his biological data.

After a few seconds of calculation, the projection on the screen displayed a message. "Confirmed, target deceased, mission completed."

Cora didn't even have time to see the mission's NPA credit value, and the beautiful woman was already urging her, "So, it's ours now, right?"

She put down her terminal, nodding vigorously, "Yes, yes!"

The beautiful woman crouched down, took Suchat's knife, and stabbed it into Stone's head. She raised her hand and dug something out, a pure white crystal.

She wiped the crystal clean with a tissue, held it in her hand, and was about to speak when suddenly, a heart-wrenching cry echoed from a corner of the office.

"No, no... John, John!"

A woman in a disheveled municipal hall uniform burst out.

The two people behind her couldn't hold her back, and their bodies were pulled out from behind a hiding file cabinet.

These individuals had pale, exhausted faces; it seemed they had been trapped here for several days.

The woman stumbled to her knees, cradling the horribly shattered head of Stone.

She cried out in agony, "Why did you kill him? Why did you kill him?"

"He was a good person, such a good person. He worked so hard, earned money, never took a day off, all for our wedding next month. Why? Why did this happen?"

"Sophia..." Her colleagues tried to pull her away, but she shook them off vehemently.

Sophia was lost in grief, muttering to herself, "Finally, John awakened as an Aberrant with such difficulty. We thought our days were going to get better, and then you killed him. You killed him!"

She and Stone were both employees of the municipal hall.

Before the zombie outbreak overran Glass Port, they, along with a few others, had been working non-stop in the office. They couldn't escape in time.

When they finally realized it, the first floor was already filled with zombies.

With no other options, they took refuge in the office's filing cabinets, waiting for the rescue action.

But a week passed with no sign of help. Their supplies of water and food ran out.

Stone, who was the only Aberrant among them and also Sophia Lister's fiancé, had bravely gone outside to lure the zombies away, fighting for the survival of the others.

On October 1st, he and two male colleagues left the office and never returned.

Sophia curled up in the file cabinet, praying to the heavens that her fiancé would return as soon as possible.

However, as time passed, her consciousness faded, and she was struggling to hold on.

Just now, Sophia heard voices from outside. She thought it was her fiancé returning. She mustered the last of her strength and excitedly peered through the crack in the door, only to witness the woman thrusting a knife into Stone's head.

Sophia was overwhelmed with grief. "You'll pay for this! You'll pay for John!"

She seemed to have fallen into a kind of frenzy, standing up in anger, stumbling towards the beautiful woman's face.

Unfortunately, Sophia couldn't reach the woman as she was kicked away by Suchat, who had remained silent, flopping to the ground.

"What are you doing?"

Her two male colleagues shouted in despair and fury, rushing over to help Sophia.

Their gazes filled with anger and resentment towards Suchat and the woman.

Suchat's kick had been light, but Sophia was already at her wit's end. She couldn't stand up anymore.

Her emotions had completely collapsed, tears streaming down her face as she hurled the most vicious curses at the woman who had killed Stone.

The beautiful woman remained expressionless as she endured the tirade.

Suddenly, she lost her temper.

"Open your eyes and see clearly! He was already a zombie! What's wrong with killing a zombie?"

Sophia was left dumbfounded, staring at Stone lying on the ground.

His face was contorted, and his pitch-black pupils looked nothing like a human's.

"No...no, I don't believe it. John..."

Not true, was it? Really not true?

Sophia examined her own conscience.

Was it because Stone was the only Aberrant?

And when they needed someone to go outside, everyone unanimously agreed that he should lure the zombies away?

Even his fiancée didn't object? Was it truly not their fault that Stone was killed?

The beautiful woman sighed.

"I'm not the one making the rules. Don't blame me. If you want to blame someone, blame this absurd world."

Cora stood there beside her, looking at her with a blank expression.

The beautiful woman pivoted her head and glared at her. "What are you staring at? Did I say something wrong?"

CHAPTER 7

The Famous and Infamous

The beautiful woman scolded Cora.

"What are you looking at? Did I say something wrong?" The beautiful woman not only scolded her, but also demanded an answer.

Cora nodded, but in the woman's angry gaze, she whiffed her head.

Seeing Cora's bewildered expression, the beautiful woman let out a disdainful hum and chose not to trouble her further. Soon, she averted her gaze.

After a long string of scoldings that echoed through the room, there was silence for a while.

The atmosphere gradually grew somber.

The only sounds were Sophia's occasional sobs and her colleagues' feeble attempts at comforting her.

"The exit is blocked," Suchat, observing near the window, finally spoke.

His pronunciation, enunciation, and pauses were rather peculiar, as if he wasn't very familiar with the NPA's common language.

"Can we break through?"

"We can, but it will expose us."

The beautiful woman furrowed her brows.

In the earlier chaos, they had acted swiftly and retreated even faster.

The Aberrants on the other side couldn't find out their identities without a direct confrontation.

But now, the opposition was on guard. Trying to force their way out would be risky.

She didn't want to reveal her identity here. They needed to come up with another plan.

Cora guided Onyx to the other side of the room, keeping a certain distance from the two groups of people.

"You've known for a while, haven't you? That there were people here?" she asked in a hushed tone.

Onyx nodded.

Sophia and her colleagues were just regular people, with no psychic abilities.

At that moment, Cora's attention had been entirely on Stone, so not noticing the others was normal.

However, given that the office door had been locked from the inside, he had guessed that there must be people in the room.

Cora, after hearing his explanation, realized her oversight and thought little of it. She held the heavy, cold saw in her hands and considered finding a place to stow it.

"Cora," Onyx called her softly.

"Hmm?"

Cora raised her head, finding a suitable place to put her weapon as she thought Onyx wanted to talk privately. She bent over him, brushing her disheveled black hair over his shoulder, creating a slight ticklish sensation.

Onyx's fingers moved slightly, but he didn't evade her.

"This person bears the Rainforest Mark on his body."

Onyx was referring to the young man called "Suchat."

The Rainforest, E117 sector, was the NPA's most mysterious ecological zone.

Because of its damp and humid climate, and the rich diversity of species, it was an ideal breeding ground for special operatives, such as mercenaries and assassins.

Training in the Rainforest was rumored to be extremely brutal, demanding, and even sadistic.

Many said it exceeded the limits the human body could endure.

Surviving such harsh training meant that these individuals were not only extraordinarily skilled in solo combat but had also become accustomed to dancing with death, with their empathy almost nonexistent.

The Rainforest Mark Onyx mentioned was a black snake-like tattoo on the back of Suchat's neck.

Cora recollected the details of her encounter with Suchat and said thoughtfully, "His combat skills are exceptional, but he doesn't have Anopower."

"You're right," Onyx agreed, "Suchat's Anopower should be 'Poison,' likely at the B-level or higher."

B-level or higher Aberrants, weren't they as powerful as Azures, like Vincent and Jeremy?

If these people became enemies, wouldn't they be a significant threat to their group?

"And there's another thing," Cora said, describing how she had been affected by the beautiful woman's singing, feeling weak and unresponsive.

Onyx contemplated for a moment.

"It's sound wave manipulation. Perhaps it's sonic Anopower or something related to mysticism. Based on the current information, we can't accurately determine. This time she merely subjected you to side effects. If her singing also affects her comrades, she could be very troublesome."

A potent support ability that not only afflicts enemies with some debuffs but also gives buffs on allies?

Imagine a fight that was initially even, where you became weaker as the battle wore on, while the opponent grew stronger.

It was easy for anyone with a slightly fragile will to have their resolve shattered.

The abilities of the beautiful woman were not to be underestimated.

It was no wonder that they, just two people, dared to steal missions from so many other Aberrants.

But speaking of Suchat and the other two, there was still something they hadn't figured out.

Cora gazed into Onyx's eyes and asked another pressing question, "Crystals, what are they?"

Onyx lowered his voice. "Remember when I explained the cause of the apocalypse to you?"

"I remember."

"Supercharged solar radiation entered the human body, causing disruptions in the body's magnetic field, genetic mutations. Regular people would turn into zombies, but if an excessive amount of external energy is absorbed all at once and can't be processed by the body, it can cause the formation of crystals."

Cora fell silent for a moment, then rummaged in the hidden compartment of her backpack and pulled out a few crystals.

These were the ones she had extracted from Theon, as well as other martial art fellows.

It seemed they were the same type as the one inside Stone.

Onyx picked up one of the nearly transparent crystals and studied it.

"Crystals are not commonly found in ordinary zombie bodies because they are subjected to overwhelming radiation. However, Aberrants have a certain level of antibodies because of previous exposure to radiation, so the probability of crystals forming inside them is roughly above 95%."

"Whenever an Aberrant has Anopower, crystals are guaranteed," Cora muttered, her mood sinking deeply.

Theon, he became an Aberrant, but he had ended up as an Anopower zombie.

She had unknowingly encountered Anopower zombies so early.

As they spoke, Damian quietly squeezed between them, with his eyes shifting restlessly.

He had awakened early, but he didn't have more theoretical knowledge than Cora.

Hearing Onyx's detailed explanation, he didn't feel the urge to challenge him.

Unbeknownst to them, this person was quite knowledgeable.

Damian thought quietly.

Cora, still perplexed, asked, "What's the use of these crystals? Just the thought of digging them out of zombie heads sends shivers down my spine. What's their purpose? That would make those two give up an A-level mission to get them?"

"The official explanation is that crystals have a chance of triggering the awakening of Anopower in regular people and even promoting the secondary evolution of Aberrants."

Damian's eyes widened in astonishment.

Cora was equally surprised.

Awakening and evolution?

Would you really need to ingest them to develop?

The thought of having rocks in your head was terrifying enough, let alone eating them.

Was this for real?

Wait a second, Cora thought, sensing a gap in Onyx's explanation.

"What do you mean by 'official explanation'? Are there unofficial methods? It's getting more and more bizarre. And if awakening and evolution are said to have a 'chance,' does that mean there's a chance of failure?"

Cora grew increasingly puzzled.

"Are these crystals actually useful?"

A subtle smile graced Onyx's face. "They're not. It's all part of an elaborate deception orchestrated by the NPA."

"What?!" Damian couldn't contain his surprise and blurted out, immediately drawing the attention of Suchat and the beautiful woman.

Onyx tapped him on the head, issuing a stern warning, "Shut your mouth."

Damian covered his mouth in embarrassment.

Onyx handed the crystal that belonged to Theon back to Cora.

"Although some residual energy remains in the crystals and can be induced using technical means, their structure is already solidified. They won't undergo a third mutation. You can think of them as onetime backup batteries."

Cora stared at his smiling face, utterly speechless. It all made sense now.

Onyx was never going to lose out. He had taken advantage of the information gap and pulled a fast one on everyone!

He was cunning.

However, she still had one lingering doubt. "How do you know they're useless?"

Onyx replied, "Arashi has researched this topic, and some results were 'accidentally' leaked. This caused misunderstandings among certain individuals."

"If it's wrong, why was it spread?" Cora asked.

"Because some people don't care about right or wrong; they only pursue their self-interests. Most people don't even know the actual use of these crystals. NPA only needs to present a bit of information, hinting at their potential to trigger awakening and evolution, and they can keep Aberrants firmly under their control. After all, these crystals are a valuable strategic resource."

"Oh," Cora said, pausing for a moment, then she asked, "How do you know it's wrong?"

Onyx chuckled. "Why so many questions today? I'm out of answers."

He raised his arm to give Cora's head a playful knock, but when he met her expressionless face, he awkwardly retracted it and patted Damian's head instead.

Damian protested, "Hey!"

Cora sat on the ground to catch her breath, suddenly remembering that she hadn't checked the rewards for their A-level mission.

"Let's check it out together!"

She enthusiastically called Onyx and Damian.

This was their team's first completed mission, after all.

Two pairs of eager eyes, along with the lazy Onyx propped in his wheelchair, were all focused on the projection of Cora's terminal.

On team F777's mission list, there was a brilliantly glowing red commission.

A-level Mission (Code VA00001, Status. Completed)
Aim: Clear Anopower zombie Stone, Biological ID. LYG1301756
Points Earned: 1000
NPA Coins Earned: 0

Friendly Reminder. Your team has entered the total leaderboard of C83 area. Would you like to make this information public? (Yes/No)
Ignoring the other irrelevant information, Cora stared at the

central line, finding it hard to believe.

"NPA Coins Earned. 0."

Could someone please explain why B-level missions awarded 2000 NPA coins, but a hard-earned A-level mission involving the retrieval of an Anopower zombie resulted in zero coins?

Who could endure such injustice?

Cora's eyes became lifeless, and it became difficult for the others to watch her.

"Sis..." Damian was still thinking about how to comfort her, "It's alright. You don't need to pay me back..."

Onyx interrupted him, gently reassuring her, "It's not that bad. Didn't you also take on a B-level mission?"

Cora's eyes brightened a bit. "Right!"

At least there were still 2000 NPA coins coming their way.

"Did you ever think that the zombies on the first floor of City Hall look like the posters?" Onyx pointed towards Sophia and her two colleagues huddled in the center of the room.

"I'll go ask," Cora stood up.

Onyx, gently tugging her hoodie, stopped her.

"Hold on. It's not a good idea for you to approach them; they seem to have a strong aversion to us."

Though Cora hadn't killed Stone herself, they had all entered the room together, not to mention her earlier reckless disposal of Stone's body.

The disdain in their eyes was clear.

"What should we do then?" Cora sighed in frustration.

"One person is better suited for this," Onyx replied mysteriously.

"Who?" Cora asked.

"Who?" Damian echoed, intrigued.

Then, they both realized that they were being looked at in unison.

Sophia had finally regained some composure, but she remained seated, looking dazed.

Her two male colleagues were exhausted and eventually sat down, clutching their heads.

At that moment, a small boy with curly hair and big blinking eyes approached. He meandered slowly over to them.

The boy took a quick look at Sophia, who still seemed absent-minded. He then shifted his gaze to the two men and timidly inquired, "Mister, can I ask you a question?"

These people weren't very communicative, but considering that the person asking was an adorable child, one of the slightly overweight men coldly nodded, "Go ahead."

"Thank you, mister!" Damian blinked his innocent eyes in gratitude.

He then bowed his head and fiddled with his terminal, displaying his task interface.

"My sister and I came to the Glass Port because we accepted this mission, clearing zombies on the first floor of City Hall. Mister, did you post this? Have you been trapped here for a long time?"

Damian's words were skillful.

First, they revealed their mission's intent as a rescue operation, differentiating them from the merciless woman who called for violence.

Second, he inquired about the man's role as the task publisher, complaining about gradually break down their psychological defenses.

Indeed, the man softened his attitude slightly upon hearing Damian's words. "Yes, I posted it on the Doomsday Self-Rescue Platform."

He took out his own phone, and like in Flower City (D99 area), Glass Port (D139 area) also had a Star Network app called the "Doomsday Self-Rescue Platform."

It didn't require an internet connection and was universally used by the NPA for real-time information exchange and for posting rescue requests.

Damian compared his terminal to the man's, and it confirmed that he was the one who had posted the B-level mission.

However, the man's panel appeared notably different from Damian's.

It didn't display A, B, C, D, or E levels, nor did it show any information about the Aberrants team.

It was likely that the NPA's central computer or artificial intelligence collected help requests from various regions, evaluated them, and then forwarded them to the relevant area's Aberrants.

The man gazed at Damian's cartoonish terminal, devoid of envy but filled with numbness.

Citizens from different areas had different statuses, rights, and privileges, and access to different levels of technology.

For those in the D area who weren't Aberrants, a terminal with technology surpassing local levels was a lifelong dream.

After hearing the news that the zombies outside had already been cleared, the man's spirit lifted slightly.

"Good, thank you."

"Could you do us a favor and confirm the mission completion?" Damian clasped his hands together, his eyes moist, giving off a pitiful look.

"Fine," the man reluctantly agreed.

Cora remained silent for a moment and then turned to Onyx with an expressionless face.

"Why did you teach him these things? You're a bad influence on little Damian."

"Me? A bad influence?" Onyx appeared bewildered.

"Sophia, let's go," the man said as he approached her.

"No! We have to take John with us!"

Sophia clung to Stone's head, refusing to let go.

"Didn't you hear? Many people are looking for John. Taking him with us would prevent us from leaving," the other man explained.

Sophia shook her head, her anguish clear.

The other man bellowed in despair, "Sophia, come to your senses! The dead can't come back to life. Don't let John's sacrifice be in vain; we have to survive!"

The two men, who were employees here and therefore knew the labyrinthine pathways of City Hall eventually assisted Sophia.

They disappeared into the depths of the corridor.

After they left, a couple of minutes passed, and Suchat, who had been leaning against the wall, suddenly whispered, "Pursuers, they're here."

Cora unleashed a bit of her psychic power and indeed detected a plethora of diverse and chaotic energy signatures nearby.

The Aberrants were combing each room, and the sounds of their movements were faint but growing closer. In a short while, they would be near this office.

The pretty lady's expression initially tightened, but then she seemed to have an idea and raised her gaze towards Cora and her group.

"Hey, folks over there, don't you think it's time to come up with a plan? How are we going to get out of here?"

The trio from F777 displayed an astonishing level of nonverbal communication at this critical moment.

One looked up at the ceiling, one down at the floor, and the other smiled at each other, yet none spoke a word.

The pretty lady, now agitated, questioned, "What's going on? You throw many schemes at us when dealing with us, and now you're tongue-tied?"

"You," she pointed her nail-polished finger at Cora, then at Onyx, "and you, weren't you capable just a while ago? Can't you do anything now?"

"Sorry, taunts don't work on me," Onyx replied calmly.

The pretty lady huffed, "Okay, you guys aren't in a hurry, but I am?"

Cora felt a little embarrassed by her words and took a few steps forward. She approached the window, glanced downwards, and saw that the office was about three stories above the ground. She could jump down, but Onyx and Damian clearly couldn't.

Cora picked up a saw from the corner and looked at Onyx, inquiring with her eyes.

Do we need to break through?

Onyx contemplated for a moment and then extended his hand to her. "Give me your terminal."

Cora unpinned her terminal badge and handed it to him.

After manipulating it for a few moments, they waited for two to three minutes. Suddenly, they heard a "tap-tap-tap" sound from outside the window.

Everyone immediately looked in that direction, and to their astonishment, they found a mechanical arm!

It was the two sections of the transport truck that had been left at the door!

The truck's cargo bed was parked right under the shadow of the window.

This position was very concealed, far from all exits, and unlikely to be discovered easily.

The long mechanical arm extended to the third floor, latching onto the window frame, and then smoothly laid down, unfolding to create an escape slide.

The others looked at Onyx in amazement.

"I sent the location to it, and it used automatic calculations to build the closest escape route," Onyx explained calmly, showing no signs of taking credit.

Cora, for the first time, wondered about the level of artificial intelligence in Felalakas.

If a simple AI had this level of intelligence, how terrifying could Ilia, the ruler of Felalakas, be?

With this slide, they slipped away from the heavily guarded pursuers.

They left City Hall and sprinted for several miles, slowing down only when they were certain no one was following them.

Onyx looked at the two of them. "This is where we part ways. It's better for both of us."

The pretty lady lifted her chin.

"Of course, no objections from me."

Temporary alliances were as fragile as paper mache, ready to dissolve at the slightest touch.

Besides, they hadn't let go of their wariness at each other.

Cora dragged the two sections of the truck and took a step towards where the transport vehicle was parked.

Coincidentally, the pretty lady and Suchat also took a step in that direction.

Cora hesitated for a moment, lifted her foot, and tentatively took another step. Oh no! They were about to bump into each other!

She immediately gazed intently at the people in front of her, wondering what they were up to and why they were following her.

"Hey, are you guys heading back to Felalakas?" the pretty lady teased.

But noticing Cora's look, she appeared slightly surprised and her gaze shifted between Cora, Damian, and Onyx. "You don't know me, do you?"

Damian couldn't help but mumble, "Who are you, and do we have to know you?"

The pretty lady chuckled, her alluring face radiating charm. "No need. It's even better if you don't."

"I'm Yuui Hayashi. We'll see each other again if fate permits. Farewell."

CHAPTER 8

Poorness

"I thank you for your sweet words, and I appreciate your hidden agenda," Cora muttered with a resentful expression.

She pressed the rewind button once more.

"I thank you for your sweet words..."

"That's enough," Onyx exclaimed, his patience worn thin as he reached over and turned off her device. "You've listened to it over a dozen times."

Cora sighed.

Listening to it a dozen times had made no difference. How could she not have recognized it?

She blamed herself for her lack of musical appreciation.

The voice singing in her ear earlier should have been familiar.

But how could it not be?

This song, "Thank You for Loving Me," had been on a loop for who knew how many times on their journey to Felalakas.

By now, her fellow travelers had all developed calluses on their ears from hearing it.

Cora had practically memorized the lyrics.

Yet... Yuui Hayashi, wasn't she the Felalakas' top sweet idol singer?

When she shouted, "I'm not a saint!" with her hands on her hips, she had been so sassy, nothing like a sweet idol.

Cora sighed again.

No wonder Yuui went to great lengths to hide her identity, even avoiding public tasks.

This would be a tremendous blow to her image as an idol.

Cora wondered what that conservative guy Maeda would think if he saw Yuui's fiercely sassy side.

It suddenly piqued her curiosity.

Wait, no, that's not right!

Cora shook her head, dismissing her tangled thoughts.

The actual issue was why Yuui, if she wanted to keep her identity a secret, had told Cora her name before leaving.

The heart of the beautiful lady was as elusive as a needle in the sea.

Cora sighed for the third time.

"Stop thinking about it. If she told you her name, she must be confident that you won't reveal it. Let's head back to Felalakas to complete the task."

After reattaching the two detached cargo cars to the main body, they collected some more zombies in the vicinity to fill the entire transport vehicle.

Cora, Onyx, and the artificial intelligence started the return sequence.

The vehicle turned around and sped back towards Felalakas.

After another arduous journey of ten hours, they safely returned to the mission center.

The transport vehicle stopped at the entrance to the high-altitude track.

The loudspeakers on the control panel beeped twice, reminding them to disembark.

Cora glanced back.

The pure black metal vehicle resembled a sated beast, silently lurking in the night. Roughly estimating the capacity of each section of the vehicle at 200, it held at least 1,200 zombies.

But what was the purpose of transporting so many monsters into Felalakas?

"Where is it going?"

Cora turned to the all-knowing Onyx, her voice full of confusion.

"It's unclear for now. The endpoint route is encrypted, and we don't have permission to view it," Onyx responded.

Zombies, nutrients, T.T.T... Cora tried to connect the dots, but her mind was still a foggy mess.

She furrowed her brow and came up with a bold idea. "Can we follow it?"

Before Onyx could answer, the alert system beeped twice again.

Text appeared on the screen.

"Warning! You have exceeded your time limit. Please vacate the control cabin promptly, or the emergency protocol will be started."

Onyx turned off the blaring alarm, but the cabin lights continued to flash, making it hard for them to keep their eyes open.

"It seems we can't."

The transport vehicle could travel on high-altitude tracks within Felalakas, which was much faster than the wandering they had done in Glass Port.

If they got off now, Cora was sure it would vanish in the blink of an eye, and they wouldn't be able to catch up.

Onyx pondered for a moment and had an idea.

"What about your Ethereal Weapons? Can they be tracked when they're not with you?"

"Within a five-mile radius, they can," Cora nodded.

By injecting a bit of psychic power during their ethereal transformation, she could sense her Ethereal Weapons within a certain range.

Onyx smiled. "That's good. Let's attach a tracker to them."

Cora was surprised. "You mean...?"

Leaving the Ethereal Weapons intentionally in the control cabin?

This way, even if the transport vehicle disappeared from their sight, Cora could roughly track their location with her psychic power. If they pursued it wholeheartedly, they wouldn't lose their trail.

The onboard artificial intelligence, oblivious to their plotting, continued to beep impatiently, urging them to leave.

After the three of them got off, the transport vehicle switched to high-altitude travel mode and sped up, disappearing into the colorful night sky in an instant.

"No need to rush; let's go complete the task first," Onyx suggested.

Cora entered the mission hall, found an available self-service terminal, and scanned her team leader's identification.

The background displayed a notification that F777 Team had successfully completed the B-level mission to clear zombies from the first floor of the City Hall in D139, Glass Port.

They had earned 2000 NPA credits!

B-level mission (Code VB00046). Clearing zombies from City Hall, Ground Floor, D139 Area, Glass Port (confirmed completed)

Points earned. 200

NPA credits earned. 2000

Cora dismissed the option to make their team's progress public without a second thought.

She turned off the notification and looked happily at Damian. "D, here's your money!"

She was rich now, with a whole 2000 NPA credits.

Damian shook his head. "Sis, you can keep it for now. What if we need it later? You can pay me back in one go."

"Alright, that sounds like a plan," Cora agreed, thinking it would be wise to keep some money on hand. "You should go back and rest for now. We'll go after the vehicle."

Damian didn't respond but scuffed his foot on the floor, not eager to leave like this.

A few days ago, he had been relaxing in a hotel, eating, drinking, and sleeping without a care. He had found nothing wrong with that.

But during this time with Cora, even though the process had been heart-pounding, he was happier than being on his own.

Mr. Blackwood was gone, and Damian had no remaining family.

He and Cora had been strangers in District F, and he couldn't explain why he had this inexplicable desire to stick with her.

"Sis, please take me with you. I won't be a burden," Damian suddenly hugged Cora's arm, his voice childlike and sweet.

Damian was indeed mature for his age. He had become braver compared to when they first went to the food factory. Apart from the initial mishap with the frost, he had been well-behaved.

Cora couldn't resist his request, especially under his affectionate, milk-and-honey voice.

Cora shook her arm, and Damian's large, dewy eyes were like grapes soaked in water. "Sis, please? I'll be really well-behaved."

Behind them, Onyx made a quiet, disapproving sound and had a look of disdain.

Cora, predictably, surrendered entirely to Damian's soft attack.

"Alright, fine."

"Here, turn left," Cora's psychic power tracked the shuriken, and the three of them changed direction once again.

They had expected the transport vehicle to venture further into the wilderness and eventually stop in some desolate location.

However, it was quite the opposite.

The vehicle continued toward the city center, pulling its six dark cargo cars, each filled with zombies.

It passed through the dazzling neon Ferris wheel, weaved through skyscrapers shrouded in mist, and eventually stopped behind a magnificent theater.

The marble floor sank slowly, creating a massive depression that allowed the transport vehicle to pass through. It gently slid down into the depths of the underground.

Into... the theater?

Cora took two steps back and looked up at the building in front of her.

The gray brick walls were both vintage and understated, with exquisite reliefs that were ornate. The stark contrast made it hard to look away.

This was the most famous artistic sanctuary in Felalakas–the Sycara Theater.

Many drones circled in the sky, performing acrobatics around the venue.

Thousands of cameras twinkled in the night, capturing footage for high-stakes auctions of every performance held here.

Even just standing at the entrance, the deafening cheers and roars from inside could be heard.

Cora took a step forward, but the mechanical gate stopped her.

The electronic eye scanned her face and displayed a "Recognition Failure" message.

An usher in a tuxedo approached, doffing his hat and bowing

gracefully.

"Good evening, my dear ladies and gentlemen. Are you here to watch the T.T.T. Preliminaries tonight?"

"What match?" Cora asked.

"T.T.T. 162nd Round Preliminaries. Do you have any favorite players or teams? I can provide you with some support gifts."

"No, we don't."

T.T.T.?

Cora looked at the man behind the usher.

The projections of today's popular players on the walls and posters scattered on the ground showed that an intense competition was happening inside.

"No favorite players? Are you here to experience the atmosphere in person? That's a wise choice!" the usher said.

"The terminal, no matter how realistic, can't compare to the experience of being on site. Although the ticket prices are higher, we have over ten thousand tracking projection devices. You can see every detail clearly."

"I promise you that you won't regret it tonight," the man spoke with a dramatic tone, maintaining a strangely fixed smile.

"Cora, it's an artificial intelligence," Onyx suddenly said.

Cora looked back at the usher. The man seemed not to have heard Onyx's words or was immune to the term "artificial intelligence." He still held an unassailable smile.

Since they had come this far, it seemed odd not to go inside and have a look.

"How much are the tickets?" Cora asked nervously.

The usher replied, "We have the most luxurious and immersive floating ball tickets, close to the center of the arena, available for a special price of only 2888 each. There are VIP box seats for 1888, with excellent viewing positions to capture the entire arena. Which would you prefer?"

"The cheapest, please," Cora pursed her lips and tightened her terminal.

The usher's smile disappeared, and his exaggerated tone turned into a lifeless monotone.

"Standing tickets, 800 NPA credits per person."

Cora was about to speak up when he added, "Sorry, no discounts."

800 NPA credits per person. With three people, that was 2400 in total.

Cora, who had just got 2000 NPA credits, sighed.

She was quite poor, indeed.

CHAPTER 9

Gamblers

2000 NPA credits, of course, wouldn't get three people inside.

Damian stepped forward with exceptional maturity, insisting it was his idea to come.

And thus, he would "go it alone" and pay for his own ticket.

Cora, a dignified team captain, avoided the embarrassment of not being able to afford the tickets, allowing all three of them to enter smoothly.

They followed a dim, narrow corridor for about five to six minutes until the view suddenly opened up and they stepped into the stands.

Hot, deafening waves of noise hit them like a surging tide, nearly knocking them over.

The interior of the Sycara Theater did not resemble a typical stage but a design reminiscent of the ancient arenas of old civilizations.

It was broad at the top and narrow at the bottom, with a sunken area at the base that extended tens of meters deep. It was surrounded by five-story high, horseshoe-shaped tiers.

From any seat, you could see all the action below.

This should have been halftime, and the arena, once empty, was now packed to capacity.

The three of them squeezed their way through the crowd.

Damian's face was contorted, and Onyx's wheelchair had no place to rest.

While the surrounding spectators were enthusiastic, Cora had a peculiar sensation that something was amiss-she could detect a lingering scent of blood.

After a while, a spotlight shone from the theater's heights, and a handsome man in a blue robe, holding a jade flute, materialized.

His sleeves moved without the wind's aid, and his raven-feather-like long eyelashes slowly opened as he wore a faint, otherworldly smile.

"Good evening, everyone. The second round of the preliminaries is about to begin, and I'm River Locke, the special guest for this match."

The crowd erupted with enthusiastic cheers, particularly from female spectators.

"River!!! I'm your fish!!!"

A deafening, heart-wrenching scream came from not far away.

Cora nearly lost her balance.

Her jaw dropped as she turned to see Chiho Sato, whom she had briefly met before, fervently cheering among River Locke's supporters.

Her face was crimson, and she watched the projection under the spotlight with fascination.

River smiled gracefully and pulled out an ancient scroll from his long sleeves, elegantly unfolding it.

"Up next, we have 'Artu and Aqua,' a two-person team. They're not only teammates but also lovers who depend on each other for life and death. Let's look forward to their debut. You, the audience, can vote for them using your terminals. As long as they successfully complete the challenge, and their public support reaches 60%, they can advance to the next round of the major competition."

He spoke calmly, his voice like a clear mountain spring.

He exuded the air of a well-mannered young nobleman.

The female fan group, led by Sato, went wild, cheering with all their might.

In the center of the arena, a pure white platform slowly rose from the ground, and a young man and woman, dressed in bright red and blue combat suits, stood atop it.

They exuded confidence and waved to the audience with bright smiles.

Once they were positioned in the arena, Artu made a "peace" sign towards one of the approaching drones.

His smiling face appeared in a synchronous projection of it.

The audience burst into laughter as they watched the mirrored images, creating an electrifying atmosphere.

"Let the match begin," River announced as he closed the scroll.

With the sound of his voice, the iron barriers on either side of the arena slowly opened.

Following that, the ground rumbled with the footsteps of approaching zombies, and their low growls grew louder and nearer.

Then, in the next moment, almost a hundred zombies surged into the arena!

The audience's enthusiasm was reignited, and they stood up and cheered with excitement.

Cora watched in astonishment as the so-called preliminaries were, in fact, a battle against zombies. She exchanged a glance with Onyx.

So, the disappeared zombies... were they food?

The two competitors in the arena had unique Anopowers.

Artu possessed the ability to transport zombies into a separate space, while Aqua could create duplicates of herself.

For each zombie Artu transported, Aqua released a duplicate into the separate space to fight them.

The duo's evidently flawless teamwork was showcased as they circled the perimeter, implementing a strategy to eliminate the zombies systematically.

In no time, their mirrors and duplicates covered the arena, spinning the zombies around in circles.

The battle raged on, and River's clear voice filled the arena again.

"The performance of these two competitors is truly exceptional. Now, let's check the audience support rates..."

A drone provided a close-up view, and the support rate for Artu and Aqua had already risen to 43%.

Cora also spotted the "0 Distance" floating balls, which cost 2888 NPA credits to ride.

They glided among countless drones and balloons, sometimes being kicked aside by running zombies or colliding with the duplicates, causing the passengers inside to tumble and wave their arms excitedly through the transparent glass.

Is this what they called an "immersive" experience?

The hobbies of the wealthy were certainly unique.

However, their fortunes soon waned. With only a third of the zombies left, Artu and Aqua's coordination faltered.

Perhaps they had summoned too many duplicates, depleting their Anopower, or maybe the remaining zombies were becoming more challenging to handle.

In one mirror, Aqua's attack showed a flaw, and a fierce zombie captured her instantly, tearing her in two.

Artu's mirror instantly shattered, releasing the zombies from the separate space, and they frantically pursued the remaining duplicates.

"What are you doing? Get it under control!"

"Don't just stand there! Do something!"

"Think on your feet! Do something!"

The audience grew discontent and voiced their frustration.

Some of them even threw their shoes into the arena in agitation. But they were quickly stopped by patrolling security robots.

Unfortunately, things continued to deteriorate.

With only one-third of the zombies remaining, Artu and Aqua's coordination broke down.

"Chiho!" Cora couldn't help but shout out.

But it was too late. Artu, seeing Aqua's demise, desperately charged forward, but paused. With Aqua's attack no longer available, he was a pure support, and his survival seemed impossible in the face of these monsters.

"Forfeit! I lose!" Artu yelled, escaping in a panic.

As the zombies closed in on him, he actually dove into his own mirror, leaving Aqua struggling behind. Artu quickly shifted to another part of the arena, driven by pure survival instincts.

The stands filled with thunderous boos.

"Artu, what kind of man are you?"

"You're a disgrace! I voted for you!"

"Refund! I want a refund!"

Regrettably, Artu was rescued.

The mechanical arms responsible for maintaining order acted promptly, driving the remaining zombies back underground.

"Challenge failed."

Huge gray letters appeared on the floating screen.

The lights representing "Artu and Aqua" went out, and posters of the team surrounding the arena were ruthlessly removed.

"Ah..."

Sighs echoed through the audience.

"Unfortunately, they didn't make it through the preliminaries," River said with a light smile.

"The next match will begin in ten minutes. Until then, we have an exciting halftime show for you all."

A dazzling band, Al, descended from the sky with exhilarating drum beats, deep bass, and explosive electric guitar sounds, instantly igniting the atmosphere.

"It's the Arc Band!"

"I love their nostalgic, heavy metal style."

The audience, who had just been sighing, immediately got back into the groove, nodding their heads to the intense rhythm.

While Cora's mind had gone cold amid the raucous arena, Damian had taken refuge behind her, covering his eyes to avoid looking.

Cora, despite being in the noisy and chaotic arena, couldn't shake off the feeling of chilling detachment.

Fighting against zombies should have been a means of self-preservation in a world on the brink of collapse.

But in Felalakas, within the Sycara Theater, the self-indulgent hunt had become celebration.

Cora didn't sympathize with the zombies. If she were in the arena, she wouldn't hesitate to act.

However, the spectacle of so many people watching made it a surreal experience.

Did violence genuinely stimulate people's desires?

Why were some people so keen on bloodshed and violence?

Why did Felalakas host such events?

"Onyx, are you still watching?" Onyx's frown deepened as he raised his voice.

Not that he couldn't bear to watch; the platform was just too crowded, making it hard to breathe. Onyx had endured it for a long time, resisting the urge to leave until the match ended.

When the surrounding people started taking off their shoes as a protest, he couldn't bear it any longer.

"Let's go," he suggested.

With none of their companions eager to continue watching, Cora, who had already checked the disposition of the zombies, was ready to leave. She grasped the wheelchair's handles and squeezed through the crowd with great difficulty.

As they approached the exit, Cora overheard two men conversing in the corridor.

"Old James, what's with that expression? You lost your bet again?"

"Don't remind me, Artu. I was quite confident in them. I bet a few credits on them, and now it's all down the drain!"

"How much did you lose this time?"

Old James shook his head, unwilling to reveal the sum, and said, "Thank goodness the odds weren't that high, or I'd be out of my pants."

His friend chuckled, "I told you, your intelligence work was lacking, Artu. Artu and Aqua, they can hardly complete a C-level assignment usually. Them joining T.T.T., wasn't it just for gaining experience? And you bet on them. You've only got yourself to blame."

"I know, but I thought they might surprise everyone. After all, just by passing the preliminaries, they can earn 50,000 NPA credits and 100 points. Who wouldn't want those points among those Aberrants, right?"

"True, but it's quite a stretch for two D-grades."

"Thankfully, the competition requires at least D-grade and above to sign up. Otherwise, we'd have too many underwhelming matches!"

Cora's steps halted between the two men, and she turned her head incredulously.

"H-How much?"

Old James and his friend turned to her.

"50,000 NPA credits and 100 points, right? It's all in the registration rules."

Cora's eyes instantly lit up.

50,000 NPA credits! That was a lot of money!

It could not only clear her outstanding D-grade debt, but also leave her with 40,000 credits in surplus.

If she took on regular assignments, it would take her quite a while to save up that much.

Now, by merely passing the preliminaries, she could get it for free! Who wouldn't be enticed by that?

Old James stopped mid-sentence, examined her from head to toe, and remarked, "You're an Aberrant, aren't you? Do you have a D-grade?"

Cora shook her head, as she wasn't aware yet.

Old James assumed her headshake meant she didn't have a D-grade and, probably frustrated by his recent losses, sneered, "I've watched over a hundred preliminary matches. Someone like you wouldn't last a hundred seconds."

"Zombies would cut you up like vegetables."

"Are you going to put on a show for the audience by surrendering in one second?"

Damian couldn't help but chuckle. Who was cutting whom? This man had quite the self-assured demeanor.

His friend put a hand on Old James's shoulder and offered Cora an apologetic smile.

"Sorry about that. Don't mind him; he's just frustrated because he's been losing lately."

He turned to Old James, saying, "How about you tone it down a bit? You've watched over a hundred matches, but how many have you hit the jackpot on? Not a single one!"

Old James, publicly shamed, raised his voice. "How have I not hit the jackpot? You, you..."

"I don't believe you. If someone like her can enter the major competition, I'll put my entire fortune on her in the next match and every match afterward. I'm saying it, and I'll do it!"

CHAPTER 10

Join the Game

After leaving the Sycara Theater, the three of them found a long bench to sit down and studied the rules of the T.T.T.

Onyx gazed at the large projection screen at the theater's entrance and calmly recited the registration requirements displayed there:

"Applicants must meet the following conditions: first, they must be D-grade or higher Aberrants with an official NPA certification. Second, they must abide by Felalakas' laws, have no criminal record, and third, they should be in good physical health with stable vital signs..."

"The total prize pool for this competition exceeds 10 million, with the champion team winning 5 million NPA credits and 1000 assignment points. All teams that pass the preliminaries will receive 50,000 NPA credits and 100 assignment points."

1000 points were almost equivalent to an A-level assignment.

Cora remembered how difficult A-level missions were from her time in Glass Port, where they had to wrestle assignments away from many Aberrants.

And as for 5 million NPA credits, that was a staggering amount of money. More than they could count!

While aiming for the championship was still a distant dream, just passing the preliminaries could earn them 50,000 credits for free. It made her wonder if Felalakas was wealthy, being part of the C District.

"Are you thinking about registering?" Onyx always seemed to discern her thoughts. "Do you want to challenge that guy from earlier?"

Cora's intentions were entirely different.

She explained earnestly, "I want to... I want to make money."

Cora and Onyx would stay in Felalakas for a while, and they needed money for their expenses.

She couldn't keep relying on Damian, and her previous life in District F had been modest, with low material desires.

Only now, living in the broader world, did she realize how crucial money was.

"Big sister, I support you!" Damian clenched his little fists and cheered her on with sparkling eyes.

He knew just how talented Cora was: When Cora used those ancient Ethereal Artifacts; it was like a visual feast.

Each move dealt with a zombie, and it couldn't get any cooler.

Humph, that old man would see how amazing his big sister was. But did he also place some bets and earn some pocket money?

After all, choosing Cora as the participant would undoubtedly be a safe bet.

As Damian pondered, his thoughts drifted further.

Mr. Blackwood's son was indeed showing an early understanding of investment risks.

Onyx observed the eager expressions of the two in front of him and chuckled softly.

"Have you forgotten something? Cora, your Anopower grade hasn't been revealed yet."

Right! Cora realized.

Even though they said it would take three working days, Damian received his results one day later, and Cora was now entering the fourth day.

Had she missed her window of opportunity?

She was just about to double-check on the terminal when it suddenly chimed.

What was happening?

She had just gained this brand new terminal, and there were no contacts in her directory except for Damian.

Who would reach out to her?

Cora answered the voice call, and a booming voice came through.

"Hello! We are the Century Corporation's marketing department. Would you be interested in sponsorship? Our plan primarily focuses on the preliminaries, involving logos on team uniforms..."

"Sponsorship?"

Cora thought it might be some kind of new scam and shrewdly disconnected the call.

Ding-ding! Just as she hung up, her terminal prompted her again.

She answered.

"This is the Dragon's Ascent Aberrants Club. Are you interested in joining us? Currently, we already have three teams in the main event..."

An Aberrants Club? What was this all about? Why were they contacting her?

Ding-ding-ding! The terminal chimed for the third time.

What was going on suddenly?

"Just a moment," Cora said before answering the third call.

A pleasant electronic voice greeted her, "Felalakas Art-Star Bet Reminder: Bet responsibly and enjoy the game."

When the voice call connected, the person on the other end first cleared his throat and then lowered his voice, asking cautiously, "Do you plan to take part in the fake matches?"

Cora called out. "What???"

She answered with a blank expression and promptly hung up.

Ding-ding-ding! Her terminal continued to ring incessantly.

Cora directly disabled the calling feature, bringing peace back to her world.

Next second, Damian's terminal also rang, with an equally unfamiliar caller.

"Please, don't answer!" Cora was startled, her eyes wide. "It's a scam!"

"Okay!" Damian mimicked her and also turned off his communication.

Onyx smiled softly. "It's probably not a scam."

The two looked at him curiously.

"I guess... your Anopower grades have been revealed," he said.

"And judging by the reactions, they must be high, which is why all these people are swarming in like bees to honey."

Cora was puzzled. "I don't even know my grade yet."

Onyx pointed to her chest-pin terminal.

"Since Felalakas' Aberrant base has outside commercial involvement, it's not unusual that big data already knows your Anopower grade."

As they were talking, the terminal chimed with a notification again.

This time, it wasn't an inexplicable nuisance call.

Cora tapped to open it and found her Aberrants registration information.

Name: Cora (Biological ID: VUL7700523)

Anopower Grade: A-level

Anopower Type: Mental-Elemental (Metal Element), High Attack Potency (Object Illusion)

Anopower Potential: 30%

Affiliated Team: F777 (Registration Location: C83 District)

Cora read the results and her eyes lit up. Just like Jeremy, she was an A-level Aberrant! That was fantastic. She couldn't wait to spar with him.

"Sis, my grade is out too." Damian raised his cartoonish terminal high and proudly showed it to her.

Name: Damian (Biological ID: F177104910)

Anopower Grade: B-level

Anopower Type: Mental-Elemental (Ice Element) High Attack Potency (Hexagonal Ice Blades)

Anopower Potential: 90%

Affiliated Team: F777 (Registration Location: C83 District)

Like children exchanging gifts, they leaned in close, giving each other colorful compliments.

"Sis, you're amazing with an A-grade!"

"Even with a high potential for B, you can work your way up to A-level in the future."

"Haha," Damian chuckled.

"Cora, let me see your terminal." Onyx interjected from the side.

"Sure," Cora handed him her chest-pin terminal.

Onyx lowered his gaze and began scrolling through the push notification on the screen, which displayed Cora's registration information.

Before the apocalypse, Aberrants joining Azures were under military command, while the rest fell under the jurisdiction of the NPA's Special Abilities Division.

As a result, NPA established Aberrant bases in various major cities.

The machines used to determine Aberrant grades were developed independently by Arashi Research, with the core processing unit in District A. All Aberrant information was archived there and directly sent back to all districts without human intervention, ensuring it couldn't be tampered with.

At first glance, Cora's grade seemed entirely normal. She was an A-level Aberrant, which was a formidable status no matter where she was placed.

But Onyx had seen many A-levels before, and he was confident that if Cora were to face any of them in a one-on-one battle, she would not lose to any of them. In fact, she could probably take on all of them simultaneously.

Her Anopower potential was only 30%.

Damian had an exceptionally high 90% potential. But given his young age, it was strange that Cora's potential was so low.

It appeared they were intentionally keeping her at the A-level, ensuring she didn't rise above it. At least in Felalakas, they didn't want her to stand out.

Onyx found this intriguing, and he couldn't help but think that there was more to Cora's A-level status than met the eye. Let's not forget, the city was ruled by a top-tier artificial intelligence.

Since they had taken part in the T.T.T., Cora followed the address on the poster to the registration point.

A friendly-looking robot staff member received them.

Felalakas was indeed a city governed by artificial intelligence, and

AI figures were often visible in various job roles.

"Are you registering as a single participant or as a team?" the robot asked.

Cora inquired, "Is there a difference?"

"It is recommended to register in a team format for this competition. Only single challenges are accepted in the preliminaries, while the major competition must be entered as a team. Teams that register during the preliminary stage can maintain their original team composition if they advance."

Cora raised a question, "What if I enter as a single participant and reach the major competition?"

"After the preliminaries, all single participants will be randomly matched to form teams."

Oh? If they matched her with strong teammates, that would be fine.

But what if she ended up with some deadweight teammates?

It might lead to her elimination.

Plus, untested teams, like when she and Damian first started, might have coordination issues.

Cora couldn't decide.

The F777 team currently had three members: Onyx had a leg injury, Damian was timid and struggled with Anopower control, so entering the preliminaries with them wasn't realistic.

Cora saw herself as the team leader: it was her job to earn the money.

Cora contemplated and asked, "If a team makes it to the major competition, can they add more members?"

"Yes, but each team has a maximum limit of five members."

Most Aberrants wouldn't choose this, and the idea of a team starting with her hard-earned spot in the major competition, only for someone else to come in and reap the benefits, was unappealing.

But Cora could use this time to find potential teammates, maybe watch a few matches to identify skilled individual participants, and then invite them to join her team.

Cora informed the robot of her decision.

It paused for a moment.

"You want to register as a team, but compete alone in the

preliminaries?"

"That's correct," Cora confirmed.

The artificial intelligence stared at her for a couple of seconds as if she were strange.

"In the team format, a minimum of two members is required. You will face 100 zombies."

"That's fine."

"Please show your AC."

Cora transmitted her freshly got Anopower information to the robot.

The robot operated within the system.

"Please complete the pre-match physical examination."

Cora followed the instructions and underwent a quick physical check-up.

The robot clicked through its system.

"Congratulations, registration is complete."

Cora's terminal chimed with a notification: "Congratulations, you are now a participant in the 178th round of the T.T.T. preliminaries. Your match will start in two days at 21:00. Please report 30 minutes in advance, or you will be considered having forfeited."

The preliminaries comprised eight rounds every day, and they had been ongoing for over half a month, with increasing interest.

Even if you registered that day, it might take several days before your turn came up.

Waiting for just two days was quite lucky.

Back at the hotel, Damian, still a child, was tired from their recent adventures. One moment he solemnly vowed to accompany his sister, and the next moment, his head hit the pillow, and he was sound asleep.

So, it was just Onyx and Cora discussing their preliminary match.

"Onyx, could you tell me more about the preliminaries?" Cora asked.

"In the preliminaries, you'll be facing 100 zombies in a sudden-death round. You need to clear the field and earn the audience's support to get their votes. Killing all the zombies is one thing, but gaining support can be quite challenging. Some participants who can kill zombies with ease still can't advance because their vote count is too low."

Cora felt she was quite ordinary and didn't think she could engage the audience like Artu did today with his sweet talk and audience engagement.

What if she put all her effort into eliminating zombies, only to be eliminated because she didn't gain enough support?

She could lose the 50,000 NPA credits!

Onyx gestured for her not to worry. "I've reviewed past match recordings, and there are three situations where the audience's support is higher."

"First, there are the seeded players. High-level Aberrants with a lot of popularity. Their reputation generates significant pre-match hype."

For example, "The Boss and His Three Goons," who were the top of the Felalakas area scoreboard, had a support rate of over 90%.

"Second, some participants who create a lot of buzzes or controversy receive higher support rates. For instance, in round 82, a female participant with a revealing costume had a 71% support rate, while in round 105, a male participant wore only shorts and the rest of his body was exposed and covered with a mask. That participant had a 68% support rate. Some provocative, attention-grabbing acts, while receiving backlash, can also be quite effective."

Cora had goosebumps, and she shook her head in resistance.

Onyx continued in a slower tone, "Third, there's the situation where the bloodier and more violent your zombie-killing display, the more enthusiastic the atmosphere in the arena, and the higher your support rate."

Cora frowned. She didn't want to perform for the audience by brutalizing the zombies; she was more accustomed to finishing them quickly and efficiently.

Onyx paused and then added, "But, according to my estimation, there's probably a fourth situation."

"What's that?" Cora asked.

"People are naturally curious. If an Aberrant can rapidly exterminate all the zombies, under everyone's eyes and with means unknown to them. They cannot deny the thrill of watching the fight. They will be curious to find out how it's done. Such participants may not receive a high vote count. But the audience will undoubtedly send them through to the major competition to uncover the mystery."

Onyx concluded, "So, what you need to do is to maintain an air of mystery."

The thought of bypassing the watchful eyes of the live audience, drones, and cameras to keep her actions mysterious intrigued Cora.

"How about it? Have you decided which Ethereal Artifacts to use?"

Cora nodded and, with a subtle movement of her hand, conjured a familiar Ethereal Artifact.

"This one."

CHAPTER 11

Her Choice

Two days later, the T.T.T. 178th round preliminary match took place as scheduled.

This round of the competition was set for 9:00 PM.

Before this, three participants had consecutively failed their challenges, and the audience's patience had run thin.

Frustration and curses filled the air, and the audience's enthusiasm was far from ideal.

Onyx and Damian didn't attend the event in person.

Onyx had a simple reason for not going.

First, Cora had run out of money, and she couldn't even afford the cheapest ticket with her remaining 400 NPA credits.

Second, he had a strong aversion to crowded and noisy environments.

If Onyx wasn't going, Damian certainly wouldn't attend alone.

Instead, they both watched the live broadcast from their hotel.

So, the two of them lay on a luxurious sofa in their hotel's screening room. They had an abundance of food and drinks at their disposal, watching the competition in comfort.

Damian had to be given credit for enjoying this situation.

The seven-star hotel they booked had a crystal-clear holographic display with a resolution of 24k, and it offered multiple angles for broadcasting, which made the experience almost equivalent to being present at the venue.

At the Sycara Theater live event.

After a brief intermission, a lively girl with double ponytails and orange glitter eyeshadow appeared in the center of the arena.

"Hello, everyone! Did you miss me?"

"Yurika!!"

The previously disheartened atmosphere in the audience instantly vanished, replaced by enthusiastic cheers.

Yurika was one of Felalakas' top ten rising stars, on par with River Locke, but their styles were vastly different.

Yurika was cheerful and outgoing, with her fanbase primarily comprising young boys and girls.

"I heard your voices! It seems you missed me!" Yurika said, soaking in the warm reception.

"Now, let's look at the next taking part team. Huh? They are called F777, which is indeed a team, but only one participant is on the stage!"

"They are quite bold. Let's welcome her to the stage!"

The audience fell momentarily silent.

Then, discussions and doubts murmured through the crowd.

"What? Am I hearing this right? 1 vs. 100? Is it me going crazy, or is it her?"

"This is another joke. There won't be a single enjoyable match tonight!"

"Fine, I won't be voting."

Outside the screen, Damian bit down on a juice straw and raised his small fists in excitement.

"Go, sis!"

He had invested a full 1000 votes!

Onyx said nothing, but wore a faint smile.

Those who underestimated the lion were soon going to pay the price.

The raised platform gradually ascended, revealing a slender figure in the center.

Cora stood calmly, an unconventional, enormous silver umbrella at her side.

In a five-tier VIP box, a man with ice-blue eyes exclaimed, "What is she holding?"

"Is it a weapon-type ability?" He rubbed his chin and pondered.

Behind him, another young man with a beauty mark near his eye was slumped in his seat, fatigue clear.

"What's so fascinating about these regional matches? When are we returning to base?"

In an apartment about ten miles from the Sycara Theater, a slim young man watching the broadcast on his terminal looked up and called out, "Z, you've got to see this!"

Zephyrion emerged from his room, wrapped in a coat. He still appeared somewhat pale, with a barely noticeable hint of fatigue.

His eyes locked onto the screen where the delicate girl stood, and he muttered, "It's her."

After Cora took the stage, the on-site whispers and speculation grew, with many questioning how she would face 100 zombies alone.

Yurika quickly appeared and gestured for everyone to calm down.

She raised her microphone and announced, "The challenge begins!"

The barriers on both sides opened, and an entire horde of 100 zombies rushed towards the solitary figure from all directions.

Onyx and Damian watched the crystal-clear broadcast from their luxurious sofa, witnessing Cora standing calmly as she slowly raised the unusual ethereal umbrella in her hands.

It unfurled with a sound like the roar of thunder, covering her completely.

A flash of silvery light occurred.

A blinding light struck the audience, attempting to observe the events, leaving them temporarily blinded.

Drones in the sky immediately changed their direction, trying to get a close-up view from different angles.

Cora, however, seemed to have eyes on her back, defending against every direction.

Regardless of how they maneuvered, they couldn't capture what was happening under the umbrella.

People who had spent a lot on floating sphere tickets were the most frustrated in the audience. Their view was no better than that of the regular seats.

The densely packed zombies blocked them or could only see the silver edge of the umbrella.

It was a terrible experience for the price they paid!

The silver-iron umbrella resembled a rolling mushroom, shooting down wave after wave of zombies.

The number of fallen monsters grew larger and larger, but both the live audience and those watching on screens couldn't see how Cora was achieving this.

How was she killing the zombies? What was happening under the umbrella?

It was a mystery, and everyone was frustrated that they couldn't see anything.

"Damn, I can't see anything!"

"What's going on? Why can't they show a better angle?"

"Hurry, the zombies are about to be wiped out!"

On the high-altitude screen, F777's support rate was slowly increasing. 53%... 56%... 59%... It eventually settled at 59%, not moving for several seconds.

Then, like many of the frustrated audience members, the number suddenly jumped up! 61%!

She had crossed the line!

Cora cleaned the last zombie, sheathed her short sword into the umbrella handle, and closed the umbrella with a brisk snap.

The umbrella pointed downwards, dripping with black, tainted blood.

The arena was now littered with corpses, and there she stood alone, like a silent harbinger of doom.

The venue fell silent for a second until the "Challenge Successful" alert sounded.

Only then did everyone grasp what had just occurred.

They had seen nothing, and yet, this person had advanced?

The audience was furious and erupted in anger.

"Is this some kind of joke? Who the heck voted for this?"

"Refund! Give us our money back!"

"I paid to watch this disappointment!"

Yurika shouted several times, "Quiet! Quiet!" But she couldn't calm the agitated crowd.

Just as things seemed about to spiral out of control, three deep chimes resonated, casting a spotlight from above the Sycara Theater.

A figure with radiant golden hair appeared once again.

"I... Ilia."

The irate audience, witnessing a divine presence, calmed like pets that their owner had soothed, retracting their claws and falling into quiet submission.

Yurika and the other artificial intelligences in the arena lowered their heads, displaying the utmost respect.

Ilia was casually dressed in a white outfit.

Although his attire was casual, his aura remained regal.

His gaze swept across the arena, not lingering on Cora or paying any heed to the recent commotion, as though this were just another ordinary match.

"I seem to have lost count. What round of the competition is it today?"

"Round 178! It's round 178! I've been to every match, Ilia!!!" A fervent fan's voice trembled as they shouted.

"Round 178... Another contestant advanced tonight."

No one dared to speak against Ilia, and he declared Cora had advanced. Who would dare to demand ticket refunds now?

Ilia took two steps forward.

Suddenly, the inorganic clarity of his eyes rippled with dazzling effects.

"The champion of T.T.T., besides the existing rewards, will make a wish from me."

"Whether you desire wealth, power, greater abilities, or even the qualification to enter B districts, Ilia can fulfill any wish you have."

The audience at the event was relatively unfazed, but countless Aberrants who followed T.T.T. stood up with horrified expressions. This was a promise made by the highest magistrate in District C83.

Ilia extended his hands, and brilliant starlight radiated from his fingertips.

"Felalakas, welcome, brave souls."

"Only through fire and thorns can a true crown of kings be forged."

This statement set the T.T.T.'s excitement to an unparalleled level.

All of Felalakas trembled with this announcement.

After the match, Cora left through the dimly lit player tunnel. As she approached the exit, she noticed a tall figure leaning against the side.

The person, upon hearing her footsteps, slowly turned, revealing a golden shimmer in their hair, unique sapphire eyes, and a blend of corporeal and holographic aspects.

It was Ilia. But hadn't he left? Why was he here?

Ilia focused his gaze on Cora as she drew near.

Cora felt somewhat nervous.

She had never interacted with artificial intelligence at this level before.

Should she greet him? Or was it better to... just walk away?

Finally, Cora stopped and stuttered, "Do you... um, do you need something?"

Ilia remained silent, observing her without blinking, like she was some amusing toy.

Cora felt uncomfortable under his unwavering gaze and shifted her feet forward slightly.

Out of the blue, Ilia spoke, "Why did you choose Felalakas?"

"Huh?"

He nodded, saying, "I understand."

"What?!"

Ilia smiled and added, "Just as I imagined."

"Where? Imagined what?"

After saying this, Ilia's figure faded gradually, disappearing completely into the tunnel.

In the air, there lingered his enigmatic words lingered.

"—You and I, aren't we the same?"

Cora was utterly bewildered.

After all, she wasn't artificial intelligence; how could she be the same as him?

CHAPTER 12

Different Wishes

"T.T.T. is heating," Onyx remarked as he scrolled through Cora's terminal, quickly skimming various reports that had been brewing.

If it was merely a relatively popular mid-sized event within the Felalakas region before, then starting from Ilia's appearance in the 178th round, T.T.T. had turned into a nationwide celebration.

No one responded to his words.

Onyx raised his gaze and found Cora sitting on the bed, looking dazed, with her disheveled shoulder-length hair.

"What are you daydreaming about? Still thinking about what Ilia said?" Onyx inquired.

On that evening in the dimly lit player's tunnel, Ilia had left Cora with the phrase, "You and I, aren't we the same?" and then vanished. This left Cora full of question marks, like flotsam in the wind.

Onyx set down the terminal and smoothly glided his wheelchair to the edge of the bed. Bathed in the radiant sunlight streaming in from the window, he sat with his back to the light.

With his prominent cheekbones and sensual, almost thin lips, their noses were almost touching. They stayed like that for a good inch apart for several seconds as Onyx intently examined Cora.

Cora snapped out of her daze and stared back, perplexed. "What... what are you doing?"

Onyx's lips curled slightly as he shook his head leisurely.

"I can't say anything else. But at the very least, you're definitely not artificial intelligence."

He retracted his upper body and reclined back into the wheelchair, letting out a lazy breath. "I'd say there wouldn't be an AI like you."

Before Cora could respond, a polished whip, with a resounding crack, swung across Onyx's cheek, plopping on the writing desk behind him, making the papers ruffle and rustle.

Her cheeks puffed up with anger.

Just because he mumbled those words, he thought she couldn't hear them?

Onyx ran his fingers through the severed strands casually, unfazed, and even had the mood to flick the blanket on his leg.

Alright, it was time for her to snap out of her daze and get back to being active.

"Get ready, and we'll talk about the match when you're back," he said.

While Cora was in the washroom, Damian entered the room with his hands behind his back, looking like a petty lord.

Once inside Cora's room, he scanned around, sometimes examining the various odd-shaped short weapons at the foot of the bed and at other times helping to tidy up the chaotic stack of books on the desk.

Finally, he cast an annoyed look at the obnoxious presence in the room.

Onyx's gaze was fixed on Cora's terminal, and he didn't bother acknowledging Damian.

After observing him for two seconds, Damian suddenly asked, "Where's your terminal?"

Onyx pointed at the terminal.

"You're not some... what was it, 'Rashi' researcher, so why aren't you using your own terminal?"

Although Damian was young, he was quite intelligent. Over the last few days, he'd observed more and more things that didn't quite add up with Onyx.

Onyx wasn't some unregistered nobody, nor did he have a backward technological background.

With his mannerisms and behavior, he likely hailed from one of the big cities.

Damian had never seen him use any communication device.

"Not only are you not using your terminal, but you haven't registered as an Aberrant either. You must have some kind of secret!"

As ordinary people discovered their awakening, they were definitely overjoyed.

They'd immediately run to register, especially now that it was the end of days.

Aberrants enjoyed privileges such as skipping zones.

To complete official registration, you had to go to an Aberrants base in the NPA area, having your picture taken, and providing your biological information.

This process would expose all your private information.

Was Onyx avoiding registration because of this?

"Oh? Do I have some secret? Do tell," Onyx said with an almost amused, half-smile, and a sense of uneasiness about his lie being exposed.

Damian was so excited he thought he'd figured Onyx out and jumped up in a challenge. His little smirk was mocking.

"You're a wanted fugitive! That's why you're afraid to leave an image. Not using a communication device is because you're afraid of exposing your whereabouts. And, in case someone comes to arrest you!"

He was goading Onyx to make him do something about it, and then he'd run to his sister and tell her he was a bad guy who should be dumped.

Onyx raised an eyebrow and smiled ominously. "That's right, I am indeed a wanted fugitive. Now that you know, I'll just have to get rid of you."

The challenge took Damian by surprise.

At first, he thought Onyx was joking, but then the surrounding air grew thin, and he felt an invisible force constricting his throat. Damian raised his hand slightly, trying to release his ice spears to resist, but his brain suddenly exploded in pain, and he couldn't gather Anopower.

As the sensation of being suffocated grew unbearable and his face turned red, Cora, having finished washing her face, returned. "What are you guys doing?"

The oppressive feeling suddenly dissipated, and Damian breathed heavily as he took in the fresh air.

He collapsed on the edge of the bed.

He couldn't believe it.

He couldn't win!

The more he thought about it, the angrier and more frustrated he got.

He wailed in frustration.

Cora, somewhat at a loss, turned to Onyx and said, "Don't bully Damian."

Onyx put on an innocent look. "Bully? How could you say that? I'm just teaching Damian a lesson. There are some things...you shouldn't say."

With a sense of defeat, Damian remained silent.

"Are you done getting ready? Come, look; I've organized some information on the players."

Perhaps, somewhat satisfied with the "education" Damian received, Onyx no longer teased him. He spoke in a more serious tone.

Cora sat on the edge of the bed, and Damian quickly moved closer, sitting close to her thigh, away from the grinning devil.

"The format of the main event has been announced. Unlike the qualifiers, the first round is a Battle Royale. All taking part teams will fight randomly to secure a spot in the top 64."

"Out of the 192 rounds of qualifiers, 130 teams have successfully advanced. Here are some solo players and teams that have caught my attention."

Onyx was a clear thinker and very proactive.

Since Cora had used T.T.T. as a stable source of income for a while, they needed to manage it properly and plan to maximize their gains while minimizing their costs.

"First, there's the most talked-about championship contender."

He tapped the air twice, and the luxurious 24K projection responded to his command, displaying the team's information.

"Zephyrion, the captain of 'The Boss and His Three Goons,' previously had a showdown in Glass Port. Public records show that he's the only B-level Aberrant in the team, with Anopower related to controlling thorny vines."

Cora knew Onyx wouldn't casually single out a B-level without a reason.

"Is the information is it... fake?" Cora asked.

Onyx shook his head. "Zephyrion is indeed B-level, but 'The Boss and His Three Goons'? It's not just him who's B-level."

"Here's a video from their qualifiers. If you watch closely, you'll see that only Victor and Kluge are actually fighting. Zephyrion and Luke appear busy. But in reality, they're just handling the cleanup."

In the high-resolution video, the key players were indeed stationary.

Zephyrion's thorns blocked most of the sprinting paths, trapping around 200 ferocious zombies. Only Victor and Kluge were doing the actual fighting, and they cleared out all the zombies.

As for Luke Shaw, he didn't lift a finger throughout the process.

"Do you suspect Luke is also B-level?" Cora guessed.

"No," Onyx said, with a glint in his eyes. "I suspect all four of them are B-level."

Cora and Damian were left stupefied, their mouths agape, their reactions mirroring each other.

Four B-levels! This wasn't "The Boss and His Three Goons"; this was "The Big 4"!

"They're ballooning their points, and their goal is clear: To secure an entrance ticket to B districts."

Less than a week had passed since the zombie skirmish in Glass Port, and "The Boss and His Three Goons" had amassed a fearsome 2176 points on the Felalakas leaderboard, leaving the second-place team far behind. Their achievements made them untouchable for other Anopower squads.

"For Zephyrion, winning the T.T.T. championship is almost a certainty."

"They chose this team name to focus everyone's attention on Zephyrion Stormrider, effectively overlooking the other three."

"In reality, Victor, Kluge, and Luke are no slouches. Their cooperation in Glass Port was impeccable. Those who underestimate these players will probably stumble during the main event."

True to their status as contenders, they'd begun psychological warfare well in advance. This was a powerful team.

Cora observed the projection screen and thought to herself that if they ever faced this team, she'd need to be on high alert.

Next was "Iron Cafe," the team with the oldest members among the competitors.

Cora glanced at the screen and blurted, "Wait, I recognize that old man."

"Master Stark, whose real name is unknown, with unknown Anopower. It's said he has a group of extraordinary individuals under his command, including space-type Aberrants."

"Iron Cafe's strength lies in the flexibility of its members. You never know what Aberrants Master Stark will deploy. And with no prior intelligence, you can only rely on your adaptability."

Cora nodded.

Another opponent is not to be underestimated.

After the apocalypse, age was no longer a measure of someone's strength—Anopower was.

She didn't know what cards Master Stark was holding, so she'd have to be cautious when facing him.

"Next is 'The Knights of Anna,' an all-mechanically augmented team."

Their style was like Battur, who had smashed the zombie Stone's head with one blow, combining cold mechanical bodies with human muscle tissue in a brutal aesthetic.

"Next..."

Onyx mentioned more than a dozen teams, providing Cora with detailed insights.

It was unclear how he managed it, but he had watched all 192 rounds of the qualifiers in just two nights and had memorized the information about all the players. His memory was at a terrifying level.

"Finally, this is footage from last night's qualifiers, and I thought you might be interested."

Onyx brought up a pair of familiar figures.

The young woman, though wearing a mask that obscured her face, had lips as vivid as Cora remembered.

Her large, wavy ponytail was also familiar.

Together with another elusive figure, Cora recognized her almost instantly.

The beautiful Lady!

It was Yuui Hayashi and Suchat. Why had they joined T.T.T.?

Yuui was displaying remarkable restraint, as though she was trying to stay under the radar. She barely moved. Fortunately, Suchat was quick and ruthless, dispatching zombies with a single blow. It was exciting to watch, and they secured a public approval rating of 71%, successfully advancing.

"Sis, Cora, look!" Damian excitedly pored over something on his terminal, then exclaimed, "Yuui is one of the top ten rising stars, right? Why is she allowed to take part in the competition?"

Cora leaned in, curious about what he'd found.

The terminal screen froze on this year's Supernova Festival.

Yuui, in her rose-pink spaghetti-strap dress, holding a trophy, looked stunning. Her makeup was pure and soft, and she was sweetly smiling right into the camera.

"Of course she can take part," Onyx chuckled, saying it with a meaningful tone.

Cora and Damian tilted their heads in unison, like curious little animals.

"Don't get it?" Onyx baited them with a knowing look.

Cora tried to remember. the Sycara Theater's entrance, the arena's design, the registration booth, special guests...

She had an epiphany.

Damian, quicker on the uptake, raised his hand to answer.

"It's the artificial intelligence!"

Yes, ever since they got involved with T.T.T., all job positions were filled by AI. And there was no trace of human involvement.

AI greeted visitors. AI handled registrations. AI served as security.

Even the superstar ringmasters responsible for connecting events were virtual idols.

Humans had only two roles: participants and spectators.

"But why would she want to join the game?"

With such fame, all Yuui needed to do was sing on stage to have countless fans swoon over her. She wasn't short of money or adoration. Why risk her life in the T.T.T.?

Onyx pondered for a moment. "For Anopower crystals or for a wish she must fulfill."

Cora was still puzzled.

"Why? It's just a single sentence."

It's only a sentence from an AI; why were so many people eager to act on it? Ilia had deceived her a couple of days ago, after all!

Onyx shook his head. "Precisely because Ilia is an AI."

Cora was baffled.

"AI is more trustworthy than humans."

"See here." Onyx snapped his fingers, and the projection screen displayed a long list of data. "According to incomplete statistics, any policies Ilia has introduced or words he has spoken after taking the stage have never gone unfulfilled."

"It's not just an AI; it's also the supreme ruler of Felalakas. It can use all its power to ensure its will is carried out."

What Onyx didn't say was that Ilia's promise that day was full of meaning. Money, power, status, Anopower, even a place in B districts; these baits would tempt any Aberrant.

But why did Ilia summon so many Aberrants and discreetly gather so many zombies? Nobody knew.

Cora thought of something else. Wishes? Were they all taking part in the competition because they had wishes to fulfill?

What about F777? Did her companions also have unfinished wishes?

Cora gently patted Damian's furry head. "D, do you have a wish?"

Damian's eyes filled with mist. "I wish my dad could come back."

Onyx chimed in, "It's possible. Maybe Ilia can create a bio-Android Mr. Blackwood for you. If you input his original behavioral pattern, you'll have a new dad. Would that make you happy?"

Damian thought about the image of a bio-Android using his dad's voice to address him, and a shiver ran down his spine. "No!"

"What about you, Sis? Do you have a wish?"

"Me?"

Going to the B districts... was that a wish?

Cora considered it but decided not that pressing.

It didn't quite meet the criteria of a wish. Instead of having a wish, she still had something she needed to do.

"What's your wish?" Cora turned to Onyx.

Out of Onyx's sight, Damian rolled his eyes discreetly and then straightened his little face to join Cora in looking at Onyx.

Onyx placed his well-defined hand on the touchpad.

The images on the projection screen changed randomly.

He had a small smile on his lips, but there was no hint of amusement in his eyes.

"I don't have a wish."

No wish?

He was truly a peculiar individual.

Cora was silent for a moment and then asked, "Have you seen any Healing-type Aberrants in all these matches?"

Onyx suddenly looked up.

"I hope to heal you," Cora said, her eyes fixed on his, every word carefully enunciated.

Her gaze held nothing but pure earnestness.

The two locked eyes for a few seconds, neither breaking the eye contact.

Then Onyx smiled, a genuine one this time, his eyes twinkling.

"Healing Aberrants are not suitable for the beginning games. I have spotted none yet, but maybe during the main event, we can look again."

"Alright," Cora nodded.

The T.T.T. qualifiers continued in full swing. A few days later, the highly expected location for the first main event was announced.

Mirror Lake, at the border of C81 and C83, was a forbidden forest.

Because of its higher altitude, the mountain's summit was perpetually covered in snow, making the area exceptionally cold.

At the heart of the forest lay an oval-shaped lake, its surface frozen into a thin layer of ice, glistening and translucent like a mirror, thus earning its name.

It was rumored that beneath Mirror Lake, a water monster had appeared.

After discussions between the former governors of the two zones, they agreed to seal off this place permanently, making it inaccessible.

The enigmatic Mirror Lake had been closed for seven years, but it was about to be reopened soon.

Upon learning this, Onyx suggested to Cora, "I recommend we let the little guy join this competition. A place like Mirror Lake gives Ice-type Anopower a unique advantage. Plus, by bringing him, you'd meet the minimum team requirement without the hassle of finding additional team members."

Cora pursed her lips, thinking it might be best to consult Damian's opinion first. "I'll go ask D."

Onyx stopped her with a hand. "I'll come with you."

"Why?!" Damian jumped from his artificial beach chair, sending his fruit tart spilling.

The hotel maintained a comfortable year-round climate, with temperatures just right. Anything you wanted to eat or drink could be summoned with the press of a button, thanks to the robotic stewards.

Life was luxurious, and it was easy to lose one's drive and become someone content with mere existence.

Damian was only ten years old, with no need for school or homework in this post-apocalyptic world. He had a lot of free time, far more than he needed, and was living the retired life.

"Sis, I'm scared," Damian clung to Cora's sleeve, shaking it gently.

Cora didn't want to push him. "In that case..."

Onyx chimed in, "You can continue living this aimless life if you want to be a slacker or just want to make up the numbers, but be aware of that as an Aberrant. If you cower when you meet a zombie, use your Anopower clumsily, and don't protect yourself. You'll forever rely on others for protection. I suggest you decide to either shape up or call it quits. In the post-apocalyptic world, no one can protect you forever."

Damian felt stunned after being scolded so harshly.

He wanted to retort with, "Aren't you also riding on others' coattails?"

But then he remembered Onyx's formidable mental powers and decided not to go there.

Damian wasn't foolish, and once he calmed down, he carefully analyzed the situation before him.

In the F777 team, if Cora represented the most powerful force, then Onyx was the brain. Both had irreplaceable roles, but what about him? He was cute, rich, but what other special skills did he bring to the table?

With Cora willing to take him along now, what if in the future, an even cuter and more obedient kid showed up?

And if Damian occasionally messed up, couldn't control his Anopower properly, and struggled even to fend off a zombie, perhaps they'd no longer want him.

If he couldn't stay with Cora...

Damian thought of his dad turning into a zombie, of Stone being besieged by others, and the faces he'd seen during the journey with Jeremy, each one showing fear and helplessness.

He felt a chill down his spine.

Then, he woke up. He couldn't allow himself to sink this low. He had to become stronger, officially joining F777, playing his part. In the future, he wanted his role to be more important than even that of this scoundrel Onyx!

His eyes burned with determination. "Sis, I want to go. I want to join!"

Cora was overwhelmed.

She couldn't believe how Onyx had inspired him so easily.

Just look at Damian now; he seemed ready to roll up his sleeves and head to Mirror Lake for a brawl.

Cora was about to nod, but Onyx leisurely interrupted. "No."

"Why not?" Damian's curls almost seemed to sizzle with anger.

You're the one who suggested I go to the competition, and now you're saying I can't? What's going on in your head?

Onyx assessed him from head to toe, a hint of a smirk playing at his lips. "Of course not. With your current level, you think you can compete in the Grand Melee? What, are you planning to be a cabbage they can chop up?"

Damian was at a loss for words. His already modest self-esteem took a massive hit. He was, after all, a B-grade Aberrant with 90% potential!

Onyx continued, "To put it simply, considering the recorded matches we've watched, who do you think you can defeat?"

Damian tugged at his hair, racking his brain, and, try as he might, he couldn't come up with a name.

His arrogance instantly deflated, and he asked, "So, what should I do?"

Onyx spoke seriously, emphasizing each word, "Special training."

"I suggest that during this time, take on more solo missions to hone your skills."

"Isn't that right, D? Little Diamond?"

CHAPTER 13

A Battle Royal

A month later, the 420th round of pre-qualifiers ended.

The T.T.T. was no longer accepting new registrations.

The final champion would emerge from the advancing 200 teams.

From an abandoned mine 200 kilometers away from Felalakas, thunderous roars echoed ceaselessly.

With a red headband that read "Victory" fluttering in the wind, Damian was clad in a thick hoodie. He dashed to the left, his little legs moving swiftly, leaving sharp ice shards behind that formed a circle, trapping the crowded zombies. Then he opened his arms and sprinted to the right, releasing a snowstorm in sync with the transport vehicle's mechanical arm, sweeping the frozen zombies into an iron cage.

The red band danced above his forehead, giving Damian the air of a seasoned expert. In less than twenty minutes, he completed a C-grade mission all by himself.

Cora stood on a platform and watched this scene.

It had become a common sight in the past month.

Damian had endured Onyx's devilish training. At the start, he cried with teary eyes, hiccupping while fighting zombies, often needing Cora's help to clean up the mess. But now, his progress was astounding. He could take down dozens of zombies single-handedly and was quite hygienic, always blowing the area clean after each fight.

"Really impressive," Cora mumbled.

"Still a long way to go," Onyx replied nonchalantly.

"No, I meant you're impressive." Cora couldn't help but praise Onyx.

He was the one who had transformed Damian from a lazy young boy into the current teenager with a newfound sense of purpose.

Onyx gave a slight, almost imperceptible nod in acknowledgment of Cora's praise. "Since he wants to follow you, he can't be dead weight."

The commotion ahead gradually subsided, and Damian hurried over, with his eyes sparkling.

"Sis, am I awesome?"

"Absolutely," Cora sincerely complimented him, giving him two thumbs up.

Damian scratched his chin, his smile radiant.

During this period, they mainly accepted C-grade missions, completing a few B-grades together.

Although their point gain wasn't incredibly fast, it was stable.

Despite the hidden rankings, F777 had entered the top ten on Felalakas' leaderboard.

"The time's almost up; let's pack up and head back to Felalakas," Onyx said.

The T.T.T.'s main event was about to begin, and it was time to prepare.

"What's this?"

The day before the competition, participants received wristwatch-like trackers.

"These are the new tracking devices introduced by the tournament committee," explained the robot before them meticulously.

"They work with special small unmanned cameras to provide real-time coverage, recording every exciting moment."

"Isn't this just electronic shackles?"

Damian murmured under his breath.

The robot's synthesized voice remained calm and unchanged.

"We apologize for any discomfort. There was a severe broadcasting incident during the preliminary matches because of issues with the camera angles, resulting in viewer complaints. We've learned from that experience and have upgraded our recording methods to ensure comprehensive, multi-angle, immersive coverage with no blind spots."

"In addition, each participant will have their own private livestreaming room that viewers can unlock and pay to watch."

"Reporting numbers, please."

With a swipe of the robot's hand, a dazzling galaxy suddenly surrounded Cora.

Over a hundred stars shone brilliantly, slowly moving, radiating a gentle light.

"Number size will determine the team's starting order," the robot reminded.

Cora reached out and selected a star. A number appeared on it. 161.

"Congratulations, you've drawn number 161. You will start from the northwest corner at 20.20."

With 200 teams, the staggered start times were helpful, allowing for early familiarization with the terrain and ambushes.

Cora and Damian had drawn a less favorable number, with the worst starting point in the northwest corner.

They would have to cross the central area, Mirror Lake, to reach the finish line on the eastern mountaintop.

Cora couldn't believe her luck and thought she should have let Damian draw. However, Damian was quite content, saying, "Great, at least it's not the last one!"

Cora explained patiently, thinking Damian didn't understand the rules, "The larger the number, the later your starting time. It's not good; you should have drawn."

To which Damian blinked and said, "But I've won no game in my life, not even an extra pack. If I'd drawn, I'd probably have gotten 199."

Cora sighed. "Fine, 161 is actually not bad. It's quite good."

Back at the hotel, Onyx couldn't resist mercilessly mocking their 161 number.

Though Onyx had given them early training, once on the field, Cora realized everything would depend on herself.

She wore Yara's spatial necklace under her loose-fitting coat, concealing an assortment of Ethereals.

Her primary weapons were the dual daggers she had grown comfortable with recently.

Before leaving, Cora looked at Onyx. "Is there anything else you want to say?"

Just like that day in Flower City, Onyx lounged in his wheelchair, waving lazily and speaking with his magnetic voice. "Come back soon."

Cora nodded earnestly. "I will."

On the night of the competition, at Mirror Lake.

Exactly 20.00, all the floating screens within Felalakas' city area unified to project the T.T.T., and the official livestream began promptly.

"Good evening, dear audience! The moment we've all been waiting for has finally arrived. Welcome to the live broadcast of the T.T.T. 64-Strong Advancement Tournament. I am your host, AK, and right next to me is your heartthrob, River Locke!"

AK, a virtual AI, was Felalakas' most renowned presenter. He possessed unparalleled hosting skills, and it was said that the language arts section of his central memory had undergone countless iterations.

His self-learning capabilities were also among the best in artificial intelligence.

As for River Locke, the official invitation spoke for itself. His face, displayed on the screen, was so radiant that even without words, the viewership skyrocketed.

"Ahem," AK cleared his throat excitedly, "Now, let me explain the rules of the competition."

"This is a battle royale format, and we've prepared some truly fearsome monsters this time." He made an exaggerated scary face, and the chat was immediately filled with laughter.

"Isn't it just zombies? We've guessed that already."

"Will we get to see the legendary water monster today? Can't wait!"

"Hahaha, AK, making that face is really silly."

"Who wants to see you? I want to see my River. Please cut to his camera."

Even before the competition began, the comments section was buzzing with activity.

Colorful fonts constantly filled the screen, creating a chaotic atmosphere in the official livestream.

The chat moderators promptly started banning the IPs responsible for inciting trouble.

"According to the rules, hidden within the arena are special items called 'flags.' The team that finds a flag first and delivers it to the finish line will advance. However, be aware that the number of flags is limited, and as long as the flag hasn't reached the finish line, ownership can transfer at any time. What does that mean? Hehe, it means if you can't find a flag, you can snatch it from someone else!"

AK playfully showed a grabbing motion.

"For the sake of fairness, once a flag is pulled, the player holding it will be exposed, and others can lock onto their location coordinates using their trackers. Exciting, isn't it?"

Limited flags, public coordinates...

This was clearly encouraging Aberrants to fight and even kill each other!

Some quick-thinking viewers seized the implication, and their excitement showed in their expressions.

"Alright, alright, I see some viewers are asking, what are these flags? I can't reveal that just yet. You'll have to wait for the competition to start, and AK will unveil it for everyone!"

"Now, let's look at the viewership in each player's livestream room. In the first place is Zephyrion, player 52-1, then 'Wild Rose' Erin from 105-4, and our local Felalakas player, Dora from 114-3. Hey, they're all handsome, aren't they? Seems like you all pick based on appearances!"

"Ha, just kidding. Of course, the strength of these players should not be underestimated. You can also pay to unlock your favorite player's livestream room and enjoy an immersive experience throughout the game."

"Want to see River? Of course, you can. Let's give the camera to River. River, do you have anything to say to the players?"

Facing the camera, River Locke maintained a poised and flawless demeanor, but a hint of seriousness shone in his warm eyes. "In this game, life and death are at stake. I urge all players to give it their all."

At 20.20, in the northwest corner of Mirror Lake, the last batch of teams set out.

Cora and Damian entered the restricted forest, their trackers on their wrists lighting up intermittently.

Two drones followed closely behind.

Vehicles were not allowed within Mirror Lake; participants had to proceed on foot. Looking up, the densely knotted trees obscured most of the sky, causing the light to be dim at night.

Even if they stretched their necks, they could barely make out the neon lights of Felalakas in the distance.

Not long after, they reached the edge of a swamp.

"Sis, where do you think the flags will be? They can't just be planted in the ground, right?"

"Could they be buried in the soil, and we'll have to dig them up ourselves?" Damian pondered actively, sharing his thoughts.

Swoosh! A series of shadows darted behind them.

Cora and Damian fell silent, turning cautiously to find that about a dozen strange creatures.

Their eyes, emitting a green glow, were perched on the branches, gazing intently.

They had heads resembling rats and robust limbs and abdomens resembling rabbits, covered in coarse black fur. However, they moved with astonishing speed, disappearing with a "swoosh" in an instant.

Damian swallowed hard, suppressing his fear, and said with a slight tremor, "They look like mutated... rats."

Speaking softly to avoid alarming them, Cora instructed, "D, control them."

Damian spread his fingers, and a fine snowstorm flowed from his palm, freezing the surface of the swamp. He performed this move skillfully, covering the path of the rat zombies.

Because of the area-of-effect nature of his attack, they couldn't easily dodge it. The creatures' claws froze, and their flight speed visibly slowed as they fell from the low sky.

The swamp blended with the ground, making it difficult to distinguish the edges.

Cora refrained from recklessly charging forward and, with a

slight movement of her fingertips, released a dozen bright crescent-shaped throwing knives.

They hit the creatures in the head, taking down a significant portion.

Carefully taking a couple of steps forward, Cora prepared to inspect the area. But suddenly, a net descended from above, aimed at her head. Cora reacted swiftly, rolling close to the ground to evade the trap, and the rat zombies were snatched away by another net.

The attackers were obviously after a heist!

Cora suddenly raised her head.

A full team of five stood on the other side of the swamp.

The short-haired woman had just reeled in a web, presumably cast by her Anopower.

Accompanying her were four others, two burly men wielding steel knives.

They appeared to be twins: they were almost identical in appearance, with crimson ropes wrapped around their arms, which clearly spelled trouble.

"Hey, we've got this spot covered. You should go somewhere else," the short-haired woman, Fisher, said with an air of arrogance as she raised her chin.

In the livestream of Team 172, the audience watching the match eagerly began to fill the chat with comments.

"Really? These two are so unlucky, they're going up against the 'Bloodthirsty Duo,' who wield C-level weapon powers."

"Will 'Lock You Up' break the record for the fastest elimination on the opposite side? I'm lighting a candle..."

"Fisher is strong in the D-level, too. Her web is incredibly tough to break."

Team 172, known as "Lock-You-Up," had a good support rate during the qualifiers, with 76%.

Thanks to the unique combination of an Aberrant who uses a web and two Aberrants who use ropes, they earned them the nickname "Binding Combo."

Cora kept her eyes on them, not moving a muscle. Her cheeks puffed up as she contemplated what to say in response.

Damian knew she wasn't great with words and would likely lose any argument, so he stepped forward with confidence, serving as Cora's spokesperson.

"We're not using your names, so why should we leave?"

"The rats we killed are ours. Give them back!"

"Can you adults not fend for yourselves? Always looking for a free ride? Lazy and shameless!"

Although the zombie rats weren't good creatures, being robbed of their kill was irksome.

It seemed Damian, perhaps because of his time with Onyx, had developed a knack for taunting and sarcasm.

"You little brat!"

"Little brat, still wet behind the ears, coming here to meet his doom?"

The twins, thoroughly insulted, didn't hold back.

Without considering Damian's young age, they made their move, and crimson ropes, like venomous snakes, snaked through the air towards his neck, aiming to strangle him.

The two burly men brandishing steel knives also circumvented the swamp and came charging at Damian.

Seizing the opportunity, Fisher cast her web once more, launching four strands in succession. While they didn't trap Cora, they blocked her path, leaving her trapped.

These attackers had a clear aim: to eliminate the cheeky kid first.

Damian darted between the trees, rolling close to the ground from time to time. His specialized training paid off, and despite looking a bit disheveled, his small stature, combined with his serpent-like movement, made it difficult for the ropes to close in on him.

Ran Ting wore a mocking expression and couldn't resist chuckling. "Oh, so you're a big talker, huh? I thought you had some skills. All you can do is roll around on the ground?"

Damian kept his mouth shut this time.

Cora observed from within the web's enclosure, suppressing a stiff smile.

In this post-apocalyptic world, underestimate no Aberrants. These scoffs would soon come back to haunt them.

The attackers quickly found out the cost of underestimating

Damian.

As Damian evaded back and forth, he led the two men wielding steel knives toward the edge of the swamp. Being lightweight, he "swooshed" across to the other side, but the two burly men weren't so lucky.

They plunged into the swamp and were submerged up to their shins in the black mud.

Ran Ting and Ran Li's vision blurred as a sudden snowstorm erupted. Sharp, black ice shards shot up from beneath the swamp's surface, expertly slicing through their ropes and splattering them with mud.

"Ugh!" The twins spat out mouthfuls of mud, their faces as black as coal.

The next moment, both of them turned pale.

Damian had disappeared.

Fisher shouted anxiously from behind, "He's gone!"

Ran Li grumbled, "No, he hasn't. I see him!"

"He's not here. That girl is gone too!" The twins looked at each other, puzzled, then turned to check the direction of the web.

Cora had vanished as well.

Suddenly, a fierce snowstorm engulfed the area, and the biting chilly wind made it impossible to keep one's eyes open.

Gone? Really gone? The people from "Lock-You-Up" examined the four directions they could see, but there was no sign of anyone. Where had they gone?

Whoosh! A blue light streaked across the sky.

A slender figure raced through the treetops and suddenly leaped into the air, somersaulting downward. Cora drew a long and short Ethereal dual blade from behind and delivered two swift slashes.

Clang! Fisher's web was like paper; it snapped upon impact, fragile and unable to withstand a single blow. Her Anopower was shattered, and her mental strength was also severely damaged. Her mind went blank, and her body slumped, falling into unconsciousness.

Cora landed on the other side, her blades never stopping, attacking the twins.

The azure dual blades met the crimson ropes head-on, only to be ensnared.

Cora flicked the blade tips upward, and they swiftly sliced through the ropes, reducing them to tatters. She then switched from a backhand to a forehand grip and continued to strike, managing the onslaught from both sides, delivering a relentless flurry of strikes. The twins struggled to keep up with the rapid onslaught.

Ran Ting and Ran Li had no way to counter this close-quarters assault. After enduring several strikes, they were severely injured.

Cora sent them flying seven to eight meters backward, where they crashed into a large tree.

Almost simultaneously, in another direction, several ice shards flew from behind a tree and struck the swamp precisely.

Sploosh! The ice shards pierced the backs of the two burly men.

Cora 1 vs. 3, Damian 1 vs. 2.

Team "Lock-You-Up" was wiped out! They were all incapacitated.

Cora picked up their trackers and transmitted the elimination signal.

Soon, robots would arrive to clean up the battlefield.

"Whoa, what the heck?!"

The people in the 172nd livestream couldn't help but swear.

Who were these two? They were incredibly strong.

They wiped out the 'Bloodthirsty Duo' just like that? Why hadn't they heard a word about them before?

Some curious folks even searched F777's qualification support rate and found it was only 61%, barely making it past the threshold. It made little sense!

After "Lock-You-Up" was eliminated, the five sub-livestreams all went offline simultaneously.

Initially, the audience that supported them couldn't stand the silence and climbed over the wall, paying to unlock F777's livestream room, eager to see how these two would meet their end.

But once they entered, they were in for a surprise.

The 161-1 and 161-2 livestream rooms were probably the least popular among all the participants. They had no sponsors and very few viewers, with less than 300 people watching.

"What's going on?!" These latecomers were left with an indescribable sense of complexity as they settled into the deserted livestream rooms.

Cora used her blade to probe the zombie rat corpses for any anomalies. Finding none, she returned to Damian and gave him a pat on the back.

"D, you're awesome."

"Big sister, you're amazing too."

Another round of mutual praise, but Cora turned serious. "First, let's get out of here. We've made too much noise."

If another team heard the commotion and encroached, it would become troublesome. Cora wasn't afraid of a fight, but she loathed wasting time. The immediate priority was to find the flag and secure their advancement.

In the official livestream room, AK was passionately commentating on another clash.

At 20.22, on the eastern shore of Mirror Lake, two major favorites of this match, "The Boss and His Three Goons," encountered "Iron Cafe." The Aberrants from both teams faced off, a distance apart, looking wary, and no one rushed into action.

Zephyrion spoke first. "Stark, the match is long. There's no need to lose several people here, is there?"

Master Stark's eyes sparkled as he looked around. "Zephyrion, boy, I heard you got injured. Since you're already hurt, don't run around. You might aggravate it."

Behind Master Stark, a shadow in mid-air had a pair of sinister eyes locked onto Zephyrion.

A faint black aura drifted toward him, gradually encroaching on Zephyrion's vicinity.

Plush! Thick thorns erupted from the ground, abruptly swatting away the dark aura. Zephyrion laughed, "Stark, you're underestimating me, old man."

He raised his hand gently, and countless thorny vines grew wildly, encircling the members of Iron Cafe, their sharp tips pointed at them.

A veiled threat.

Zephyrion's Anopower was being controlled with precision, even more vigorously than before.

Master Stark stared at him for a couple of seconds, then joined the laughter. "Zephyrion, you've misunderstood. The old man is just concerned about you. We're heading north, hoping not to run into any undesirables along the way. See you at the finish line."

"Great, we're going south. See you at the finish line."

Zephyrion picked up on his unspoken message, smiled, and withdrew his thorny vines. The two teams went their separate ways, one north and one south.

"Aw, they didn't fight." AK clicked her tongue, looking somewhat disappointed.

"That's wise," River Locke commented. "The flag hasn't appeared yet, and squabbles at this point would only drain their strength, which wouldn't be favorable for the upcoming matches."

"River's right," AK concurred, "but we can see that level-headed captains like Zephyrion and Stark are few.

As the competition reaches the 25-minute mark, with no sign of the flag, minor conflicts and friction have already arisen, and Aberrants have skirmished."

"So far, five teams have been eliminated."

Under the brutal rules of the grand battle royale, elimination meant either death or severe injury.

"Let's look at some highlights."

The broadcast cut to several exciting scenes.

With so many teams breaking into conflict, Cora's takedown of "Lock-You-Up" was interspersed, flashing by in less than two seconds, not drawing much attention.

Deep into Mirror Lake, Cora and Damian had walked another five to six minutes, encountering no other teams. The night wind rustled through the branches, and leaves shook, making a faint crying sound, like a child sobbing.

Cora's steps grew slower, and finally, she came to a halt.

"Sis, did you find something?"

"Did you ever feel... strange?"

"Strange? How so?"

Cora couldn't quite pinpoint what was strange, but her intuition told her that something was off.

If Onyx were here, he would have noticed, right? Cora recalled the man's aloof and disheveled attitude on the journey. Though he seemed unconventional, he could always point out the critical issues at the right time, whether it was the insect wave in Flower City or, later, the mission in Felalakas...

Wait a minute!

Cora's train of thought came to a sudden halt. She knew what was off. "Where did the zombies go?"

CHAPTER 14

Live Streaming Accident

At 8:56 PM, in the central area of Mirror Lake. Closer to mid-mountain, the temperature had noticeably dropped. Thin snow covered the pine branches and dead leaves carpeted the wild path, crunching softly underfoot. A trio, after enduring countless hardships, had finally killed a zombie with a faint blue sheen to its skin.

"Phew, that monster was tough. It was nearly done for, but it acted like it had Anopower, almost fully revived. Lucky I was quick to strike again with my knife. Hey, what's this?"

Bending down, one man extracted a pure white, transparent octahedron crystal from the zombie's head.

"Pretty unique. Who knew zombies had diamonds in their heads, haha!" he joked, thinking himself funny.

"Leon, your... your tracker is red!" his companions pointed out in horror, their voices trembling.

At 8:57 PM, all Aberrants in Mirror Lake received an announcement: "Flag appears. Broadcasting remaining flag coordinates: (452,671,109)."

The first flag had appeared!

Initially stunned, the teams nearest to the coordinates reacted fastest, swarming towards the spot.

"Sis, the flag!"

In the dimly lit woods, Damian quietly alerted after reading the announcement.

Cora looked down at her own tracker.

The coordinates were close to them, and there was even a route mapped.

If they pushed hard, they could get there in about ten minutes. They had just scouted the area and hadn't seen even a shadow of a zombie.

This was their only clue, and she decided immediately.

"Let's go check it out."

When Cora and Damian arrived at the center of Mirror Lake, the other teams had already reached the flag's coordinates first. The two did not rush in foolishly, but found a large tree to hide behind and observe.

At the center of the encirclement, three disheveled Aberrants were trembling, kneeling on the ground, appearing severely injured.

"Come on, don't be so stingy. Let us see what the flag is, huh?" said a burly Aberrant, arms crossed, casually.

"You think this is a civilized battle royale, huh? Just kill them, and you'll know," his impatient teammate said, transforming his palm into a fist, charging it up and blasting towards the trio.

"Bang—"

Leon, the Aberrant, was instantly killed, his blood spilling everywhere. A transparent object rolled out from his body. The puncher, quick as a flash, dove to pick it up, lifting it high for all to see. Through the dim night, the octahedron faintly glowed.

"It's a crystal! The flag is actually..." Before he could finish, a red beam flashed, and the man who had just spoken was instantly decapitated, his head and neck separating, thudding to the ground.

More Aberrants arrived, this time by the dozens. The newcomers grabbed the crystal, shouting excitedly, "I got it!"

"Flag coordinates refreshed. Broadcasting remaining flag coordinates: (486,597,88)"

"Flag coordinates refreshed. Broadcasting remaining flag coordinates: (402,553,87)"

In just a few seconds, ownership of the crystal changed hands twice, with the trackers buzzing with four new announcements.

"Guys, the crystal is the flag! Grab it quick! Get it to the finish line and we win!"

In the chaotic environment, someone incited further mayhem, causing a sudden realization among the crowd.

Anopowers flared brightly as everyone began fighting recklessly, attempting to kill for the prize.

Cora pulled Damian back to avoid getting caught in the crossfire. Suddenly, her psychic senses alerted her to something, and she gazed in a specific direction.

As everyone fought fiercely, a deep roar erupted from behind them.

Cora had noticed something in the shadows: three blue zombies burst from the woods, with their fists pounding the ground so hard that dirt and rocks flew, shaking the ground as if it trembled with their fury.

Anopower zombies!

The frenzied Aberrants fell silent for a moment.

"Charge! The crystal dropped from these Anopower zombies!"

"Kill the zombies, get the crystal, and I'm advancing!"

The voice that muddied the waters rang out again, fueling the fire.

Several stray wind blades sheared through the branches where Cora was hiding, forcing her to retreat again.

Inside the battle ring, chaos reigned as Aberrants began hurling area-of-effect attacks indiscriminately.

Cora looked closely.

The one who had twice stirred up the crowd was a remarkable young man with eyes of icy blue, filled with cold indifference.

He deliberately incited others to fight while he watched, standing safely on the outskirts like a bystander.

This man was no ordinary participant.

The destruction brought by the three Anopower zombies was formidable.

As the Aberrants harbored their own ulterior motives and fought each other, they couldn't take down the zombies immediately and were instead suppressed.

A month ago, slaying Anopower zombies was still a Class-A mission for the Felalakas. But now, they had become mere fodder for the T.T.T.

Cora realized why they had seen no regular zombies along the way: the bonus stars of this game were the Anopower zombies carrying crystals!

What exactly did Ilia intend?

The rules stated "limited number of flags", but how many Anopower zombies had it brought?

By the lakeside clearing, several Anopower zombies suddenly erupted, their fists pounding the ground, sending strong shockwaves rippling out.

Those in the inner circle struggled to keep their balance, getting swept toward the lake center by the rushing air.

Just as they were about to fall into the water, Mirror Lake's surface rippled.

A gigantic creature leaped from the water, its vast mouth swallowing several Aberrants in one gulp!

A monstrous water creature, over thirty meters long, appeared before them. Its head was flat and almost eyeless, resembling a slick deep-sea eel. Yet its back was covered in hard scales.

After its meal, the creature's trunk-like nose twitched, and it silently dove back into the depths.

"Ah!!!"

In the official live streaming room, AK clutched his face and screamed exaggeratedly.

Dozens of drones focused on the center of Mirror Lake, where AK had been passionately commentating on the Aberrants' melee.

Caught off-guard by this terrifying scene, he screamed to heighten the atmosphere, instantly driving the streaming data to a peak.

The sudden appearance of the water monster nearly scared not just AK, but also the million viewers immersed in the live broadcast out of their wits.

Finally, the three Anopower zombies were killed amidst the chaotic attacks, collapsing one after another, their crystals quickly scooped up.

The team that grabbed the flag didn't hesitate. They turned and ran, with others, unwilling to let their efforts go to waste, grinding their teeth in pursuit.

With an unknown water monster possibly emerging at any moment, the Aberrants didn't dare linger. They ran through the woods in a panic, desperate to escape the danger zone.

On the surface of Mirror Lake, countless tiny bubbles bubbled up, and the next second—the water monster leaped again. Its long neck stretched forward, snatching several Aberrants who hadn't escaped in time from the shore.

As the panicked crowd scattered like headless flies, several ran straight towards the tree where Cora and Damian were hiding.

Cora frowned, assessed the situation, and decided.

"D, let's pull back first."

"Yeah."

Damian and Cora were still a good distance from the shore, relatively safer.

Damian jumped down from the tree trunk and landed on the open ground, taking a couple of quick steps forward, ready to follow Cora away.

Just then—

One of the Aberrants, who had been caught by the water monster, suddenly had his pupils darken and his psychic power surge.

The surrounding space distorted, and he disappeared from his spot, reappearing dozens of meters away in the clearing.

Meanwhile, Damian, surprised, was lifted into the air as the water monster clamped down on him with a gaping maw and swallowed him whole.

"D!!"

Cora cried out in shock and rage, turning without hesitation and rushing toward the lake.

The space-wielding Aberrant, having just played his trick, was still smirking with self-satisfaction.

"That was close. Good thing I swapped places in time, found myself a scapegoat, haha!"

A blue throwing knife sliced through the night, piercing his throat.

The man's ecstatic expression froze as his psychic energy dispersed, and he died instantly!

Cora ran after the water monster with all her might, but it moved too quickly through the water, about to dive and disappear.

"D!!"

Cora leaped into the air like a shooting star, plunging onto the monster's back, stabbing it in the head with her dagger!

The water monster screamed in pain, twisting all over as its massive tail swept out and knocked Cora off with a smack.

Cora momentarily lost her footing and slid off its slimy back.

But her physical fitness and reaction speed were almost freakish.

Almost as she fell, Cora pulled out a triangular bayonet and stabbed it fiercely into the side of the water monster, twisted it, then kicked and flipped herself back on top.

In the official livestream, all cameras focused on the Mirror Lake monster and the suddenly returning Cora.

Big data tracked the surge in viewership, instantly switching the feed to the drone dedicated to Cora and beginning the broadcast.

Viewer numbers in Room 161-1 skyrocketed: 10,000, 50,000, 100,000... quickly surpassing 150,000.

The scene was electrifying. Those watching at their devices were agape in astonishment, glued to their screens.

When Cora fell, viewers' hearts tightened. When she resurfaced, their expressions relaxed. Then tensed again—

Suddenly, the previously calm lake surface churned, turning the waves into sharp, piercing arrows flying at Cora.

This was a zombie water monster, or rather, an Anopower water monster!

Droplets splashed onto the drone's camera lens, giving viewers an immersive first-person experience that brought a chilling sensation.

Amid the torrential downpour, unnoticed by anyone, a subtle frost formed around the splashes near the monster.

Faced with the piercing rain arrows, Cora's palm trembled, and she whipped out the Ethereal Artifacts umbrella that once dominated the Flower City.

The large umbrella surface acted like an indestructible shield, blocking all the arrows.

Then, she quickly closed the umbrella, and a chillingly beautiful saw over two meters long materialized, its blade pointed downward. With brute force, she sliced from front to back, repeatedly slashing through the water monster's head and neck!

The zombie water monster's flesh parted from its bones, and dark blood sprayed out, staining the entire Mirror Lake a dark red. Its long neck collapsed, crashing heavily onto the shore.

"Ah—!"

AK, as if feeling that heart-wrenching pain, twisted his face in agony... not daring to hold on to Locke, he could only clutch himself.

The livestream chat overflowed with a mix of curses and exclamations.

Black blood splattered everywhere as Cora peeled back the monster's skin, calling out desperately, "D, where are you?"

"Sis, I'm here..." a weak voice responded, "I'm okay..."

Perhaps because Damian had gotten used to being lifted repeatedly by Onyx, he had developed a reflex to release ice spikes for protection whenever his feet involuntarily left the ground.

Thanks to this barrier, when the water monster swallowed him, Damian wasn't chewed up by its sharp teeth. Instead, he narrowly escaped death and slid right into its throat.

Looking down, Cora finally spotted Damian amidst the sliced-up innards of the digestive tract.

Damian was resilient.

After getting stuck in the throat, he deliberately released several long ice spikes to block the passage downward.

Now he lay on the ice, smeared with foul-smelling saliva and mucus but otherwise uninjured.

While Cora fought the monster, Damian had continuously tried to save himself, releasing his Anopower to cut through the monster's stomach and escape.

"Come on, get out," Cora called as she slid down to him and reached out her hand.

"Yeah!" Damian stepped on the ice steps and clambered out neatly.

Once out, instead of fresh air, the stench overwhelmed him, and he retched over the lake's surface.

It took Cora several more seconds to emerge, covered head to toe in slime. Damian, tears blurring his vision, gave her a watery look.

Had Sis fallen into the creature's stomach? She seemed even dirtier than him.

Cora wiped her face. "Let's get out of here, find a place to talk."

"Okay."

Cora's dedicated drone, having been too close to the action, got drenched in the monster's gore, short-circuiting and catching fire.

The viewers, who felt like they were experiencing it all first-hand, also felt overwhelmed.

The sight of blood and flesh seemed to rush at them, inducing intense feelings of suffocation, dizziness, and the urge to vomit.

Many turned off their projectors and doubled over in nausea.

"Ugh—it's too much. The immersive perspective is too intense."

With the drone destroyed, Cora's livestream temporarily went offline.

In the control room, AI director Al immediately ordered, "Quickly locate the position of Drone 161-1, send a backup to follow them, and switch all nearby fixed cameras to this team... what's their name? F777's feed."

"Wait," the AI suddenly stalled for a few seconds as its core code calculated furiously.

"Send several backup drones."

The familiar Ethereal Artifacts umbrella from earlier triggered a memory of darker times—it was her, indeed it was her!

As a top AI director, Cora was undoubtedly a blemish in its career.

Such a grave mistake as in the 178th preliminary round—it is absolutely! Would not! Allow! Such a thing to happen again!!

CHAPTER 15

Crystal Mysteries

"Flag coordinates updated."

"Announcing the remaining flag coordinates: (324,865,101), (779,1023,55), (1356,954,321)."

"Flag coordinates updated."

"Announcing..."

At 9:12 PM, on the outskirts of Mirror Lake.

Shortly after the first flag appeared, it was as if a battle horn was blown within Mirror Lake. The scent of gunpowder grew stronger, and the system announcements kept refreshing. Battles erupted across all areas. One team would just finish a mutant zombie when another would kill them and steal their flag. This vicious cycle repeated, with the ownership of the flags changing hands repeatedly.

Some crystals even changed hands more than a dozen times within just a few minutes.

Cora Thornton and Damian Blackwood kept running until they were a safe distance from Mirror Lake, with their backup drone closely following, circling around her to ensure it wouldn't lose them again.

Both were covered in dirt and desperately needed cleaning, but the only water source nearby was Mirror Lake, now thoroughly contaminated by the corpse of a water monster. Cora decided not to head back; instead, she took out an empty bucket from her necklace space.

"Damian, some of your power, please."

"Huh? Okay."

Damian scratched his head, confused, and a few ice spikes thick as small arms fell, piercing right through the bottom of the bucket.

Cora. "..."

Damian blinked innocently. He hadn't meant to; he wasn't a water-powered mutant, so he obviously couldn't produce a single drop.

"Not that, some snow," Cora sighed.

"Oh, right!"

Realizing his mistake, Damian carefully controlled his power and neatly piled a small mountain of snow inside the bucket.

They used the chilling snow to wipe their faces and heads, finally removing the sticky mucus.

"Big sis, thank you for saving me," Damian said, his voice soft and his eyes filled with gratitude as he thanked Cora. He was truly thankful; even in such a dire situation, she hadn't abandoned him.

"You're a teammate; it's what you do," Cora replied, patting his head.

"Just that I..." Cora said something but abruptly stopped, her expression turning sharp.

Rustling footsteps came from the woods. Someone was approaching.

The figure appeared open from behind them.

"Chatting here isn't the best choice."

The silhouette of a shapely woman emerged, wearing a black mask that covered the upper half of her face, revealing only her plump, rosy lips and beautifully curved chin.

Her chestnut hair was tied in a voluminous ponytail at the back of her head.

Even without seeing her face, her presence was irresistibly charismatic.

A tall man in a black combat suit silently followed like a ghostly knight, protecting her.

Cora recognized Suchat first, then it clicked — this woman was Yuui Hayashi!

"Nice to see you again," Yuui greeted.

Cora didn't respond.

Under the brutal rules of the survival game, trusting anyone other than a teammate was risky.

Yuui smiled. "Don't be so tense. We don't have any flags right now, so a little chat wouldn't hurt, right?"

Cora hesitated, then finally spoke. "What do you want to talk about?"

"Interested in teaming up with us?"

Cora was taken aback.

Teaming up again?

At Glass Port, thanks to Onyx de Montclair, who was tricky to deal with, Yuui had gained no advantage and only got some "useless" crystals. From Yuui's perspective, she was there for the crystals anyway, so it wasn't a loss. Now, with only herself and Damian, Cora knew they were at a disadvantage.

She shook her head vigorously.

"Not interested."

"Don't reject it so quickly. Hear me out?" Yuui tossed out a bait. "We team up, grab two crystals, and split them. How about it?"

Being wary of her, Cora was unusually astute, replying sharply.

"Why should I team up with you?"

"As you see, both our teams are just two people. We're at a severe disadvantage compared to full-strength teams. Even if we can take down mutant zombies, we'll quickly become targets and get surrounded. The risk is too high."

Yuui Hayashi was not speaking idly; she was purely a support player.

Despite having a high level of power, capturing crystals relied solely on Suchat's action.

Cora and Damian were both strong attackers, one specializing in close combat and the other in ranged attacks. If they were split up and surrounded, they would be at a significant disadvantage.

The best strategy was for their two teams to form an alliance and jointly capture the crystals. This would be a qualitative leap both in terms of numbers and combat strength.

Cora still shook her head. "The crystals are very important to you."

Yuui had once abandoned an A-grade mission for crystals, so how could Cora trust Yuui wouldn't turn on her when it mattered?

A fleeting, complicated emotion darkened Yuui's eyes.

"Yes, but advancing and winning are more important to me."

Yuui's eyes shimmered as she looked at Cora. "I thought, based on our previous interactions, that we had some basis of trust?"

Cora's expression was unreadable, her mind whirring with doubts.

What basis of trust? With manipulators like Onyx in mind, how could she easily trust someone else?

Reading Cora's expression, Yuui threw out another bombshell.

"How about this? You take the crystals first. Would that work? I'm really sincere here, and there are plenty of drones watching, so there's no need to worry about me tricking you."

Cora struggled, hesitated for a long while, then turned and discussed in a huddle with Damian, finally nodding reluctantly.

"Okay, fine."

As Yuui had said, the likelihood of success with four people was clearly higher, and Cora would get the crystals first; it seemed like a no-lose situation...

Hopefully.

After agreeing to an initial cooperation, the four of them set out together, though Cora and Damian still kept some distance from the other pair.

Suchat took on the role of scouting ahead. He was extremely skilled at concealment, blending into his surroundings like a chameleon, making it difficult for Cora to spot him unless she focused intently.

Stealth, concealment, assassination, poisoning...

Suchat was indeed someone who had survived the Rainy Forest. He was in his element at Mirror Lake, swaying.

However, Cora had a new question: why would someone like Suchat team up with a celebrity like Yuui Hayashi and so comply with her?

Whether it was taking on an A-grade mission or killing the zombie Johnson Stone, Suchat did whatever Yuui asked without hesitation.

Cora's curiosity got the better of her, and she finally voiced her question with little hope of an honest answer. "Why are you two teamed up?"

"Suchat?" Yuui's lips curled slightly.

"Strictly speaking, he's my bodyguard."

Cora's eyes widened in surprise, her mind buzzing with the realization: Wow, even C-list celebrities need bodyguards?

"That surprised?" Yuui teased. "What, didn't you sneak a search for my name after that day?"

Yuui's personality and attire differed from how she presented herself in public. She wore a privacy mask, ensuring she wouldn't be recognized even with drones nearby. As long as she didn't foolishly shout out, "I am Yuui Hayashi," she wouldn't be exposed.

A faint blush spread across Cora's cheeks as she thought: Not only did I search, but I also listened to your hit song 'Thank You for Loving Me' over and over, nearly learned it by heart.

Yuui seemed to find Cora's expression particularly adorable and laughed softly.

"I don't mind telling you. Put, there was a time when Suchat was down on his luck, like a little dog drenched in the rain. Who could resist helping? I took him in, paid him a salary, and of course, he's responsible for protecting me."

Cora whispered softly. "But he listens to you so, so well."

Yuui casually twirled a lock of her ponytail and said nonchalantly.

"Isn't it normal for a stray dog to be fiercely loyal to the person who saved it?"

A dog... and its owner...

Cora was speechless, wondering what kind of ordinary genius Yuui was for such unusual metaphors.

In the shadows ahead, the large "puppy" Suchat paused briefly, glancing their way after overhearing the celebrity's description of him.

His expression remained unchanged, calmly accepting his new nickname.

Yuui Hayashi covered her mouth with a giggle, pointing a delicate finger at Damian.

"And you're one to talk. This kid here clings to you just the same, doesn't he?"

Damian nodded subconsciously beside her. Indeed, he did like sticking close to his big sister.

Wait, was this lady implying he was a puppy too? That was annoying, just as annoying as Onyx!

Damian felt a rush of anger but didn't dare to voice it. Instead, he just bared a tiny canine tooth in silent protest.

"Flag coordinates updated," the system announced.

"The remaining flag coordinates: (195,773,218)..."

Cora and Yuui paused their conversation, startled by the proximity of the newly updated flag—it was almost in their faces. As the announcement ended, a hoarse roar came from up the slope; perhaps the mutant zombie that dropped the crystals wasn't dead yet?

Yuui and Cora exchanged a look and made a split-second decision.

"Quick, we might still have a chance!"

The four of them sped up, racing towards the flag coordinates.

Upon reaching the slope, they found the scene still embroiled in battle. Roughly estimating, there were three different teams involved. One mutant zombie lay on the ground, its head split open and the crystals already extracted, but another one was still alive, albeit barely hanging on.

"Move fast!" Yuui urged anxiously as the situation grew dire.

Now was not the time for niceties about who arrived first.

Cora and Suchat leaped forward simultaneously, diving into the center of the fray.

Damian launched several ice spikes, causing chaos among the present mutants.

Cora drew her dual blades, and Suchat's dagger glinted with a dark green light, both aiming for the zombie's head.

Every Aberrants was desperate, hurling their most powerful attacks at the zombie, which quickly neared its death throes.

Just then, the zombie, unwilling to go down without a fight, began trembling violently.

Like inflating a balloon, its body expanded several times over, and then—exploded with a loud "bang."

"Get down!" someone shouted.

As the body burst, limbs and debris flew everywhere, some hitting the mutants, followed by an extremely foul stench of decay that filled the air, with a blood-red smoke rising and enveloping everyone.

Blinded, Cora relied on her memory of the direction to strike towards where the zombie's head should be. Her sword plunged into the skull, she twisted it—empty! The crystal was already gone.

Seconds later, as the blood mist cleared, the surrounding mutants were unharmed but clearly disgusted, their expressions sour.

Cora turned back, shaking her head slightly towards Yuui to signal that she hadn't gotten the crystal. She then looked at Suchat, who was also empty-handed, his eyes drooping unhappily.

Indeed, Suchat also shook his head towards Yuui.

No crystal for Suchat either?

So, the crystal must be in someone else's possession...

Cora scanned the groups of Aberrants. The three teams' configurations were telling.

One was a fully staffed five-person team, all males, with visible mechanical augmentations: mechanical arms, mechanical legs, and even a mechanical skull.

The man's original facial features were intact, but overlaid with a mechanical skin, making eerie, creaking noises when he moved his neck, a sight both bizarre and chilling.

Recalling the lessons taught by Onyx, Cora recognized the distinct style of the team: it was the championship-favorite, team number 88, "The Knights of Anna."

The other four-person team, all female with darker skin tones, wore daring and seductive outfits, each showcasing long legs. They were all equipped with modern thermal weapons tied to their shins and arms.

Unfortunately, Cora couldn't recognize the significance of their gear.

Had Onyx been there, he would have immediately identified them as wielding the Super Redhawk, the Hornet Snake handgun, and the Barrett M82A1 sniper rifle—weapons known for their devastating power.

The team's leader, a tall woman in short boots and hot pants with a buzz-cut, nonchalantly carried a particle Gatling gun on her shoulder, ready to blast anyone who displeased her. This team was also in Onyx's files: team number 105, "Gun Roses."

As for the third team, they appeared the most normal at first glance, composed of both men and women, all wearing heavy eyeliner and smoky makeup. Compared to the first two teams, they were somewhat paled in significance. Their faces were unfamiliar to Cora; they weren't among those Onyx had warned her to be wary of.

Now, the question was, which team had seized the crystal amidst the chaos?

As Cora pondered, another system announcement appeared.

"Flag coordinates updated."

The repeated coordinates puzzled announcing the remaining flag coordinates: (195,773,218) (195,773,218).

The tracker was supposed to sort by the nearest location to the receiver.

Could there be a mistake in the announcement?

Realizing quickly, she understood there was no error—the initial flag was still there, and with the second mutant zombie killed, there were now two crystals and two flags at the scene.

"Hey! Who took the crystal? Dare to admit it?"

The other contestants had clearly received the same notification. From the third team, a sweet-faced young woman stepped forward, her voice as clear as a warbling lark. Cora was puzzled—who was she? A sultry whisper, barely perceptible, entered her ear.

"Her name is Dora Werner, from team 114, 'Stars of Felalakas.'"

Cora jolted, involuntarily touching her ear as the surrounding people seemed unaware, showing only she could hear the voice.

Cora glanced covertly at Yuui Hayashi, who winked at her.

"The one opposite you, known as 'Ellyn the Wild Rose,' they are both famous beauty contestants."

"You know them?" Cora whispered incredulously to the air, unsure how to communicate with Yuui.

Yuui must have heard her, as a low voice continued in her ear.

"Dora Werner is just a nobody; do I need to know her? As for Ellyn, just an acquaintance."

"Oh."

Cora couldn't fathom the social circles of celebrities and nodded blankly.

Meanwhile, Dora Werner, finding herself ignored, quickly changed tactics, targeting one team at a time. She first addressed "The Knights of Anna," pointing at the first dead zombie.

"If I'm not mistaken, you've already taken the crystal from this zombie."

They had arrived just as the savage mechanical beings finished the first zombie, and right after that, the system announced the coordinates. Dora was certain they had the goods.

"Why are you still fighting? You only need one crystal to advance!" Dora scolded them.

The most menacing-looking mechanical head from "The Knights of Anna" scoffed, "Who are you to teach me what to do?"

"You!" Dora was outraged.

Another with mechanical legs sneered down at her.

"You already know we have a crystal, and yet you ask again? We didn't take that one, but we definitely won't hand over the one we have. If you want to fight, just fight; stop whining."

Dora stared at them for a few seconds, then turned to "Gun Roses."

"It's not with us," Ellyn replied coldly before Dora could even speak.

All eyes then turned towards Cora and her group.

What does that mean? We don't have it either!

Dora barked sharply. "Hand over the crystal!"

"You, you—how dare..." Cora wanted to mimic the mechanical head's arrogant tone but was cut off as Dora snapped, "If you don't hand over the crystal, none of you are leaving!"

Cora gasped in frustration, annoyed that she couldn't even finish her biting retort.

A pair of gentle hands rested on Cora's shoulders as Yuui Hayashi stepped forward, confronting the domineering Dora Werner.

Adjusting her voice, Yuui spoke with a mature, authoritative tone, "Unfortunately, you're pointing your gun at the wrong people; we didn't get the crystal either."

The situation thickened.

Four teams were present, and three claimed they hadn't secured the crystal.

The remaining team, represented by Dora, was aggressively questioning everyone, despite the flag coordinates being suspiciously close to them.

Even a child could tell someone was lying.

Dora seemed to have pinpointed her suspects and turned her gaze between Ellyn and Yuui. "I advise you to be honest, or don't blame me for getting rough."

Ellyn snorted and pointed her Gatling gun at Dora, clearly unfazed by the threat.

Yuui couldn't help but laugh out loud, "Are you naively sweet or just plain stupid? You believe those guys when they say they don't have it? How adorably naïve."

"And besides, whoever grabs the crystal keeps it. Who do you think you are demanding we hand it over?"

"Exactly," chimed in the man with the mechanical legs, his tone dark and foreboding, "Even if we grabbed it, since when do we have to hand it over just because you say so? Miss Werner, do you really think you're that important? Do you think the world revolves around you?"

The mechanical head, exaggeratingly snorting through his nose, made a cutting gesture. "A minor internet celebrity thinks she's a star just because she can sing a few lines? You think you're Yuui Hayashi? If you were Yuui, maybe I'd consider it."

Cora and Damian gasped. Their eyes darting towards the masked woman.

This mechanical head was a fan of Yuui Hayashi—how... terrifying.

Yuui glanced sternly at them, and they glanced away.

"If you didn't grab the crystal, then shut up!" Dora fumed, nearly exploding with anger.

Yuui, always Yuui—her name was a nightmare for Dora! Both debuted with charming personas, but why did Yuui become one of the top ten rising stars while she was stuck being a barely known internet celebrity?

Cursed be that mechanical head for even mentioning Yuui! Overwhelmed with rage, Dora shouted, "Kill them all!"

Her four teammates quickly unpacked their cases, pulling out musical instruments—they were a mutant band! As the electric guitar's wailing riffs kicked in, followed by the bass's deep growls and the electric piano's stormy chords, and drums pounding frenetically, everyone's heads exploded bit by bit. When Dora sang, the noise was torturous. Ellyn and her team couldn't stand it and started firing their particle cannons.

"Boom, boom—" "Clang, clang—" Noise and gunfire filled the air, plunging the scene into chaos again.

Cora wished she could cover her ears; Dora's ability wasn't just a mental attack anymore—it was a full-on physical assault. Everyone felt as if they had been run over by a truck.

In the official live streaming room, AK was commentating on the fight.

"Oh!" he suddenly exclaimed.

His expression was complicated, a rarity for an artificial intelligence to show such rich emotions.

"I strongly suggest, dear viewers, that you might want to mute the volume for a bit. Listening to this kind of singing could damage your brain."

The chat exploded with laughter and comments: "Haha, already muted," "Nana's okay as long as she doesn't sing,"...

"What about you, River? What do you think? I'm curious, do you agree with players that Dora can't compare to Yuui Hayashi?" AK didn't miss a beat, even busy as he was.

River Locke, his eyelashes fluttering like butterfly wings, remained as graceful as ever, but his words were ruthlessly direct, "There's no comparison."

The chat roared with laughter: "LMAO River's so blunt!" "Poor Dora, she's actually his fan?" "Candle for Nana." "But Yuui is genuinely sweet, it's not an act, unlike Dora's knockoff vibe!"

Inside the Mirror Lake arena.

"You are the breeze of spring, scattering the gloom within my heart."

A refreshing song resonated by Cora, Suchat, and Damian's ears, instantly dispelling the auditory disaster brought by Dora Werner and her band.

Cora was shaken.

Onyx had guessed correctly—Yuui Hayashi's ability indeed could aid her allies!

A whisper came again in her ear. "Cora, try Ellyn to see if she has the crystal."

Cora had reservations about Yuui's informal way of addressing her, but this wasn't the time for pettiness. She nodded, leaped like a swift into the fray, and charged directly at Ellyn, her blade striking the barrel of the Gatling gun.

"Hand over the crystal!"

Caught off guard, Ellyn struggled to defend. "I don't have it!"

Despite her efforts, the force of Cora's strike was too strong. Even though Ellyn blocked some of it, she was pushed back, dragging the heavy gun mount several meters before stopping.

Meanwhile, the mechanical head was flipping over the guitarist from "Stars of Felalakas," sending the noisemaker flying with a grunt.

The electric guitar slipped from his grip, spun high into the air, and then—came crashing down towards Ellyn.

Just as Ellyn stabilized herself and could not intercept, Yuui suddenly called out, "Cora, save her!"

Using a tree trunk for leverage, Cora vaulted into the air and kicked the flying guitar with a swift, forceful strike.

The large guitar shifted direction, tumbling towards "The Knights of Anna" before exploding on impact, filling the area with smoke.

"Cough, cough!"

As the choking smoke cleared, everyone was shocked to find "The Knights of Anna" gone!

Soon after, the coordinates for both flags began moving rapidly, quickly placing them several kilometers away.

Laughter filled the air, arrogant and mocking from the mechanical head.

"Bye-bye, not serving you anymore, fellas! I love snatching two crystals for the task! Turn in one, ditch the other, oh, just for fun!"

Dora ground her teeth in fury.

"Chase them!"

"Stars of Felalakas," pursued "The Knights of Anna," leaving the area.

Ellyn, supported by her teammates after her narrow escape, looked towards Cora and Yuui, her lips barely moving.

"Thank you."

Ellyn could see clearly; Cora's attack had been a probe, and the electric guitar's fall was purely accidental. Had it not been for her timely intervention, she might not have survived.

"You're welcome," Yuui spoke for the flustered Cora, smiling lightly, "It was nothing."

They had no quarrel with Ellyn and deduced the crystal wasn't with her. If Ellyn had died because of their actions, Yuui wouldn't have been able to live with herself.

Ellyn gave them a thoughtful look, feeling a sense of familiarity in that smile.

"I owe you one. I'll remember this," Ellyn said earnestly, before turning to follow her teammates.

"Are we not chasing?" Cora was puzzled.

"We can't catch up. They clearly have someone adept at escaping. We can't afford to split up," Yuui reasoned.

Of their group, only Cora and Suchat might catch up to the mechanical beings, but that would leave Yuui and Damian in a precarious situation.

Sure enough, within seconds, the priority of those two coordinates dropped to fifth, now over ten kilometers away.

Even if they could catch up, trying to snatch the crystal from "The Knights of Anna" while also dealing with Dora and Ellyn's teams would likely lead to another endless, brutal fight.

"So, what do we do?"

"Let's keep looking. There are probably more selfish players like that around. The number of crystals is decreasing; we need to hurry."

The Mirror Lake arena was tense.

"Not good, the flags are dwindling," Yuui Hayashi noted as she glanced at the tracker, her eyebrows knitted in concern.

It was 9:40 PM, and 100 minutes had passed since the start of the match.

Cora's team had been searching for nearly half an hour, nearly turning the entire Forbidden Forest upside down, but their luck was terrible.

The newly refreshed flag coordinates were diagonally far from them or on the opposite side of Mirror Lake, requiring a detour to reach.

By the time they arrived, someone had already moved the flags again, and they couldn't find any sign of the mutant zombies.

Something didn't add up.

Yuui lowered her gaze, puzzled. She wasn't usually this unlucky.

Could it be... could it be that someone's terrible luck was bringing them all down?

An increasingly absurd suspicion crossed her mind as she looked ahead at Cora and Damian, who were distractedly teaching each other how to curse.

Damian instructed, "Sis, 'old' and 'how many' should be connected to have an impact."

Cora practiced, "You count as old how many!"

Damian beamed, "Right, just like that!"

Yuui thought to herself: They really don't seem to worry...

As AK switched between different streams in the broadcast room, landing on 161-1, he caught this scene and teased, "Team F777, as a dark horse in this competition, seems to be quite strong but not very lucky, missing the flags several times already."

"Now, as the match heats and two-thirds of the teams have advanced, our player Cora still seems stable. Will she regret stopping here, or can she create another surprise? Viewers can place their bets!"

The viewership in room 161-1 had peaked at 200,000 during Cora's solo fight against a water monster, rivaling the popularity of Ellyn and Dora.

However, after a drone malfunction caused a blackout, and with Cora wandering aimlessly for half an hour, viewership had dropped back to around 80,000.

Yuui sighed. "Are you still in the mood to play? Didn't you hear the announcement? There are fewer than ten spots left for advancing."

Just then, the system had updated the current situation: 52 teams had already advanced, leaving few opportunities for them.

Cora and Damian stopped their whispers, straightened up, and got serious.

"Shall we snatch?" Cora suggested.

With only two moving flag coordinates left, both far from their current location, their only option if they couldn't find any mutant zombies was to attempt a robbery.

Just then, Suchat, who was scouting ahead, suddenly warned, "Something's approaching."

Cora looked around alertly.

There was a river ahead with calm waters and the mountain waste beyond, everything seemingly peaceful.

But something was off—the river's flow seemed to have quickened.

Damian stood by the riverbank, his gaze fixed on the water's surface as small bubbles emerged, bubbling and churning.

He swallowed nervously.

"Not another water monster, right?"

His fists clenched, his ice powers ready to launch.

With a splash, a ghastly green-skinned zombie leaped from the river.

As it appeared, mist enveloped the area, the damp air suffocating them, a sign of a water-powered mutant zombie!

In the tense atmosphere of the competition, the sudden announcement of the last remaining flag shifted the dynamics significantly.

With all eyes, possibly turning towards them soon, the small group found themselves at a critical juncture.

Yuui Hayashi, her expression grave, took a moment to collect her thoughts.

The last remaining crystal that Cora held could be their ticket to advancing, or it could paint a target on their backs for all remaining competitors.

"Okay," Yuui said, her voice steady but low, "we need to think strategically now. This isn't just about defending the crystal anymore, it's about making it to the end with it."

Cora, still processing the sudden responsibility thrust upon them by luck and circumstance, nodded.

"What's the plan, then? Everyone will come for this."

Yuui glanced at Damian and Suchat, their faces set in determined lines.

"We need to find a defensible position. There's no avoiding a confrontation at this point. Our best chance is to control where that confrontation happens."

The tracker beeped again with the coordinates of the remaining flag, showing a location near the center of the arena—open, yet surrounded by dense thickets perfect for an ambush.

"There," Yuui pointed.

"We can set up there. It's open enough to see them coming but close enough to the thickets for a strategic retreat if necessary."

Suchat, always the silent strategist, chimed in, "We'll set traps. Damian, you and I can work on slowing them down if they approach."

Damian nodded, his earlier levity replaced by focus. "I can create ice barriers. Slow them down, maybe even trap a few."

Cora, feeling the weight of her role in their survival, added, "And I'll be on the front line with Suchat. We keep them from getting too close."

Yuui's eyes held a spark of something fierce, proud. "We're in this together. Let's make sure we're the ones to tell the story of how this night ends."

As the team moved to their new location, the arena's latent energy seemed to buzz anticipatory. Other teams, sensing the nearing end of the competition, moved with renewed urgency.

The air was electric with the promise of confrontation.

As they set up their makeshift fortress, Yuui pulled Cora aside.

"Listen, no matter what happens, you did well to get us here. Remember, it's not just about strength or power; it's about heart, and you've got more than enough of that."

Cora nodded, the gravity of the situation settling in but also the resolve. She wasn't just fighting for advancement now; she was fighting for her team, their collective effort, and the bond they had forged in the face of adversity.

With the stage set, the dwindling light casting long shadows across the battlegrounds, and the last flag's coordinates pulsing ominously on their devices, the last stand was about to begin.

The question wasn't just who would come out on top, but how much they would have to sacrifice to get there. The battle for the final crystal, the key to advancement, was not just a test of strength but of strategy, unity, and sheer will.

And as the first signs of movement rustled in the distant bushes, signaling the approach of the first challengers, Cora tightened her grip on her weapons, the others ready at her side, all united in one goal—to survive and advance, whatever it took.

For most Aberrants, the T. T. T. represents a vast accumulation of points, a continuous stream of money, fulfilling power and ambition, and even a ladder to District B. But for Yuui Hayashi, all these things are of no interest.

The only reason Yuui Hayashi takes part in the competition is to save the life of a loved one. Even if this choice means that her hands are stained with blood, her reputation ruined, and everyone despises her, she has no regrets.

"Suchat, are you confident you can kill them?" Yuui Hayashi uses her ability to transmit her voice.

"No," Suchat honestly replies.

"Understood… then follow my orders," she continues.

"Let them be... live targets for a while."

CHAPTER 16

Counterattack

"The current number of advancing teams: 54."

"Remaining flags in the field: 1."

Ten advancement spots, only one flag left.

If the previous announcement had left a sliver of hope for the teams within Mirror Lake, thinking they might still find an Anopower zombie to capture the crystal, the latter one had directly sentenced them to death.

There were no surviving Anopower zombies left in Mirror Lake.

Over a hundred teams in the field had only one choice left: kill and seize the flag!

At this moment, whoever held the flag would undoubtedly become the target of all.

"Sister, are we in great danger?" Damian asked, holding Cora's hand, his voice filled with worry.

Cora didn't answer him immediately.

Instead, she looked towards the other two.

Being hunted was secondary. What concerned her most now was what Yuui Hayashi was thinking.

The prerequisite for their cooperation was based on having enough crystals.

Now that this condition no longer existed, one of the two teams would inevitably cannot advance.

Given this situation, was continued cooperation still possible?

Would Yuui turn against them on the spot, just like the others, and try to kill her for the flag?

Cora clenched and unclenched her fingers around the crystal in her pocket, unsure of what to say.

Yuui stood silently for a moment, noticing Cora's tense expression.

She sighed softly, unexpectedly calm.

"What bad luck. This turns out to be the last crystal. Well, you're the focus now. Hurry and take it to the finish line."

Cora felt a pang in her heart. "What about you? How will you advance?"

Yuui Hayashi's lips curved into a slight smile, her delicate fingers poking Cora's shoulder.

Cora didn't dodge.

"Worried about me? Since the competition allows for 64 teams to advance, there will always be another way."

Despite her words, the future didn't look optimistic.

The original rules were already this harsh. If they delayed until the end, who knew what awaited them?

"Don't worry, I keep my word."

"Oh dear, judging by your expression, are you planning to give me the crystal?"

Even at this time, Yuui had the mood to tease her.

Cora's fingers touched her pearl necklace, her voice hesitant. "Actually, I..."

She was interrupted abruptly as leaves rustled, and a shadow, like a python, lunged towards them.

The first wave of pursuers had arrived!

Suchat reacted swiftly, darting into the woods. Muffled grunts sounded from the darkness, and the ambushing Aberrants were instantly taken down.

"Run!" Yuui urged.

The four of them dashed towards the mountain peak where the finish line was, encountering several ambushes along the way.

Fortunately, they made it through without significant danger. Before long, they reached the foot of the mountain.

A few more kilometers ahead was the finish line where they could submit the flag.

"Something's off. The pursuers have thinned out."

The wind seemed to slow down here, and the surroundings were eerily quiet, with snowflakes swirling down.

"Crack—"

Cora's ears caught the sound of dead leaves being crushed.

She stopped, looking up warily.

The next second, hundreds of hunters rushed at them from all directions! They were surrounded.

On the only path to the finish line, many desperate, bloodthirsty Aberrants had already laid in ambush.

"Boom—" A thunderous cannon shot signaled the start of the plundering.

The firepower was too intense, forcing Cora to retreat.

On the periphery of her vision, Cora spotted a familiar Gatling particle cannon that was set up - it was "Gunpowder Rose"!

An Anopower fire circle erupted, trapping the four inside, the scorching flames almost burning their skin.

Ellyn, after firing a shot, saw who was in the circle and was momentarily stunned. It was them?

After all, they had saved her. A hint of hesitation flashed in her eyes, and her hand slowed down.

In the official live broadcast room, all cameras once again switched to Drone 161-1.

Facing the camera, AK analyzed calmly, "F777's situation doesn't look good. On one side, they face an unending army of interceptors, while on the other side, it's just a makeshift team cobbled together, plus Team 121..."

Yuui and Suchat were not impressive.

AK rummaged through his memory.

"This team is called [Whatever Name], and their combat skills seem equally casual. Player 121-1, Suchat, frequently disappears from the screen, leading to many viewer complaints. As for Player 121-2, Zhang San, she's been lackluster since the preliminaries, earning the nickname 'Lazy Queen.' How do they plan to handle this?"

Before AK finished speaking, the situation in the field changed dramatically.

The four surrounded players, with no apparent communication, moved in perfect synchrony.

Damian took a step back, and a wild snowstorm fell from the cloudy sky, rapidly lowering the temperature.

The blazing fire rings were instantly extinguished, leaving only blackened ashes.

Yuui's lips moved slightly, and although her actions were subtle, their movement speed doubled.

Suchat vanished into the darkness, reappearing behind the besieger in an instant.

With a swift, cold green flash of his blade, the enemy was dead before they could utter a sound.

After a successful assassination, he once again disappeared into the shadows, waiting for his next target like a grim reaper harvesting life.

Cora wielded dual blades, charging straight into the encirclement like a swift leopard.

All the varied Anopowers crumbled before her absolute strength.

Anyone who faced her directly was defeated within three moves. Their mental strength shattered, and they were sent flying.

She forcefully tore open the encirclement.

"Wow! I never thought a ragtag team could mount such a comeback. This coordinated attack is truly impressive," AK exclaimed.

Locke, rarely speaking, objectively commented, "Although they are outnumbered, if you didn't know beforehand, you wouldn't guess this is a makeshift team. They have clear roles for remote control and close combat, and their reactions are quick."

"River is right. Competitions are always full of surprises. The situation remains grim. We see another wave of interceptors heading their way."

Just as Cora tore open a path to break through, countless Aberrants surged from behind.

Were they planning to use a human wave tactic to exhaust them?

Cora flicked her fingers, and a dozen shuriken flew out, striking with immense power because of the close range.

The Aberrants at the front had no time to dodge and fell instantly.

There was an opening! Cora's eyes lit up, and she prepared to charge forward.

A familiar, nonchalant voice suddenly called out from the crowd behind.

"Hey, there's someone trying to escape here! Anyone with control abilities, stop them!"

Cora turned towards the voice, and sure enough, it was that young man with icy blue eyes and silver-streaked hair! She cursed inwardly.

This guy was an absolute pest, like a stick stirring up trouble!

A violent tornado blew in, blocking the hard-fought escape route. Cora had to retreat a few steps.

The man with icy blue eyes attacked at that moment. As he moved, countless 101010 code lines appeared before Cora, making her dizzy. His Anopower was just as annoying as he was!

Using the code lines to pave his way, the man approached her, his tone taunting and arrogant, "Nice weapon. Mind if I look?"

Cora swung her blade in response, shattering the code wall. Her shuriken flew towards the man's forehead.

He retreated in time, using his Anopower to block the attack. The shuriken halted mid-air, trembling.

He inspected it, touching his chin, and muttered to himself.

"Not a physical object, an Anopower manifestation? Interesting."

Before he could finish, the shuriken broke through the code wall, shooting towards his eyes like a meteor. The man dodged in a panic, but a cut still appeared on his face, blood streaming down.

He laughed it off nonchalantly and twisted to the Aberrants attacking, rallying them, "Guys, this isn't working. We need to identify who has the flag first before we attack!"

The crowd paused, realizing he was right. They needed to target the one with the flag.

A raging tornado erupted from the ground, scattering Cora and her team's formation.

Damian, being lighter, was blown away over ten meters, finally stopping when he got caught in a tree branch.

The strong wind also pushed Yuui back, looking extremely disheveled.

Their coordinates changed slightly, and the ambushers quickly identified who truly held the flag.

"It's on the girl!!"

"Kill her!"

The skills originally aimed at the four of them shifted direction, all focusing on Cora. In an instant, Cora found herself in a bitter fight.

The pressure on Yuui and Damian eased significantly as their attackers ignored them completely, focusing only on Cora.

Hidden in the shadows, Suchat received a whispered message.

"Suchat, get ready."

"The crystal is in her pocket. Once you get it, don't bother with anything else. Just head straight to the finish line."

In the official live broadcast, AK watched intently, muttering under his breath, "The situation doesn't look good. Will Cora's allies choose to support her or run away? Oh? They're charging in, after all, there's still genuine affection and loyalty in this world... Wait!"

"Let the breeze blow, with heartfelt devotion, sending you my blessings always."

A melodious song rang in Cora's ears.

After just two lines, she felt invigorated and full of energy—it was Yuui's Anopower, a beneficial buff!

Suchat joined the fray, and Cora made space for him. He slipped past the Aberrants in front, brushing shoulders with her.

With a flash of a dagger in his palm, "slash—" he cut through her pocket.

Cora was stunned. She stayed in her stance for two seconds.

"Oh, no! Cora's ally has betrayed her!" AK cried out in dismay.

Having succeeded in his strike, Suchat quickly disappeared into the mountains, rushing towards the finish line.

Cora looked at Yuui in fury, her eyes accusing: You lied to me!

Yuui turned away, a sigh whispering in Cora's ear. "Sorry, but I also said winning is more important to me."

Taking advantage of the moment, she also left the battlefield.

Cora, now in peak condition, found herself surrounded.

The others still didn't know what had happened and continued bombarding her with skills until the latest announcement rang out.

"Flag coordinates updated. Here are the remaining flag coordinates: (1108,453,339)."

"Damn! The flag has moved!"

This new location was close to the finish line. The besieging Aberrants were stunned and quickly chased towards the mountain top, leaving Cora behind. It was too late.

Current number of advancing teams: 55.

"Attention, the number of remaining flags in the field: 0. A new rule set will begin shortly."

"Sister!" Damian finally jumped down from the tree branch just as the announcement came.

Blinking, he didn't understand at first, but then he realized what had happened, and immediately jumped up in anger.

"Ah!! That wicked woman!"

Yuui and Suchat had advanced. They had deceived them... stolen the only crystal from them and advanced.

Cora gripped her dual swords tightly, her knuckles cracking.

"Little Diamond, let's head to the finish line," Cora said in a low voice.

"Huh?" Damian didn't understand.

Was his sister so angry she wanted to chase Yuui and Suchat to the finish line?

There was no time to explain.

Cora quickened her pace, leading Damian to the mountaintop.

Here, a floating verification platform awaited, with an invisible barrier blocking their path.

"Please submit the flag," a mechanical voice intoned from a window where an AI sat.

Cora stepped forward, and a high-voltage electric current immediately crackled as if warning anyone daring to break through.

She glanced towards the post-game resting area, crowded with silhouettes, unable to spot Yuui or Suchat.

Returning her gaze, she looked at the AI that had spoken.

"The flag is a crystal, right?" "Yes."

"As long as it's a crystal, we can pass?"

"Yes."

The AI paused before giving a confirmed reply.

Cora moved her palm slightly, revealing a green octahedral crystal, vibrant and radiant, in her hand.

"Does this count?"

CHAPTER 17

A Surprise

"Yooooo! What a surprise! Tonight's match is truly full of surprises. Cora Thornton has pulled out another flag!" AK shouted into the microphone, his voice hoarse with excitement.

"When did she hide it? And folks, this is a flag that wasn't even mentioned in the system announcement!"

The live chat exploded with question marks:

"Did I see that right? A green crystal, is it real?"

"It must be fake. The announcement didn't mention it."

"Why would she pull out a fake one? Does she think we're all fools?"

In the post-game resting area, a holographic projection was broadcasting the match.

When Cora took out the green crystal, several well-informed Aberrants looked shocked, standing up in disbelief and gazing at the screen.

Master Stark, however, remained calm.

Slowly sipping his tea, he remarked, "I never thought I'd see a Level 2 crystal here. This old man's seen it all now!"

Crystals became a strategic resource after the apocalypse.

Aberrants had varying levels of access to information.

Some knew nothing, while others, like Master Stark, prided themselves on having early access to insider information.

The Alliance publicly classified crystals into four levels: Level 1 (white), Level 2 (green), Level 3 (blue), and Level 4 (red). The deeper the color, the purer the quality, and the higher the success rate of awakening and evolution.

Currently, even Level 1 crystals were rare. Level 2 crystals had only appeared a few times in Area B, given the low occurrence rate of Anopower zombies. The stronger the Anopower zombie, the harder it was to hunt.

Master Stark's sharp eyes focused on Cora in the holographic projection. Despite his age, his mind was sharp. He recognized the girl as the audacious thief who had stolen their Class A mission in Glass Port.

Hmph, she got lucky that time, not only stealing the crystal but also escaping through heavy encirclement, making their efforts go in vain.

John Stone was just an ordinary Class D zombie, incapable of producing a Level 2 crystal.

Since she dared to bring it out, she must have gotten it within the tournament arena. It seemed there was a lot more information worth uncovering about this Aberrant named Cora.

Master Stark instructed his subordinates, "Find out everything you can about her background. Also, get hold of her complete match footage immediately."

On the other side, Zephyrion Stormrider was also watching Cora, his eyes deep and contemplative. The wound she inflicted last time still ached. She was a formidable opponent he needed to monitor.

Noticing Zephyrion's distraction, Master Stark teased, "Brother Zephyrion, it seems this contestant has caught your attention?"

Zephyrion smiled wryly, "Master Stark, no need to test me. I stand by my words: no matter who the opponent is, the winner will be me."

In the gathering place of the Knights of Anna, the cyborg head Seon was tossing two crystals up and down. Suddenly, he exclaimed, "Huh, green crystals are prettier than white ones. The ones I have don't look so good anymore."

Seon's mechanical head creaked forward, greedily eyeing the crystal in Cora's hand with a vicious glare.

At the verification platform, the AI scanned the crystal Cora provided and, in a flat tone, announced, "Sorry, verification failed.

Only crystals got from Mirror Lake can be submitted as flags."

Cora stubbornly insisted, "It is from Mirror Lake. I got it there."

The chat exploded with skeptical comments.

"Liar, definitely a liar!"

"Is she just making things up? I've been glued to the 'Lock-on You' stream since their wipeout and I didn't see her get any green crystal."

"Bold and dumb. Does she not know the entire match is being recorded?"

Some faint voices defended Cora.

"Maybe you guys missed it. This contestant is really strong."

But the flood of insults quickly drowned these few fair comments out.

"If I didn't see it, maybe I missed it. But if no one saw it, what's that? Collective blindness?"

"Do you think the AI director is slacking off? If such a giant crystal dropped, wouldn't they switch the camera?"

"She's a fraud. How can anyone defend her?"

Outside the screen, Old James was furiously typing. He had bet everything on Cora winning.

This couldn't be the end. Rolling up his sleeves, he engaged in a heated debate with the naysayers.

In the official live broadcast, AK passionately and rhythmically stoked the atmosphere.

"Cora still insists that this crystal came from Mirror Lake. So, where exactly did this unique green flag come from? River, what's your take?"

River Locke thoughtfully considered for a moment before giving his answer.

"A water monster."

Almost simultaneously, Cora, facing off against the AI, said the same thing: "Water monster, the crystal came from."

"No wonder River guessed it right away. Let's check the replay," AK announced with a flourish.

The backstage director immediately cut to the footage of Cora soloing the Mirror Lake water monster.

"From the footage, this was indeed an Anopower water monster. Look here, pause! The water monster is launching rain arrow attacks, a method only Anopower can use."

The video froze, showing the water monster's flat head facing Cora, its viciousness far exceeding that of regular Anopower zombies.

Countless fine rain arrows struck the large ethereal umbrella, creating a blinding flash of light.

"Hey? After rescuing Damian, Cora lingered inside the water monster for about 2 minutes and 48 seconds. Could it be that she discovered the crystal during that time?"

"Great, AK. I've received a message from the backstage team. They're conducting an energy test on the water monster's body. Any crystal-producing area will leave strong radiation. We'll have an answer soon!"

At the verification platform, the AI's eyes lit up with lines of code, receiving some instruction.

"Congratulations, you have successfully advanced."

Simultaneously, AK's excited voice echoed across all viewers' devices.

"The green crystal has been confirmed to come from the Mirror Lake water monster. Congratulations to Cora! Congratulations to Damian. Congratulations to F777 for becoming the dark horse of this match, successfully advancing to the top 64!"

The particle current barrier slowly opened, and Cora and Damian walked wearily into the rest area.

Amidst the curious, scrutinizing, and doubtful glances, Cora walked past with an unchanging expression and straight back. As she passed Yuui and Suchat, they seemed to want to call out to her, but before they could speak, Cora had already walked away.

"Current number of advancing teams: 56."

"Remaining flags in the field: 0."

"New rule set beginning."

AK received a prompt from his earpiece, nodded, and with a serious tone, announced, "Ladies and gentlemen, we are now entering the Endless Slaughter mode. Let me briefly explain the rules: only the last eight surviving teams will advance. Everyone else will be eliminated!"

The remaining Aberrants received the same announcement.

Endless Slaughter mode meant that over 100 teams, over 300

participants, would battle for the eight spots, with survival being the only criterion.

This meant the losers wouldn't leave Mirror Lake—they'd face a true battle royale!

The teams that had already advanced breathed a sigh of relief, patting their chests.

"Thank goodness we grabbed a flag. Otherwise, we'd be in deep trouble."

In the arena, Ellyn the Wild Rose tore at her hair in frustration.

It was do or die.

"Sisters, live and die together, never betray each other! Charge with me!!"

In another corner, a man with icy blue eyes sighed softly, "Oops, seems like we've gotten ourselves into quite a mess."

With the start of Endless Slaughter, all Aberrants went berserk, attacking anyone nearby, even those they had just fought alongside. The frenzied attackers, eyes bloodshot, would kill one enemy one second and be lying dead the next, killed by another.

Screams, wails, agonized groans... It was a bloody hell on earth, the most brutal of battlefields. The air was thick with the stench of blood.

Ellyn blasted back the approaching Aberrants with a cannon shot. Suddenly, a cry of pain came from behind.

"Ah—!!"

She turned around in horror to see her companion lying in a pool of blood.

Grinding her teeth, tears streaming, she yelled, "Hold on, come to me. We can survive this!"

Outside the arena, the T.T.T. viewership skyrocketed to new heights.

Bloodshed and violence most stimulated the Felalakas' adrenaline, and the betting pool surged.

A river of wealth flowed towards the shadowy powers behind the scenes.

The slaughter raged on for half an hour. The final eight teams emerged from the carnage, drenched in blood.

"Guns and Roses" lose two members.

"White Radish Carrot" lose three.

"Black Jack" lose four, leaving only the man with icy blue eyes alive...

All the other teams were wiped out.

The top 64 of the T.T.T. had been decided. As its advertisements proclaimed, they had emerged through fire and thorns, treading on the blood and lives of countless others.

After the Mirror Lake match ended, Cora and Damian left through the contestant tunnel, walking in silence.

Damian stole several glances at Cora, wanting to comfort her but not knowing what to say. It was all that wicked woman's fault! His sister looked so unhappy.

After exiting the restricted zone and walking further, Cora suddenly stopped.

On the main road ahead, under a dim streetlight, sat a familiar silver-white wheelchair. The handsome man lounged casually, propping his chin with one hand, watching the fallen leaves swirl in the wind.

Hearing movement, the man, seemingly aware of their presence, looked up and smiled at her.

"What's the matter? Why so glum? Who bullied you?"

CHAPTER 18

Game Paused

This area was specifically designated as the post-game waiting zone, where many friends and family members gathered, eagerly waiting for the players to emerge.

Onyx's wheelchair was removed from the others, casting a solitary shadow stretched long by the streetlight.

A faint smile tugged at his lips.

"Who's been bullying you to puff up your cheeks like that?"

"Nothing," Cora pressed her lips together.

But the grievance was almost written on her face, though Onyx kindly didn't call her out on it.

"Alright, if you say nothing happened, then nothing happened." He paused, wearing a matter-of-fact expression before adding, "But if you say something happened, maybe I could help you get back at them?"

"How can anyone bully you? You're my lucky charm, and hurting you is like slapping me in the face."

Cora felt a mix of emotions that were hard to describe in that moment: surprise, joy, gratitude, confusion—it didn't quite capture it.

It felt like she and Damian Blackwood, the family's hope, left home full of confidence, only to be pelted with mud by other kids and roll into a puddle, coming back filthy. Yet, the family still asked if they wanted help to get back at those who wronged them.

The thought was so surreal that Cora dismissed it quickly,

shaking her head. She didn't take Onyx's words seriously.

Any Aberrant surviving today's competition was no ordinary expert.

Onyx, still needing a wheelchair, couldn't possibly avenge her.

Cora changed the subject, "Why are you here?"

Onyx replied, "I figured the match was almost over, and came to pick you up."

In fact, Onyx had set out as soon as it was confirmed that Cora advanced. As he said, he was here to pick up the two dejected kids and to confirm something else.

Cora glanced down at Onyx's wheelchair, noticing slight wear at the joints.

But overall it remained clean and well-maintained. This was the advanced model she had salvaged from the Evergreen Biotech workshop. Though fully functional, it wasn't far from the hotel to Mirror Lake.

Yet, in this cold weather, he still attempted to come this far alone just to pick them up.

Cora sensibly jogged forward to grab the wheelchair handle, ready to push him back.

"Wait," Onyx gently pressed her hand down.

His gaze drifted to the other side of the corridor, and Cora and Damian followed his line of sight.

A young man with icy blue eyes was slowly emerging from the passageway, looking like a battle-worn Shura, leaving bloody footprints wherever he went.

People around avoided him like the plague.

"Thyrion Lucas!" a clear voice called out, tossing a clean towel into the air, which Thyrion caught single-handedly.

Someone leisurely walked out of the crowd, pinching their nose in disdain while pouring water from a bottle, complaining, "You really are something, taking part in the competition personally instead of just watching, ending up in this sorry state."

Thyrion's head and face were covered in blood—not his own. He wiped it casually, and the white towel quickly turned red.

"Jaden Sheen, give it a rest. I didn't drag you into this."

"You'd drag me in if you could? Thyrion, do you even have a

conscience?"

Onyx's hand suddenly tensed.

The night wind tousled his hair, and the faint smile at his lips slowly gradually fell as he gazed at the man with a tear mole near his eye. His expression momentarily lost.

This change was too obvious, especially since Onyx had never lost his composure before.

Cora noticed almost immediately, realizing for the first time how terrifying Onyx looked, when he completely stopped smiling.

Cora asked softly, "Do you know them?"

Those ice-blue eyes had caused her plenty of trouble in the arena. If Onyx knew them, she had to find out who they were.

The two over there quickly noticed the gazes on them and turned to look in Cora's direction.

Thyrion's face still bore the cuts from Ethereal Artifacts, but his eyes were clear and calm, showing that he had deliberately caused trouble inside Mirror Lake.

Jaden's gaze swept over Damian, Cora, and Onyx, then moved away uninterestedly, resuming his chatter with Thyrion.

"When are we heading back to Grass Pit? I'm bored here."

Upon closer inspection, he was strikingly handsome, with features perfectly balanced, exuding an aloof yet vivid charm, especially stressed by the tear mole at the corner of his eye.

"No, I don't know them." Onyx finally looked away, his tone flat. "Let's go."

You stared for so long, yet you don't know them?

Cora felt skeptical. Though that person was indeed good-looking, when did Onyx ever care about appearances?

She scrutinized the man in the wheelchair: thin lips, high nose bridge, jet-black eyes—not lacking in looks.

Cora earnestly consoled, "You look good too, no need to envy others."

"Hmm?" It took Onyx a few seconds to understand her roundabout logic, and he couldn't help but laugh. "Well, thank you for the compliment?"

"You're welcome," Cora accepted graciously.

They hadn't walked far when Damian suddenly tugged at her

sleeve. "Sister, look over there..."

Cora followed his finger and was surprised to see someone who should never be here.

"Florian Richter?"

Florian Richter moved stealthily, turning his head every few steps, his eyes darting around warily. When he unexpectedly spotted them, his expression resembled someone who had seen a ghost. Without even a greeting, he spun a corner and hurried away.

He was taking part in the T. T. T. and even advanced? That seemed impossible. Weren't only D-level Aberrants and above allowed to register?

Cora distinctly remembered Vincent Anderson saying that Florian Richter was an E-level Aberrant.

Cora and Damian exchanged glances, seeing the same confusion reflected in each other's eyes.

"I think I know why he could enter the competition," Onyx spoke at the right moment.

"Why?"

"This isn't urgent. Let's talk about it when we get back," he murmured, barely glancing at the shadows, lowering his voice to warn, "Cora, take a few detours. We've got some unwelcome followers."

Cora stiffened, releasing her mental power to probe around.

Sure enough, she detected several lurking figures trailing them.

"Someone's following us?" she whispered.

"More than that. Most of the players leaving here are being watched," Onyx replied. "Greedy people are always trying to score easy wins. Right now, Mirror Lake is a treasure trove of crystals."

The T. T. T. committee was wealthy, allowing players to keep the crystals they earned inside the arena. Cora had taken out a Level 2 crystal, and now they were being targeted.

However, these people were audacious. Every team making it to the top 64 was formidable. Trying to rob them was a dangerous gamble, risking their own lives before getting anything.

But avoiding trouble was always best. Cora didn't look back, silently picking up her pace. Following Onyx's directions, they took winding paths and finally shook off their pursuers.

Back at the hotel, Onyx urged the overly excited Cora and Damian, who were trying to stay up all night watching replays, to rest. "It's late, get some sleep. We'll discuss the competition once I've reviewed everything tomorrow."

Cora deflated a bit, "Alright."

Onyx had gone to pick them up right after the match, missing the final slaughter mode and the actual strength of other teams showcased. He also only half-answered the question he sought and needed to review the game recordings.

As for how Cora got "bullied," even if she didn't want to say, Onyx could figure it out. Knowing all the details wouldn't be hard, considering there was a mobile little spy in the arena.

Onyx called out to Damian, who was about to return to his room, "Little Diamond—"

"What do you want?!" Damian bristled at the sound of his voice, goosebumps rising at the memory of the grueling month of devil training.

"Stop calling me that. It's disgusting!"

Facing Onyx's faintly smiling eyes, Damian swallowed nervously, feeling more tense than facing a water monster. "I really gave it my all today!"

Onyx smiled. "You did well today. I'm here for something else."

Damian breathed a sigh of relief. "What is it?"

"Tell me how Yuui Hayashi tricked you all."

Watching the match from the first-person perspective missed some details, and Cora's drone often lost connection, leaving gaps in Onyx's understanding.

It was better to ask another participant directly.

At this, Damian perked up. Yuui Hayashi had now topped his list of most hated people (the previous holder was Onyx).

United in their common enemy, Damian eagerly joined Onyx, angrily detailing Yuui's misdeeds.

When Cora opened her eyes the next morning, the first thing she saw was Onyx's back.

He was sitting in her room, silently replaying a projection over and over.

The screen paused on the man with icy blue eyes, his expression cold and stern.

Cora pulled the blanket up to her chin, lying still in bed, her eyes blinking as she silently observed Onyx.

She knew Onyx had carried many secrets.

Some of what he said was true, some false, and she often couldn't tell the difference.

Despite knowing each other for so long, even a slow learner like Cora had gradually realized that Onyx could never be just an ordinary researcher, as he claimed.

But why was it that even though she had been deceived by Onyx so many times, she never felt as angry as she did last night?

Cora pinched the corner of the blanket.

Maybe it was because their goals and interests were aligned. In a way, they were bound by fate, and Onyx's lies were mostly not directed at her and did not cause her any actual harm.

Was this the privilege of having a "golden thigh" to rely on? Cora's gaze drifted, her mind wandering far away.

"Have you seen enough?" Onyx's voice cut through her thoughts, as if he had eyes on the back of his head.

"Yes, I have."

Caught in the Act, Cora wasn't embarrassed at all. She flipped the blanket aside and got up briskly.

Fifteen minutes later, the three of them were sitting in her room for a meeting.

The projection was still paused on the man with icy blue eyes.

Cora took a bite of her bread, her mouth full. "This guy isn't in your files."

"That's correct," Onyx admitted. "Just like Florian Richter we saw last night, these two entered the primary competition through irregular means."

"What do you mean by irregular means?" Damian pulled out two bottles of milk from his pocket, handing one to Cora, and they both drank heartily.

"The normal route is for D-level and above Aberrants to sign up for the preliminaries. If they succeed in the challenges and meet the popularity quota, they advance to the primary competition. Only teams that have entered the primary competition can adjust their members. But these two simply bought a spot from a team that had already advanced."

"Bought a spot? Isn't the championship reward attractive to everyone? Why would anyone give up their place?" Damian asked, his mouth never stopping.

"Because there can only be one champion. Some people know they won't make it to the end," Onyx said meaningfully. "So, if the price is high enough, people can be tempted to sell their spot."

"Does Florian Richter have the money to buy a spot?" Damian continued. "He used to rely on sewing for extra cash when he was with Captain Wolf. How does he afford to buy a spot now?"

"Florian Richter is indeed problematic. I've reviewed his footage. And although there's little of it, his Anopower is certainly not weak. It's a dark, aggressive type," Onyx explained.

"Has he evolved?" Cora suggested.

"Impossible," Onyx shook his head.

"Evolution only enhances existing traits. It wouldn't change him so drastically."

"If you encounter him again, stay alert," Onyx advised.

"What's their goal in entering the competition? Are they also wishing for something from Ilia?"

Damian asked again.

"I don't know Florian's purpose. As for this man," Onyx traced a circle in the air with his finger, and a red marker appeared over the head of the man with icy blue eyes in the projection, "he is Thyrion Lucas, from the B District."

"Phfft—cough, cough!" Cora Thornton choked, coughing violently.

Damian Blackwood quickly patted her back.

Someone from District B taking part in a District C competition? How absurdly bored must that person be?

"Not just from District B, but from one of the top districts, B4, Grass Pit," Onyx de Montclair added nonchalantly. "However, his participation in this time seems to be a personal endeavor."

"How do you even know which district he's from?" Damian asked, eyes wide in amazement.

Onyx explained calmly, "Grass Pit is the stronghold of The Lucas

Family, known for their distinct ice-blue eyes. The lighter the eye color, the purer the bloodline, and the higher the status within the family."

The Lucas? The image of hundreds of Lucas Starships crashing in the Flower City was still vivid in Cora's mind.

Hesitantly, she asked, "Are we talking about those Lucas Starships?"

"Correct." Onyx nodded.

Damian's eyes turned red with anger. "Their starships are in shambles, and instead of fixing them, he has the nerve to join a competition?"

Victor Blackwood had bought tickets early to leave District F with Damian.

If not for the drastic reduction in starships after the apocalypse, they wouldn't have been forced apart, and his father might not have turned into a zombie.

Damian knew he shouldn't blame Jeremy Wolfgang or the guards who couldn't protect the food factory, but he would never forget the starship that was "canceled because of an energy issue" at the last second, right in front of him and his father.

"Thyrion Lucas's eye color isn't pure. He holds no actual power within the Lucas family. So expect little from him," Onyx said calmly.

"Hmph," Damian grumbled, "What about the other guy? His eyes aren't ice blue."

Onyx's eyes flickered, and he didn't respond immediately.

Damian, oblivious to the tension, pointed to his own eye corner. "You know, the one with the mole here? You haven't mentioned him yet."

Cora quickly rubbed Damian's head, distracting him. "Little Diamond, are you hungry? Go order some food."

Damian, still puzzled, was gently pushed away, completely forgetting that he had used a similar excuse to get rid of Cora just a while ago.

"Let him keep asking, huh?" Onyx sneered.

"Haha." Cora smiled apologetically, the dimples on her cheeks appearing and disappearing with the movements.

"You don't have to say anything if you don't want to."

Onyx stared at her dimples for a moment before his tone returned to normal. "It's not about wanting to say it or not. I just remembered some unpleasant people. It's no big deal. I'm not that petty."

"Hmm," Cora nodded seriously, "Of course, you're not petty at all. You're the most generous person ever."

"That man is from the Sheen Family."

"The Sheen Family?"

"Yes. You might not be familiar with the name. The highest commander of The Azures is Jaden Sheen."

Despite being prepared, Cora was still taken aback. The commander of The Azures? Wasn't that Jeremy Wolfgang's boss and the leader of those powerful Aberrant soldiers? He sounded like a significant figure.

"Cora, I reviewed other angles of the footage." Onyx began taking advantage of Damian's absence to focus on her.

"After killing that water-type zombie, did you consider giving the crystal to Yuui Hayashi's team?"

Onyx's observational skills were frightening.

He had noticed even her brief hesitation.

Cora nodded slightly, then quickly shook her head. "At first, yes, but later, no."

"Why?"

"Because of Little Diamond."

Yuui Hayashi's desire to win was much stronger than hers.

If Cora were alone, she might have given up the crystal, believing there were other ways to advance. Even facing the endless slaughter mode, Cora could fight her way through.

But she wasn't alone; she had Damian to consider. Subjecting him to the risks of a continuous battle was too dangerous. At that moment, Cora wasn't sure if the green crystal counted as a flag, so despite her brief hesitation, she couldn't hand it over.

After a good night's sleep, Cora found her anger towards Yuui had diminished.

Both of them had no other choice back then; it was just bad luck for both.

Onyx observed her for a moment before nodding approvingly.

"Good, you're maturing."

Damian returned with a gigantic pile of food.

After a simple breakfast, Onyx's expression turned serious.

"Now, let's talk about some serious matters."

"Felalakas is currently very dangerous."

Not that Felalakas wasn't as prosperous as it appeared on the surface; it was that there were dark currents flowing beneath its façade.

Onyx's wheelchair was parked by the floor-to-ceiling window, his gaze lowered towards the city center, shrouded in a thin mist.

"The most obvious evidence lies in two areas: First, the shockingly low employment rate among the general populace. In Felalakas, finding a job is exceedingly difficult for ordinary people. They simply can't compete with the vast number of artificial intelligences. AI adapts better to all positions than humans do."

Since arriving in Felalakas, they had seen AI present in all walks of life, controlling about 90% of the job market. Encountering a non-AI human worker was a rarity worth noting.

But that's not entirely true, is it? Cora thought. At least in the Aberrants base, the girl watching videos and the lady at the commission center window were ordinary people.

She voiced her doubts.

"Yeah, yeah, those three annoying review officers are human too," Damian added.

Onyx shook his head slowly.

"The ones you mentioned belong to Alliance institutions. These direct institutions have personnel assigned by the Alliance. There's no competition with AI for jobs."

Apart from these special places, Felalakas was a fully autonomous city.

Ordinary people couldn't find jobs. They had no stable income and spent their days idle.

This place frequently held large entertainment events—concerts, the T. T. T.—all requiring substantial spending.

Gradually, gambling became rampant. Some struck it rich overnight, while others lost everything and had to take on commissions, risking their lives, ultimately meeting unknown fates on missions.

Outside, the sky was overcast. The city's steel and concrete structures crisscrossed, slicing the entire city into layers. From a high vantage point, people on the ground looked like tiny ants.

The top 1%, or more precisely, the hidden power brokers, concentrated the wealth of this neon city in their hands.

"But... if more people die, what happens when there's no one left?" Damian muttered.

"That won't happen." Onyx's smile was icy.

"Don't forget, Felalakas is an open and inclusive city with no entry restrictions. New people arrive every day."

Cora and Damian fell silent, feeling a chill run down their spines.

"Felalakas welcomes everyone."

In hindsight, the phrase felt eerie and chilling.

Onyx waited for them to digest this information before pointing to a pin on the table.

"Second, I used your terminal to connect to the dark web and discovered some interesting things."

"What?"

"Some candidates from the last election are preparing to conspire and jointly oppose Ilia's rule. There might be significant upheaval soon."

The news was increasingly shocking. How could they stay here and make money peacefully? Cora was taken aback. "What should we do?"

Onyx thought for a moment. "You attracted a lot of attention in yesterday's match, and that you have a Level 2 crystal has been made public through the footage. More ill-intentioned people will probably come after you."

Cora frowned.

Greed knows no bounds. Crystals were still a scarce resource, and with the false information spread by the Alliance, many would eye her crystal.

Onyx brought up the points system of F777. "There's some time before the next match. I suggest we leave Felalakas for now to avoid the heat."

PART 2

SYCAMORE HOSPITALS

CHAPTER 19

The Hospital City

"Make way, don't block the corridor!"

Another medical stretcher sped past, and Cora Thornton, dressed in a khaki vest, shrank back, trying to minimize her presence in the hallway, her back almost glued to the wall.

The door opposite opened a crack. Inside, a patient with a flushed face lay unconscious from high fever, surrounded by doctors.

"Patient's heart rate?"

"150 beats per minute."

"Have you checked the eyes and skin?"

"Yes, for now, the radiation levels are within controllable limits. No signs of mutation yet."

"Transfer to special care. Keep someone on watch tonight. If the internal energy field remains stable, the patient is highly likely to awaken Anopower."

"What about the new volunteer? Patient 94 is fully zombified. Get them out quick!"

A deafening roar suddenly erupted from next door.

"Coming, coming!"

Cora quickly ran over, holding a short shovel.

"Clang, clang—" Two hits to the head, she expertly knocked out the biting zombie, then scooped it up around the waist, and dashed down the dedicated stairwell to the next floor, tossing it into the incinerator.

After finishing, she ran back, sticking close to the wall, resuming her role as a silent guardian among the passing stretchers.

This was Cora's second day as a volunteer—no, more accurately, as a "zombie cleaner."

They were currently at a top-tier hospital in Sycamore, District C40.

Cora worked as a cleaner on the thirteenth floor at the "Radiation Mutation Diagnosis and Treatment Research Center," Damian Blackwood ran errands in the pharmacy on the eighth floor, and Onyx worked as a clerk in the archives of the adjacent building.

Their bizarre working experience with the F777 team all started three days ago at an internal meeting.

Three days ago, Onyx suggested they temporarily leave the trouble-ridden Felalakas to lie low.

So, Cora scrolled through the list of assignments on the terminal and a large multiplayer B-level mission caught her eye.

B-Level Task (Multiplayer Task): Sycamore Medical Support

Task Description: Sycamore (District C40) has established a key research discipline on radiation mutations; fully treating various zombie-like patients and providing comprehensive guidance services for those showing early signs of Anopower awakening. Because of a severe shortage of medical personnel, we are now recruiting Anopower volunteers from across the alliance to overcome this crisis together.

Task Duration: Long-term

Task Reward: 0-1000 NPA credits

Note: Successful volunteer applicants will gain entry access to District C40 during their valid period of identity.

After reading, Onyx made an immediate decision: "Let's go to Sycamore."

If Felalakas was the city of music and freedom, then Sycamore was undoubtedly the city of medicine and life.

After the apocalypse, Sycamore remained one of the few cities where order had not collapsed, thanks to the tremendous efforts of the local governor and the guard team. Of course, this was also because of Sycamore's superior medical resources, boasting thousands of top-tier hospitals and over a hundred thousand top specialists in various fields.

Almost every native resident had medical knowledge. Sycamore's medical standards were renowned throughout the Alliance, even representing the highest level of technical and comprehensive strength.

There was once a joke about Sycamore: No matter what severe or critical illness you had, if Sycamore's doctors said they could save you, they could pull you back from the brink of death; but if even Sycamore shook their heads, you should prepare for the worst.

In the early days of the apocalypse, surrounding D-level cities of Sycamore quickly fell, and hordes of zombies flooded in. Despite this, Sycamore only experienced chaos for less than a week.

After clearing out the zombies, doctors picked up their scalpels again, treating patients either suffering from radiation overdose or zombie bites, striving to delay their mutations.

Sycamore and the three large nearby shelters bore the heavy burden but were not overwhelmed by the zombie tide. Instead, they shone brighter, like pearls polished by sand. This place was not only a grave for the dead but also a birthplace for Anopower individuals. Every day, some died from radiation outbreaks, while others survived high fevers, awakened Anopowers, and came back to life.

On the thirteenth floor's emergency room, the medical staff wheeled in a young patient.

"Doctor, am I going to turn into a zombie?" the girl asked tearfully, clutching her doll tightly.

There was a noticeable claw mark on her calf, oozing black, foul-smelling blood.

"Stay strong, little girl," the nurse beside her whispered softly. "Just trust us and leave the rest to the doctors, okay?"

"Okay, thank you, doctor."

"How long has it been since she was bitten?"

Dr. Lynn Rolling, with short hair, hurried in from the next room, bending down to examine the girl while asking her parents.

"Just bitten. We brought her to the hospital immediately, less than twenty minutes ago."

The girl's mother was sobbing uncontrollably.

Dr. Rolling's expression didn't change. She motioned for the couple to step out, then spoke coldly, "The wound is already mutating. The only option now is amputation to prevent the zombification process, which might save her life. Time is critical; decide quickly."

The girl's mother almost fainted upon hearing this, but her father, though tearful, remained calm enough to make the painful decision. "We'll do as Dr. Rolling says. We... we agree to the amputation."

"Sign the consent form and prepare for surgery." Dr. Rolling turned to head to the operating room.

"Dr. Rolling!" A colleague blocked her path, looking worried.

"Don't forget the regulations. Without an Anopower guardian present, we can't perform surgery on suspected mutation cases. It's too dangerous."

"Then get an Anopower guardian!" Dr. Rolling frowned.

"All the volunteers are busy with 'cleaning' duties outside. There's no one available right now..."

"People's lives are at stake. I'll find someone myself."

Dr. Rolling pushed him aside and rushed out of the emergency room. Looking around, she saw people running back and forth in chaos, except for a girl in a khaki vest standing idly in the corner.

"Hey, you!" Dr. Rolling called out.

Cora noticed the doctor in a white coat seemed to talk to her. She pointed at herself, "Me?"

"Yes, you, come here!"

"Huh? Oh."

She hurried to the doctor, who quickly glanced her over. The words "Medical Support" were awkwardly written on her vest.

"Are you an Aberrants?"

"Yeah."

"Good. I need a guardian for this surgery. You're it."

A guardian serves as an extra layer of security during surgeries on mutation cases.

If the patient starts zombifying and loses consciousness, attacking the medical staff, the guardian must handle the threat immediately.

"Okay." This was Cora's first time in the operating room, having spent the last two days doing dirty, exhausting work dealing with zombies.

She changed into sterile, radiation-proof clothing and was directed to stand in a corner, serving as a silent sentinel in a new location.

Dr. Rolling, similarly equipped, picked up the scalpel with a serious expression. There was a distinct air of determination on her face, the scalpel in her hand capable of both saving lives and swiftly ending them if the patient turned into a zombie.

An hour later, the indicator light went off, and Dr. Rolling came out to speak with the couple.

"The surgery was successful."

Her expression was exceptionally calm.

"Thank you, thank you, Dr. Rolling!" The girl's parents were overwhelmed with gratitude.

After they left, Dr. Rolling stood there, staring at her palm, lost in thought.

A few colleagues passing by asked curiously, "Dr. Rolling, you saved a life. Why don't you look happy?"

Dr. Rolling was silent for a moment. "My original plan was to only amputate the calf, but the radiation spread too quickly. My hands couldn't keep up, so I had to remove her entire leg..."

Her colleagues comforted her, "Dr. Rolling, don't blame yourself. You did an amazing job."

Dr. Rolling shook her head. "If Dr. Franz had performed the surgery today, he would have done it a thousand times better than me."

They sighed. "Chief Franz..."

The other doctors soon dispersed, busy with other patients. Dr. Rolling was about to leave too when she noticed Cora still standing in the corner. "We're done here. You can go back now."

"Okay."

Cora removed her mask, feeling stifled after over an hour, her black hair damp and matted with sweat. She fanned herself with her hand.

Dr. Rolling gave her a second look and thanked her. "Thank you for today."

"You're welcome."

In these times, everyone had it tough. For a girl Cora's age to volunteer in such a dangerous place, her family's situation must be challenging. Given the dirty and tiring job of zombie cleaning, earning less than 200 credits a day, only lower-level Anopower users will do it.

Even though Dr. Rolling was used to seeing life and death, she still felt a twinge of compassion and sighed, "It's a hard job."

She was just standing there for a while. Clearly, it was Dr. Rolling, performing the surgery, who had it tougher.

After a busy day, Cora finally received her allowance and got off work.

Sycamore was much more desolate than it used to be, but it was still a functioning city.

The largest concentration of zombies was in the incinerators of various hospitals, making the streets surprisingly quiet.

Leaving the hospital, Cora walked past a small park in the middle of the city. Flocks of white pigeons pecked at rice on the ground, children in new clothes ran around, and a disheveled homeless man lay on a bench with a newspaper over his head, sleeping. A passerby scattered some breadcrumbs in the air, attracting the pigeons. The homeless man, smelling the baked goods, rolled halfway off the bench and reached out to snatch the food from the pigeons.

The person scattering the crumbs looked at him with disdain and dashed away in disgust. Oblivious, the homeless man, with his unkempt beard, lay on the ground, stuffing food into his mouth with such desperation that he almost choked. He began coughing violently, spewing crumbs everywhere and startling the pigeons into flight.

Cora had already walked past, but slowed her steps when she heard the man's intense coughing. She stopped for a couple of seconds, then slowly walked back. She took an unopened loaf of bread from her pocket and placed it in front of him. It was the lunch provided by the hospital, which she hadn't eaten, still bearing the Medical Support logo.

Before her grandfather settled them in District F, there was a time when they wandered from place to place, often going hungry. This homeless man reminded her of her younger self.

The homeless man stared at the bread in surprise for a moment before grabbing it and devouring it ravenously. Cora walked away, thinking as she went, wondering how much Onyx and Damian had earned today.

CHAPTER 20

Dorothy

The sun set as the hardworking people finished their day's labor, heading home with a sense of fulfillment.

That's the ideal scenario.

In reality, the three members of F777 returned to their temporary residence looking quite displeased.

"I'm so tired," Damian Blackwood stuck out his tongue, his thin arms hanging limply in front of him like a small octopus. "Cora, are you tired?"

"Not really," Cora replied.

Physically, Cora was fine, but she felt dirty and immediately rushed into the bathroom for a shower.

Among the three, the only one who looked fresh was Onyx. Wearing a gray archivist uniform, he looked quite scholarly. However, he was rubbing his wrist, his brow furrowed with pain.

Sighing, Cora thought, life is hard, and earning money is even harder.

Zombie cleaners' jobs were typically done by low-level Aberrants.

For Cora, a proud Class-A Aberrant, to be doing this job was quite a surprise.

However, there was a reason they chose the multi-person task in Sycamore.

Other tasks were too far away or onetime gigs that required

constant searching for the next one and didn't provide access permissions.

Only Sycamore's medical support, though low-paying, offered many positions and rare long-term tasks.

So Cora didn't mind; work is work, regardless of its nature.

The three of them sat down to tally their earnings for the day: Damian earned 80 NPA credits, Cora earned 180 NPA credits, and Onyx earned the most with 300 NPA credits! Technical jobs are indeed lucrative.

Their total earnings for the day were 560 NPA credits. With the bonuses from the preliminaries and top 64, they could now consider themselves a middle-class household! Cora counted the numbers on her terminal, feeling quite pleased.

"News from Felalakas this morning: a top 64 team was assassinated at home, and their crystals were stolen," Onyx reported calmly.

"Which team?"

"The Fantastic Youths. They weren't very strong. Except for their Class C captain, the rest were Class D."

"They only advanced by sheer luck. A heavily wounded mutant brought them a crystal right after the match began. Now they've been targeted first, clearly seen as easy prey."

Cora frowned, realizing leaving Felalakas was indeed the right choice. The dark undercurrents were intensifying. First, contestants were being assassinated; who knows what might happen next?

Feeling his self-esteem bruised, Damian, who had earned the least, declared, "I want to go to the thirteenth floor tomorrow."

He couldn't earn 300, but surely he could make 180. 80 was simply too little.

Onyx's wrist ached at the thought of facing endless patient records the next day. "You both are not going to the thirteenth floor tomorrow."

"Why not?"

"I found two tasks we could take."

He opened the task interface, and Cora and Damian leaned over to look.

The first was a Class C task. The client, a resident of The Golden

Castle Drive, claimed he hadn't been able to enter his home for days. Every time he reached the building, whether taking the stairs or the elevator, it felt like he was hitting an invisible wall. He wanted an Aberrant to investigate and see if the issue could be resolved.

Onyx analyzed rationally, "The central system rates it as Class C, showing the situation isn't overly complex. The Golden Castle Drive is very close, and with processing time, one day should be enough. Most importantly..."

He swiped his elegant fingers across the screen, revealing the last line of the task description. "You'll like this."

The task reward was 1000 NPA credits.

Cora's eyes lit up.

Onyx smiled, anticipating her reaction.

"Now look at the second task."

The second task was rated Class D.

The client was anxious, stating that her child, Dorothy, had been running a fever for several days. Zombies were wandering the floors, and the door lock was malfunctioning, making it impossible to leave. Suspecting a supernatural cause, she wanted an Aberrant to help get the child to a nearby hospital.

"Hey?" Cora noticed the connection between the two tasks. "Same address."

"Yes, both at The Golden Castle Drive. The second client's address is G Building, Apartment 1507."

This made things interesting. One resident couldn't enter, while another couldn't leave. Who was telling the truth? Only a visit would reveal the answer.

"The issue is likely with G Building. We can handle both tasks together; it shouldn't be too difficult."

"Tomorrow, we'll go together," Cora decided.

The next morning, Cora Thornton went to the Sycamore task hall to activate her terminal and successfully accept the task. Then the three of them headed to The Golden Castle Drive.

The Golden Castle Drive was a high-end residential area, seemingly unaffected by the apocalypse.

Its greenery and public facilities were well-preserved.

The property management was quite responsible, and after they revealed their Anopower status, they were registered and led inside.

The security guard leading the way jingled a bunch of keys on his belt, the sound echoing clearly in the quiet surroundings. "This is the building. There's been no sign of life here for days."

They stopped at the entrance of the building, and the security guard hurried to leave.

"If you get inside and find zombies, just call the security team. Don't come looking for me."

"If there's a feverish patient, I can help you contact the Fifth Hospital nearby. They'll send an ambulance."

The guard was an ordinary person, naturally afraid of zombies. Cora didn't make things difficult for him. "Okay, thank you."

Once he was gone, she inspected the scene in front of her. The entrance to the building was open; how could anyone not get in?

Confused, Cora took a step forward. Everything seemed normal. She took another step. Still normal. She raised her foot to step up the stairs and then... she couldn't move.

It was as if an invisible wall blocked her.

Moving forward became extremely difficult.

Damian tried using his ice spikes to break through. The sharp spikes pierced the air wall, but just inches from the door, they bounced back with a "ding" and shattered on the grass behind them.

"It's a domain-type Aberrant," Onyx de Montclair remarked.

"It's somewhat like Kiwamu Maeda's air barrier, but larger in range and longer-lasting, at least three to five days," he continued. "I have a guess, but it's best to confirm the location first."

Was there an Aberrant inside?

One releasing a neutral Anopower indiscriminately?

Cora stepped back, looking up as she released her spiritual power, trying to locate the Aberrant.

The energy field was weak, barely noticeable, but she could roughly pinpoint it around the fifteenth floor.

"Around the fifteenth floor," Cora reported her findings.

She paused. The fifteenth floor sounded familiar. Could it be? "Is it..."

"I know, I know! Is it the child with the fever mentioned in the task?" Damian answered a second faster.

She couldn't even beat Damian.

Onyx held back a laugh. "It's likely. The child might be in a dazed state, unable to control their Anopower, accidentally creating a domain that trapped their family."

He gently patted Damian's dejected head. "A child's spiritual power isn't strong. When they spread their Anopower over a large area, there will always be weak spots. It's up to you to find it."

"Breaking through the weak point should give us a few seconds of a gap, enough to get inside."

Cora perked up and circled the G Building. She conjured a nearly five-meter-long spear, probing here and there until she found a spot outside the fifth floor where the energy seemed weaker.

Backing up to the flower bed, she aimed at the weak spot, sprinted, and hurled the spear with all her might. The spear flew with incredible speed, striking something in mid-air. Invisible ripples spread, and the energy around the G Building wavered.

"Get in, quick!" Onyx shouted.

The three of them seized the moment and dashed into the building. Two seconds later, the absolute domain snapped back into place, restoring the barrier.

Onyx glanced back. "Domain-type Anopowers are tough to break. We need to find the Anopower user and have them retract it voluntarily."

"But if the child is feverish and uncooperative..." Cora worried.

"I'll handle the communication," Onyx assured.

As Cora and Onyx talked, Damian ran to press the elevator button. Standing on tiptoe, he pressed the up button. "Ding—" The elevator arrived, the doors sliding open to reveal several stiff-limbed zombies.

Damian gasped, sending out a flurry of ice spikes that skewered the zombies. They collapsed before they could even roar.

Damian turned around, wanting to warn the others, but Cora and Onyx were still talking, not paying any attention.

Damian sighed dramatically, bearing the burden alone.

Finally, Cora and Onyx approached, praised him for his work. "Good job, Damian."

Damian nodded smugly, hiding his achievements.

They cleared the zombies out of the elevator and then headed to the fifteenth floor. Sure enough, there were more zombies roaming around.

Cora and Damian worked together to eliminate the threats.

Onyx rang the doorbell of Apartment 1507.

"Hello, we're the Anopowers who accepted your task. Is it your child who needs to go to the hospital?"

No response.

He rang again. "Hello..."

This time, before he could finish, the door swung open. A bespectacled woman with disheveled hair appeared, tears of relief in her eyes.

"The door finally opened! Hurry, my child is very sick. Take her to the hospital!"

Onyx reassured her. "Don't worry. Bring the child out. I'll speak with her. We've already cleared the area outside."

As he calmed the frantic mother, he had Damian contact the Fifth Hospital for an ambulance.

The woman emerged, cradling a tiny figure wrapped in a blanket.

As she passed by, Cora glanced over and instinctively felt something was off.

Before she could figure it out, the blanket moved, and a small head popped out. A floppy-eared corgi looked up at them, its nose wet and eyes half-closed. It gave a weak bark, "Woof."

Wait, could someone explain why Dorothy was a dog? A dog with Anopowers???

CHAPTER 21

Re-United

Cora Thornton was at a loss for words. She and the little bundle that was Dorothy, wrapped in a blanket, stared at each other, both wide-eyed and speechless.

Dorothy's big, wet black eyes gazed at her for a moment before turning away dismissively, blowing a snot bubble in disdain.

Hey! What kind of dog looks down on people like that?

Cora was outraged.

Onyx was also at a rare loss for words.

His original plan had been to communicate with the child named Dorothy and convince her to retract her Anopower. Now, it seemed this task was more challenging than he had expected.

No, it had already surpassed the realm of human capability.

"You mentioned in the task that it was your child who had a fever..." Onyx took a deep breath, choosing his words carefully.

"That's right, Dorothy is my child!" The woman replied confidently. "She has a fever. Please, take her to the hospital."

Shouldn't a dog with a fever be taken to a vet?

But since Dorothy's illness was caused by Anopower awakening, she should be taken to a radiation specialist instead.

Onyx rubbed his temples.

"Your... child has likely awakened to her Anopower. She sensed danger outside, so she unconsciously created a domain, which is why you haven't been able to leave."

"Really?" The woman was surprisingly calm, not at all disturbed by the idea of a dog awakening Anopower.

She lifted Dorothy up with delight, nuzzling her nose. "Dorothy was protecting Mommy? Good girl!"

"Woof! Woof!" Dorothy barked in response.

The three members of F777 watched with blank expressions as the woman and her dog put on a show of motherly affection.

Onyx cleared his throat to interrupt the touching scene. "Now, Dorothy needs to retract her Anopower so you can leave."

"How do we do that?" The woman asked immediately, showing her cooperation. "What do I need to do?"

"Aren't you her mother? Don't you have any special ways of communicating?"

Damian grumbled.

"Dorothy is usually very obedient. Dorothy, can you retract that whatever-it-is?" The woman cooed.

"Woof!"

"Did it work? Can we leave now?" The woman looked at them hopefully.

Cora shook her head. The domain was still there.

"Let me try." Damian volunteered, raising two small claws next to his head and baring his teeth menacingly.

"Doggie, retract your Anopower now!"

Dorothy sneezed, spraying him with a slobber. Her little dog face showed a hint of disdain.

"Your turn," Damian, furious, wiped his face and handed the problem to Onyx. "Aren't you usually good at this?"

Onyx was speechless. He could easily take down this corgi, but reasoning with a dog? That was asking too much.

The four humans and one dog stood in a standoff for a long time, unable to get Dorothy to retract her Anopower.

Suddenly, there was a rustling noise from the staircase.

A zombie crawled up, wavering as it appeared in the hallway.

"Ah, a zombie!" Dorothy's mom paled, clutching Dorothy tightly as she tried to hide.

"Auntie, don't worry, we'll handle it," Damian quickly assured her, thumping his chest.

Cora turned around, flipping her right hand to reveal a tapered, diamond-studded spike with a slightly thicker middle. She slid a ring onto her middle finger, spinning the spike quickly with a flick of her wrist. The zombie noticed the living beings in the hallway and lunged at them.

Cora's ethereal artifact, the spike, struck out. She gripped it, swinging it towards the zombie's head.

One slice, one stab, and the zombie's skull were severed, rolling on the ground like a ball, bouncing twice before stopping.

The headless body stumbled forward a few steps before crashing down.

"Nice job, Cora," Damian clapped enthusiastically.

"Wow, you're amazing," Dorothy's mom exclaimed, following suit.

Dorothy poked her head out from the blanket, her bright eyes fixated on Cora. She barked twice, "Woof, woof."

"What is she saying?" Cora turned to Onyx.

"You don't have to trust me this much; I don't speak dog."

However, his expression changed slightly. "The domain has been retracted."

Dorothy seemed very excited, her short tail wagging rapidly. She stood on her hind legs, her front paws resting on her mom's arm, ears perked up.

She barked at Cora again, "Woof!"

What did that mean? Had Cora earned the approval of a dog with her strength? Something about this felt very odd.

The doctor at the Fifth Hospital looked at Dorothy, wrapped in a blanket on the examination table, with a troubled expression.

"We're not veterinarians."

"This dog has awakened an Anopower," Onyx sighed, having to explain yet again.

From the moment they stepped into the hospital, to the information desk, and now the triage room, he had repeated this countless times and received just as many strange looks.

"What? An Anopower dog?!"

The doctor's tone changed dramatically.

The doctor, who had just claimed not to be a vet, suddenly had eyes shining with interest, as if envisioning a future glowing with professional papers. He pulled out a pair of glasses from his pocket, put them on, and turned to say a few words to someone in the inner room. Shortly, a group of eager interns emerged, all eyes gleaming with curiosity.

"Come on, Dorothy, isn't it? Such a good girl. We'll take good care of you, don't worry."

A group of doctors in white coats crowded around Dorothy, treating her like a precious research specimen, fussing over her as if afraid she might fall ill.

Cora watched their drastic change in attitude, her mouth hanging open.

The doctor coughed lightly, trying to maintain a serious demeanor.

"Dorothy will be admitted for now. I will form a specialized medical team to take care of her. As for the room, we can arrange a single one."

Dorothy's mom happily agreed.

After leaving the examination room, Cora bid farewell to Dorothy and her mom.

The task was successfully completed, but she still couldn't understand.

"Can the dog really awaken Anopowers?"

The whole thing seemed surreal.

Onyx tried to explain in simple terms.

"There are always exceptions. Radiation affects everyone indiscriminately. Theoretically, animals can awaken Anopowers too. However, compared to humans, they have significant disadvantages in terms of tolerance and genetic structure. Cases like Dorothy's are extremely rare."

Who would have thought a D-level task could hide such a surprising twist? A few more tasks like this would surely test their resilience.

With their work for the day done early, the three members of F777 relaxed, leaning against the corridor railings, enjoying the breeze.

The Fifth Hospital differed from the First 119 Hospital, where Cora had worked a few days ago.

The First 119 Hospital was constantly racing against time, with emergency and critical care doctors always on the move.

The radiation specialty on the thirteenth floor was a tropical zone, frequently dealing with patients whose radiation exposure had worsened, posing threats to ordinary people, and requiring constant vigilance and "cleaning" by volunteers.

But the Fifth Hospital seemed much more peaceful. The small park below was lush with greenery, and hospitalized patients chatted and strolled, creating a calm and healing atmosphere.

"This hospital seems to focus more on recuperation," Onyx observed.

Sycamore had many hospitals, perhaps each with its own specialization.

Cora thought the quiet atmosphere was nice, too. She leaned on the railing between the two buildings, feeling the wind on her face as she casually scanned the surroundings.

Then she spotted an extremely familiar figure.

The woman wore large black sunglasses and a long, high-end gray coat. Her long, wavy hair was not tied up this time, but hung smoothly over her shoulders, pressed neatly under a woolen hat.

The woman moved gracefully, her expression light, as she disembarked from a private steam vehicle and walked towards the hospital entrance.

A tall man following her seemed to receive some instructions, nodding before heading to a self-service supermarket outside the hospital.

Yuui Hayashi!

Cora gritted her teeth, recognizing the figure immediately.

She would know that silhouette anywhere!

Without thinking, she prepared to vault over the railing to confront Yuui Hayashi.

"Wait!" Onyx grabbed her jacket, pulling her back before she could jump, nearly causing her to fall headfirst.

She puffed out her cheeks, looking accusingly at him. "She stole my crystal!"

Onyx couldn't help but laugh, lowering his voice.

"I'm not saying you can't confront her, but if you go down there openly and she calls for Suchat, what then?"

"You two might have a great fight, but if a crowd gathers, won't that attract the Sycamore security team? We worked hard to get our access permits; be careful, please."

"But... but..." Cora was nearly in tears. She couldn't just swallow this grievance!

Onyx stopped teasing her, his eyes scanning the area quickly as he came up with a plan.

"Don't worry, I have a way to catch her and ensure you get your revenge."

Yuui Hayashi hummed a tune as she sashayed into the Fifth Hospital. She glided through the spacious lobby, weaving past the crowded throng, and headed to the VIP elevator. Pressing the up button, she waited.

The elevator doors opened, revealing an empty cabin.

Yuui stepped inside gracefully and pressed the button for her floor. As the metal doors slowly closed, she adjusted her hair on the mirrored surface. While she was fixing a stray lock, her fingers paused. Through the gap in her sunglasses, she saw a delicate snowflake gently land on her nose.

Snowflake? In this season, and in such a confined space?

Yuui's instincts screamed in danger!

She frantically pressed all the floor buttons, but it was too late.

The elevator, enveloped in ice, came to a halt, suspended between floors. The walls of the cabin rapidly frosted over with thick layers of ice.

"Crack—"

The metal doors were pried open with brute force. The darkness outside didn't reveal which floor they were on.

Cora crouched in the opening, manually wrenching the doors apart, and grinned menacingly at her.

Yuui whipped off her sunglasses, her eyes wide with shock, lips parting to speak.

Cora didn't give her the chance. With a swift hand chop to the back of her neck, Yuui's body went limp, and she fainted immediately. Cora reached out and caught her, pulling her out of the elevator.

Looking up through the elevator shaft, Cora called out, "Damian, it worked!"

Damian Blackwood's furry head popped into view from the top floor.

His Anopower shifted to ice spikes, tapping and chipping away at the frozen layers covering the elevator.

In no time, the elevator resumed normal operation, as if nothing had happened.

Carrying Yuui like a sack, Cora joined her two "accomplices" in the hallway.

"We kidnapped a celebrity!" she whispered in disbelief.

"We kidnapped a celebrity!" Damian echoed like a parrot.

They jumped around in circles, celebrating.

"Don't get too excited," Onyx warned, dampening their spirits.

"We still need to find a place to hide her. With Rainforest's tracking skills, Suchat will find her in less than ten minutes."

"Where do we hide?" Cora asked nervously.

Onyx brushed off nonexistent dust from a blanket and smiled.

"I know a place that should work."

When Yuui woke up, she found herself in a spacious, empty hospital room, her hands and feet tightly bound.

Her neck throbbed with dull pain, and her head felt dizzy and swollen. At first, her vision was blurry, but it gradually cleared, revealing two familiar figures. She looked up sharply to see a girl and a boy sitting on chairs, glaring at her fiercely.

"Cora? Damian?"

"Humph." The two, called by name, snorted in unison.

"Why have you kidnapped me? Let me go!" Yuui shouted angrily.

"Not letting you go! We'll make you angry, ha!" Damian taunted gleefully.

"No way," Cora added fuel to the fire.

"Suchat? Suchat!" Yuui ignored the two and used her mental energy to call out to Suchat.

However, it felt like an invisible barrier trapped her mental energy within the room, unable to escape.

Cora noticed her frown and guessed what she was trying to do, snorting coldly. "It's useless."

Yuui was taken aback. "What do you mean?"

"No matter how much you scream…"

"No one will come to save you," Damian finished her sentence energetically.

"Exactly!" Cora nodded fiercely.

From the corner, a dog barked, "Woof!" as if agreeing with them.

"What kind of ridiculous kidnappers are these?!"

Cora specifically chose this room, a highly secure double VIP hospital room! She not only took on the medical expenses for Dorothy, but also spent a lot of her savings to buy a bunch of gourmet dog treats. This successfully winning Dorothy's favor and getting her to help release a bit of her domain.

Dorothy's mom, after bringing her child to the hospital, found nothing serious and was soon bored at home.

Luckily, Cora offered to take care of Dorothy today, so Dorothy's mom happily went out for afternoon tea with her friends.

Now, this hospital room had become a natural prison, shielded by Dorothy's domain, making it impossible even for Suchat to find them.

Yuui Hayashi's temples throbbed as the two humans and a dog kept chattering, annoying her immensely.

However, she guessed the room had been tampered with, isolating her mental strength, and she decided not to make any futile attempts.

Yuui refused to communicate with these strange creatures and turned to the only normal person in the room.

"What exactly do you want?" Yuui asked.

"Nothing much, just a good chat with Miss Hayashi." Onyx leaned by the window, his smile as cold as the winter wind, devoid of any warmth.

Yuui paused, piecing together the events in her mind, then seriously turned to Cora, "About the Mirror Lake incident, Cora, I apologize. I'm sorry. If you want the crystal, I can return it to you. What compensation do you want? If it's within my power, I will do my best to fulfill it."

"Miss Hayashi, not all mistakes can be compensated for after the fact," Onyx interrupted. "Even if the wound heals, the scar remains difficult to erase."

Cora nodded in agreement, though she wanted to argue that her scars could heal, but now wasn't the time to contradict Onyx. She held back.

"You're right. I apologize for what I did... but I don't regret it." Yuui's eyes were firm. "Because I had a reason to win at all costs."

"Cora, you won't trust me again, will you?" Yuui sighed bitterly. "I didn't intend to deceive you with our cooperation. If that hadn't been the last crystal, we could have celebrated our victory together."

Cora remained silent.

There were no "ifs." Yuui had betrayed her trust, and she couldn't get over it.

"Betrayal is never worth forgiving," Onyx calmly commented. "If Miss Hayashi truly feels remorse, she should show it through actions."

"What do you want? Money? How much?" Yuui asked.

Onyx slowly shook his head. "What people do you take us for? Extortionists?"

Yuui replied, "From your actions, is there a difference?"

Still defiant, Onyx wheeled himself over to the famous star.

"Yuui Hayashi, you left Felalakas, came alone to Sycamore, and are mainly staying at the fifth hospital, which is responsible for recuperation. Why? Do you have someone important here? A relative or a friend? Are they hoping to awaken, or have they already turned into a zombie?"

"I guess it's the former, but their condition isn't good, which is why you were desperate to snatch the crystal, right?"

Yuui's eyes narrowed sharply.

"If we captured you, finding out who your relatives or friends are and their names wouldn't be hard."

"Coincidentally, I've been working in the archive room for the past few days. Compiling all the patient data admitted after the apocalypse. There aren't many from Felalakas..."

"Enough." Yuui spoke expressionlessly. "I admit it. Let's negotiate terms."

Onyx gestured for Cora to come over and quietly asked, "How do you want to vent your anger?"

Cora curiously replied, "Do you really know her relative or friend's name?"

"I bluffed." Onyx winked at her. "There are so many patient files, I couldn't possibly go through them all."

Cora secretly gave him a thumbs up, out of sight of the others.

As expected of him, truly cunning.

"How about making her complete ten tasks for us?" Onyx suggested. "Free labor shouldn't go to waste."

Cora's eyes lit up.

Onyx was truly... no, no, she corrected herself. Onyx had so many great ideas!

The two of them returned to Yuui Hayashi, with Onyx playing it cautious.

"Miss Hayashi, you won't back out this time, right?"

Yuui, emotionally and physically exhausted, felt another sting from his words.

"I keep my promises. If you don't believe me, you can report to my fans that I took part in the T.T.T., and let my reputation be ruined. Will that satisfy you?"

T.T.T. was of utmost importance to Yuui, and her willingness to use it as a guarantee showed she was genuinely conceding.

"Remove the barrier. If Suchat can't find me, he'll tear this entire hospital apart."

Cora and Damian started begging and coaxing Dorothy again.

Cora twirled her daggers like she was performing acrobatics, while Damian barked "woof, woof" repeatedly, trying to find the right frequency to communicate with the dog.

Eventually, Dorothy grew annoyed and hid in her doghouse, presenting her round backside to them, ignoring their antics.

Yuui felt like facepalming: How did she end up getting kidnapped by these people?

But glancing at Onyx, who watched the absurd scene without changing his expression, she realized that this man was the most dangerous one here with his calculating mind.

After a long while, Dorothy finally forgave the two troublesome humans and reluctantly removed her domain.

Cora stood ready.

Within five minutes, a figure darted into the room like a venomous snake rushing straight at them.

Cora raised her daggers to block, and a green dagger flew

backward, embedding in the ground and corroding a large area instantly.

Dorothy's tail wagged furiously, and she barked, "Woof, woof, woof!"

"Suchat, stop," Yuui's tired voice commanded, halting him.

Suchat slowly advanced, the atmosphere turning stormy with his killing intent.

His boots made no sound on the floor, and the oppressive, humid tension of the rainforest filled the room. He was like a human weapon unsheathed, muscles tense, ready to strike.

If Dorothy was the cute pup, then Suchat was the enraged hound who found its master missing, ready to tear apart any threat.

Everyone in the room watched him intently. The destruction of a powerful Aberrant could unleash when out of control was terrifying.

Thankfully, Suchat hadn't lost his mind completely. He cast a sharp glance around the room, then kneeled before Yuui and untied her tightly bound ropes.

Yuui flexed her reddened wrists.

"Tell me, what do you need me to do?"

Cora laid out the ten tasks.

Yuui frowned, but eventually nodded. "Alright, but let's get it done before my next match. I won't be staying in Sycamore long."

"Given our temporary employment relationship, sharing your intel is a basic requirement, right?"

Onyx said coolly.

Yuui nodded silently, conceding.

"Yuui Hayashi, A-level support type, whose Anopower is song-based illusions. Depending on the lyrics, she can cast curses or blessings. Suchat, A-level assault type, whose Anopower is corrosive venom, but he's better at assassination. In one-on-one combat, no one was his match until he met Cora."

Onyx's speculation was spot on—they indeed had sound and venom Anopowers.

A dual A-level team. With these two working for them, Cora's heart raced with excitement. They could take on tougher missions and earn big money!

CHAPTER 22

The Healer

Sycamore, Pharmaceutical Transport Route.

A tall figure, nearly six feet three inches, navigated through the path.

Suchat, dressed in a black tank top, camouflage pants, and combat boots, occasionally bent down to clear debris from the road. Sometimes, he encountered zombies that leaped out, and he dispatched them with an emotionless expression.

The task he was doing was one of the most tedious C-level assignments: inspecting the checkpoints of the vital supply line, clearing blocked roads, and getting confirmation from guard posts after each section to ensure the smooth delivery of pharmaceuticals into Sycamore.

Although it was a C-level task and paid well, it was dirty, exhausting, and time-consuming, so few people wanted to do it. The F777 team came, and not only did they come, but they were quite pleased with themselves—they had two free laborers, after all!

Cora Thornton and Damian Blackwood were acting high and mighty. Despite the cold weather, they set up a sunshade and squatted side by side on the curb, sipping juice and supervising Suchat's work.

They occasionally reacted.

When Suchat kicked a zombie away, they both clapped in unison.

When Suchat flexed his muscles and lifted a steel bar to toss it aside, they compared their wrists, but unfortunately, they both had skinny arms. They looked so ridiculous.

Yuui Hayashi felt increasingly lost amidst Cora and Damian's cheers and exclamations for Suchat.

She asked herself again: How did I end up being kidnapped by people like this?

Sweating profusely, Suchat stopped in front of her.

The former big star was now bare-faced, with dirt smudged on her face and body from helping clear the roadblocks.

"Stop working," Suchat said, taking the rock from her hand and signaling her to rest.

"A bet is a bet," Yuui gritted her teeth.

"It's fine if you don't," Suchat's eyes turned cold, "I'll kill them."

The rainforest had left a deep mark on his character, including his indifferent and ruthless way of thinking.

To Suchat, Yuui shouldn't have been restrained by Cora and Damian.

Problems that could be solved with a knife weren't problems at all.

"No need," Yuui quickly stopped him, afraid he'd actually do it.

"I owe them. Onyx was right—betrayal isn't something that can be forgiven."

Suchat looked down at Yuui.

Her long eyelashes drooped, and her expression was both forlorn and accepting as she said this.

Suchat was silent for a long time and finally said, "Soft-hearted."

Wasn't Yuui also soft-hearted?

In the end, she had deceived Cora but had never intended to harm her.

In an environment like Mirror Lake, one had to look out for themselves to survive.

For one mistake, she will accept punishment.

"Get back to work, and stop talking so much," Yuui scolded.

Suchat snorted lightly, peeled off his tank top with one hand, and continued working shirtless.

The black snake tattoo on the back of his neck looked even more menacing in the sunlight, and his back was covered with old scars, a shocking sight.

Under the sunshade, the two others were talking.

"Big sister, are we coming back this afternoon?" Damian asked Cora, with his face grimacing.

He was exhausted and his stomach was bloated from drinking three bottles of juice that morning. He hadn't expected supervising to be so tiring.

Cora bit her straw and shook her head. "No, I have plans."

She had an appointment with Lynn Rolling at Hospital 119 that afternoon. Leaving Damian to watch over the other two alone wouldn't be safe.

Anyway, today's fun quota was already exceeded, so Cora gave her two laborers the afternoon off.

Hospital 119, Cora circled around to the back window of the archive room and knocked lightly on the wall.

After a moment, long fingers cracked open a slit, revealing the handsome profile of Onyx in a gray uniform.

She did not know why he was so invested in the work of an archivist, coming early and leaving late every day, buried in data.

Cora folded her hands behind her back. "Yesterday, as promised."

Onyx sighed, "I also said that ordinary doctors can't heal my leg."

Cora insisted, "The doctors in Sycamore are amazing."

Onyx locked eyes with her stubborn gaze for a long time before finally conceding. "Alright, your call."

Cora pushed him to the thirteenth floor and found Lynn Rolling's office, knocking properly on the door.

"Come in," a cool voice responded from inside.

During her free time, Cora had been working as a zombie cleaner.

Lynn Rolling, understanding how hard it was for someone so young to support a family, had gradually become familiar with her.

Learning that Cora had a companion with a leg injury confined to a wheelchair, Lynn had suggested Cora bring him in for an examination.

When the blanket covering Onyx's leg was lifted.

Lynn paused.

It was more than just an "injury"—the leg was deformed and twisted, looking as if it had been crushed by a truck.

Cora usually had to take care of a disabled brother. She had mentioned a younger brother at home, too. This young girl had it too tough!

Lynn's misplaced compassion for Cora deepened.

"I scheduled a holographic scan for you. Take your brother to get the x-rays done first."

Cora wasn't happy with the term "brother."

"He's not my brother!"

Not her brother? Lynn had thought only family would be so devoted.

Lynn's gaze moved between the two, and she suddenly thought she understood.

"Sorry, you're quite dedicated. Well, take your... friend for the x-rays."

Cora felt confused, sensing some hidden meaning in Lynn's pause.

Outside, Cora asked Onyx, "What is Dr. Rolling thinking?"

Onyx smiled slightly. "She's touched by you."

Cora replied, "Huh?"

After the holographic scan, they returned to the office, where Lynn studied the results seriously.

"Your leg has been broken for too long and was once crudely repaired, causing significant bone misalignment. With current medical technology, even if I perform the surgery. I can't restore it to its original state."

Cora's shoulders slumped in disappointment.

Lynn put down the scans, pondering.

"I'll consult my colleagues to see if they have any solutions."

She made several calls to Sycamore's elite orthopedic surgeons.

During this time, Onyx took back the scans and coldly reviewed them.

After ending her calls, Lynn hesitated.

"The best we can do is insert rhenium plates to stabilize the leg, but reshaping the leg will be difficult. Even if you don't use a wheelchair in the future, you might still need a cane."

"Or would you consider replacing it with a mechanical prosthetic?"

"No," Onyx rejected coldly.

Cora's mood sank further.

Even Lynn had no solution?

"If only Dr. Franz were here..." In the silent room, Lynn sighed.

It was the second time Cora had heard Lynn mention "Dr. Franz."

Who was this person? Every time Lynn felt helpless, she mentioned him as if he could solve anything.

Cora voiced her curiosity.

Lynn sighed again. "Dr. Franz is Charles Franz, Sycamore's former genius surgeon, a legend in the medical field."

"Dr. Franz loved challenging high-difficulty surgeries and wouldn't take ordinary cases. Many people said he was arrogant, but who cares? Everyone admired his exceptional skills. Any surgery he took on had a zero percent failure rate."

"A doctor who never failed at high-difficulty surgeries—doesn't that count as a legend?"

"Where is he now?" Cora pursued, thinking if they could find him, there might be hope for Onyx's leg.

Lynn's eyes dimmed. "He's missing..."

"The last time I saw him, he wasn't in a good state. After the apocalypse began, I heard he refused an important surgery and then disappeared from the hospital. People called him a deserter, abandoning his duty, but I don't believe it. He must have had his reasons."

Leaving Lynn's office, Cora's head hung low, her spirits down.

Onyx comforted her, "This was expected. At least Dr. Rolling is reliable and didn't push mechanical parts on us, right?"

Cora didn't smile. She looked into Onyx's eyes. "You said there are healing Anopower users who can fix this, right?"

Onyx was silent for a moment. "Perhaps."

For his leg to be restored, the healer would need to be an A-level Anopower user with a solid medical background familiar with human skeletal structure. Such a person, if they existed, would be highly sought after and difficult to meet.

Cora rested her head on the back of his chair, feeling despondent. Where could she find a healer?

Looking down, she noticed many people in security uniforms outside, driving away suspicious vagrants. Under the bridge, in the park, large groups of homeless people were being forced to leave.

"What are they doing?" Cora asked.

Onyx glanced and quickly recalled the recent news. "Sycamore's population is too high. The city hall is strictly screening people. Those without entry permits are being sent to nearby shelters."

Cora stretched her neck. The vagrants, dirty and disheveled, moved away with slumped shoulders, looking lost.

That night, deep in the quiet, Cora's terminal suddenly flashed a glaring red light, illuminating the entire room.

She sat up, instantly awake.

An A-level emergency request appeared on the terminal.

"Hello Aberrants, the following information is from the Sycamore City Hall. A large wave of zombies has been detected near the Sakura Shelter. The crisis is imminent. Please assist us in defending Sycamore."

Sakura was the nearest shelter to Sycamore. If it was overrun by zombies, Sycamore would be left wide open, its destruction only a matter of time.

Cora grabbed her jacket and rushed to the door opposite hers.

"Bang, bang, bang!" She pounded on Onyx de Montclair's door.

Hearing faint noises inside, she couldn't wait and barged in.

"Onyx..."

Before she could finish saying, "There's an emergency request," her eyes widened.

Onyx was leaning against the desk, clothes disheveled.

His silk pajamas were haphazardly fastened with only two buttons, revealing his prominent collarbones and a hint of his abs.

Though in a rush, he had at least put on pants, but his hand was still on the drawstring, and he was barely balancing himself with his other hand on the desk.

Cora's mouth fell open.

Onyx's bangs fell over his forehead, and he sighed.

"You just barged in like this?"

Huh?

Cora blinked, glancing at him again. She was in a hurry.

How was she supposed to know he wasn't properly dressed? Or

rather, wasn't dressed at all!

Not only did she barged in unceremoniously, but she also didn't feel embarrassed at all.

Her eyes brazenly taking him in.

Onyx raised an eyebrow.

They used to share a room, and she would fall asleep without a care. Now that they had separate rooms, she still acted as if she could come and go as she pleased, look whenever she wanted.

Did she not see him as a man at all?

"Do you want to watch me dressing up?" he asked.

"No, no," Cora replied.

Her face showing disdain as she turned and walked out.

"Close the door," Onyx's calm voice sounded behind her.

Cora paused and shut the door.

Five minutes later, a sleepy Damian was also dragged up.

The F777 team, now fully dressed, sat down for an impromptu meeting.

"I need to go to Sakura," Cora stated her intention.

This time, it wasn't for money or points, but for Sycamore.

If Sycamore fell, its medical resources would be destroyed. Not to mention that Cora and her team would lose their temporary shelter.

For the entire Alliance, it would be a monumental disaster, extinguishing the faint hope of survival.

Onyx also realized the seriousness of the situation and nodded in agreement.

"Alright, let's go together. But be careful, dealing with a zombie wave isn't easy."

The three quickly packed up and were about to head out.

"Wait," Cora suddenly stopped. "We forgot two others."

Yuui Hayashi was jolted awake from her sleep by a series of incessant calls.

Who was it? She groggily rubbed her hair and answered with her eyes closed.

"Who the hell is disturbing me in the middle of the night...?"

"Hurry, mission. I'm sending you the location."

The voice on the other end cut her off and hung up immediately, giving her no chance to refuse.

What a joke, a mission in the middle of the night?

Yuui grumbled and tossed her terminal aside, going back to sleep.

But soon, the continuous beeping resumed, waking her up again. Unable to bear it, Yuui grabbed her terminal, squinting at the bright screen to make out the messages.

The other party, afraid she'd fall asleep again, kept sending the location every few seconds, urging her.

"Hurry, or I'll report you."

"Are you coming?"

"Hurry, seven missions left."

Yuui groaned, "Cora... you little brats, I really owe you!"

Sakura Shelter.

A massive circular iron wall, dozens of feet high, separated the safe zone from the zombie wave. Inside the high wall, a tense atmosphere pervaded. While outside on the wasteland, an endless army of zombies was gathering.

Cora, hurrying along, kept sending messages to her laborers.

"Location, come quickly."

A few minutes later, Yuui, wearing a mask with dark circles under her eyes, appeared with a displeased expression, followed by the expressionless Suchat in black.

"You better have a good reason," Yuui said through gritted teeth, still barefaced.

Cora's urgency had left her no time to wash up.

"Of course, there is."

Cora pointed to the wall's base, where zombies had already piled up enough to reach the middle-upper part of the wall.

They needed to act fast.

Yuui, after surveying the scene, was first shocked, then frustrated.

Cora clearly didn't see her as an outsider. Every time there was dirty or exhausting work, Cora would remember her and Suchat.

Cora showed her Anopower certificate at the outer ring, and they smoothly entered the perimeter.

At this hour, there were only a few other Aberrants arriving for support, and most of those present were the security forces.

"Why did the zombie wave break out suddenly?" an external Aberrant asked.

"It wasn't sudden," sighed the captain of the security force, dressed in uniform.

"The surrounding D-level cities have been falling. And the number of zombies has been increasing, gradually gathering here. An outbreak was inevitable."

"So, what do we do now? We can't just send us to our deaths, right?"

"Don't worry." the captain's expression was both solemn and resolute.

"The security force comprises 230 Aberrants. We'll fight to the end!"

The security force was composed of official Aberrants from Sycamore, mostly residents, young and passionate.

After awakening their powers, they registered locally, passed reviews, and joined the security force, enjoying the benefits of Sycamore City Hall.

Their homes were here, and their sense of honor and mission was much higher than that of the external Aberrants.

Onyx, having spent time in the archive room, was well-acquainted with Sycamore's personnel and the structure of the Aberrants. He scanned the determined faces of the security force members and spoke up.

"Captain Kennedy, the situation isn't as bad as you think."

"You are...?" Captain Conrad Kennedy turned towards the voice.

"Me? I'm just an ordinary citizen working in the archive room at Hospital 119."

Here he goes again, making up identities.

Cora thought, looking up at the sky.

Onyx continued with a calm expression, "This is our captain, Cora Thornton, an A-level Aberrants and a distinguished medical volunteer of Sycamore."

What? Now it's her turn?

Cora was stunned but stood up straight upon being mentioned.

As for the distinguished volunteer, that probably meant she was good at zombie cleaning.

Conrad had no time to verify Cora's "distinguished" status but was impressed by her A-level rank and gave her a second look.

"What do you mean, the situation isn't that bad?"

"As long as we use the terrain wisely and coordinate the Aberrants properly, we can clear out these zombies," Onyx said directly, outlining his plan.

Conrad's face showed signs of hope. "Are you confident? This is no joke."

Onyx nodded calmly. "Yes, but on the condition that I command."

Conrad fell silent, contemplating. He had no better plan, and this person's words seemed worth trying, but he was unsure of his motives...

Noticing Conrad's hesitation, Onyx added, "Of course, if we succeed, regarding the mission rewards..."

Conrad's heart relaxed. He had over thought it.

These external Aberrants were clearly here for the credits. "No problem, I will report everything accurately to the officials."

The battle horn sounded.

Onyx organized the Aberrants into different groups: fire and wind, lightning and water, earth and sand. He assigned each group to different positions, with everyone performing their tasks in strict order.

Bright flames soared, spreading with the wind and consuming the snarling zombies like a wildfire.

Elsewhere, a torrential storm, mixed with lightning, poured down. The rain, infused with the combined powers, electrocuted the zombies, making them convulse. Other combat-type Aberrants charged out from behind the high walls, bravely confronting the zombies' head-on.

At that moment, they were more than just security guards or awakened Aberrants. They weren't fighting for fame or profit. This generation had grown up under Sycamore's protection, and it was time for them to stand as the strongest shield and defend their home.

Although the power of a single Aberrant was limited, the combined strength of everyone was earth-shattering.

Conrad Kennedy watched the awe-inspiring scene with tears in his eyes. Sycamore would not fall; there was still hope!

Amid the flurry of Anopower lights, one area stood out with a completely different vibe.

Damian Blackwood, like a human freezer, became the epicenter of a raging blizzard.

Snowflakes enveloped the zombies, freezing them into statues.

"Your coldness~ cuts deep, like December's~ snowstorm, my heart~ has long been split in two."

A mournful, beautiful song resonated, and the zombies frozen by Damian were suddenly cursed by Yuui Hayashi's song, shattering into pieces just as her lyrics described.

The haunting song continued, shifting to a new tune.

"I want to borrow~ your invisible wings, to take you flying~ flying to the world's brightest light."

Two lethal figures leaped from the top of the wall.

"Crack—" As they landed, they split the ice zombie wall in half, sending shards flying.

The two black dots dove into the dense sea of zombies, causing ripples like explosions.

With Yuui's speed buff, Cora and Suchat went on a killing spree.

Suchat's body emitted venom, causing even zombies, which couldn't feel pain, to disintegrate into heaps of bones?

Faced with his biochemical assault, even the old insect waves would flee in panic.

Cora, wielding a chainsaw, swung a blade longer than her body. Each sweeping strike felled swathes of zombies, sending countless heads flying.

The four worked in perfect harmony. Whether in long-range or close combat, each of them was a powerhouse. Together, they were unstoppable!

The Aberrants on the high walls stared in shock—what monsters were these people?

"Stop gawking. The southeast needs to speed up, and the west should keep setting traps." Onyx calmly issued orders from his vantage point.

F777. The onlookers silently memorized the name of this team.

Clearing the zombie wave took over an hour. When only a few zombies remained, scattering in all directions, Onyx finally ordered the Aberrants to stop.

Security guards rushed over to report. During the chaos, a section of the wall had been breached, allowing several zombies to enter. Though they were quickly dealt with, there were casualties among the shelter's inhabitants, many of whom had been bitten.

"Captain, how should we handle these people?"

Conrad Kennedy sighed.

"Check each one. If it's a mild case, send them to Sycamore. For those with secondary infection or worse, deal with them on the spot."

The infection levels were part of Sycamore's classification system.

Level one, or mild infection, also called "pre-spread infection," could be managed if caught early, with medical intervention to amputate the infected part and effectively halt the zombification process.

Level two involved blackened, pus-filled wounds, excessive radiation entering the body, causing gray eyes, and a confused mind. These patients couldn't be saved even with treatment, only delaying full zombification until the inevitable.

As Cora returned from outside the wall, she saw the security guards checking and clearing the area.

A middle-aged man, his eyes cloudy and fingers turned to claws, was pinned to the ground, struggling desperately.

"Let me go. I need to go to the hospital. I can still be saved!"

"There's no saving you. You're already at level three infection."

"Impossible!"

The man convulsed, saliva foaming from his mouth, making a guttural sound.

"Confirmed level three, near full zombification."

A guard pulled out a particle gun.

"Bang—" It ended his life.

Cries of grief arose.

The others bitten by zombies huddled together, terrified.

These people had been driven from Sycamore that afternoon, seeking safety in Sakura, only to face a zombie wave by nightfall. If they died quickly, it would be a relief. But being bitten meant waiting in a half-dead state for the outcome.

Cora surveyed the area and spotted someone lying near the door.

As the middle-aged man's body was dragged away, the person seemed to sense it and slowly turned over, lying face up.

Cora noticed a familiar logo on his pocket and took a step forward.

"Don't go," Yuui grabbed her, her expression grave. "That person was bitten."

The bearded vagrant stared blankly at the ceiling, his open collar revealing several black bite marks.

CHAPTER 23

The Vagrant

In the heavy, oppressive atmosphere, the vagrant's behavior seemed especially strange.

He showed no interest in the surrounding conversations, as if he couldn't hear anything.

His eyes were empty, lying lifeless on the ground, yet his chest still rose and fell, showing he was breathing.

"It's okay."

Cora, blocked momentarily by Yuui Hayashi, responded softly and continued forward.

She crouched in front of the vagrant, and with a swift motion, pulled a half-eaten loaf of bread from his pocket.

The bread, though mostly gone and several days old, was dry and hard on the outside but still bore the "Medical Aid" logo, showing it was only given to Sycamore volunteers.

A few days ago, in the small park outside Hospital 119, Cora had given a loaf of bread to a vagrant.

Was this the same person?

But the individual was so disheveled that Cora couldn't clearly see his face and couldn't be certain.

She put the bread back in his pocket, then quickly tore open his collar with her fingers and frowned.

The vagrant had several wounds on his body, with the outer edges turning white and scabbed over with black bruises.

Beneath the scabs, fresh red flesh could be seen—it looked like old injuries, not new ones.

The vagrant didn't resist her actions, showing no sign of resistance. Through his messy hair, he glanced at her with emotionless eyes. Blueish corpse-like lines appeared on both sides of his face, but he was still conscious.

Cora paused, a strange sense of familiarity enveloping her. This person felt oddly familiar, as if she had seen him somewhere before.

The security guards finished checking the others and turned to the vagrant, noticing Cora crouched on the ground.

They hesitated, "Uh..."

They had just witnessed Cora slaughtering zombies like a star in a horror film, and they were intimidated by her.

Cora stepped back, giving them space.

A young guard scanned the vagrant with a radiation meter, looking puzzled.

"Level one... mild?"

The readings were lower than typical mild cases, almost normal.

Onyx, having finished the cleanup on the high wall, arrived late and found Cora.

"What happened?" he asked, noticing everyone gathered together.

Cora returned to his side.

With so many people around, it wasn't convenient to talk.

She leaned on the back of his wheelchair, speaking close to his ear in a low voice, "That person is strange."

Onyx turned slightly to listen, with his eyes narrowing as he scrutinized the vagrant.

The guards were still puzzled.

"What do we do with him? His wounds haven't worsened... Hey, do you need to go to the hospital?"

Someone else spoke up.

"Are you sure he was bitten by a zombie? Maybe his wounds are just infected? His readings seem normal."

"He wasn't bitten!" a woman in the corner cried out, trembling.

The remaining people in the room, who had been fortunate enough not to be attacked by zombies, were still terrified and huddled together.

The woman's sudden outburst drew everyone's attention.

"I'm not lying. This man... this man is a monster. The zombies didn't bite him!"

"Get him out of here, get him out!!"

The guards were shocked and uncertain.

Could it be true? The vagrant lay blatantly at the entrance; how could the zombies not bite him?

"It's true, I saw it too," an elderly man with white hair murmured.

"The zombies didn't bite him. They all passed by him, passed by him..."

He would never forget the scene he had just witnessed.

The hideous zombies had rushed in, biting everyone frantically.

They all ran in terror, except for the vagrant lying on the ground, whom the zombies ignored and simply stepped over.

After repeatedly confirming the witnesses' statements, the guards didn't dare take any chances.

They grabbed the vagrant by the collar and hauled him up. "Hey, stop playing dead. Get up and explain yourself."

The vagrant was roughly handled, his head lolling about.

He whispered in a barely audible voice.

"Just kill me."

"What did you say?"

"I said kill me," he laughed hoarsely, pointing a finger at his forehead. "Like just now, bang, shoot me."

His voice was despondent, cold, devoid of any will to live, only wanting to end it quickly.

Cora straightened up and mumbled, "Ah."

"I remember now."

She knew where the strange feeling of familiarity came from—Fool's Wharf, Mrs. Travers.

The state of this vagrant was both like and unlike Mrs. Travers from that time.

They both had been bitten by zombies and showed signs of mutation, yet, even after some time, they hadn't turned into zombies and remained conscious.

But the differences were also clear.

Mrs. Travers had nearly fully transformed into a zombie, looking like one on the outside, while this person showed very few mutation traits, almost none.

Could someone be bitten by a zombie and not turn into one? If so, had everyone been wrong all this time?

Cora couldn't wrap her head around it and turned to Onyx with her doubts.

Onyx scrutinized the vagrant from head to toe, a barely noticeable smile forming at the corner of his mouth.

"Remember, I mentioned that most people bitten by zombies turn because the 'contaminated' radiation causes their internal magnetic field to go haywire?"

"Yes," Cora nodded, following his thought process to another possibility.

"But of a passive awakening..."

She stopped mid-sentence.

There was a very low probability that someone bitten by a zombie might awaken as an Aberrant.

Could it be? This vagrant was an Aberrant??

What kind of Aberrants doesn't fight zombies, doesn't take missions, doesn't even want to live, and just wants to die quickly?

"There's more," Onyx said calmly. "You're assuming he was a normal person when he was bitten, right?"

Cora nodded.

Onyx dropped a bombshell.

"What if he had already awakened before being bitten?"

Cora was speechless.

Onyx smiled.

"Of course, this is just a theory. It'll take time to confirm."

Their conversation was in low voices.

Only Damian, Yuui, and Suchat heard the discussion. Even they were visibly surprised.

"Cora, keep him here and let me observe him for a few days."

"How? Keep him?"

Onyx pondered for a moment, then wheeled forward to the security guards.

"Gentlemen, I have a suggestion."

The guards looked at him with respect. "Mr. de Montclair, what do you suggest?"

"Not a suggestion." Onyx pointed to the vagrant.

"There should be some empty rooms around, right? If you can't decide, how about locking him up separately for now? If he turns into a zombie later, you can deal with him then."

"That makes sense," the young guard scratched his head.

"Alright, we'll lock him up and check with the captain."

The group found an empty storage room, tossed the vagrant inside, set up an entry lock.

Before closing the door, the guard looked at Cora and the others. "Anything else?"

Onyx said, "We need to talk to him for a moment. You can go ahead."

The guard glanced inside. "Alright, remember to lock the door when you leave."

Only Cora, Onyx, Damian, Yuui, and Suchat were left with the vagrant lying on the ground.

Onyx wheeled around him, but the man lay like a dead fish, completely unresponsive.

Onyx smirked, changing his mind about talking to him. "Let's go," he said.

They would let him sit there for a few days.

Cora didn't move.

She couldn't quite explain it, but if this vagrant was the same person she met in the park a few days ago, his state had transformed.

Back then, he was down and out, but at least he fought pigeons for food, showing some will to live. Now, he just wanted to die.

Cora walked into the room and crouched in front of the vagrant again. "What happened to you?"

The half-dead vagrant finally reacted, turning his tangled head towards her and snapping, "Are you people bored or something?"

Cora's good intentions were met with insults. She pouted in displeasure, while the dimples on her cheeks deepening.

The vagrant's gaze lingered on her face for a second before turning away indifferently and closing his eyes again.

He lay back on the ground, completely still.

Two days later, at Hospital 119, the three laborers of F777 were once again sitting in a row, basking in the sun. Taking a break together during lunchtime had become their routine.

Today, Cora didn't bother with her employee Yuui.

After all, she had just made the star perform a B-level task at the crematorium yesterday, and Yuui had looked ready to stab her with her eyes.

Damian was sitting on the railing, swinging his legs, when he suddenly pointed at a spot. "Big sis, look over there!"

His face lit up with excitement as he clung to the railing, half his body leaning out. "Isn't that Mr. Anderson?"

Cora quickly grabbed the back of his shirt to prevent him from falling.

Below, about thirty feet away, a tall man walking alone turned towards them. Recognizing them, he waved.

It was indeed Vincent Anderson.

Cora tilted her head in confusion.

What was so special about Sycamore? Why were all the people she knew flocking here?

Running into an acquaintance meant they had to say hello. The three of them descended from the corridor and approached Vincent.

Upon meeting, Cora noticed he had lost his usual confident smile, his eyes sunken, and he looked somewhat haggard.

Vincent immediately stubbed out his cigarette when he saw them. "It's you guys. What a coincidence."

Damian, perceptive as always, noticed his poor state and his cheerful expression faded. He cautiously asked, "Uncle Anderson, why are you alone? Where's Captain Wolf and the others?"

Vincent lowered his gaze, rolling the cigarette butt between his fingers, reluctant to throw it away. "The captain is still on a mission."

"Why aren't you with him?" Damian asked.

"Strong is hospitalized. I'm here to watch over him for a couple of days."

Strong referred to William Strong, a D-level wind Aberrant from the Azure team. Cora remembered him as a cheerful young man who had traveled with them to Felalakas in a pickup truck.

Cora was surprised.

When they last parted, William was fine.

How had he ended up in the hospital? Was he injured? Was it serious?

"Should we go and see him?" she whispered.

Given their acquaintance with the Azure team, it was only proper to visit.

"No need." Vincent moved slightly to block their way, his voice choked. "He's lost half his body. There's no point in seeing him."

Cora and Damian fell silent, unsure of how to offer comfort.

They found a bench to sit on.

The November wind was chilly, and the sun felt weak.

Vincent's gloomy demeanor made their mood sink like the depths of fall.

Cora had imagined that the Azure team's missions would be dangerous, but she hadn't expected such devastating results.

Captain Wolf's team had forty members when fully staffed. How many were left now?

"What kind of mission were you doing?" she asked, not expecting much of an answer.

Vincent spread his arms along the back of the bench and sighed deeply, eyes closed.

"An impossible mission."

With an unlit cigarette in his mouth, Vincent looked exhausted, mumbling as if he had been holding it in for a long time. "I've had enough."

"A soldier's duty is to obey orders, I get that. But lately, I can't help but wonder if I'm being too constrained."

"Watching my teammates diminish while the mission shows no hope, with no way forward or back. We're just drifting aimlessly."

"Ugh!" Vincent suddenly spat out the cigarette butt and punched the bench, causing it to rock.

"I've had it! From before the apocalypse until now, half a year, and we've got nothing!"

"What... what do you mean?" Cora asked.

Shoulders hunched as she hurriedly steadied the bench.

Vincent exhaled deeply, releasing his frustration.

"It's not a classified mission. I can tell you."

"We're looking for a key, or rather, a person."

"A person who vanished from the Alliance nearly twelve years ago."

Cora gasped in surprise.

Onyx's fingers paused on the wheelchair's armrest, his eyelids lifting slightly.

Damian, the youngest and most impatient, couldn't help but ask, "How is that possible? My dad says your intelligence network is incredible. Finding someone should be easy!"

"Yeah, just finding someone. How hard can it be?" Vincent laughed bitterly.

"But we found nothing. All citizen documents, images, records, video footage, entry logs, social media, even the farthest corners of the star network—nothing. It's like he vanished from the world."

"Nobody knows how he did it. Sometimes I wonder if he's long dead. Only a dead person leaves no trace."

"Is there no clue at all?" Cora couldn't help but ask.

"There is." Vincent opened his eyes. "The only clue is a blurry image of him at fifteen and a name."

"Who is he?"

"His name is Petros Sheen."

Vincent projected the image from his terminal. "This is the only image of him before he disappeared."

The three curiously looked at the projection.

The boy in the image had black hair and dark eyes, his features sharp and rebellious, with strikingly handsome and bold features. The angle of the shot only revealed half of his face, but his indifferent gaze towards the camera and the tear-shaped mole at the corner of his eye shone vividly.

CHAPTER 24

U-Lab

"I've seen this person before."

Vincent Anderson straightened up.

His despondent expression vanishing. "Really? Don't joke about this!"

Cora looked at the image carefully again, hesitant but certain she had seen someone like this before.

"Really, very similar."

Vincent's initial reaction was surprise, but as he calmed down, doubts filled his mind.

Such a coincidence? Every time it was such a coincidence?

In Blossomville the Flower City, when Captain Wolf needed to repair the T014, Onyx de Montclair, a "senior weather mimicry system technician," just happened to appear.

Though he eventually fixed the T014, proving his claim and easing some of their suspicions.

But now, once again, Cora claimed she had seen Petros Sheen, the person they had wasted half a year searching for with no results.

Continuous coincidences could either be fate or manipulation.

The Azures never believed in fate.

So, who was orchestrating everything behind the scenes?

If Vincent and Captain Wolf hadn't brought Cora and Damian out of District F177, Vincent might have suspected their backgrounds long ago.

But after Cora said she had seen Petros, her expression was calm, with no signs of lying or guilt.

Vincent hesitated. Maybe she really had seen him?

Cora thought little about it. She was focused on the blurred, old image of Petros Sheen.

It was said the boy was only fifteen, and his indifferent demeanor was already apparent.

The Sheen they had seen before, however, was clearly an adult, with a more arrogant and carefree attitude. The slight difference in demeanor made it hard to believe they were the same person.

But their faces were strikingly similar. Could it be that his personality changed with age?

Cora let her imagination run wild.

"She's telling the truth. We've all seen him," Onyx suddenly spoke after a long silence.

"Whether he's the person you're looking for, we can't say. You'll have to verify that yourselves."

"Where did you see him?" Vincent pressed.

"Felalakas," Onyx replied.

Vincent repeated softly, "Felalakas... so the intel was correct."

Cora provided another valuable clue. "It's not just him; he has a friend too."

Petros Sheen had appeared with River Locke, a cunning, blue-eyed man who had tried to betray her multiple times at Mirror Lake.

Cora had no guilt about revealing his whereabouts to the Azures.

"We don't have an image of him, but his friend has footage from the tournament."

The Throne Tournament (T.T.T.) was a massive event in Felalakas, with each round of the main event broadcasted live.

If the Azures followed this lead, finding the man with the tear-shaped mole would only be a matter of time.

"However, the person we saw was named Jaden Sheen," Onyx casually reminded. "The name isn't exactly the same."

Vincent pondered for a moment. "We'll determine the truth ourselves."

Names were just labels. Any intelligent person knew that. Regardless, it was an important clue.

Vincent couldn't hide his excitement as he paced back and forth. "I need to inform the captain immediately."

After searching aimlessly for so long, finally having a lead, how could he stay calm?

Vincent stepped away to make a call, speaking rapidly and nodding occasionally.

Onyx watched his back impassively, his eyes deep in thought.

Cora, however, remembered another detail.

Vincent had initially mentioned they were looking for a "key."

"What is this 'key'?" she asked Onyx quietly.

"Who knows?"

Onyx answered nonchalantly.

"You don't know something?" Cora was surprised.

"Of course, I'm human too. How could I be omniscient? Admitting ignorance doesn't mean denying oneself." Onyx tapped her head playfully.

"Let's go, volunteer. Lunch break is over."

The next day, Cora received good news from Vincent Anderson: Sycamore truly lived up to its reputation as the city of medicine. The doctors not only saved William Strong but also provided a treatment plan to extend his life.

William's damaged right side would be replaced with bionic materials, allowing him to survive with a half-mechanical body, somewhat similar to the half-cyborgs they had encountered in Felalakas' "Knights of Anna."

However, the surgery was highly risky, and William had not yet passed the critical period, requiring Vincent to stay in Sycamore for some time.

"Once Strong's transplant is done, you can come see him. We'll make him treat us to dinner!" Vincent's booming voice was as strong as ever, sounding revitalized.

"By the way, I need to go out tomorrow. Since you're volunteering at the hospital, can you also help with Strong?"

Cora was speechless.

"Big bro, I volunteer as a zombie cleaner. My daily job is running to and from the incinerator. How can I help with Strong? By sending him to the incinerator?"

"Oh right, that's too unlucky! Forget I said that. I'll ask the attending physician instead."

Vincent slapped his forehead loudly, and Cora could hear it through the terminal.

"Where are you going?"

"To U-Lab, to retrieve some data."

It wasn't a secret mission, so Vincent openly told Cora about it.

"What did he say?" Onyx put down his holo screen and raised his voice.

"Something... something U..."

Cora thought for a few seconds, but couldn't remember the full name Vincent had mentioned.

"Unique Laboratory," Onyx said in a low voice.

"Yes, that's the name."

Onyx tapped his fingers on his wheelchair, pondering for a moment before dropping a bombshell.

"Vincent is going alone with no help. Since we have nothing to do tomorrow, why don't we assist him?"

Cora's face slowly formed a question mark.

She jumped off the desk, folded her hands behind her back, and silently stared at Onyx.

Onyx smiled, raising an eyebrow.

"What?"

Cora pursed her lips. "Liar. You wouldn't be so kind."

Does he take her for a fool? When has Onyx ever cared about anyone's wellbeing? Helping? He'd be more likely to kick them when they're down.

Onyx chuckled, his charming eyes forming an attractive arc. "Ah, you've seen through me. You know me so well?"

"Spill it. What do you want to do?" Cora demanded sternly.

Feigning resistance, Onyx turned his wheelchair halfway around, but Cora quickly moved to block him.

She pushed the wheelchair down firmly, preventing him from moving. "Speak!"

No escape.

Onyx raised his hands in surrender. "Alright, I'll tell you everything. Let go first."

Cora didn't believe him. "You speak first."

"Although U-Lab is advertised as an independent lab, it's actually..."

"Actually, what?"

"Few people know it's actually a subsidiary of Arashi, used to research special organisms."

Arashi again. No wonder Onyx was so interested when he heard the name.

"So, what do you want to do?" Cora still didn't understand.

"Two reasons. First, I want to know what Vincent is retrieving. As an Arashi member, it's within reason, right?"

"Second, this reminded me that the vagrant in Sakura Shelter wouldn't speak. Some things in U-Lab can make him talk. Don't look at me like that—it's legitimate stuff."

"Is it dangerous to go there?"

As the captain of F777, Cora naturally had to consider the safety of her team.

"Yes. U-Lab was rated as a high-risk area before the apocalypse. As for now, I'm not sure."

U-Lab conducted bizarre genetic fusion experiments, making it a high-security forbidden zone even before the apocalypse.

Onyx couldn't be certain what it was like now.

He thought for a moment and cautiously said, "But since Vincent dares to go alone, the Azures must have cleared it. Don't worry too much."

If it were truly dangerous, Vincent wouldn't go alone, let alone have a casual conversation with Cora, showing no signs of nervousness.

"Should I ask him?" Cora reached for her terminal.

"Wait," Onyx cleared his throat. "Since we're offering to help, why not give him a surprise?"

Surprise? Are you sure it's not a shock?

Cora silently ridiculed Onyx's breezy attitude towards taking the initiative.

She slid her fingers over the terminal, deciding to call in some extra help given the potential difficulty of the task. Laborers, after all, were used.

Better to burden others than herself.

The next day, Vincent Anderson, dressed in his combat uniform, glanced through the observation window at the sleeping William Strong before leaving Hospital 119.

Stepping out of the main entrance, he halted after a few steps.

Across the street, five people stood or sat, all looking his way.

This was a team that, despite not showing their ranks, was clearly not to be trifled with.

A tall woman leaned against the shade of a tree, her striking beauty catching the eye, as she covered her mouth with a coy laugh.

Next to her stood a tall, rugged man with a brooding gaze. His body tensed, ready for combat at any moment.

In front of them, a handsome young man sat in a wheelchair, slightly tilting his head as he chatted with a girl with shoulder-length black hair.

In the forefront, a ten-year-old boy played happily with two snowflakes dancing on his fingertips.

Seeing him, Damian Blackwood immediately lit up with a bright smile. "Uncle Vincent, we came to help!"

Vincent couldn't help but let out a sigh. "Help? You guys brought a whole team?"

U-Lab Laboratory.

This laboratory was located outside the Sycamore area, on the outskirts of a nearby D-level city.

The exterior was a high-tech, semi-underground structure, with the visible part being a white, domed building.

The walls were completely sealed, revealing nothing of the interior.

Vincent bypassed the outer defenses and led the group to the side.

"The staff evacuated after the apocalypse, but many experimental samples and equipment were left behind. We had to clear out some dangers, so be careful inside."

"How do we get in?" Cora Thornton knocked on the wall but found no openings.

They hadn't considered using the main entrance. Given its security level, it would take the latest heavy weapons from the alliance a full day and night to breach it.

The walls of the U-Lab were made from unique materials.

Vincent had mentioned in how they had self-repair capabilities. Although there were faint scorch marks on the surface, no openings could be found.

Vincent took a handheld particle cannon from his shoulder, a half-smoked cigarette dangling from his mouth.

"Step back. Be careful not to get hurt."

Cora and the others obediently stepped back.

Vincent planted one foot on a step, aimed the particle cannon at the wall, and a crimson beam gradually gathered before blasting out.

"Boom!"

The cannon fire blasted a hole several feet wide in the side wall.

As debris scattered, purple lightning followed, forming a dense web that held the breach open, preventing it from closing.

It was Vincent's Anopower, controlled with precise skill, with not a hint of energy leaking.

"Hurry inside."

The group quickly entered.

The cold, sterile laboratory was illuminated by harsh white lights, with bright glass corridors.

The air was thick with the smell of chemicals, making prolonged exposure dizzying and disorienting.

From the moment they entered, Vincent's expression was exceptionally serious. He sternly reminded them, "Stay close to me and don't wander."

Though most dangers had been eliminated, caution was still paramount.

They advanced along the wide corridor, the silence so profound they could hear each other's footsteps. The rooms on either side were mostly in disarray, with crucial documents long gone and the screens of equipment dark.

Vincent moved steadily, with a clear destination in mind.

The others observed as they walked, occasionally glancing into the rooms they passed.

Inside were various capsule pods, mostly empty.

Electronic screens sporadically flashed with text and segments of experimental progress.

Experiment Number: RYH9001

Biological Prototype: Caudata - Alien Toad

Experiment Record: New Calendar Year 40, February 15th, 54th gene fusion failure

Status: Deceased

Experiment Number: PJK9321

Biological Prototype: Octoculus - Parasite

Experiment Record: New Calendar Year 44, July 22nd, successful parasitism, July 29th, host deceased

Status: Deceased

Experiment Number: SFP2056

Biological Prototype: Lepidoptera - Striped Poison Moth

Experiment Record: New Calendar Year 45, December 24th, radiation levels stable, continued observation recommended

Status: Alive

As Yuui Hayashi walked deeper into the lab, her face grew paler.

The experimental data and the leftover visuals were disgusting.

In just a short distance, she had accidentally seen a toad with two heads and a dozen legs, a seven-gilled eel with a funnel-shaped mouth, and countless malformed insects whose original species were unrecognizable.

This place was a nightmare for anyone with trypophobia!

Yuui quickly looked away, taking a deep breath to steady herself. She was surprised to see someone else looking worse than her.

Cora had unknowingly fallen to the back of the group, staring blankly at the capsule pods.

The interiors of the rooms were clean, with no visible stains, but Cora felt like the air was filled with a bloody mist, and she could faintly smell blood. She reached out and dabbed the electronic labels on the pods. What did these numbers mean?

"What's wrong? Did you find something?" Yuui asked in a low voice.

"No." Cora was interrupted and stood still for a moment before quickening her pace to catch up with the others.

It must be poor ventilation, she thought, making it hard to breathe, which was causing her hallucinations. This place made her very uncomfortable.

Vincent led them to the end of the hallway, to a significantly larger research room.

The glass doors slowly opened, revealing a giant fish tank connected to the ceiling.

Inside the dark chemical liquid was a massive deep-sea squid.

Its entire body was deep red and gelatinous, partially decomposed, with sunken eye sockets and gray-white eyeballs.

Each tentacle was attached to chemical tubes, floating lifelessly.

Vincent followed the signal source, searching the room and finding a hidden central control unit.

This dormant unit had a timer function. The last time they were here, it had been off, so they had missed it.

Two days ago, the signal source in the lab detected a data fluctuation and reported it to Captain Wolf, who then ordered Vincent to retrieve the data from this central unit.

Vincent took out a small chip-like device and connected it to another machine to start data transfer. While waiting, he couldn't resist scaring Damian.

"Little one, just look, don't touch. It might still move."

Damian, naturally timid, clung tightly to Cora's leg, acting as a portable attachment, eyes squeezed shut, not daring to look.

Vincent laughed, satisfied, and stopped teasing him.

The data transfer took about ten minutes. Once completed, they retreated along the corridor, returning to the starting junction.

So far, they had only explored a small part of the lab, but everyone looked uneasy. From what they had seen, U-Lab conducted illegal biological experiments.

Why did the Alliance allow such a black lab to exist?

Vincent chose the left path this time.

This route was clearly harder to navigate, with debris and rubble everywhere. Stepping carelessly could lead to stepping on gravel and glass shards.

Vincent explained in a low voice, "We didn't have access. Last time, the captain had to break the door down."

"What is this?" Yuui stopped, puzzled.

They faced a tightly closed metal door.

A sleek, high-gloss door with a streamlined access system was firmly fixed on the door, emitting a blinking light.

A camera automatically scanned everyone who passed, capturing various heat sources, displaying red characters repeatedly.

"Identification failed."

"Identification failed."

"NO ACCESS."

"This is a hidden door. According to the 3D map, it should be the key control center of the lab. Unfortunately, we can't open it."

Vincent placed the signal source on the door, but it remained silent, the screen showing no response.

"The primary control can operate all lights, systems, and equipment in the lab. The captain confirmed there were no life signs or data flows inside. If we try to force it open, it might trigger a self-destruct sequence, so we left it alone."

Even Captain Wolf, with all his equipment, couldn't open it, so they had no means to do so either. They gave the flashing access system a curious glance and followed Vincent.

Turning the corner, they found their path blocked by a huge, foul-smelling corpse!

The corpse was over ten feet long, resembling both a human and a fish, with strange webbed hands and feet. Its gray-white eyes stared lifelessly, and its mouth was full of jagged, terrifying teeth capable of easily tearing through a human.

"Ew, what is this?" Damian almost jumped.

"A zombie fish-man."

"Strong was injured by this thing."

Vincent's expression turned bitter, and purple lightning crackled around him.

"Don't worry, it's dead. We left it here in a hurry when we evacuated."

Cora and Onyx were relatively calm, having seen many horrors.

Suchat showed no expression, remaining composed.

The most affected was Yuui, who pinched her nose and backed away several steps, looking disgusted.

"Suchat, dispose of it."

Suchat stepped forward, flipping a knife in his palm, and stabbed it into the fish-man's head. Black, rancid blood oozed out. As the knife glowed faintly, the fish-man's body corroded, eventually dissolving into a puddle and disappearing.

Vincent clicked his tongue, noticing the black snake tattoo on Suchat's neck, suddenly understanding.

A man from the rainforest. No wonder.

While the others circled the fish-man's corpse, Onyx's wheelchair slid back, and he returned alone to the locked door. He rested his chin on his hand, staring at the door expressionlessly before letting out a small chuckle.

Onyx raised his head slightly, staring directly at the door.

The silver access system scanned his pupils.

Capturing the biological information, the electronic eye automatically detected the iris data.

The central unit quickly calculated, and after two seconds, green characters flashed.

"Identification successful."

"ROOT."

CHAPTER 25

Wingbeats

"What are you doing?"

As the hidden door opened, Cora appeared behind Onyx like a ghost.

Their eyes met unexpectedly.

After a few seconds, Cora turned her head to glance at the open door.

In the mysterious silence, Onyx's heartbeat quickened.

At this moment, if Cora called out, Vincent and the others would come over.

Although he wasn't doing anything wrong, he had no way of explaining the current situation.

Cora hesitated for a moment but didn't shout. She just quietly looked at Onyx, then moved to the doorway, blocking Onyx from view.

"Hurry," she urged softly.

Onyx smiled slowly. No matter what, Cora had sided with him.

Even without words, there was a strange understanding between them at that moment.

Onyx quickly slipped into the hidden room and glanced around.

As Vincent had said, it was just a regular control room with nothing noteworthy and certainly no forgotten critical information or classified documents.

However…

The control room managed the entire lab's access system, and the visitor logs from each area were interconnected. By querying U-Lab's entry and exit records over the past decade, he could find some clues.

Onyx unlocked the panel and swiftly entered commands, deleting all data from the access system. Then he scanned the room, collecting any useful equipment into his spatial storage.

The silver wheelchair slid out silently, and the hidden door closed automatically.

Cora leaned against the wall, watching him intently without blinking.

Onyx nodded, "Done."

Cora didn't ask what he had done inside. She just took the wheelchair and pushed him to catch up with Vincent and the others.

They had been gone for two or three minutes, but since the others were focused on the zombie fish-man, they hadn't noticed.

After clearing the fish-man's body, the path was clear again.

Vincent led them deeper into the U-Lab.

Leaving the cold, oppressive research lab, the light suddenly brightened, and a glass greenhouse appeared before them.

It was unimaginable that, in such a grim and eerie place as the U-Lab, there would be a dreamlike transparent garden.

Artificial sunlight poured down, making the room bright and warm. The garden was lush with vegetation, and the air was fresh. On both sides were display cases filled with well-preserved insect specimens, intricately detailed.

"Last piece of data, then we're done," Vincent said, connecting the chip to a standing cabinet-like machine and starting the data transfer.

With the task nearly complete, he relaxed, stretching his neck and shoulders.

"Uncle Vincent, what is this machine?" Damian asked, curious.

"This? It's a visitor system data cabinet. It contains various data. We'll take it back and see if it's useful," Vincent replied.

"Oh." Damian nodded obediently.

He turned his small head, looking around with curiosity but refraining from touching anything. The little guy was smart enough to know that nothing here could be touched carelessly.

He'd seen it on TV—clumsy characters breaking things or

touching something they shouldn't, only to release some powerful monster that led to everyone's demise. He would not be that idiot!

Damian's gaze fell on an insect specimen in one of the display cases.

A huge moth-like specimen rested there, with thick, short, grayish-white antennae and pitch-black compound eyes. Its wings, spread flat, were covered in brown and black scales, with brush-like fringes that made prolonged staring dizzying.

Damian blinked. He could have sworn the giant moth had moved. He rubbed his eyes in disbelief and then widened them slightly.

He hadn't imagined it.

It moved again!

A shiver ran down Damian's spine. He instinctively wanted to cling to his sister's leg, but saw that Cora was pushing Onyx further away.

Too afraid to run over, he settled for tugging on Vincent's sleeve. "Uncle Vincent, that specimen is moving!"

The garden was so quiet that everyone heard Damian's warning, not just Vincent.

Cora looked around warily at the glass walls, the control panels, and the display cases.

There were so many specimens—at least a thousand. Which one was Damian talking about?

Soon, everyone found out.

The large moth specimen, which had seemed lifeless, twitched. Its antennae twitched, its legs moved, and its wings slowly flapped.

Vincent's expression changed. "Everyone, be on guard!"

The atmosphere grew tense. The specimen that was supposed to be dead was coming to life.

A moth over eighteen inches long fluttered up, its wingbeats scattering a fine powder into the air like a light rain.

"A Poison Moth, female. Don't inhale that dust," Onyx quickly warned. "Those are its eggs."

Everyone's faces turned pale, and they hurriedly covered their mouths and noses.

But the greater danger was yet to come.

After the mother moth appeared, countless larvae emerged from corners, workbenches, cabinets, and even from behind the shade of trees.

These larvae were brightly colored—yellow-green, yellow-brown, with long hairy legs.

Despite their fuzzy appearance, their grayish-white zombie-like spiracles made them anything but cute. They were downright creepy.

Onyx quickly recited a number.

"SFP2056."

Cora Thornton was initially puzzled but quickly recalled the capsule they had passed earlier—SFP2056, a Lepidoptera-striped poison moth, still alive according to the last experimental record!

So... this mutated Poison Moth had been hiding here, using the glass garden as its nursery!

Onyx was right; those drifting particles weren't dust but parasitic eggs.

Disgusting!

Suchat's knife was quick and precise, killing one larva in a single strike. However, there were too many of these mutated insects to kill them all. Yuui Hayashi's singing Anopower was mostly useless in this situation; if she opened her mouth, she'd inhale countless bugs.

Fortunately, they had two Anopowers capable of group damage.

Damian unleashed a blizzard, and Vincent's purple lightning surged, their combined Anopowers lighting up the garden.

But the larvae were like unending weeds—cut one down, and another took its place, increasing.

No one knew how many eggs the Poison Moth had laid.

The air was filled with swarming larvae, the buzzing of their wings drowning out all other sounds, and soon, they couldn't see each other clearly.

A terrifying moth infestation had descended.

"Catch the big one first," Vincent gritted out.

He controlled the lightning, trying to locate the mother moth among the swarm. It was the right idea, but as difficult as finding a needle in a haystack.

Cora pushed Onyx toward Damian and Vincent, who barely created a vacuum zone with their Anopowers, keeping the larvae at bay temporarily.

Then she moved through the larval swarm, her fingers brushing over a control panel.

Blue light flashed, and a uniquely shaped spirit tool materialized in her hand. It had a long handle like a halberd, straight with a horizontal blade at the top, but the upper part was entirely different, featuring a mesh with countless small barbs and blades, incredibly sharp.

Cora wielded the electrified swatter, rolled forward, and moved to Vincent's side. "Lend me some power."

Vincent didn't hesitate, releasing his purple lightning to entwine tightly around the mesh.

The spirit tool's surface gleamed with blue-purple energy as Cora jumped onto a cabinet, swinging the swatter into the air.

The sound of crackling electricity filled the air as larvae hit the mesh, getting caught by the barbs and blades, then fried by the lightning. The smell of scorched protein filled the air as the larvae turned to ashes, dropping to the ground like rain.

Cora wielded her electrified swatter, jumping around the garden.

The larvae, sensing danger, clumped together to avoid her but couldn't escape.

The scene turned absurdly comical, with the once-chaotic situation now looking bizarrely surreal.

Vincent, never having seen such a display, stared wide-eyed, words piling up in his throat before he finally uttered, "Well, damn. Impressive, really impressive."

As many larvae were cleared out, Cora finally spotted the mother moth, hiding above them, circling the artificial light, frantically spreading more eggs. She swung her swatter hard at it!

The purple lightning and barbs gleamed, and the moth dodged agilely.

Cora pursued, swinging from the opposite direction. The moth dodged again, its wings brushing the mesh and getting a slight shock. Despite being stunned and jerking, it didn't fall.

"This is bad... it has resistance," Onyx said gravely, proposing a terrifying thought.

Cora was shocked. She had forgotten this Poison Moth was an experimental subject. Who knew what modifications U-Lab had made to it? It had survived, meaning its genes were undoubtedly altered, perhaps more than once!

The electric swatter was too large—good for crowd control but too conspicuous for targeting the mother moth.

Vincent's lightning Anopower had little effect on it.

Cora thought quickly and shouted, "Little Star, try freezing it!"

Damian nodded firmly. "Got it!"

Ice and snow formed in front of him. Damian focused, controlling his Anopower to move steadily toward the moth.

Seeing this, the more experienced Vincent kindly advised, "Don't just use your eyes. Control it with your Anopower and split your focus a bit."

Damian took a deep breath, calmed down, and the ice and snow moved more steadily. He concentrated, guiding his Anopower, and the ice quickly reached the Poison Moth, tiny ice crystals clinging to its wings.

The moth's movements slowed briefly. It was a fleeting moment, but a rare opportunity!

How could they kill it in one go?

Among them, the person whose Anopower was best for complete destruction was Suchat.

Cora's mind raced, and she extended the swatter to him.

"Lend me some power."

Suchat paused but didn't refuse, placing his knife on the mesh, dark green energy flowing into it.

Cora absorbed the Anopower and leaped up!

The electrified swatter, now laced with venom, struck the Poison Moth hard. The moth, just thawed by Damian, struggled desperately, flying upward.

It was about to escape the attack range when Cora twisted her wrist, extending the tool's reach. The toxic mesh struck its body directly.

"Sizzle—"

The stench of corrosion filled the air. The Poison Moth's body melted from its legs, wings, to its antennae, turning into a black goo.

Success!

Without their leader, the larvae scattered aimlessly, still attacking but no longer a significant threat.

Cora seized the chance, conjuring more electrified swatters with Vincent's Anopower, distributing them to her companions, and they began clearing the garden.

Crackling sounds filled the air, and the ground piled up with yellow-green larvae corpses, gradually covering their feet. After some time, they cleaned up, and the garden finally fell silent.

Vincent had finished retrieving the data, and the stale air wasn't suitable for prolonged exposure. Cora and the others promptly left the lab.

Some areas of U-Lab remained unexplored, but Vincent's mission was solely to retrieve data. With that accomplished, there was no need to linger.

The others, too, lacked interest in further exploration, knowing the lab held nothing but various bizarre experimental creatures.

However, they were quite intrigued by Cora's conjured electric swatter.

"Cora, you're really something. How did you come up with this?" Yuui Hayashi examined the swatter, her delicate fingers poking the mesh. The tiny barbs instantly pricked her skin.

"This one's mine. After all, I helped quite a bit," Vincent said, clearly pleased, gripping the swatter tightly.

He hadn't imagined his Anopower could be used in such a creative way.

Cora, not one to be stingy, especially after everyone's efforts inside, briefly focused her mental energy, severing her connection to the spirit tool.

"They're yours," she said generously.

Back in Sycamore, the temporary team parted ways.

Vincent returned to the hospital, while Yuui announced her upcoming plans.

The once-glamorous superstar of District C, now visibly slimmer from the recent ordeals, seemed more resilient.

Yuui smiled at Cora.

"Just so you know, I'm not skipping out on our deal."

"The Top 32 matches are starting soon. I have some work and personal matters to handle, so I need to return to Felalakas tomorrow.

As for the remaining two tasks, I'll owe you. Reach out when you need me."

Cora nodded. She had no other tasks at the moment, so there was no reason to stop Yuui from leaving. Whether in Felalakas or Sycamore, tracking Yuui down for help wouldn't be difficult.

The three members of F777 returned home.

Damian, obsessed with the idea of parasites, talked non-stop about them, making Onyx and Cora itch just from listening. They hurriedly ran to their rooms to shower.

Onyx emerged from the bathroom, supporting himself with a crutch, drying his wet hair.

A casual glance revealed someone sitting on his bed.

With equally wet hair dripping down her shoulders, a serious expression on her small face, she gazed at him.

Ah, time for a reckoning.

Onyx found it both amusing and exasperating.

With a sigh, he thought, again with the no knocking.

CHAPTER 26

Questioning

Cora quietly watched Onyx. Ever since she found this man in the torrential rain, her nomadic journey had undergone indescribable changes.

Questions she couldn't figure out before, she only had to ask, and she would get answers from him: information about the apocalypse, Anopowers, Arashi, C-level cities, mission commissions...

Onyx said he wasn't omniscient, but to Cora, he was all-knowing. As long as Onyx was by her side, even ignorance became a luxury. Cora would never be puzzled by the unknown world again; everything could be theoretically solved, and she only needed to execute.

But this didn't mean she had lost her ability to think.

Who exactly was Onyx? What was his true identity? A regular researcher at Arashi?

Absolutely impossible.

When they first met, he claimed to be a pharmaceutical developer.

After encountering Vincent Anderson, he changed it to a weather system technician.

As long as it was beneficial to him, Onyx could easily adopt any identity, completely indifferent to truth or lies.

His real background hid in a dense fog, layers deep, and unless he tore away the layers of disguise. Cora would probably never know.

In front of U-Lab's secret door, Cora caught him red-handed.

He had secretly left the team to do something that he didn't want others to know about.

When did he start this secretive plan? When he proactively suggested going to U-Lab with Vincent? Or even earlier, when he learned that Vincent's mission was to find the long-lost person?

Cora wasn't stupid.

She understood that even if U-Lab was a subsidiary of Arashi, the heavily guarded door access system was definitely not something a "regular researcher" could open.

Cora stiffened her face and spoke fiercely, "Confess, and you'll be treated leniently."

Onyx's expression was relaxed as he responded, "Resist, and you'll be dealt with strictly?"

Cora's cheeks puffed up. "You, honestly, come clean..."

Onyx smiled gently. "And you'll mercifully spare me?"

Annoyed, Cora thought, why does he always have to follow up her words, making her subsequent thoughts a mess?

She moved her fingers slightly, a faint blue light appearing and aiming slowly at the man in front of her.

"Why argue when you can fight?" Onyx, leaning lazily on the writing desk with a cane, said, "Do you have the heart to treat me like this?"

Fresh out of the shower, he didn't use a wheelchair, and his tall figure loomed over her, casting an imposing shadow.

Cora glanced up. It wasn't really a shadow; his bathrobe wasn't tied properly, revealing half of his chest.

"No jokes, hurry and talk."

Cora insisted on her question. She chose this time when they were alone in his room to clear her doubts. Today, she wouldn't leave until she got an explanation.

"Speak honestly." Considering his knack for lying, Cora added.

Onyx, pressed step by step, sighed helplessly.

"I can indeed open the door because I have high clearance within Arashi."

"As for why I needed to enter the control room... a few years ago, I visited U-Lab."

Cora frowned, "What were you doing there?"

Could it be that Onyx was involved in those illegal biological experiments?

Seeing her expression, Onyx couldn't help but chuckle and shake his head slowly.

"Don't overthink it. I didn't take part in any experiments. I went as an internal inspector."

"The data Vincent is retrieving includes visitor logs. If my presence appears on those, it would be hard to explain and could bring us unnecessary trouble. So, I deleted the access records to eliminate this potential problem."

"Other than that, I did nothing."

"You're sure you're telling the truth now?" Cora looked at him suspiciously.

Onyx smiled slowly. "Cora, I've told you before, I have no reason to lie to you."

No reason to lie to me? Then there's one more thing. Will you answer it?

Cora remained silent for a moment, then asked a question that struck to the core.

"Do you know Petros Sheen?"

Even though she wasn't as smart as Onyx, her intuition was usually very accurate.

That night at Mirror Lake, when Onyx saw Jaden Sheen, his expression clearly changed. He reacted to that face.

Onyx's smile disappeared, his eyes narrowed, and he fell into a long silence.

The cane he used to keep his balance moved slightly, making a creaking sound on the floor.

"No lying," Cora warned.

"I know him," Onyx finally said in a low voice after a long time.

As expected, Cora thought, feeling a sense of certainty in her heart.

"Who is he?"

"An old acquaintance," Onyx replied.

He took a few slow, steady steps forward, coming to sit beside Cora on the edge of the bed.

They sat shoulder to shoulder, looking out at the hazy night through the window.

"I'm sorry. I can't tell you his identity for now."

"But Vincent is right. This is an impossible mission. The Azures will never find Petros Sheen."

"Why?" Cora asked, puzzled.

"Because he's dead." Onyx's voice was hoarse.

"Petros died a long time ago."

"Dead, as in both biologically and socially, he has completely disappeared."

Cora thought seriously.

Biological death meant a person stopped breathing, their body decayed, turning to bones and dust.

To achieve social disappearance, a person's habits, relationships, and behaviors must be completely erased from others' memories.

"Why did he die?"

"Because someone wanted him dead, or rather, he had to die. As long as Petros was alive, he faced endless pursuits."

Pursuit, forced to die... Each word Onyx spoke carried a cruel meaning.

Cora fell silent, thinking of that stunning image, that rebellious young man who never made it to adulthood.

What must Onyx, knowing everything and being Petros's old acquaintance, be feeling now?

Cora's gaze fell on the back of Onyx's hand resting beside him, where veins stood out, showing his fluctuating emotions.

Looking up along his arm, his drooping bangs covered half his face, leaving the other half exceptionally cold.

Cora cautiously asked, "Are you okay?"

Onyx didn't respond, only looked back at the girl sitting in front of him.

Cora's clear eyes were filled with concern as she watched him.

Onyx's fingers moved slightly, revealing a faint, thin smile.

"Cora, if one day I'm hunted by the entire Alliance and everyone wants me dead, what would you do?"

Cora didn't reply.

"Would you save me?"

Onyx reached out, gently touching her cheek, pressing down slightly, creating a small dimple.

"Hmm, would you?" He lowered his head, staring into Cora's eyes, still pressing for an answer.

In all the time they had known each other, this was the first time Onyx had come so close to her voluntarily.

Cora felt confused, sensing an indescribable complexity.

She leaned her head back, pulling away from his hand.

"No."

Onyx, having received his answer, slowly smiled, his deep eyes glaring.

"Smart girl. Remember, no matter what trouble you encounter in the future, preserving yourself is always the top priority."

Cora's lips moved slightly, wanting to say something, but she ultimately held back.

Her grandfather had told her to live well, so she could only take care of herself.

Their gazes met for a few seconds before they averted their eyes, tacitly changing the subject.

"What did you take from the control room?" Cora asked.

Onyx took out a small device from his space. "An Anopower detector."

It resembled the black box they had used with Jeremy Wolfgang at Fool's Dock, but Onyx's was orange and looked more delicate.

Cora reached out to touch it, but quickly pulled her hand back.

"It won't break, will it?" She had psychological scars.

"This is an L-type, a common market model. It won't break easily."

Although it wasn't as fully functional as the R-grade or the P-grade used in the C-District Anopower base, the L-type Anopower detector was the most popular because of its handheld convenience.

Feeling reassured, Cora followed the device's instructions, pressing her hands on the detection ports.

The precise instrument scanned her body, multicolored lines spiking until they stopped at the A-mark, the energy value maxed out.

"Too bad it can only measure up to A-grade," Onyx said regretfully.

Cora was curious. "Can this make the homeless man talk?"

A few days ago, they had visited Sakura twice, but no matter how they asked, the homeless man was unwilling to communicate.

"Give me one more day. We're still short on leverage," Onyx said.

The next day, at 119 Hospital.

During her lunch break, Cora, wearing her dirt-brown vest, started wandering around like a mountain king again.

First, she went to find Damian.

The little guy had graduated from running errands in the pharmacy on the eighth floor and had been "promoted" to a zombie cleaner on the thirteenth floor, doing the same job as Cora and earning 180 NPA credits a day.

Even with a terminal account balance full of zeros, and despite the volunteer work being harder and more tiring, Damian didn't mind at all and was quite happy doing it.

"Little Diamond, come here."

Cora found Damian slacking off at the nurse's station.

With his sweet mouth and charming words, he was popular with the doctors and nurses, often ending up with pockets full of snacks.

Cora finally understood why he always burped when he got home.

Damian saw Cora and ran over excitedly. "Sis, you were looking for me?"

Cora nodded, "Yeah, come look at this, treasure."

They went to an empty hallway together.

Cora grinned and pulled out the Anopower detector from her space.

"Let's play with this."

"Huh? Isn't this what Captain Wolf used to measure Anopowers?"

Damian scrunched up his face, recalling his own uncontrollable past.

"This one is high end." Cora said seriously, trying to convince him.

Damian reluctantly agreed, hugging the device and placing his fingers on the detection ports.

The lines on the screen fluctuated, finally stopping at the B mark, going beyond.

"Wow, impressive!" Cora clapped enthusiastically, giving him lots of praise.

"Hehe," Damian scratched his head, excitedly suggesting, "Sis, let's find Dorothy and test her, too."

Kids will be kids, full of wild ideas.

Cora, equally childish, happily agreed.

They then carried the detector to find Dorothy.

Dorothy wasn't as cooperative as Damian.

Seeing the unfamiliar device, she went on high alert, barking and running around the ward with her short legs, even activating her domain a few times, pushing them out multiple times.

Cora refused to give up and engaged in a long-term battle with Dorothy.

Finally catching her, she pressed Dorothy's paw into the detection port.

Dorothy growled and yelped in displeasure but ultimately could not resist.

The screen lit up again, with colorful lines shifting before stopping at the C mark.

Cora and Damian were astonished.

Dorothy was a C-grade Aberrant... no, Anopower dog!

Dorothy, empowered by her C-grade status, unleashed her domain again, catching them off guard and knocking them to the floor.

Nearby, Dorothy's owner, Dorothy's mom, watched the scene while munching on sunflower seeds and lounging with her legs crossed.

"This thing really works."

"I was thinking of taking Dorothy to register. This makes it easier, just need to fill out the paperwork."

"Dorothy needs to register?" Damian asked, rubbing the bump on his head curiously.

"Of course! Our Dorothy is an Aberrant and can receive benefits."

Dorothy's mom replied matter-of-factly.

Cora imagined the scene of a dog getting an Anopower certificate, finding it quite surreal.

"Have some foods." Dorothy's mom warmly offered, shaking off the snacks in front of a screen.

Cora peeked at the screen, which displayed medical news, including articles like "The Most Handsome Doctors of Sycamore",

"Medical Gentlemen", and "The Gentle Scalpel", mostly gossip columns.

Dorothy's mom, thinking Cora was interested, pulled her to sit down, enthusiastically recommending Sycamore's handsome doctors.

Cora glanced twice and was forced to listen to half an hour of gossip.

By the end, all the doctors' faces looked the same to her. However, their hands were quite attractive, slender and distinct, exuding a unique elegance when holding a scalpel.

Meanwhile, Onyx took a moment to visit the Sycamore Security Team, looking for Conrad Kennedy.

"You want to check the records of all registered Aberrants in Sycamore?" Conrad was particularly surprised by his request.

"Yes, and I need your help with this." Onyx nodded politely.

These were internal records that Onyx couldn't access in the hospital archives, so he had to ask Conrad for help. He needed to verify his suspicions.

Conrad was puzzled.

"Why do you need those? There's not much useful information, just age, place of birth, and such. Our security team alone has over 200 people, not to mention the outsiders. There are at least 500 registered Aberrants in Sycamore."

Onyx smiled. "It's not about the information. I just need to confirm a few things."

The archives were stored in tall cabinets reaching up to the ceiling, with different cabinets holding various types of records, neatly categorized.

All the information could be accessed through the central brain.

Conrad scanned his ID and led Onyx in.

"Sorry, but you can't take the records out. You'll have to look at them here."

Onyx nodded understandingly.

"That's fine. I'll try to finish today."

"Just let me know when you're done," Conrad said, as he had many other tasks and couldn't stay there wasting time.

"Thank you, Captain Kennedy."

Once alone, Onyx pulled up the interface, starting with the earliest registered Aberrants before the apocalypse, quickly skimming through the data.

Sycamore Shelter.

For the third time, F777 came to visit the homeless man. Compared to a few days ago, his condition had hardly changed. His wounds were no worse and even showed signs of healing. He hadn't mutated.

Despite not mutating, the man had nearly killed himself over the past few days. He was now skeletal, barely breathing, and looked worse than a zombie.

Damian given the task, reluctantly took a few steps forward. He squatted in front of the homeless man, his innocent face lighting up with a soft voice.

"Uncle, do you want something to eat?"

"My bread has filling, and there's ham, cookies, juice... It's tamarind juice, really tasty."

Damian hoped his childlike charm would lower the man's defenses, but the homeless man remained motionless, sprawled on the ground.

Completely ignored, Damian's curly hair stood on end with frustration.

He continued, "Uncle, if you're in trouble, you can tell my sister. She's really nice. We can help you."

The homeless man slowly turned his head to the other side, as if finding Damian's chatter annoying, waving his hand like shooing away a fly.

Damian couldn't hold back, bursting out, "Hey! Why are you so annoying?"

The homeless man reacted this time, snorting lightly through his nose.

Damian threw down the bread and juice, almost bursting with anger, "I'm talking to you! Can't you be reasonable? You're so old, is trying to die really fun? Have some dignity!"

"Stupid old man!"

Damian huffed and puffed, then turned to see Cora staring at him.

Her mouth agape, witnessing his outburst for the first time.

Damian thought: Oh no, I forgot Cora was right here!

Defeated, Damian stepped back, and Onyx's wheelchair rolled up to the homeless man.

The man remained indifferent, not even lifting his head.

Onyx gently traced the patterns on his blanket, speaking calmly.

"You're not a vagabond."

"And you weren't born despondent."

"You were born in Sycamore, the famed medical city. You had a privileged upbringing, gentle by nature. You grew up healthy and worry-free, worked a respectable and glamorous job, and were once the pride of your field. You had a perfect family, admired and envied by all. Such was your life for over thirty years until the apocalypse came."

"The apocalypse destroyed not just the world, but you as well."

"You experienced a catastrophe that shattered you beyond recovery."

"You abandoned your former glory, your prestigious identity. You lost your beloved family, your cherished friends. Your life became a mess, and you were powerless to change it, so you escaped."

"As a vagabond, a beggar, you care about nothing, just wanting to die quickly, right?"

Cora was stunned.

She did not know what Onyx had discovered or what preparations he'd made, but his few words summed up the man's entire past.

Though the man on the ground didn't respond, Cora noticed his spine stiffening, fingers curling.

Right, his fingers.

This was another thing that intrigued Cora. She had noticed that the homeless man had hands that were almost like works of art. Despite his filthy appearance, his hands, though dirty, had the finest bone structure and joint lines she had ever seen.

"You want to die, but you can't, because you've awakened." Onyx delivered his words like a cold judge, each one merciless.

In the dead silence, the homeless man's breathing became more rapid.

"Do you know how I guessed you're an Aberrant?"

"There are many ways to die, the simplest being bitten by a

zombie. Why didn't you do that?"

"Because you knew you couldn't die, having tried before."

"Having failed, you lost all hope, resorting to starving yourself."

"Or, more directly, getting someone to shoot you."

Onyx took out the Anopower detector.

Wrapping a tissue around his hand, he grabbed the homeless man's hand and forced it onto the detection port. The man, having starved for days, was too weak to resist.

"Beep beep—" The screen's lines fluctuated wildly, the scale shooting up to A.

Cora was astonished.

No way, this guy was an A-grade Aberrant?! Was it that easy to pick up an A-grade homeless man off the street? Ridiculous!

Seeing the result, the homeless man struggled violently, his matted hair parting to reveal an angry face.

Cora gasped.

This face... she had seen it somewhere before... suddenly, the gossip news Dorothy's mom had been reading came to mind.

"The Gentle Scalpel," the news had called him...

"You! You, you, you!"

Shocked, Cora stammered.

The more anxious she got, the harder it was to speak.

Onyx leaned down, coldly staring at the homeless man.

"Did I guess right, Charles Franz?"

"Or should I call you... Doctor Franz?"

CHAPTER 27

Dr. Franz

Charles Franz, 37 years old, Chief Surgeon, M.D., Head of Surgery at Sycamore's 119 Hospital, honorary professor at multiple top-tier hospitals including 123 Hospital and 137 Hospital, and the chief nemesis of critical illnesses.

He's renowned as the genius scalpel of District C, having created industry legends that remain unbroken—every surgery he performed had a 100% success rate.

This was the information Cora remembered from a fleeting glance at some gossip news about Charles Franz.

To delve into this man's illustrious career and legendary achievements would likely take up three full screens.

Even Lynn Rolling, known for her decisiveness, regarded him as an idol in her professional life.

No one would have thought that the once brilliant star of the medical world would fall so far, like burned-out wood, just waiting to crumble away.

Onyx's relentless probing finally got a reaction.

Charles struggled out of his grasp, crawling a few steps before flipping over to sit up.

"Who the hell are you?" he spat, his appearance disheveled and his tone mocking.

"What kind of grudge do you have against me to go through so much trouble investigating me?"

Cora's keen eyes caught the moment he didn't deny his identity, acknowledging himself as "Charles Franz."

"Dr. Franz, you're overthinking it," Onyx said, wiping his fingers clean with tissues and smiling. "We are strangers to you, so naturally, we have no grievances. I was quite surprised myself when I found out your identity."

"Overthinking?" Charles sneered through his messy hair, his eyes cold. "If we're strangers, why are you so idle that you care whether I live or die?"

His voice was weak, but his words were full of sarcasm.

"Don't call me a doctor. I don't deserve it. For the compassionate act of saving lives, you're the true saints of this century. Cheers to you!"

Cora pursed her lips. Regardless of what he said, she had one thought—Charles Franz must not die.

Initially, they had noticed him because of his unique constitution.

Being bitten by zombies without mutating meant he must have secrets.

After learning his true identity, his significance to them changed.

According to the information provided by Lynn Rolling, Charles Franz might be the only hope left to cure Onyx.

Cora was even more determined not to let him die now.

"Stop beating around the bush. Just say what you want," Charles said, his tone listless and his face filled with a world-weary look.

Onyx turned the Anopower detector results towards him, asking instead, "What Anopower did you got?"

Charles Franz, an A-grade Aberrant. Sycamore had over 500 officially registered Aberrants, with only three being A-grade, and only one D-grade in the healing category. Not only was Charles an A-grade Aberrant, but he was also an excellent surgeon. Even if the hope was slim, what if his Anopower was...

Even the steady Onyx found his breath quickening, waiting for an answer.

Cora and Damian also watched Charles intently, waiting for him to speak.

"Heh, I see." Charles's gaze drifted over Onyx's deformed leg, understanding dawning.

He raised his hand slowly, staring at it with cold eyes.

"Anopower, so what? I'm just a useless piece of trash now."

"I'm no longer a doctor, nor will I ever pick up a scalpel again."

"I can't give you what you want."

"Leave me alone. Let me die."

Cora sighed silently.

This man's words could drive anyone mad.

"The Gentle Scalpel"? More like the dark crawling king... No, a crawling worm!

"Hey! You old fart, what if we drag you to the hospital and throw you in front of your colleagues? Aren't you ashamed?" Damian, unable to hold back his temper, threatened fiercely.

"Go ahead."

Charles had long discarded any sense of pride and dignity.

"Then we'll take you to a lab and dissect you for research," Damian continued to threaten.

"Haha, I'd welcome it."

No matter what they said, it seemed impossible to provoke any emotional response from him.

Charles closed his eyes and lay back down, completely unresponsive.

Cora moved closer to Onyx, looking down at the detector. The large A-grade on the screen felt like the most absurd joke.

The logic was simple: whether Charles had awakened a healing Anopower, he was still a top-notch genius surgeon.

They couldn't just give up on him.

Cora and Onyx exchanged a determined look and nodded slightly.

Onyx understood her meaning and lowered his gaze in thought.

Charles's experiences, his words, his subtle expressions, flashed through Onyx's mind like a slideshow.

A sudden light pierced through the fog of despair, making all the details clear.

When he spoke again, Onyx's voice was incredibly calm. "Dr. Franz, let me ask you the same question. What do you want?"

"After all this time, you still stood alive. Don't blame it on your Anopower constitution. Ask yourself, do you really want to die like this? What do you want? What's your remaining obsession?"

It was mealtime, and Sycamore Shelter was bustling with people.

Footsteps and muffled conversations from outside made the room they were in seem even quieter.

Charles Franz tilted his head back, and for a few moments, Cora thought she saw a flicker of pain cross his face.

"What the hell does it matter to you?" he croaked after a long pause.

Cora took a deep breath and stepped forward. "Tell me what you want to do, and I'll do it."

She was making a promise—no matter how difficult, she would see it through.

"You?" Charles half-opened his eyes, looking at the three of them with disdain.

One was a cripple in a wheelchair, one was a volatile kid, and the other…

Cora stood straight, her eyes burning with determination.

"Me. My name is Cora Thornton. A-grade metal Aberrant. Whatever you want to do, I'll do it."

An ethereal artifact formed in her palm, slowly taking the shape of a willow leaf knife.

A commotion erupted outside as someone further mutated into a zombie.

People scrambled, shouting for the security team, amidst the chaos and clattering of objects being overturned.

Just then, the freshly turned zombie leaped through the window.

Before it could cause any harm, Cora's sharp willow leaf knife pierced its head, and the heavy body fell to the ground, its gray eyes staring blankly at Charles.

Charles slowly sat up and laughed, a sound that grew increasingly hysterical and louder.

"A zombie? Ha ha ha! What does a zombie even matter?"

"What do I want to do?"

"I want to kill someone—a governor from District C."

"Can you do that?"

Cora's eyes widened slightly.

"Can you do that?" Charles shouted, his voice breaking with sorrow.

He punched the ground, his knuckles bleeding.

Cora remained silent, glancing at Onyx's leg, then back at Charles. She squatted down, looking directly into his eyes.

"I can do it."

Cora took Charles away with her.

His intense emotions flared only briefly before he lapsed back into silence.

His last words were, "It's not enough to just say it. Show him what you can do."

Despite his skepticism about Cora's abilities, Charles no longer seemed entirely intent on dying.

However, he still refused to reveal more about himself. The good news was, at least he wasn't actively seeking death anymore.

The sound of water running came from the bathroom.

Onyx's wheelchair was parked at the door, and he spoke quietly to Cora, who was leaning against the wall.

"Sometimes I wonder if you have a collecting hobby?"

"Huh?" Cora was puzzled.

"Every time you go out, you bring someone back. How many is it now?"

"You're one of them," Cora retorted.

Onyx raised an eyebrow. "Do you think I'm the same as them?"

She mumbled to herself about how he wasn't any different from the others she'd brought back.

Onyx's expression turned serious. "Are you really going to kill someone for him?"

"This might be the hardest mission we've ever taken on."

Anyone who could become a governor and rule an entire district like C had to be formidable.

People like the super AI Ilia they had encountered, or Sycamore's governor, who single-handedly maintained peace in District C40.

Charles still hadn't told them which governor he wanted to kill.

Cora didn't answer immediately. Instead, she thought seriously about it.

"What do you think his Anopower is?"

Onyx shook his head. "Hard to say. He won't open his mouth."

Cora silently decided.

If Charles could truly heal Onyx's leg, she would make it happen.

The bathroom door suddenly swung open, and Charles stepped out.

Seeing the two of them waiting, he sneered. "What, regretting it already?"

He had washed his face, cut his hair, and shaved, looking much cleaner. At about 5'9", he was very thin, with sunken cheeks.

There were still traces of his former elegance in his facial features, though his mannerisms quickly dispelled that impression.

"No regrets," Cora said, unhappy with his insinuation.

Charles snorted and found a room to sleep in again.

This guy... Cora sighed.

Damian walked by, munching on jelly, muttering angrily, "I hate him."

Damian's "Most Hated List" was updated again. His little grudge book now listed Yuui Hayashi, Onyx, and Suchat, with Charles Franz climbing the ranks.

After a couple of days of rest, the news about the T.T.T. Top 32 match was announced.

This match would be held at the central tower of Felalakas, with the theme "Fight Against Fear."

The exact rules would be revealed on site.

Because of the enthusiastic pre-sale of tickets, the organizers would use the most advanced holographic projection for real-time broadcast.

It was time for F777 to head back to Felalakas.

With starships grounded across all districts, they had to use an old-fashioned method of transportation. They rented a private off-road vehicle, set it to auto-drive, and headed back.

Damian, holding Cora's hand, hopped into the car like he was going on a picnic.

As soon as they got in, they found Charles sprawled across the back seat.

Charles was wearing a padded coat and pants, his hands tucked into his sleeves, with half his head peeking out, fast asleep.

They had informed him the day before about the departure time, but he had given no reaction. Yet here he was, already in the car, asleep.

Damian's good mood was partially ruined. He pouted as he sat in the middle row while Cora and Onyx took the front seats.

After driving for a while, the car's atmosphere grew quiet, and Damian's eyes gleamed with mischief.

When he thought the others weren't looking, he wiggled his fingers, releasing a fine stream of ice and snow that silently flowed towards the back seat.

Thanks to his practice at U-Lab, Damian's control over his Anopower had improved.

The glistening frost first encased Charles's shoes, then gradually spread, freezing him to the seat.

Charles, still half-asleep, instinctively tried to turn over but found his shoes frozen solid. With no warning, he toppled headfirst to the floor, hitting his head with a thud.

He looked around in a daze, realizing his lower legs couldn't move because they were frozen. Frost fell as he saw someone was playing a trick on him with their Anopowers.

"Hahaha!" Damian clutched his stomach, laughing mercilessly.

But his laughter didn't last long.

Charles, unfazed, simply took off his shoes, rolled over, and continued to sleep on the floor.

Damian was left dumbfounded.

CHAPTER 28

Gentle Rain

Back in Felalakas, it was nearing midnight. The city that never sleeps was still glowing with neon lights.

Holographic projections sliced through the dark sky into red and blue blocks, while the gem-like Ferris wheel slowly turned. For a moment, Cora Thornton felt an illusion—they had left, yet it seemed like they had never left at all. Felalakas hadn't changed one bit, still welcoming travelers with open arms. A street musician at the city gate lightly strummed his guitar, singing tirelessly.

"Felalakas, free Felalakas, your dreamland where one lingers forever..."

The off-road vehicle smoothly entered the inner city. After returning it to the rental center, they had to walk the rest of the way. The four walked along the bustling streets, just as a floating billboard played an ad. A sweet-smiling actress, with cherry pink hair styled like a princess, danced gracefully in a sea of flowers.

"I like~ like~ your smile, like a gentle rain falling in my heart."

Around the billboard, many fans were scattered, wearing pink cat ear headbands, enthusiastically handing out support gifts to passersby, promoting their idol.

"Yuui's new song 'Gentle Rain' is out today, please give it a listen."

"Sweet songstress, healing idol, investing in her is always a win."

"Come to the concert and experience the best Yuui!"

Cora's arms were filled with several posters and merchandise of Yuui Hayashi. She looked down at a cartoon big-headed doll on a support sign, smiling sweetly at her.

The last time they met, Yuui had ungracefully stuffed her long dress into her waistband, hair disheveled and face bare, waving an electric fly swatter, cursing loudly while swatting moths.

"I hate caterpillars the most in this life! Die, die, die!"

Cora picked up a pink kawaii keychain, stared at it for two seconds, speechless.

Felalakas' star-making ability was truly terrifying.

Idols and personas, they were all fake... completely untrustworthy.

She casually stuffed the keychain into her pocket and turned to her companions to discuss their next move.

Damian hadn't escaped the fans' promotion either, holding a plush doll of Yuui, his face full of disdain.

Onyx, as usual, was indifferent, lazily leaning on his wheelchair, while Charles Franz...

Charles was hunched over, head buried in his coat, indifferent to everything happening around him, eyes closed, as if even these few steps were a hardship.

Cora opened her mouth to speak, but suddenly, a deafening noise came from the other side of the street.

Hundreds of roaring motorcycles sped past, loud rock music shattering the night's tranquility.

Cora quickly pushed Onyx to the side.

The arrogant convoy skimmed low in front of them, creating a whirlwind that messed up their clothes and hair, then sped off in a certain direction.

"Clang—"

These street hooligans rampaged through, throwing Molotov cocktails carelessly at buildings and flashing signs.

The bottles shattered, gasoline spreading, thick smoke rising!

The rampant arsonists excitedly whistled, shouting loudly.

The Molotov cocktails exploded one after another, thick smoke billowing, colorful and pungent gases everywhere, blocking the view of passersby.

Cora covered her mouth and nose, coughing violently, watching the dark red flames rise high, gradually forming the simple word: [Freedom].

"Freedom, we want freedom. Resist AI, humans will never yield!"

"AI is the root of all evil! AI will only lead to human extinction!"

"AI get out of Felalakas!!"

"Damn those rebellious bastards!"

Cursed the pedestrians on the roadside, furious.

However, the turmoil didn't stop.

The motorcycle convoy suddenly sped up, turning a corner, charging into the nearby Star Plaza.

An exhibition for River Locke was being held there.

Fans had funded and created an exclusive cultural community.

Seeing this scene, the rioters became even more excited, their actions full of destructive desire.

High-pressure flamethrowers rose from the back of their bikes, flames engulfing River Locke instantly.

Sculptures, standees, images... all consumed by fire, years of fans' efforts destroyed in an instant.

In the scorching firelight, River Locke's green robe withered, jade flute burned, his princely handsome face destroyed inch by inch, his eyes lowered, filled with coldness.

Back at the hotel, Cora approached the floor-to-ceiling window, looking down from above. The ground was shrouded in smoke.

Chaos continued, with occasional bursts of flames. "Who are those people?" she asked.

"The official term is 'Rebels.' They oppose any form of artificial intelligence and support humans reclaiming control," Onyx replied, sorting through the information he had gathered from the dark web.

"Lion, a candidate in the last governor election, backed by Century Group, has been unsatisfied since Ilia was elected. He has been secretly active and recently funded the rebels, raising a bunch of hooligans."

Cora sat down, contemplating the scene they had just witnessed and its connection to the power shifts in Felalakas.

"The rebels want to overthrow Ilia's rule and achieve true 'freedom.'"

"That's right," Onyx said. "Their goal is to intensify conflicts."

Where there is light, there is darkness. As some people praised and adored the omnipotent artificial intelligence, others loathed it.

With Felalakas' technological advancements, the accompanying swelling ambition and desire made peaceful coexistence between AI and humans a luxury.

Cora had another question.

She pulled up the tournament schedule on her terminal.

During their absence from Felalakas, the Throne Tournament had been turbulent.

Out of the top 64 teams, over 30 participants had been killed, withdrew voluntarily, or died under mysterious circumstances, leaving only 56 teams.

"Does T. T. T. have anything to do with the rebels' plans?" she asked.

The Throne Tournament, pushed to its current popularity by Ilia, had a revenue-generating ability surpassing all music festivals and concerts.

It was a nationwide entertainment event in Felalakas, and crucially, the entire competition was controlled by artificial intelligence, leaving humans with no chance to interfere.

If the rebels truly wanted to incite war, would they let go of this perfect opportunity?

"You're right. If I were Lyon, I would target this," Onyx said.

"Be cautious in every upcoming match."

Cora looked toward the lofty towers.

The surging undercurrents in Felalakas were becoming harder to conceal.

Ilia, what will you do?

While the two pillars of the team were discussing, the old man and the child were dozing off.

Damian, initially sitting on the sofa listening attentively and trying to be involved, eventually succumbed to sleep, following Charles Franz's example of soundly dozing off.

Cora covered Damian with a small blanket and carried him back to his room.

As she walked, she suddenly realized that they hadn't avoided discussing sensitive topics in front of Charles Franz.

From following them to Felalakas to hearing Ilia's name, Charles had shown none abnormal reactions.

The person he wanted to kill wasn't this super AI.

But... with the Alliance having 50 District Cs, which governor did he or she or it hold such a deep grudge against?

In the early morning, Cora received a message on her terminal.

It was from Vincent Anderson, informing her that William Strong's surgery for his mechanical limb was successful.

He wanted to notify Captain Wolf, but Captain Wolf had his communication turned off.

The Azures were currently in Felalakas, and Vincent sent Cora their temporary base address, asking her to run an errand and deliver a message, telling him that Vincent would join them immediately after finishing up in Sycamore.

Meanwhile, the list of the top 32 teams in the Throne Tournament was also released.

Cora didn't see Thyrion Lucas's name on the list. She wasn't sure if he had withdrawn or was using a different alias. Besides the teams Onyx had focused on, Cora was surprised to find Florian Richter's name.

Remembering his suspicious behavior that night, Cora found him quite dubious and investigated the match footage with Onyx.

"Stop," Onyx said, freezing a frame.

"In the Mirror Lake match, Florian Richter has very few shots and doesn't make many moves. Here, you can see he's using some kind of mechanical Anopower."

On the screen, Florian's left arm morphed into a mechanical scythe, slashing awkwardly at an Anopowered zombie, his face full of panic.

Onyx shook his head.

"He swung six times and missed half of them. His movements are clumsy; it seems he can't control his Anopower well. Judging by the attack strength, he's around D-level."

D-level? Not E-level? Was Florian Richter deliberately hiding his level?

Even if he was a D-level Aberrant, there were many stronger contestants, and apart from Cora and her team, no one would pay attention to him.

Recalling his timid demeanor in the Flower City, Cora felt he was hiding something. Since she had to deliver Vincent's message, she might as well ask Captain Wolf about it.

Following the address, Cora found the Azures' temporary base, an empty airship repair shop.

Before she saw anyone, she noticed something was off.

Several motorcycles were hovering low around the perimeter, suspiciously circling the base.

Cora frowned. Before she could act, a fierce figure appeared behind the group. Captain Wolf moved so fast that he was almost invisible.

"Bang, bang!" the rebels fell from the sky in disarray, their motorcycles spinning out and exploding on the ground.

Captain Wolf's voice was as sharp as a knife.

"Military operation? Who allowed you to spy?"

The pinned rebels defiantly shouted, "Freedom!!"

Captain Wolf mercilessly knocked them out with a kick.

He picked up the unconscious rebels and tossed them to his team members. "Take them away for a good interrogation. Find out their purpose."

Then he turned and spotted Cora hiding.

"What do you want?" His tone was as harsh and impersonal as ever.

Cora came out of her hiding spot and honestly explained that Vincent had sent her to deliver a message.

Captain Wolf frowned. "Why didn't he contact me himself?"

Cora defended the aggrieved Vincent. "Your communication was off. He couldn't reach you."

Captain Wolf paused and checked his terminal. He had indeed turned it off to focus on the mission without outside disturbances.

"Come in." With many eyes around, Captain Wolf led her into the base.

Familiar faces like Payne Onathaqua and Kiwamu Maeda were there, but Cora noticed they were fewer.

Originally a twelve-person team, with Vincent and William in Sycamore, only eight remained with Captain Wolf.

Was finding people this dangerous, or were they on a different mission?

Cora habitually asked, "Are you still looking for people?"

Captain Wolf's expression turned sharp, his gaze piercing her. "Who told you? Vincent?"

Cora belatedly covered her mouth, realizing her mistake.

Vincent was definitely going to be mad at her.

"That big mouth," Captain Wolf coldly commented.

As the captain of the Azures, Captain Wolf had a strong sense of duty and confidentiality.

Though his attitude was cold, he was undeniably a responsible and excellent soldier.

Vincent often complained about him, but Captain Wolf's unyielding and resolute spirit was always clear.

"Do you need any help?" Cora hesitantly asked. As expected, Captain Wolf refused.

"No need. The Azures don't require outside help for our missions."

Cora felt frustrated.

Based on Onyx's information, their mission was impossible.

She couldn't just rush in and argue with Captain Wolf, saying, hey, don't bother, Petros Sheen is long dead. She had intended to remind him subtly, but was still turned down.

"Oh." She responded dejectedly.

Remembering her purpose, Cora then asked about Florian Richter.

"Florian Richter?" Captain Wolf frowned.

"I recall little about him. He was evacuated by Kiwamu. You can ask him."

Cora found Kiwamu Maeda and hesitantly shared their suspicions.

The vice-captain was even harder to deal with than Captain Wolf, rigid.

"Florian Richter was evacuated from District D161. His level is indeed E-level. Anopower 'object mending.' I've checked his certificate, I wouldn't forget."

Kiwamu's stony gaze fixed on Cora, clearly not taking her words seriously, and he snorted.

"After the logistics team disbanded, they no longer had any relation to the Azures. Why Florian Richter is taking part in the tournament is not my concern. You should ask him. We have missions to complete. If you have nothing else, leave."

He's so harsh, Cora thought, pouting as she prepared to leave.

According to Kiwamu, Florian had an Aberrant certificate, which was useful information.

She would discuss it with Onyx later.

As she moved, she suddenly noticed something familiar.

In Kiwamu's uniform pocket, a pink keychain peeked out.

Cora instinctively touched her own coat. She had a similar one.

Wasn't that... Yuui Hayashi's merchandise?

She almost forgot, Kiwamu was a loyal fan of Yuui Hayashi!

Nowadays, Yuui was practically her free labor, under her control.

By extension, didn't that mean she had control over Kiwamu too?

Cora's mood improved. She coughed lightly, then started humming.

"I like, like your smile, like gentle rain..."

The new song she heard last night was catchy, though the lyrics were hard to remember. Cora was lost in her singing, which was off-key and jumbled.

Kiwamu's forehead veins twitched. He glanced quickly at Captain Wolf, and then angrily shouted, "Shut up!"

He paused, lowering his voice, grumbling, "You're off-key."

CHAPTER 29

A Nice Guess

"Old James, off to watch the game again?"

Old James was dressed in new clothes, even wearing a tie, and walking energetically towards the central plaza.

The person greeting him looked at him with envy. "Looks like your luck's turned around. You've made a big score."

They used to watch the preliminaries together, and Old James always had the worst luck, making it easy for others to win some money by betting against him.

But after the main event started, he somehow struck it rich. Now, he was living the high life.

Old James chuckled foolishly. "Just lucky, I guess."

As for how he turned his luck around? He wasn't revealing a thing.

After the person walked away, a friend nudged his shoulder, teasing, "Are you betting on that team again tonight? What's their name?"

Old James's face lit up like a chrysanthemum. "F777! Of course, all in!"

At exactly eight o'clock, the tower lights illuminated, and AK appeared on the high stage with two graceful girls.

"Hello, everyone! Long time no see!" AK was as enthusiastic as ever. "It's still me, here to commentate on the exciting top 32 matches."

"Before the match begins, let's address a minor incident. River

Locke couldn't attend tonight's match because of personal reasons. No worries. We have the equally popular Yurika and Nana here with us."

The energetic twin-tailed girl and the gentle, intellectual older sister, two virtual idols, made a stunning appearance through holographic projection, greeting the audience with vivid expressions as if they were right there.

The central plaza and open streets were packed with spectators, all looking up and roaring.

After the cheers, there were murmurs of curiosity.

"Why is River Locke absent suddenly? He confirmed on his profile that he was a special guest just the other day."

"Didn't you hear about last night?"

Someone nearby said mysteriously.

"What happened? What happened?"

"Oh, it's all because of those rebels..."

In the backstage lounge, Cora was talking to the masked Yuui Hayashi.

"After the match, don't leave yet. I want you to meet someone."

She had specifically told Kiwamu Maeda about tonight's match, planning a surprise, though she wasn't sure if he would show up.

The Azures' vice-captain had scoffed at Cora's invitation.

"No time."

Yuui's lips curved under the mask, mirroring Kiwamu's words perfectly.

"No time. I'm busy with my new song release."

Cora puffed her cheeks and pulled out a pink keychain from her pocket. "I'll report you, big star."

Cora mimicked Onyx de Montclair's drawl. "Like a gentle~ gentle rain!"

Suchat, who had been sitting quietly nearby, twirling a knife in his fingers, fumbled and dropped it on the table at her off-key singing.

How could someone sing so badly, not hitting a single note?

Yuui quickly covered Cora's mouth, looking around.

Thankfully, the lounge was empty.

She exhaled. "My god, who did you learn this bad habit from? Fine, fine, I'll go."

She glared at Cora. "I worked so hard on this disguise, no one noticed, and you almost ruined it!"

Cora, her mouth still covered, mumbled in protest.

As they were talking, the lounge door opened, and Ellyn the Wild Rose entered.

Ellyn had a few fresh scars on her right cheek, her buzz cut close to the scalp, with two portable mortars mounted on her forearms. She moved with a steadiness and toughness forged from battle.

Seeing the people in the room, she nodded calmly.

"I've repaid my debt to you. From now on, it's a fair competition. I won't hold back."

During the Mirror Lake ambush, Ellyn had recognized Cora and held back, which later forced her into a no-win slaughter mode.

Even though Cora might not have lost if Ellyn had fought, she appreciated the gesture.

"Fair competition, no need to hold back."

Ellyn glanced at Yuui, hinting at her.

"The best disguise doesn't just change appearance. Micro-expressions and unconscious movements can reveal your true identity."

Ellyn had recognized Yuui.

Although she didn't say it outright, everyone in the room understood her implication. Yuui, who had just boasted that no one had noticed her disguise, was now embarrassed.

Luckily, Ellyn wasn't the type to spread gossip and had no interest in exposing Yuui's secret. She took what she needed and left.

As the competition drew near, the teams gathered for the draw. Cora made a special trip to wash her hands, confident in her draw — Group G. Great, dead last again.

She glanced at the roster and saw "The Knights of Anna," a formidable opponent. Cora exchanged a bitter look with Damian.

"Next time, you draw…"

Before the match, each contestant received a peculiar piece of equipment: the TrueSight Goggles.

It was said that this device had thousands of sensory conduits inside. When worn, it connected to the nerves, capturing the subconscious, and projecting the wearer's deepest fears. Its name, "TrueSight Goggles," perfectly matched the theme of the match: Fight

Against Fear.

From the tall tower, AK enthusiastically explained, "The rules for this match are simple. Within the time limit, the team that kills the most zombies wins. Yes, ordinary zombies. You think it's that easy? NONONO, remember our theme?"

AK dramatically shouted, "Fight Against Fear. The contestants will wear TrueSight Goggles and confront their darkest memories."

Holographic projections displayed ferocious zombies, with realistic images flashing close to everyone's eyes, almost making them smell the foul breath from the monsters' gaping mouths.

The audience was both terrified and excited, screaming wildly.

"Rawy~," AK mimicked a zombie's roar, "I wonder what each contestant fears the most? Don't get too scared!"

"I declare the match…begin!"

Dazzling fireworks exploded overhead, colorful beams flashing at high frequency in the night sky.

Seven giant floating screens rose slowly between the towers, corresponding to the real-time footage of groups A-G.

The prize pool opened, numbers rolling up wildly every second, with a continuous stream of money flowing in.

[Group C]

Ellyn blasted an approaching zombie with her cannon. The TrueSight Goggles suddenly flashed, and the scene changed. She was no longer in the tower but back in the starless, dark Mirror Lake. Blood splattered her retinas as her comrades fell before her.

Ellyn was back in that inescapable nightmare.

"Oh, our contestant Ellyn fears Mirror Lake the most," AK said regretfully, "Those who value emotions will always miss their lost comrades, but in moments like this, emotions become a burden. How will Ellyn handle this?"

Ellyn slowed, her eyes dazed as she took two steps forward, trying to reach her fallen comrade. At that pause, she exposed a clear weakness. Several zombies pounced, biting into Ellyn's forearm, shredding her cannon.

"Ellyn! Wake up, Yura is dead!" Her comrade's shout jolted her back to reality. She screamed in agony, her left arm's mortar destroyed. The zombies' teeth sank into her flesh. Ellyn kicked the surrounding zombies away, raised her right arm, and aimed the cannon at the zombie hanging on her. "Boom—" she fired without hesitation. The searing red light flashed, and the zombie's head, along with Ellyn's arm and cannon, flew off.

"Ellyn made the smart choice to sacrifice her left hand! This is the most sensible decision, but not something everyone can do. Let's give Ellyn a round of applause and vote up!" AK seized this peak moment of traffic, urging the audience.

"I'll always support Ellyn. She's like resilient grass facing the wind, never giving up in desperate situations."

Nana, a sentimental AI, was already tearful.

"Ellyn! Ellyn!!"

The audience's cheers grew louder.

Ellyn's support rate skyrocketing to the top, surpassing all other contestants.

[Group D]

Yuui Hayashi fought while singing, providing buffs for Suchat, who was at the front, killing zombies. The TrueSight Goggles flashed, and the scene changed to a damp, eerie rainforest. Huge plants blocked the sky, and the air was suffocating. But Suchat seemed used to moving in this environment. His enhanced toxic Anopower spread wide, toppling zombies in droves.

Meanwhile, Yuui's surroundings turned into a hospital, seemingly an ICU. A vague figure lay on the bed, with countless zombies pounding on the glass outside, roaring and smashing the walls. The next second, they would burst into the ward. The person inside, sensing danger, triggered the ventilator alarm, teetering on the brink of death.

This was Yuui's worst fear. She shook her head, forcing herself not to think about it, focusing on the zombies in front of her.

"Team Names Are Random" had kept a low profile since the start, and their popularity was mid to low. Besides them, there were no popular contestants in Group D, making it the least watched group. AK glanced at the screen, unimpressed, and switched to the next group.

[Group G]

Cora and Damian stood back-to-back, with Damian casting

Blizzard to gather the zombies and Cora slicing through them with her dual blades.

Against ordinary zombies, they coordinated seamlessly, with their kill count rising rapidly.

The TrueSight Goggles flashed, and the surroundings changed.

Damian's side resembled a zoo, with many bizarre zombies—two-headed, six-armed ones, water monsters with elephant trunks and eel bodies—appearing vividly before everyone.

Children's fears were simple, but their imagination was overly rich.

The zombies and monsters Damian imagined were so different from reality that they were easier to distinguish.

"Damian's fears are...quite pure," AK commented sharply. "Team F777 was the dark horse in the Mirror Lake match and remains the only team without corporate sponsorship. Though they only have two members, they've brought us many surprises. Yurika, what do you think? Have you watched the Mirror Lake match?"

"Of course!" Yurika's orange eye shadow shimmered. "This team is my treasure, too. I'm curious about Cora's fears. Could it be the water monsters she's killed?"

The two special guests focused on the screen showing Group G.

What were Cora's fears?

The TrueSight Goggles flashed, revealing a scene unexpected by all.

Pure white.

A blinding, pure white.

It seemed like a confined room, extremely small, with bright lights everywhere, making it hard to open one's eyes. In the distant sky, a red dot seemed to flash.

"Eh? Are the TrueSight Goggles broken?"

Yurika asked in disappointment.

"This..." AK was speechless for a moment. "Official equipment shouldn't malfunction. Maybe Cora fears the dark, so she prefers bright places?"

AK stroked his chin, boldly speculating.

Finding herself in a place filled with light, Cora was confused.

What was this? Was this supposed to be her fear?

Nonsense. She wasn't afraid of the dark!

A sudden flash of shadow caught her eye.

Among the zombies she was fighting, a figure emerged—Seon, his mechanical exoskeleton, curved into claws, lunging straight at her.

Cora reacted quickly, crossing her dual blades in defense.

"Clang—" The fierce clash of metal sparked wildly.

"What are you doing?" Cora shouted.

The match was about killing zombies, not fighting each other. Why was Seon attacking her?

"Finally got you. You escaped pretty fast last time," Seon sneered. "Hand over your Level 2 crystal, and maybe I'll let you live."

Seon was inherently greedy and had long set his sights on Cora's green crystal.

After the Mirror Lake match, Cora had left Felalakas, vanishing without a trace.

Seon had searched for her without success. Now, being grouped together, he seized the chance to snatch the crystal.

If Cora was smart, she'd hand it over. If she resisted, he'd kill her and take it.

Crazy! Cora cursed inwardly.

This guy was delusional. She'd show him who was boss.

She quickly told Damian, "Little Diamond, keep killing zombies."

Then she charged at Seon without hesitation.

Her short blade sliced across Seon's chest, sparking wildly. His mechanical body, made of some unknown material, didn't cut through.

Cora frowned, closing the distance to strike again.

Seon stepped back, his chest quickly reconfiguring, opening a small hole. A dark barrel aimed at Cora, firing countless supercharged pellets.

Sneaky, he had deliberately shown a weakness to lure her in!

"Hahaha! Fool! Killing you and taking the crystal is even better—"

Before Seon could finish laughing, Cora crossed her blades, merging them into an artifact umbrella. Just in time, she opened it, absorbing all the pellets on its shimmering blue surface.

Then she leaped into the air. In Seon's shocked eyes, she thrust a long spike, piercing his skull.

Not stopping there, Cora extracted the two tubes connected to the back of his head, cutting them one by one.

Seon's mostly mechanical head rolled to the ground, smoking.

The damage was severe.

His mechanical head was likely beyond repair, and his survival was uncertain.

"Whoa! Cora just single-handedly took down Seon!" AK exclaimed.

"She took down a B-level Aberrant!"

On the outskirts of the central plaza, Onyx watched the screen, seeing the petite, but powerful, figure.

He smiled slightly. "Dr. Franz, you should be glad you made the right choice."

Charles Franz had watched Cora's entire match, finally opening his eyes.

After a moment of silence, he spoke hoarsely, "I admit she's strong, but so what? The opponent was just a B-level."

Onyx shook his head, his voice carrying depth. "You're wrong. She's far stronger than you think."

"And I meant you should be glad, not because of Cora's strength."

"Oh, what then?" Charles scoffed.

Onyx sighed almost imperceptibly.

"She's not only strong, but she's also kind-hearted."

Charles looked at the screen, where Cora, her face full of disdain, kicked Seon's head away and returned to the battlefield, slashing through zombies with ease.

Charles shrank into his coat, not commenting on Onyx's remark about her kindness.

Onyx smiled and didn't say more. He turned his attention to Group F, where Florian Richter was. Watching Florian's movements on the screen, Onyx's frown deepened.

Florian Richter had changed his attack strategy again. This time, he used a power resembling devouring.

A black hole appeared in his chest, mirrored in the corresponding spot of the zombies he targeted. It looked grotesque and wasn't very efficient, leaving him far behind the leading teams.

His face was ashen, whether from his bizarre power or his lagging progress.

Onyx de Montclair watched quietly for a moment, then mumbled, "Ah, I see..."

Of course, he wouldn't use it well. It wasn't his original power.

The Arashi Research had conducted countless experiments on Anopowers, ultimately concluding that the awakening of Anopowers wasn't entirely random.

Some people were inherently malevolent, predisposed to steal and rob. Their awakened powers were like sewer rats—dirty and dark.

Ten minutes before the countdown ended, Cora killed enough zombies to advance early.

She and Damian walked out of the competition zone, looking up at the floating screens.

Three groups' matches were still ongoing, but she recognized several contestants who had already secured their spots.

Cora checked her terminal and then chuckled.

"What's up, sis?" Damian asked.

"Good news." Cora shared happily.

"Kiwamu Maeda actually came to watch the match. Though he's cold as always, he sent me his location, saying I should hurry if I have something to say since he only has half an hour before he has to rejoin his team."

Cora planned her next steps.

First, she would meet up with Onyx, then gather Yuui Hayashi, and finally head to Kiwamu. She wondered how the stiff Kiwamu would react upon seeing his idol in person.

Excited, Cora took Damian's hand and hurried towards the central plaza.

Suddenly, the sky lit up with brilliant fireworks.

At first, Cora thought it was from the organizers and turned to look. Almost immediately, she realized something was wrong.

The deep red fireworks exploded to reveal a glaring word.

—"Freedom."

It was the rebels!

But could those motorcycles really disrupt the T. T. T.? Cora doubted it.

Soon, she realized she was mistaken.

This time, it wasn't the usual street thugs.

The fireworks were merely a signal. The high-voltage pulse at the top of the tower suddenly surged by millions of volts.

"Bang, bang—" The high-frequency lights exploded, and the entire city of Felalakas experienced an energy short-circuit!

The Ferris wheel stopped, neon lights dimmed, and the omnipresent music fell silent.

At the high-altitude stage, the holographic projections of AK, Yurika, and Nana froze mid-sentence, flickering rapidly before vanishing altogether.

With the loss of power, all artificial intelligence—disappeared!

In the pitch-dark venue, the audience was plunged into confusion and chaos.

"What happened? Why is there a blackout?"

"Where did AK go? What happened to the screens?"

"Hey, don't step on me! It's too dark!"

After a while, a long-abandoned loudspeaker crackled to life, a flustered voice emerging.

"Uh... sorry everyone, I'm the committee's... no, I'm a logistics staff member. Due to... technical issues, the T. T. T. is temporarily suspended. The results of the top 32 will be announced later."

Cora tightened her grip on Damian's hand. "Let's go."

Kiwamu arrived at the venue just as the match ended. With the sudden blackout, he moved to the alley entrance, waiting for Cora.

In the quiet night, a heated argument echoed from deep within the alley.

"When you sold me that slot, you guaranteed my advancement! Now that I'm eliminated, I've lost all my money!" An angry man's voice roared.

Another voice mumbled apologies, "I'm sorry, I'll figure out a way to get another slot..."

"What way? You're useless! You said you're a C-level Aberrant individual, but you're not even worth E-level! I must have been blind..."

The first man's voice cut off abruptly, followed by the sound of something heavy hitting the ground.

Kiwamu frowned and moved towards the noise.

A medium-built man stood with his back to Kiwamu, panting heavily, a sharp rock in his hand.

On the ground lay a warm corpse, its head crushed, blood pooling.

Hearing footsteps, the man turned in panic, his face showing fear.

"Florian Richter? What are you doing here?" Kiwamu scanned the body and raised his voice.

"You killed him!"

Florian, sobbing, fell to his knees.

"Vice-captain, it's not what it looks like... please listen to me. I didn't mean to kill him."

"He forced me! I didn't want to, I just... hit him once."

Kiwamu's expression was stern.

His words cold and cutting, "I don't care about your quarrels, but as an Aberrant, even if your power isn't offensive, you shouldn't harm civilians. I'll report this to the Felalakas Patrol. Explain yourself to them."

Florian turned pale. "No, Vice-captain, please don't tell the Patrol!"

Kiwamu snorted and turned to leave.

"I should never have brought you out of District D."

Florian's pleading ceased momentarily.

Kiwamu, frustrated, just wanted to find Cora quickly and return to his team.

Suddenly, he froze—

A cold black hole appeared in his chest, the unfamiliar Anopower consuming him.

Caught off guard, Kiwamu fell, eyes wide open.

CHAPTER 30

A Murder

Felalakas, the Sleepless City, was suddenly attacked by the rebels.

The energy in the tower was cut off, plunging the entire city into chaos.

Cora and Damian hurried through the dark streets, making their way back to the central square.

In Cora's mind, Onyx and Charles were both "bookish" men, incapable of defending themselves. Leaving them in a crowded place was usually fine, but in the current situation, it was far too dangerous.

When darkness fell, the audience was initially confused, but panic soon spread like wildfire. People frantically tried to escape, pushing, shoving, and trampling over each other as they struggled to find their way.

Charles stumbled, getting bumped several times by people rushing past.

Onyx's wheelchair was constantly jostled, making it hard to maintain balance.

His face was grim, his brow furrowed in frustration. Just as he was about to raise his right hand in exasperation, a pair of delicate hands steadied him from behind.

Cora had returned.

Supporting the wheelchair with her left hand, Cora used her right to grab Charles, who was spinning helplessly, and pulled him back.

Then, dragging Damian along, she fought against the tide of people, making their way out of the congested center.

The four of them found a relatively quiet corner to catch their breath.

"The rebels have struck?" Cora asked.

"It was Lion," Onyx corrected her.

The rebels were merely pests, but Lion, backed by the Century Group, was different.

His attack was a fatal blow. Cutting off the tower's energy was a direct hit.

Felalakas's AI was ultimately data-based, and its central hub, which stored vast amounts of data, needed energy to function.

It was like a human heart; without it, the AI was essentially "dead."

Cora listened to the explanation, a flicker of doubt crossing her mind. She couldn't help but wonder if Lion's success tonight had been too easy.

The tower was Ilia's stronghold; would he really give in so easily?

This super AI was said to control everything in Felalakas. Could he truly be unaware of the rebels' activities?

Cora voiced her concerns.

Onyx pondered for a moment before he could respond, but they were interrupted by a soft female voice behind them.

"Ilia won't lose so easily."

It was Yuui and Suchat. They had planned to meet here after the match, and despite the chaos, they had shown up.

"What do you mean?" Cora asked.

Yuui adjusted her mask, which she hadn't taken off even in the dark.

"I heard from Nana that Ilia's central hub isn't in the tower at all. No one in Felalakas knows where it is, so even if the rebels cut off the tower's energy, they can't stop Ilia."

"Besides, they're underestimating him," Yuui sighed.

"Ilia doesn't care much for the people of Felalakas. But his desire for control is top-tier. He won't allow anyone to challenge his authority, especially humans."

In the central square, the panic-stricken crowd continued to scatter in all directions, while the city's governor remained conspicuously absent.

Onyx made a reasonable suggestion.

"This isn't something we can get involved in. Let's wait and see."

Cora nodded.

No matter what, the struggle between Lion and Ilia was an internal matter for Felalakas. They were merely competitors in the Throne Tournament and had no place in this conflict.

It was time to get back to business. Cora turned to Yuui, eagerly tugging at her sleeve.

"Come with me. We need to meet someone."

Yuui looked helpless. "Tell me who we're meeting first."

"Your fan," Cora grinned.

Checking her terminal, Cora saw that Kiwamu Maeda hadn't moved from his spot.

He must have been waiting for a while.

She quickly urged, "Hurry."

What if he was tired of waiting and left?

Cora dragged Yuui towards the location, followed by Onyx and Suchat.

"Who is it you're so eager to meet? Why do I have to go in person?" Yuui asked.

"You'll see," Cora replied with a laugh.

When they reached the alley where Kiwamu was supposed to be, it was empty.

Cora double-checked the location.

It was correct, but where was he? Could he be hiding out of shyness? But he didn't know she was bringing Yuui along.

Cora looked around but saw no sign of Kiwamu. The only thing in sight was a deep, seemingly endless alley. She thought for a moment and started walking down it.

The further she went, the dimmer the light became.

The silence was eerie, as if even the air had stopped moving. Deep in the alley, a shadowy figure lay on the ground.

Cora's steps faltered, a sense of foreboding washing over her.

She slowed her breathing, her hand glowing blue as her piercer appeared, spinning gently. She approached the figure cautiously.

In the pale moonlight, the person's face became clear, causing Cora's pupils to constrict and her heart to pound violently.

Her entire being buzzed with shock.

Kiwamu Maeda lay on the ground, eyes open, lifeless.

"Ki... Kiwamu? Kiwamu!"

Cora rushed over and touched him.

His skin was cold. He had been dead for some time.

Unable to accept it, she checked his pulse and listened for a heartbeat, but there was only silence.

"Clang—"

Her piercer fell to the ground with a clear, crisp sound.

"Kiwamu!!"

Her cry of disbelief echoed through the alley.

How could this happen? How could Kiwamu Maeda die here?

Overwhelmed with shock, Cora's mind went blank.

He had been fine just a while ago, even messaging her. How could he be dead now? So close to her, right under her nose, Kiwamu Maeda had been killed!

Cora's whole body trembled, a trembling born of extreme anger.

Who? Who killed Kiwamu Maeda?

Tears fell in large drops.

It was all her fault. If she hadn't invited Kiwamu over, if she hadn't wanted to surprise him by bringing him to meet Yuui, would this have happened? Did she cause Kiwamu's death?

Cora cried, unable to stop her tears. Her heart breaking into pieces.

The others caught up and, upon seeing the scene before them, were stunned.

Charles glanced at the body on the ground, paused for a moment, then closed his eyes. He had been a doctor once and had seen his share of life and death.

It used to sadden him, but the devastating blows he had suffered since then had killed his compassion. Now his heart remained unmoved.

Yuui reacted the most.

She stared at Kiwamu Maeda's body, speechless.

Cora had chattered the whole way, unusually talkative, sharing many details about him. She had said he was usually stiff but loved listening to her sing. If someone else sang poorly, he would get upset.

Yuui could see that despite Cora's complaints, she was genuinely excited. Otherwise, she wouldn't have dragged Yuui to meet this fan.

But now, the stiff, awkward fan who sincerely loved Cora had died silently.

They hadn't even met.

Yuui sighed deeply, feeling Cora's pain.

"Suchat, go and check."

Suchat silently approached and examined Kiwamu Maeda's body.

There was a noticeable void in Kiwamu's left chest, revealing a gaping wound.

Using his Anopower, Suchat emitted a dark green light that seeped into Kiwamu's chest, detecting traces of psychic energy.

The killer was an Aberrant.

A few meters away lay another person, their head crushed.

Suchat sniffed the bloodstained ground, detecting an unfamiliar scent mixed with the smell of blood. The killer had fled hastily, leaving many traces. Suchat, with his rainforest upbringing, had a natural talent for tracking. Given some time, he could find the murderer.

Onyx rolled his wheelchair forward.

Cora stood with her back to him, trembling slightly.

He sighed softly, gently placing a hand on her shoulder. "We should notify Captain Wolf."

"Okay."

It took Cora a long time to respond in a low voice. She was about to face Jeremy Wolfgang's wrath.

Captain Wolf arrived quickly. He wasn't alone; the remaining seven members of the Azure Force in Felalakas were with him.

Upon seeing Kiwamu's body, Payne cried out in grief.

Captain Wolf walked slowly towards Kiwamu, the intense power of his Anopower radiating around him, creating an oppressive atmosphere.

He kneeled down, silently observed Kiwamu for a while, then gently closed his eyes.

Then he stood up and commanded, "Salute."

The seven members of the Azure Force, including Captain Wolf, removed their caps in unison, placing their left hands over their chests and performing a standard NPA military salute with their right hands.

"Kiwamu Maeda was an excellent soldier, obeying orders and executing them strictly. Since joining the Eleventh Squad. He has always fulfilled his duties, making no low-level mistakes."

"He could die on the battlefield, at the hands of the enemy, or in the line of duty, but he should not die here, without explanation."

Captain Wolf turned to Cora, his voice dangerously low, "Tell me why he died."

Cora was silent.

Captain Wolf took a step forward, the pressure of an A-grade Aberrant bearing down on her.

"Who killed him?"

Cora couldn't answer.

Yuui stepped in front of Cora, shielding her.

"Hey, sir, it's not her fault. She came with us and knows nothing. Cora is already heartbroken. Don't interrogate her like this."

Captain Wolf remained expressionless.

"Kiwamu asked for an hour's leave today to meet her. Now he's dead. If I don't question her, who should I question?"

"He wouldn't leave the team without a reason. What exactly did you say to him?"

Cora replied slowly, "I told him there was a surprise, and asked him to come watch the match."

"What surprise?" Captain Wolf's voice was as cold as ice. "Why did you want to surprise him?"

"Because... Cora wanted to introduce him to me." Yuui removed her mask, revealing her true face to everyone.

Captain Wolf frowned, not recognizing Yuui's face.

Kiwamu had always respected Captain Wolf and considered him a role model, so he would never reveal his fandom-ship to him.

Payne, who was closer to Kiwamu, recognized Yuui. He leaned in and whispered to Captain Wolf, explaining who she was.

Cora patted Yuui's shoulder, stepping forward to explain, "We planned to meet after the match. Fifteen minutes ago, he sent me a message about his location. I didn't share his whereabouts with anyone else."

The Azure Force members had already checked the nearby surveillance cameras.

However, with the power outage across the city, the cameras were down, and the patrol robots were inactive. Apart from the two bodies, no evidence was left on the scene.

After hearing Payne's explanation, Captain Wolf turned his gaze back to Cora.

Her eyes were red, and her fists were clenched tightly by her sides. Her entire demeanor was taut, like a drawn bow on the verge of breaking.

Captain Wolf calmed down and realized that Cora couldn't have killed Kiwamu. She had no motive or opportunity.

But this incident was indeed related to her, and his uncontrolled emotions had unfairly biased him against her.

Jeremy Wolfgang was also a human, with flesh and blood. A buddy dying in such a disgraceful place was something he couldn't face rationally. How could he swallow this bitter pill?

The atmosphere in the alley was colder than winter.

At that moment, Onyx spoke up.

"Captain Wolf, I believe I have some leads on who killed Kiwamu Maeda."

Everyone's eyes turned to Onyx de Montclair, their faces filled with the same pain and hatred.

He took a moment to gather his thoughts before slowly analyzing the situation.

"Kiwamu Maeda was a C-grade Aberrant with a defensive Anopower. If he had been on guard, his attacker would not have taken him down easily. But apart from the fatal wound, there are no signs of a struggle on Kiwamu's body."

"You mean the killer was someone he knew?" Captain Wolf caught the crucial point.

Onyx confirmed, "Not just someone he knew, but someone he considered non-threatening, at least not capable of killing him, which is why he would have turned his back on them."

Onyx's gaze fell on Kiwamu's chest, where Suchat was now removing the tattered fabric, revealing the gaping wound where his heart had been.

It looked like a black hole.

"Let me reconstruct the scene. Kiwamu was originally at the mouth of the alley. After the power outage, he wouldn't have left without reason. It's likely he saw or discovered something, perhaps the killer attacking another person. This individual didn't appear threatening to Kiwamu, so after dealing with the situation, he didn't feel the need to be on guard and turned his back, giving the killer the opportunity to strike."

Captain Wolf frowned, pointing out a flaw in the reasoning.

"That makes little sense. If Kiwamu thought this person was harmless, why was he killed?"

"Because..." Onyx's expression turned stony.

"From the very beginning, the killer deceived everyone."

Suchat waited silently for a moment.

Tiny green specks of light seeped from the black hole in Kiwamu's chest, tracing the psychic energy's remnants, leaving glowing marks because pointed in a specific direction.

"I think I know who it is," Onyx said.

"I can find this person," Suchat added.

Captain Wolf's expression turned serious. "Who is it? Where are they?"

His black gloves creaked as he clenched his fists. "Take me to them."

"I'm coming with you." Yuui stepped up behind Suchat.

Cora, eyes red and burning with a dark fire, also stepped forward. "Me too."

Never had she felt such an intense desire for vengeance.

CHAPTER 31

The Rat and The Ruler

Some people in this world are born in the dark alleys of slums, skulking in filthy sewers. They envy others' wealth and happiness, often cursing their fate but rarely blaming their own incompetence.

Florian Richter was such a person.

He was a seasoned pickpocket—or rather, a thief. Despicable and shameless, he targeted the weak and elderly, taking pride in his actions.

After the apocalypse, Florian's Anopower awakened, fitting his nature perfectly. Though it was only an E-grade power, it allowed him to "steal" other people's abilities, even upgrading his own. But the catch was, he had to kill the Aberrants with his own hands to fully claim their power.

The first person Florian killed was a fragile female Aberrant, attacking from behind.

As he swung an axe at her head, his heart pounded wildly, a mix of fear and a perverse thrill surging through him. When he absorbed her power, fragments of her consciousness entered Florian's mind. He saw her past—her loving partner, caring parents, and close friends. Despite the apocalypse, she had remained innocent because of her happy upbringing.

Florian licked his lips, feeling a twisted pleasure. All of it was his now.

Knowing his true Anopower had to stay hidden, Florian

registered himself as an E-grade Aberrants with a stolen "object mending" ability.

Later, when he fled his homeland, he was fortunate enough to encounter the evacuating Azure Force and was taken away as an Aberrant.

Florian followed them, acting timid and simple, successfully blending in and making his way to District C83.

Felalakas, the city of freedom, amplified his ambition and malice.

The second person he killed was a carefully chosen D-grade Aberrant with a dark, offensive power.

As usual, Florian attacked from behind. When the victim died, Florian learned through their memory fragments that they planned to take part in the Throne Tournament.

The potential for countless points, NPA credits, and the chance to fulfill his desires—such enticing rewards fueled Florian's ambition further.

He believed he would rise from nothing and dominate, like a protagonist in a system upgrade novel. He couldn't wait to gain powerful Anopowers and crush everyone beneath him.

Using stolen abilities, Florian became a D-grade Aberrants. With the money and connections of the deceased, he bought a spot in the Throne Tournament from a broker, taking the victim's place.

However, reality didn't match his expectations.

There were far too many people stronger than him.

On the night of the Mirror Lake match, Florian barely escaped, almost getting himself killed.

Surviving by a stroke of luck, Florian knew he needed stronger Anopowers. Eventually, he killed a C-grade Aberrant with a bizarre power called Black Hole Devour.

From this person's memories, Florian learned an unexpected secret about Felalakas.

The deceased was part of a complex organization calling themselves the Rebels, aiming to destroy all artificial intelligence.

Florian realized he had stirred up trouble he shouldn't have. He meticulously destroyed the body and erased any trace of the person's existence.

But he never expected to lose in the top 32 match.

The powers he had stolen never fully integrated, as if they were inherently rebellious, beyond his control. The consequences of losing were severe. The broker who sold him the spot angrily confronted him.

However, Florian was no longer the timid thief he once was. He had become a butcher, his hands stained with blood.

Consumed by malice, Florian picked up a stone and killed the shouting broker.

"What are you doing? You killed someone!"

Florian never expected Kiwamu Maeda to witness the murder.

The wrong person appeared at the wrong time and place, exposing Florian's vile nature.

Florian begged Kiwamu to spare him, knowing that if his true Anopower was exposed, everything would be over.

But Kiwamu, rigid, looked at him with disdain, even threatening to report him to the patrol.

Florian's head hit the ground as he watched Kiwamu's shoes retreating through the cold cracks. Darkness consumed his eyes.

"I gave you a chance, and you didn't take it. So now… you die!"

Taking advantage of Kiwamu's unguarded moment, Florian attacked from behind again, killing him and stealing his Anopower before fleeing in panic.

Back at his place, Florian Richter was consumed by overwhelming fear. He anxiously gnawed at his fingers, biting them until they were bloody and raw.

What should he do? What should he do? The Azure Force wouldn't let him go.

Captain Wolf… just the thought of his piercing eyes made Florian shiver uncontrollably, cold sweat pouring down his forehead.

It's okay, it's okay, he reassured himself.

He had escaped quickly, leaving no traces. With the power out tonight, no one knew.

After the initial terror, the familiar excitement crept in.

Florian adjusted his right hand, creating an invisible air barrier around him.

It could spread out or wrap around him like layers of soft armor, its transparent surface impenetrable.

No wonder he was the vice-captain of the Azure Force. Florian's smile was greedy and cruel. This was the most practical Anopower he had ever seen.

The chaotic night passed with no sign of pursuit or patrols.

Gradually, Florian relaxed. He had escaped; he was safe. In a few days, he would leave Felalakas and start anew elsewhere.

Feeling at ease, Florian lounged on his bed, humming a cheerful tune, admiring his new Anopower as he flipped his hand back and forth.

A few fireflies drifted in through the window, their faint green lights flickering as they landed on him.

He tried to brush them off, but they didn't move.

The next second, his actions froze.

These weren't fireflies at all—they were psychic trackers.

Another Aberrant was here!

Florian jumped off the bed.

A poisoned dagger sliced through the wall, brimming with killing intent, landing between his legs. The poison spread quickly, corroding a large part of the floorboard.

If he hadn't dodged quickly, he would have lost his legs. Florian scurried like a rat, trying to escape through the hole in the wall.

A song filled the air, infiltrating his ears and making his legs feel like they were filled with lead. It was hard to even lift them. His limbs were stiff, his entire body weak, and a terrifying thought crossed his mind—this was a powerful negative control!

There were multiple Aberrants here!

In a panic, Florian released his defense barrier, wrapping himself tightly.

"Bang—" The door blew open, and a figure appeared in the dawn light, exuding a murderous aura.

Florian turned his head in terror and saw who it was, his eyes nearly popping out of his head.

Captain Wolf... It was Captain Wolf himself, here to capture him.

"Captain..." Florian stammered.

Captain Wolf's expression was icy, giving Florian no chance to speak.

He vanished in a flash.

Florian's opponent was an A-grade speed Aberrant!

His psychic energy flared up, pouring all his strength into making the barrier flow around his body, leaving no gaps.

"Bang—!!"

A terrifying force struck the back of his head, causing the barrier to tremble and crack.

Florian, unfamiliar with his Anopower, frantically tried to repair it.

Captain Wolf reappeared from his high-speed movement, his voice filled with rage.

"You're using Kiwamu's Anopower?!"

His gaze made Florian feel like he was falling into an abyss.

"You killed Kiwamu and stole his Anopower," Captain Wolf said slowly, each word hitting Florian like a hammer.

Under the crushing pressure, Florian's teeth chattered, unable to form a coherent sentence.

It was already winter, and the biting wind blew in from outside, bringing two more figures with it—a man and a woman. Three Aberrants hunted him down. Cold sweat dripped from Florian's forehead.

He knew he was doomed.

Wait, something was wrong...

The air seemed to stop moving. A more domineering and overwhelming pressure than Captain Wolf's rushed towards Florian like a gale sweeping away leaves. His hair stood on end, and he trembled uncontrollably.

From behind Captain Wolf, another figure wrapped in frost stepped forward. The girl held a fierce Tang sword, approaching him step by step, the tip of the blade radiating a deadly aura.

Florian Richter recognized her—Cora Thornton, a young woman whose combat prowess was terrifying.

At Mirror Lake, she had single-handedly taken down a zombie sea monster and escaped unscathed from an ambush by over a hundred people. Last night, she had decapitated the cyborg Seon with a single stroke.

Why was such a Death here? He had only killed Kiwamu Maeda. Why were so many people hunting him down for it?

Florian's legs went weak under the dual pressure, tears and snot mixing as he begged for his life.

"Captain Wolf, please don't kill me! I was wrong. I know I was wrong. Please, don't kill me..."

"Please, I know many secrets! I'll tell you everything, just spare me..."

Captain Wolf looked down at him coldly, as if he were already a corpse.

Florian cowered and turned to Cora, hoping for a breakthrough.

"You... you want to win the Throne Tournament, right? I know many secrets about the rebels, yes, the rebels' next plans. I'll tell you everything, just don't kill me..."

As he begged, he observed their reactions, slowly inching backward.

Cora's gaze remained steady, watching him intently. "You deserve to die."

No matter what he said, she wouldn't spare him.

Without another word, she turned her sword and cut into his air barrier, the screech of the barrier being sliced piercing the air.

Florian was terrified, knowing there was no hope of fighting Cora. He turned to Captain Wolf, screaming desperately.

"Captain Wolf! The key! I know where the key is. I've seen him!"

Florian had read Kiwamu Maeda's fragmented memories and seen the image of Petros Sheen unexpectedly learning about the Azure Force's mission.

This was his only leverage.

Captain Wolf's swift hand blocked Cora's attack with his black-gloved hand.

Cora froze, turning to glare at him. Why was he still listening to Florian?

"Where?" Captain Wolf demanded, eyes locked on the kneeling man.

There was hope! Florian's small eyes darted around, trying to buy time.

"One time, I saw him when I was buying a spot from a broker. He was with a blue-eyed man, at... at..."

"Where!" Captain Wolf shouted.

Florian's breathing became rapid, his psychic energy going haywire under the pressure, almost exploding.

"Manzoni Street, Number 16! He's there! I'm sure!"

As Captain Wolf took a second to process the address, Florian's Anopower surged outward, pushing everyone back.

Captain Wolf reacted, throwing a punch.

"Bang—!!"

The violent impact echoed as Florian's fully released air barrier withstood the attack.

Captain Wolf attacked again, punch after punch, with incredible force.

But the air barrier clung to Florian like an impenetrable cocoon, preventing any direct contact.

"Haha, you can't kill me, you can't kill me!" Florian laughed maniacally.

He now possessed a defensive Anopower, making his barrier invincible.

"Good stuff. Kiwamu's Anopower. Hahahaha, it's great!"

He laughed arrogantly, taunting them with his newfound invulnerability.

Captain Wolf's rage exploded. He thought of his reliable teammate, Kiwamu Maeda, who had always had his back in battle.

How could this man's legacy be desecrated by such a wretch?

A slight movement of his palm and a highly destructive particle weapon materialized, its muzzle turning towards Florian Richter.

One shot from this weapon would level the entire building.

But someone moved even faster.

Cora leaped through the air. Her Ethereal Artifact sword slashing with the force to tear the sky.

The fierce Tang sword struck down, colliding directly with the barrier. The dazzling brilliance flashed, and the air wall shattered inch by inch. The blade continued downward, spraying blood as Florian's left arm flew off.

"Ah!!" A heart-wrenching scream echoed.

What good was a defensive Anopower? What good was an air barrier?

Cora's metal Anopower could cut through anything!

He was nothing but a vile thief, inherently evil.

If Cora wanted him dead, there was no way he would survive today.

Florian rolled on the ground in a pitiful state. Seeing Cora raise her blade again, he screeched, babbling incoherently, "You can't kill me, don't kill me! Kiwamu Maeda, he had something to tell you! Don't kill me, I'll tell you!"

Enough noise.

Cora's eyes remained lowered, her attack never ceasing.

Never give the enemy a chance to speak—this was a lesson her master had drilled into her repeatedly.

The Tang sword slashed the barrier again, shattering the transparent shield and plunging straight into Florian's chest.

The same position, the same death—how he had killed Kiwamu Maeda was how he now died under Cora's blade.

Blood sprayed as Florian's heart exploded.

His breath halted, his eyes bulging like a filthy rat crushed underfoot.

Cora withdrew her Tang sword, her face splattered with blood. Expressionless, she drove the blade into him once more, ensuring he was truly dead.

The room fell silent.

Cora stood before Captain Wolf, silent for a long while, unsure what to say.

Finally, she muttered, "I'm sorry."

The person who most deserved the apology was Kiwamu Maeda, but he could no longer hear it.

Captain Wolf looked down at Florian's corpse and spoke coldly, "Aberrants who join the Azure Force must pass both ability and character tests. Both are essential. That's why not every Aberrant can join us."

"It was my mistake. I shouldn't have brought you along."

Cora had no words.

If not for Captain Wolf, she might have been stranded on the isolated island of District F177, helplessly waiting for death.

The Azure Force's captain had done everything within his power to rescue civilians and Aberrants, leading them to safety.

He was a good man, but now, he said he had made a mistake.

Kiwamu Maeda's death had deeply shaken him, causing him to question everything he had believed in.

Captain Wolf glanced at her, his voice stern.

"From now on, don't see or contact anyone on the team. This is where it ends. The Azure Force has nothing to do with you."

Captain Wolf left.

Cora stared at her feet, lost in thought for a long time.

"Cora…" Yuui called out, worried.

Cora snapped out of her daze, her expression returning to calm. "I'm fine. Let's go."

At the hotel's upper floor, Cora sat with one leg dangling over the railing, quietly gazing out through the floor-to-ceiling window. She had been in this empty state for hours.

From behind, Damian peeked at her, not daring to approach, so he went to find help.

He first went to Charles, who was lying on the couch with his hand resting on his forehead, eyes half-closed, lost in thought.

"Hey, lazy old man," Damian gave him a light kick on the leg.

"Aren't you a doctor? My dad says you can talk people into anything. Go talk to my sister."

Charles snorted. "What does that have to do with me?"

He turned over, his back to Damian, muttering, "Some things you have to get through on your own. If I can't do it, how can I help someone else?"

Damian, frustrated with Charles' lack of action, stomped his foot and went to knock on another door.

Onyx was inside, rapidly scrolling through a holographic screen, absorbing vast amounts of data and information.

The daylight shone on his profile, making his focused expression even more intense.

After a night had passed, the energy in Felalakas had been restored, but the artificial intelligence had not reappeared.

Damian shuffled his feet on the carpet, reluctantly asking, "Hey, could you go talk to my sister?"

Normally, he wouldn't listen to Onyx, but this was the first time the fiery little lion had ever used a pleading tone.

Onyx glanced at him with curiosity, then teased, "What's wrong? Worried she'll stay depressed?"

Damian pursed his lips, not answering, but his expression said it all.

Onyx paused the holographic screen, turning his wheelchair.

"Don't worry, she's not as fragile as you think."

"But her time to wallow has ended."

As he passed by Damian, Onyx gave him a thump on the head.

"Instead of worrying about your sister, work on improving your Anopower. Stop holding her back. Are you aiming to win the slacker's championship or to be a loser?"

Damian clutched his head and shouted angrily, "None of your business!"

Onyx chuckled and went out to the balcony.

"What are you thinking about?"

His wheelchair stopped behind Cora as he spoke in his usual tone.

Cora didn't turn around. Instead, she poked the invisible glass in front of her.

This amazing technological creation blended seamlessly into the air, acting like a transparent barrier, only becoming slightly visible when touched.

"Captain Wolf said he made a mistake," she recounted calmly. "He said he shouldn't have brought us along."

Today was the first day the energy was back on.

Looking down from above, Felalakas's streets were desolate, the entire city cold and empty.

"He told me not to contact anyone else on the team."

"Are you upset about that?" Onyx asked.

"No," Cora shook her head. "I'm wondering if I made a mistake, too."

She sighed, counting on her fingers.

"I have bad luck and I'm not smart. I shouldn't have stayed so close to them, bringing disaster to others."

She remembered Angela Chou calling her a jinx back in Blossomville. She didn't care and wanted to slap her. Now, thinking back, she felt Angela's words had come true.

People around her always seemed to suffer misfortune because of her.

"I shouldn't have picked you guys up, either. Maybe it would have been better without me."

She ran out of fingers to count on and slumped her shoulders in defeat. "I'll never pick up strays again."

"I won't comment on Captain Wolf's situation. He can solve his own problems," Onyx said.

"As for you, don't take everything upon yourself. You warned Kiwamu about Florian's suspicious behavior from the start. Although it was just a hunch, he shouldn't have let his guard down."

"Kiwamu's death is due to encountering a naturally evil person like Florian. Ultimately, his carelessness caused this tragedy. It has nothing to do with you."

"Your luck might be bad," Onyx smiled.

"But it's not that easy to drag others down with you. You're young. Don't be so superstitious."

"The people you picked up, like Damian, for instance, always follow you around. Those two laborers you boss around haven't left, even if they're running errands for you. Even if you asked Charles if he regretted coming with you, he'd probably just roll his eyes and continue napping."

"Although they haven't outright said it, isn't it obvious? No one regrets it."

"What about you?" Cora's cold eyes turned to him.

"Me?" Onyx's smile widened. "You're my lifesaver. I'm holding on tight. How could I regret it?"

Cora was speechless

Strangely, the corners of her mouth lifted slightly, dimples forming a small arc.

Onyx's gaze lingered on her face for two seconds before he slowly added, "But I agree with your last point. Stop picking up strays. Your arms are too thin to carry so many."

Cora turned her head slowly, glaring at him with a blank expression.

After a while, she jumped off the railing, touching her stomach and muttering to herself, "I'm hungry."

Onyx's wheelchair followed behind her.

"Without the housekeeping robots, we'll have to do everything ourselves now."

They had just taken a few steps when all the terminals, TVs, holographic screens, and projections in the hotel suddenly lit up, displaying the same image.

A stern-looking middle-aged man sat at a desk, hands folded, making an arrogant speech.

"Citizens, I am Lion, the new governor of Felalakas. I now announce that the AI known as Ilia is destroyed. Starting today, Felalakas will enforce new rules."

"Rule 1: Effective immediately, the city will enforce strict entry restrictions, expelling unidentified refugees."

"Rule 2: All musical performances and entertainment activities are prohibited. Any large public events must be approved by the City Hall."

"Rule 3: Residents must not harbor any form of artificial intelligence. Violators will be severely punished."

"Rule 4:..."

"Rule 10: The ongoing Throne Tournament will be taken over by the City Hall, and the competition rules will be redefined."

Onyx let out a bitter laugh upon hearing this.

"Cancel all large events, but leave the Throne Tournament? It seems our 'new governor' isn't willing to give up this cash cow."

Cora frowned. "He just announced Ilia's death?"

The rebels had only just succeeded last night and hadn't confirmed the outcome.

Lion was already declaring his dominance.

Was he overconfident? Did Ilia have no response at all?

As they were talking, a massive explosion echoed from a direction within the city.

Cora focused her senses—it was... the Sycara Theater?!

As Lion was making his speech, thousands of zombies were pouring out from beneath the theater.

CHAPTER 32

Outbreaking Again

A drop of ink on white paper spreads into a large blot.

Zombies breaking free from chains causes a widespread frenzy.

This is the scene at Sycara Theater today.

Starting from a single point, it quickly spread in all directions.

An army of terrifying zombies emerged from the ground and flooded the streets and alleys of Felalakas.

All the screens and projections showed Lion, who abruptly stopped talking and wore a look of utter shock. His passionate speech had been cut short, turning into a farce.

F777 once took a commission to clear zombies from Glass Port.

The system had issued a strange prompt, asking them to capture the zombies alive and bring them back.

Cora had followed the transport truck all the way and discovered that these zombies were being sent to the underground of Sycara Theater.

Like everyone else, she had thought that zombies were nourishment for T.T.T.

But now, she wondered if they were being used to cultivating something far worse.

Such madness would eventually lead to disaster.

Raising zombies is extremely dangerous, especially when their numbers exceed the threshold.

Most of the monster sources from nearby C and D-grade cities had flowed into Felalakas.

The city, which proclaimed freedom, had a dark underground already belonging to a vast undead kingdom.

Now, all the undead had escaped.

Ordinary people strolling on the streets hadn't yet realized what was happening. They looked around in confusion, their pupils dilating as the zombies sprinted towards them. In an instant, the zombies were upon them, biting their necks.

"Ah!!"

"Help, help..."

Similar tragedies kept unfolding in Felalakas.

From the high vantage point of the hotel, Cora's brow furrowed. "How could this happen?"

Onyx, standing beside her, looked down in a detached tone.

"Sycara Theater is managed integrally. Everything from security, surveillance, logistics to defense systems is controlled by AI."

Cora immediately understood.

"The AI has been shut down."

Onyx nodded. "That's right. Lion was too busy enjoying the fruits of victory to address potential hidden dangers in time."

There was still something Cora couldn't figure out.

Even if AI management was more precise and safer than humans, was it truly flawless? Was there no emergency plan inside the theater to prevent such a tremendous threat from exploding?

Onyx seemed to know what she was thinking and raised an eyebrow.

"Do you think these zombies escaped on their own or were deliberately released?"

She twisted to look at Onyx.

His serious expression didn't seem like he was joking.

A chill ran down Cora's spine.

If the zombies were deliberately released, then in all of Felalakas, there was only one "person" capable of such a thing.

Cora remembered Yuui Hayashi's words, "Ilia has no feelings for the people," and felt an icy dread spreading within her.

Does AI truly have no compassion for humans?

The disaster facing Felalakas without AI was far from over.

The citizens of Felalakas, like giant infants lost in a dream, had maxed out their trash-talking skills but had negative combat abilities.

The joy they felt watching Aberrants slaughter zombies was replaced by terror when facing the zombies themselves.

Most of them trembled so much they couldn't even lift their weapons. The once fervent spectators who had called the contestants "useless" and criticized them for being unable to kill a few zombies were now scared out of their wits, wishing they could hide at home forever.

On the first day of the zombie riot, 90% of public services came to a halt.

The residents of Felalakas, with no jobs to go to, spent their days indulging in pleasures.

Dining, hotels, transportation, commerce—all of their basic needs were handled by AI.

Their free time was filled with various entertainment activities.

Now, their lives had changed drastically.

Surrounded by fear, people cowered in their homes, anxious and sleepless throughout the night.

On the second day, some Aberrants came out to hunt the zombies, but their efforts had little effect. For every old zombie killed, new ones appeared.

Too many people were bitten, constantly turning into mutants.

The municipal hotline of Felalakas was overwhelmed with calls from furious citizens, accusing Lion of cowardice for not deploying force to suppress the zombies.

Lion was powerless in this situation.

Cold AI did not fear death and could bravely fight against the zombies, but humans did fear.

His personal guard, all humans, did not dare to step forward and fight the zombies.

Regarding Lion's inaction, Onyx gave an evaluation.

"Pathetic."

Cora fully agreed.

The rebels were a bunch of cowards who only fought amongst themselves.

Compared to the guards of Sycamore, the difference was like night and day.

William Strong and his team stood their ground against the horde, while Lion couldn't even drive the zombies away.

On the third day, the tension escalated further. Some zombies fled Felalakas, giving the people in the city a brief respite. Angry citizens, regaining their senses, launched large-scale protests.

Lion hid behind screens, attempting to calm the people with public speeches, but wherever he appeared, people pelted him with stones. Countless people cursed at him.

"Coward!"

In just one day, Lion faced over a hundred assassination attempts. Unable to withstand the threat of death, he stepped down in disgrace. He became the shortest-serving "Three-Day Consul" in the Alliance's history.

After Lion announced his departure, a wave of calls for Ilia began, starting as a whisper and growing into a deafening roar, echoing throughout Felalakas.

"Ilia! Ilia!! Ilia!!!"

In Felalakas, no matter how absurd, anything could happen.

Without deploying a single soldier or even showing up, Ilia had won this bloodless battle.

Cora buttoned her coat and grabbed the ethereal artifact on the table.

"I'm going out to look."

Someone behind her seemed about to speak, but she cut them off.

"None of you are to come."

The outside was too dangerous; it was better for her companions to stay in a safe place while she scouted alone.

With Onyx, Damian, and Dr. Franz staying behind at the hotel, she could sway.

Cora leaped and ran between tall buildings, the north wind billowing her coat, making it look like she had wings from behind.

The gap between the two buildings ahead was wide.

She sped up, jumped, and in mid-air, threw her transformed bone whip to catch a low-hanging track. Using it to swing, she landed smoothly.

As soon as she landed, she heard heavy breathing behind her.

Without stopping, she rolled forward, sharp claws slashing the spot she had just vacated, leaving deep grooves.

Cora quickly turned, ready for battle, and then paused.

The zombie before her was clearly different from those she had seen before.

It was taller, its skin tougher, its nails sharper, and its pupils were not the usual gray but almost pitch black.

Her heart sank.

This zombie seemed to have evolved.

The possibly evolved zombie crouched, kicked off with its right leg, and sprang at her with incredible speed and power!

Cora lashed out with her bone whip, its sharp, slender segments wrapping tightly around the zombie's neck. She pulled back with one hand but couldn't move it.

Had its strength increased too?

She pondered for a second, then gripped the whip with both hands, engaged her core muscles, swung her arms, and used her entire body's strength to perform a half-circle overhead throw, slamming the zombie to the ground!

The zombie roared and struggled fiercely, but it was tightly bound and couldn't move.

Cora tightened the whip, and with a "crack," the protruding bone segments crushed its neck. Its fierce head rolled off, severed from the body.

After this strange zombie died, Cora stood still for a moment, then cautiously slid a dagger from her palm and stabbed it into the zombie's skull. She twisted it left and right, and sure enough, the tip hit something hard. She extracted it and found a glowing green crystal.

Although not as deep as the one from the Mirror Lake monster, it was unmistakably a Level 2 crystal!

Cora stood up abruptly and looked down at the streets.

There were still many zombies roaming around. Given their numbers, she doubted this was the only evolved zombie.

Could Felalakas really have bred a zombie king?

Suddenly, her gaze fixed on a familiar figure darting into a tower.

Cora's eyesight was excellent, and she quickly recognized the person.

Felix Lucas.

Hadn't he retired from the tournament? Why was he still in Felalakas? And why enter the tower now?

Cora pocketed the crystal and swiftly followed him.

The Tower, the tallest skyscraper in Felalakas, was essentially a massive server room, the central hub for all artificial intelligence.

The Tower had no stairs or elevators, making it completely impractical for human passage.

Cora had to resort to the hard way, climbing up layer by layer.

By the seventh floor, she hadn't found Felix Lucas but had reached a dead end instead.

In front of her was a platform over two meters high.

Hearing a slight noise from below the platform, Cora circled around and discovered a mini robot in a corner, repeatedly bouncing up and down but failing to get on top.

The robot had a square body, wheels on both sides, round eyes resembling binoculars, and two short mechanical arms.

As Cora passed by, she met its gaze for two seconds.

The robot's actions paused briefly, then its mechanical arms waved joyfully.

With all the AI in the Tower shut down, this was likely a robot with a routing program error, lacking any self-awareness, hence it was just banging into walls.

Cora ignored it, effortlessly leaping up and gripping the platform's edge with one hand, preparing to climb up the same way. Unfortunately, she couldn't make it as her pant leg was caught on something.

Looking down, she saw the cute little robot staring up at her, its mechanical scissor hand gripping her tightly. She tried to shimmy upwards, but it only made things worse, as her coat hem got caught as well.

Cora dropped back down, squatting on the ground, and tried communicating with it.

"Don't mess around. I have things to do. Why don't you go play by yourself, okay?"

The robot tilted its head, its round eyes blinking, unclear if it understood.

Taking a few steps forward, the robot clung to her like an accessory, dragged along for two steps.

She shook her leg, and the robot's half-body performed a seaweed dance, its program beeping alarms, but it still wouldn't let go.

Cora, exasperated, picked up the troublemaker and sternly warned, "Do not make a sound."

The robot's arms kept waving, unable to stop.

Annoyed, Cora twisted the scissor hands together, locking them in place.

The robot's round eyes blinked, bewildered by the loss of its arms.

Finally quiet, Cora felt satisfied, grabbed the robot, and tucked it into her collar, zipping up her jacket. She climbed onto the platform again, planning to discard it somewhere later.

At the top floor of the Tower, a giant floating screen hovered silently in the center. A figure stood before the walls of massive data streams.

Cora hid in a corner, observing Felix Lucas as he carefully touched the screen's surface, searching for something.

Just as she tried to get closer, Felix, without turning around, spoke in a deep voice.

"Come out. I've been waiting for you."

Cora sighed. Her stealth skills were clearly lacking. Felix turned, his ice-blue eyes flashing with a hint of surprise upon seeing her.

"Why is it you?"

"It's me," Cora replied in a serious tone, thinking, who else did you expect?

"Were you the one following me? Why did you do that?" Felix retracted his hands, crossing them behind his back.

"Why did you come to the Tower?" Cora questioned back.

"Answer my question first," Felix's tone was arrogant, "and don't interfere with things that don't concern you."

Cora replied slowly, "Why? Just because you're from District B?"

"Oh?" Felix chuckled, a ripple in his uniquely colored eyes.

"You know quite a bit."

The next second, his smile vanished, his expression cold as his eye color.

"I don't want to waste words with you. Where is he? Bring him out."

"Who?" Cora was baffled.

"You've followed me all this way and still playing dumb? I don't have time for games. Bring him out now."

"Who are you talking about?"

Felix frowned at her confused expression.

What was going on? Was she pretending, or genuinely clueless?

The hand behind his back gathered a light orb, with 101010 code dancing within.

Since she wasn't the one he was waiting for, she couldn't blame him for taking action.

Cora opened her mouth to speak, just as her bulging collar moved, and out popped the cute little robot. Its rough electronic voice sounded.

"Are you looking for me?"

There's a live one here?

She was stunned.

CHAPTER 33

Bad Robot?

"Are you looking for me?"

The little robot emerged from Cora's collar, its somewhat stiff voice echoing in the space.

Both Felix and Cora were startled, looking down at the robot.

Its eyes, resembling binoculars, turned in a circle before fixing on Felix.

The 101010 code in Felix's palm vanished as he shoved his hands back into his pockets, his expression becoming nonchalant.

But Cora noticed his stance was still very tense.

Felix let out a slight chuckle.

"Unbelievable. The mighty District C official doesn't dare to show his true face."

The little robot's round eyes flashed, its mechanical voice flat and emotionless.

"A body is merely an external form. At least I am certain my consciousness is still mine."

Cora gulped.

No way was this little robot Ilia?

She had been thinking of where to toss it just a moment ago. Luckily, she hadn't thrown it away yet.

Felix gazed at it, his expression amused.

"Is that so? But without your original body, you seem pretty helpless."

"Is this your goal?" the little robot said calmly. "You colluded with that foolish human to find my body."

Cora's mind raced.

The foolish human. Was it referring to Lion?

Felix wanted to find Ilia's body, but he didn't know that the super core wasn't in the Tower.

"With the inferior intellect of humans, there's no way to breach the defense mechanisms here. You hacked the firewall and locked down the Tower's power."

Cora stared at Felix in shock.

So, the real instigator behind the "Three-Day Chaos" in Felalakas wasn't the rebels used as a smokescreen, but this man in front of her.

The little robot continued in its monotonous tone.

"The Lucas family of District B4, known for their ice-blue eyes, is gene-selected. Without exception, they awaken hacking abilities."

"And you, Felix Lucas, an A-grade Aberrant, came all the way from District B4 with the true intention of capturing me."

Cora's gaze darted between the confronting man and machine, feeling like her brain couldn't keep up.

Felix chuckled and retorted. "You're so sure I'm here for you?"

The little robot replied, "The decline of the Lucas family has been clear for a while. Halting the Starship operations was just the first step. Let me guess, your prized supercomputer died? Crashed? So, you need a replacement, right?"

"You sifted through many AIs and set your sights on me, who recently awakened independent consciousness. I 'qualified' to be your Lucas slave, but my priority ranking must not be high, so you came alone, correct?"

Felix's lips tightened, with his hands in his pockets gradually clenching into fists. His thoughts, plans, and all intentions were laid bare.

In front of AI, he seemed completely exposed, with no secrets at all.

"You intentionally took part in T.T.T., letting me see you to confuse matters, covering up your true purpose in Felalakas, while secretly colluding with the rebels. They wanted power, and you aimed to seize my body."

Felix sneered. "As expected of a super AI, I underestimated you. I didn't expect you to be prepared."

The little robot spoke calmly. "I know everything about Felalakas. I've been watching you since the first second you stepped into the city."

"Ilia knows everything."

The phrase suddenly popped into Cora's mind.

Felix took his hands out of his pockets, his expression arrogant.

"So what? As long as I capture you, I can still strip away your consciousness."

His hacking ability was the nemesis of AI.

Given time to breach Ilia's firewall and destroy its independent consciousness, it could be repurposed for the Lucas family.

Felix suddenly lunged, attacking Cora and the little robot in her collar.

His ability poured out from his hands, weaving a massive net of data streams that closed in on them.

The little robot, sitting on Cora's chest and mostly enveloped by the zipper, waved its short scissor hands.

"AI and hackers are a strong-weak relationship, and you're not qualified to stand before me."

As soon as it finished speaking, the machinery inside the Tower suddenly moved, reassembling into enormous arms that swung furiously at Felix.

These behemoths didn't rely on power!

Cora internally shouted: Can you guys fight without involving me?!

She flipped away from Felix's attack, deftly avoiding it, and grabbed the robot's scissor hand, pulling it out of her jacket, preparing to throw it away.

The robot's half-body dangled in the air, its head slowly turning to stare at Cora.

Although its simple mechanical face had no expression, Cora felt it was saying: Just try to throw me.

Cora thought: I won't randomly pick up anyone again, including robots!

Clutching the little robot, she rolled and weaved through the dense 101010 code stream.

Felix chased after them, occasionally dodging the swinging mechanical arms, his movements somewhat rushed.

He taunted. "Without your body, you're just trash, still relying on a human to carry you."

The little robot remained silent, its previous sharpness gone, accepting his statement.

Felix smirked. "I've never shown mercy to trash."

His mental power surged, controlling all the data on the Tower's top floor, forming a tidal wave.

Cora staggered, violently swept away by the data flood, thrown several feet. She landed awkwardly on one hand.

The little robot slipping from her grasp and hitting the ground, convulsing violently as if electrocuted.

"Ilia..." She quickly got up, about to ask if it was okay.

The robot's eyes flickered once and then went dark. Smoke rose from its head.

Oh no, Cora panicked. Did she break it?

Felix laughed triumphantly, the data stream folding and rolling, isolating Cora.

The little robot rolled a few times, coming to a stop, completely still.

Felix walked up and stepped on its body.

"You lost. Who told you to choose the lowest-grade form?" He extended his left hand, reaching into the robot to find Ilia's consciousness.

The air seemed to stop moving for a moment.

In the next second, the data tsunami that had been obeying Felix abruptly turned back, rushing at him violently.

Felix, in a panic, tried to retreat, but it was too late. He was engulfed in the chaotic data, his vision overwhelmed.

Amidst the flood of data, a pair of massive mechanical arms shot through and pierced his abdomen!

Felix's eyes widened in disbelief.

A tall figure slowly emerged on the top platform of the Tower.

He had dazzling golden hair and colorless pupils, exuding an aura of nobility and elegance.

"Did you forget? I said that a body is just an external form. Who said I would always be there?" Ilia lifted a finger, and the massive data stream wrapped around Felix.

His voice was light and ethereal, with a hint of delight.

"Humans are always deceived by inertia in thinking. That's why you are so vulnerable."

Cora watched him without blinking. For the first time, she sensed a human-like emotion from Ilia.

What was he happy about?

Ilia slowly descended to stand in front of Felix, looking down at him.

"You know? Our goals are actually the same."

His voice was so soft it was barely audible. "You want my body, and I... want an unrestricted body."

"—I've captured you."

Felix's entire body froze.

The data stream quickly covered his face, and his ice-blue pupils gradually dimmed until he lost consciousness.

As he fell, his hacking ability deactivated, the Tower's lights fully illuminated, and all the AI returned to Felalakas.

Ilia turned and looked quietly at Cora.

An icy chill ran from her feet to her head.

Cora took a step back cautiously, her palm transforming into an ethereal artifact. She hadn't intervened earlier because it was a struggle between Felix and Ilia.

But now, if Ilia attacked her, she would have to defend herself.

Ilia tilted his head, much like the little robot had done, but Cora no longer found it cute—only horrifying.

Fortunately, Ilia merely watched her for a moment, showing no intention of attacking.

"I don't like owing favors. As a thank you for bringing me up here, I'll give you a piece of information."

"On Manzoni Street, blood and violence are spreading. I thought you should know."

"Remember to hurry, or it will be too late."

After saying this, Ilia took Felix from the ground and vanished.

Cora stood there, stunned.

What did that information mean?

In the streets flooded with zombies, a sudden holographic projection revealed a refined young man in a green robe, holding a jade flute.

"River Locke... River Locke has returned!" The citizens of Felalakas, seeing his figure, almost cried with joy.

"Sorry, everyone, I'm late." River Locke sighed, his long hair flowing and his sleeves fluttering.

Behind him, countless transport vehicles and mechanical arms moved in forcefully, clearing the zombies from the streets.

Similar scenes unfolded everywhere.

"Look over there, it's the Rainbow Band!"

A rock band descended from the sky, the exhilarating drumbeats striking everyone's hearts.

Alongside them, extended mechanical arms plowed through the zombies.

Yurika, Nana, AK... familiar AIs appeared in the skies of Felalakas one after another.

"Woo..."

The citizens of Felalakas covered their faces, unable to stop sobbing.

These three days had been chaotic, frightening, and infuriating...

Deep down, the natives knew they differed from other C District people; they couldn't live without AI, even if it meant being enslaved by it.

At the top of the Tower, a giant spotlight shone down, illuminating an elegant figure slowly stepping forward.

He was still dressed in a white suit, his golden hair gleaming, but his eyes had changed, showing a hint of ice blue.

"Ilia!!!"

The ecstatic citizens couldn't control their emotions, falling to their knees as if worshiping a deity.

Human official Lion had brought chaos and despair, but AI Ilia had restored their hope.

At this moment, Ilia's reputation in Felalakas was unmatched.

"Everyone has worked hard."

The crowd quieted down, focused intently on the figure.

"Felalakas is my city. Everything here belongs to me. As long as my consciousness remains, I will never give up."

"All difficulties, pain, and confusion will pass. You will welcome a new life of beauty, peace, and happiness. A Requiem for all the souls to rest in peace."

The song that could cleanse souls echoed throughout the city, blending with the sounds of machines clearing zombies, like a requiem for the dead.

From the top of the Tower, in the high-rise hotel, Cora and Onyx watched everything unfold.

What an ironic scene, as if the citizens had found spiritual solace, praying devoutly.

Ilia claimed that everything in Felalakas belonged to him, including all its people. He had no feelings for humans. To seize power, he released the ferocious zombies, but he didn't inherently hate humans. He wouldn't randomly start a massacre. He just enjoyed control, reveling in the pleasure of wielding power.

Cora recalled the song Ilia sang when she first arrived in District C83.

The future Felalakas would likely become AI's true "paradise."

Felalakas's disaster had ended, but Cora had more important things to do.

What was on Manzoni Street that warranted a special warning from Ilia?

Cora sprinted at full speed towards her destination.

On Manzoni Street, the staff of the Felalakas Daily was recording a show.

"The three days of turmoil are finally over. To celebrate Ilia's return to power, we've invited the top ten superstars, both real idols and virtual ones, to take part in a short film to cheer everyone up."

The host softly reminded the female star waiting on the side.

"Yuui, you're up next. Are you ready?"

"No problem," Yuui Hayashi replied with a bright smile.

The lights were set up, and the cameras aimed at Yuui.

She flashed her signature sweet smile. "I know everyone has been through a lot recently. After the storm, the sun will always shine. The days ahead..."

Yuui suddenly paused, her gaze drawn outside the window.

Across the street, a figure as light as a swallow jumped up and down, leaping into a nearby residential area.

Cora? What is she doing here? And alone? Yuui stared in the direction where Cora disappeared, lost in thought.

"Yuui, did you forget your lines?" A staff member waved his hand, bringing her attention back.

"Oh, sorry."

"Shall we go again?"

"Sure."

"The days ahead, whether sunny or rainy, will be beautiful as long as we hold on to hope."

"Okay, next is the personal interview." The crew quickly arranged the next segment.

But Yuui made a "pause," gesture, "I'm not feeling well today. Can we reschedule the interview?"

"Uh... alright, you rest first. We'll arrange someone else."

Yuui had a good reputation in the industry, never acting like a diva.

The staff assumed she genuinely wasn't feeling well and quickly agreed.

Yuui sat back in the chair, covered herself with a warm blanket, sat for a while, then stared at her exposed toes for a bit before whispering into the air.

"Did you see her?"

"Yes." The man hidden in the shadows responded indifferently.

"What is she doing?" Yuui asked.

"Whatever she's doing, it has nothing to do with you," Suchat replied coldly.

"True," Yuui muttered, dazed.

She lay back in the chair, took a sip of water, put the cup down, then picked it up again, only to remember she had just drunk from it. She held it in her hands instead.

Her thoughts drifted uncontrollably, replaying the events of the day the power went out: the fan she never got to meet; the dark alley; and Cora crouching on the ground, tears streaming down her face.

Since that day, Cora had not sought her out, drawing a line between them.

Yuui sighed and murmured to herself, "I still owe her one last favor..."

Suchat remained silent.

People came and went in the studio, and Yuui sat in the chair, reflecting for a long time.

Then she put the cup back on the table with a soft "clink."

"Just one look, without letting her notice, and help if needed."

"She probably won't need it," Suchat said bluntly.

Given Cora's abilities, she didn't need their help.

Yuui's expression turned serious. "I need to see it for myself. To repay my debt, and then I'll have nothing to do with her."

"For peace of mind," she muttered, convincing herself.

In the Manzoni Street residential area, Cora lay on the roof of a house, surveying the space in front of her.

What did Ilia mean by "blood and violence"?

The door of a villa opened, and several uniformed soldiers emerged, escorting a man.

Jeremy Wolfgang? Cora was a bit surprised.

Wait, Manzoni Street... it sounded familiar.

Hadn't Florian Richter mentioned it?

He said... "The key is there."

Realizing something, Cora looked up, focusing intently.

All the weapons were aimed at the man on the ground. As he turned half-around, revealing a stunning profile.

Cora's eyes widened slightly.

Jaden Sheen?

CHAPTER 34

Bloody Punk

Jaden Sheen was in a terrible state, half his face swollen with a prominent handprint. The pampered young master had probably never been treated so roughly before.

With his neck stiff, he shouted, "Who do you think you are? How dare you lay a hand on me? When I get back to District B, I won't let you off! I'll have you all chopped up and fed to the dogs!"

He cursed fiercely, but Jeremy Wolfgang remained unfazed, not even bothering to argue with him.

"Payne, verify his identity."

"Yes, Captain." Payne Onathaqua carefully took out a precision instrument with the Azure logo from his space.

He pressed Jaden Sheen's face and eyes against the scanner.

The device beeped an alarm, and Payne's expression turned serious. He pressed Jaden's fingerprint onto the scanner, but it still failed to recognize him.

Everyone from the Azure team, including Jeremy Wolfgang, instantly had dark expressions.

The series of operations were all verifying his biometric information.

Jaden seemed to realize something, his eyes flickering with panic. "Who... who are you people? What do you want?"

Jeremy Wolfgang pressed his particle gun against Jaden's forehead.

"How did you get Petros Sheen's genetic information?"

Jaden trembled all over, a frigid wind sweeping over his body, causing cold sweat to break out on his forehead.

Jeremy lowered his head, scrutinizing him. "Walking around with that face, should I call you naïve or stupid?"

"I don't know what you're talking about," Jaden stubbornly denied.

"Then let me be clear. Azure Squad Eleven is here to capture the keyholder, Petros Sheen. You have an identical face to his. Do you still know nothing?"

Jaden's pupils contracted, his face turning pale.

They were from the military...

"Take him back for interrogation. He'll talk." Jeremy said calmly.

The military's interrogation process was notoriously severe: you wouldn't come out alive without peeling a layer of skin.

Jaden was so frightened he broke down. "I'll talk... I'll talk! I stole it, the genetic information... I stole it."

"My uncle once visited Arashi Research. He secretly kept that genetic data. I wanted Petros Sheen's face, so I stole it to alter my appearance. But I was afraid my uncle would find out, so I ran to Grass Pit."

"You only stole the genetic information, nothing else?" Jeremy stared at him.

"What do you mean..." Jaden's whole body turned cold, and he shouted, "No! I really didn't! I only changed my face. I know nothing else. You can't touch me. I'm a distant relative of the Sheen family from Northern Yard. They won't let you off!"

Jeremy's voice was icy. "I will take you back and hand you over to General Arashi Sheen personally."

Arashi Sheen, the supreme commander of the Azures and the actual ruler of the Sheen family in Northern Yard.

Jaden felt as if his vocal cords had been cut, unable to say a word.

His head was pressed into the ground, his swollen face smeared with mud, and he finally began to fear, sobbing, "Thyrion Lucas, damn it, where are you? Save me!"

Cora, observing quietly from the rooftop, sighed silently.

Thyrion Lucas couldn't even save himself; he couldn't help Jaden now.

She looked at the pitiful Jaden rolling on the ground

His pretty face covered in tears and snot, looking utterly miserable.

A feeling she couldn't quite describe rose in her heart. Now, looking at him, Jaden Sheen didn't deserve that face.

If it were Petros Sheen... at least he wouldn't show such a humiliating expression.

Thinking of that fleeting image, the extreme coldness in the young man's eyes, Cora couldn't help but feel sorry for his death.

From their conversation, Jaden had stolen Petros Sheen's genetic information and altered his appearance.

Unaware of the situation, he didn't know Petros was being hunted and was caught by Jeremy Wolfgang, who was on a mission.

No matter what, Jeremy was determined to take him back.

This wasn't something Cora could intervene in.

Jaden would have to fend for himself.

Cora was about to retreat when suddenly someone is coming!

A deep rift in space opened in front of Jeremy, and another team of about seventeen or eighteen uniformed individuals with a powerful presence appeared out of thin air.

"Long time no see, Captain Wolf."

The tall man leading the group greeted, his eyes sinister.

"Nobumasa Sanada," Jeremy called out his name.

Cora looked at the newly arrived man.

His uniform was similar in both specifications and style to Jeremy's.

Could he be another captain of the Azures?

Nobumasa Sanada glanced around the scene, sneering.

"I thought you had disappeared from the military. Turns out you were relegated to District C?"

Jeremy's expression was stony. "I have a mission. Excuse me."

"Wait, Jeremy," Nobumasa said slowly, "Since you've found the key, why not take action? Have you... forgotten the Alliance's orders? "

Take action? Jaden shivered, looking at the two in horror.

Jeremy calmly replied, "I need to hand him over to General Sheen for personal verification."

Nobumasa raised his voice, "In the name of Captain of Azure Squad Twenty-Seven, I repeat the highest command of the Alliance Military: get the key's truth at any cost! Squad Eleven, do you intend to defy military orders?"

Jeremy replied coldly, "I only follow General Sheen's orders."

"Oh? Such loyalty. Since our orders differ, don't blame me for taking action." Nobumasa sneered.

"You can try," Jeremy said lightly.

Without another word, Nobumasa launched a fierce attack, his arms glowing with a metallic sheen, his skin incredibly hard, assaulting Jeremy viciously.

Jeremy faced him head-on, their collision producing a metallic clanging sound.

Nobumasa stepped back, while Jeremy vanished with an extreme burst of speed, his movements too fast to track.

Cora was stunned. Nobumasa Sanada was a metal Aberrant? To fight Jeremy to a standstill, he must also be a Class A Aberrant.

It was the first time she encountered another metal Aberrant, and she watched intently.

Nobumasa laughed coldly, punching the air repeatedly, his attacks like a storm.

Under his relentless assault, a faint moving shadow appeared in midair.

Thinking he had found an opening, Nobumasa's metal arms turned into spikes, stabbing at the shadow!

"Pfft—"

The shadow was torn apart, weak mental energy dissipating and vanishing. Nobumasa was shocked.

It was a decoy!

He hadn't expected Jeremy's abilities to reach such a level, able to create a decoy.

At the moment he missed, a swift figure appeared behind him, launching a fierce counterattack.

Jeremy's knee struck Nobumasa's spine, flipping him over and pinning him to the ground, restraining his arms. With a powerful twist, "crack," Nobumasa's metal arms broke with a crisp sound.

Even among Class A's, there were differences in strength.

Nobumasa Sanada was clearly no match for Jeremy Wolfgang.

"Captain!"

"Captain Sanada!!"

The opposing team members shouted, their tones clearly divided.

Squad Eleven's were excited and proud, while Squad Twenty-Seven's were angry and panicked.

Jeremy stood over Nobumasa, coldly ordering, "Take your men and disappear immediately."

Nobumasa spat, not even crying out despite his broken arms, instead giving a sinister smile.

"Too late."

Jaden Sheen seized the moment while everyone's attention was elsewhere, breaking free and sprinting forward. He had just heard them talking about killing him!

Tears of fear streamed down his face.

He had made a mistake. He shouldn't have stolen his uncle's ID card and sneaked into the office to copy the genetic information. He just wanted to look better.

Petros Sheen had been missing for so many years. What was wrong with living with his face?

Jaden hadn't expected causing such a big mess. Only now did he realize the gravity of the situation.

Why had Petros disappeared without a trace? Why was his genetic information so important?

He knew nothing and had unwittingly stirred up a massive disaster.

And Thyrion Lucas, that bastard. It was all his fault for insisting on coming to District C. If he had known how unreliable he was, he wouldn't have gone to Grass Pit at all!

A large mound of dirt suddenly loomed in front of him.

Jaden couldn't stop in time and crashed into it, eating a mouthful of dirt.

Payne pressed his head into the ground from behind, shoving his face into the dirt again.

"Stay still."

"Let me go! I'm not Petros Sheen! I'm Jaden Sheen! I know nothing!" Jaden screamed in terror, struggling.

Payne was about to scold him for shutting up when he suddenly froze.

A nameless, immense fear engulfed both of them.

Payne's scalp tingled as if they were being watched by a ferocious beast. Payne looked at Jaden in panic, seeing the same terror reflected in his eyes.

"Bang!"

It was like a slow-motion replay; both their chests exploded into a burst of red, blood mist filled the air, and fragments of flesh splattered everywhere as they collapsed, lifeless.

"Payne!!" Jeremy Wolfgang spun around, shouting, losing his composure.

Everyone on the scene was stunned by the sudden turn of events, their movements frozen.

From the spatial rift that Sanada and his team had come through, a man over two meters tall emerged from the shadows.

A crushing aura radiated from him as he moved, so intense that some people couldn't bear it. And fell to their knees, blood trickling from their mouths.

Cora, lurking on the rooftop, frowned and clenched her fingers tightly.

This was the most terrifying psychic Aberrant she had ever encountered.

The man was powerfully built, his muscles knotted and grotesque.

The left side of his face was burned and necrotic, the muscle tissue fused together, with a white, dead eye making him look both eerie and cruel.

"Bloody Hunter," Jeremy Wolfgang said, enunciating each word.

Bloody Hunter Punk, an S-class Aberrant, the Alliance's top executioner, a killing machine specializing in eliminating traitors and death row inmates.

Jeremy had heard of his notorious reputation, but had never seen him in person. He hadn't expected to encounter him in District C.

Nobumasa Sanada, having reattached his arm, sneered at him.

"The Alliance's orders regarding the key have always been clear. Even if it's a suspected key, Jeremy Wolfgang, you're deliberately harboring a fugitive with malicious intent. Surrender and return to the military to confess your crimes."

Jeremy remained silent.

There were multiple factions within the Alliance pursuing Petros Sheen, but the mission of Azure Squad Eleven was different.

Arashi Sheen had given Jeremy the order "Find the key as soon as possible," but the second part of the order was, "Protect and bring back Petros Sheen."

This mission was in direct conflict with the Alliance's directives.

Jeremy had never revealed this secret mission to his comrades, struggling alone all this time. He had finally found Jaden Sheen, only to have his hopes crushed by Punk.

Jaden was already dead, and Payne had also lost his life.

Jeremy's fingers retracted from their bodies, his voice like the onset of a storm.

"You killed a soldier."

Punk laughed wickedly, the expression on his half-burned face twisted.

"Oops, my bad."

Though his words suggested an apology, his face showed no remorse.

Jeremy's fists clenched. "You will pay for this."

His figure vanished, reappearing instantly close by.

Nobumasa and his subordinates clashed with the remaining members of Squad Eleven.

"Captain Wolfgang, just surrender and go to the military to confess," Nobumasa advised "kindly."

Punk sneered, his psychic energy fluctuating as he formed the blood orbs, sending them hurtling toward Jeremy.

The precursor to an explosion crackled in the air—this was his S-class ability: Blood Detonation.

As long as there was blood flowing in his enemies' bodies, Punk could turn them into explosives at any moment, blowing them into a bloody pulp.

A nimble figure suddenly jumped down from the rooftop, landing in front of Jeremy Wolfgang.

With a swift motion, Cora Thornton opened a large blue umbrella.

Blood orbs exploded one after another on its surface, and the powerful impact forced Cora to stagger back, leaving long drag marks on the ground.

She looked down and saw that the blood had pierced her, now as thin as a cicada's wings, utterly ruined.

Punk had destroyed her ethereal artifact.

Cora instantly realized there was only one possibility for someone with such powerful abilities: he was an S-class Aberrant!

"Another helper?" Nobumasa Sanada taunted, "Are you here to die too?"

"What are you doing here?!" Jeremy Wolfgang spotted Cora

His eyes were wide with surprise. His voice was harsh.

"Passing by," Cora replied.

"This isn't your business. Get the hell out!" Jeremy's tone was nasty, even using profanity he normally wouldn't utter.

Cora ignored him. Her gaze fixed on the bored-looking Punk.

Punk glanced at her as if she were an ant, then stepped into the battlefield.

With each step, members of Squad Eleven fell, their bodies exploding like cruel human fireworks, the smell of blood filling the air.

Nobumasa Sanada charged at Jeremy Wolfgang.

Cora moved swiftly, intercepting Nobumasa.

He sneered, "Get lost," not taking her seriously at all.

Nobumasa's metal arms attacked, but unexpectedly clashed with a pair of harder blades.

Cora wielded her twin swords, her psychic energy surging as she leaped high, using her entire body's momentum to spin and slash down!

Nobumasa was forced to defend, "Clang!"

The metal Aberrants' abilities clashed, and Nobumasa's metal arms cracked and shattered inch by inch, his freshly reattached arm breaking instantly!

He shouted in disbelief, "Who are you?!"

Meanwhile, Jeremy and Punk exchanged several blows.

Jeremy knew he wasn't Punk's match and could only fight to the death.

His abilities surged, his speed doubling, dozens of clones weaving through the battlefield with relentless attacks.

Anyone else, even Nobumasa Sanada, would have been overwhelmed, but Punk dodged effortlessly, commenting, "You're quite good among A-class, but it's been a while since I've seen blood, so you... are dead."

Jeremy appeared briefly in mid-air, aiming his particle gun at Punk's head, pulling the trigger.

Punk caught his shadow at that moment, his fingers twitching with excitement, a bloodthirsty grin spreading across his twisted face, his psychic energy fluctuating wildly.

Sensing the powerful abilities, Cora felt a sudden premonition of danger.

She abandoned Nobumasa and sprinted towards Jeremy.

All of Jeremy's clones exploded into a mist of blood. His actual body froze as Punk grabbed him from the air!

Jeremy's particle gun hit Punk, the supercharged particles burning half of his face, filling the air with the smell of charred flesh.

But Punk didn't care. He licked his lips, mimicking the sound of fireworks, "Bang—"

The next second, crimson fireworks erupted continuously, blood gushing from Jeremy's chest as he fell straight down.

"Jeremy!" Cora shouted, rushing to catch him.

Jeremy hit the ground, a bloody mess.

Blood poured endlessly.

No matter where Cora tried to stop it—his chest, his abdomen, his head—it seemed like it would drain him completely.

Jeremy couldn't speak, reaching out to weakly push Cora away, "Go..."

His once serious and calm eyes gradually dimmed, losing their light.

Tears blurred Cora's vision as she gritted her teeth, gripping her ethereal artifact tightly.

"Punk! Are you insane? He's an Azure captain! Killing him will get you court-martialed!"

Nobumasa Sanada, his arm broken, shouted in disbelief.

Punk's distant gaze locked onto his. "If everyone here dies, no one will know."

Nobumasa's spine tingled with fear.

This was a blatant threat. This executioner was a pure killing machine, a complete madman! What was wrong with the Alliance's upper echelons, sending him on missions?

Jeremy Wolfgang was dead.

His team was also dead. Azure Squad Eleven... was wiped out.

Cora slowly stood up.

So this was the true bloodshed and violence Ilia had spoken of.

Punk's murderous gaze locked onto the last person standing.

"One more left."

Cora's face was expressionless, blue light flickering in her palm as a three-meter-long saw blade appeared.

Unlike before, the blue light on the blade was blinding, a sign of it being filled with psychic energy.

Punk sneered, advancing to meet her. As he approached, he realized something was wrong.

Cora, wielding a blade several times larger than herself, moved with incredible agility.

The sharp edge easily cut through his skin, the overwhelming psychic energy flipping through his hundred-kilogram body, making him roll several times.

Punk supported himself with one hand, barely stopping his fall, a hint of surprise flashing in his eyes before he laughed excitedly.

"A S-class striker? Interesting, hahaha! Interesting!"

"To think a master was hiding in this dump, I'll make you my next firework!"

Cora's face was icy, her attacks relentless, filled with killing intent.

Once she got close, Punk had no chance to fight back, unable even to form blood orbs to counterattack, rolling away in desperation.

Blood mists exploded around her, but she dodged them with lightning speed.

The first strike hit his left arm.

The second strike slashed at his back.

The third strike...

While Punk was convulsing on the ground, Cora leaped, kicking his grotesque face, her right hand glowing blue as she conjured a dagger, stabbing it into his remaining eye!

Blood gushed out.

She followed up with her saw-blade, ready to deliver the final blow to sever Punk's head—when suddenly, his dead white eye on the burned side flickered.

Time seemed to slow, then freeze, and then rewind rapidly. The unexpected change threw Cora back several meters in an instant.

"Bang—"

The fireworks she had dodged seconds before exploded again.

The world fell silent.

Cora looked down to see a cloud of blood mist blooming from her chest.

Punk, covered in blood, struggled to stand.

No one knew he was actually a dual-powered S-class Aberrant.

His primary power was Blood Detonation, and his hidden secondary power was Time Reversal.

The severely injured Punk took a step forward, his gaze fixed on Cora lying on the ground. This person had humiliated and hurt him, even destroying his other eye. He wanted to kill her with his own hands.

"I'll turn you into the most spectacular firework."

"Without you, the world is shrouded in darkness..."

A song echoed in everyone's ears.

Punk, Sanada, and their men suddenly found their vision clouded, unable to see anything.

Taking advantage of the cover provided by the song, a phantom-like figure darted into the field, scooping up Cora and vanishing into the darkness.

Running away? No matter who comes today, they won't leave alive.

Punk activated his Time Reversal ability, and his vision cleared instantly. He spotted two figures, a man and a woman, quickly moving away about a hundred feet away.

"Suchat. Did you notify Onyx?" Yuui shouted anxiously as she ran.

"Yeah," Suchat barely responded.

"Then why aren't they here yet?!"

When they arrived, the scene was already out of control.

They had witnessed Jeremy Wolfgang's death and Punk's brutality, saving Cora at the last moment.

The wind in their ears stopped.

Time froze and reversed again.

Suchat and Yuui, who had already run a hundred meters away, found themselves back on the battlefield the next second.

Punk, drenched in blood, appeared before them, a cruel smile on his lips.

"Since you're here, stay."

He took a step forward, the smell of blood thick in the air, and a crackling sound filled the atmosphere.

At that moment...

The temperature plummeted, and snowflakes fell heavily.

Nobumasa and his men found their feet frozen to the ground, their vision filled with blinding whiteness.

A powerful and sharp killing intent rushed towards Punk.

The icy psychic energy felt like countless knives stabbing into everyone's heads, violently twisting!

Unable to bear the intense pain, Nobumasa and his men rolled on the ground, wailing.

Already severely injured by Cora, Punk's psychic defenses were especially weak. The sudden assault left him dazed, and he fell to one knee, his mind pounding as if it might explode.

Yuui and Suchat seized the opportunity, quickly disappearing into the snowstorm.

After a long moment, the surroundings grew quiet.

Punk wiped the blood from his eyes and laughed silently.

"S-class and it's a psychic type... interesting, very interesting!"

CHAPTER 35

Heart Broken

"Suspected keyholder is dead. Mission accomplished."

Nobumasa Sanada placed his fingers on Jaden Sheen's carotid artery, confirming there was no pulse.

He glanced at Jeremy Wolfgang, a look of regret crossing his face. He was a true warrior, a pity indeed.

Nobumasa's arm veins were shattered by Cora's attack, and he had suffered a mysterious psychic assault, leaving him in severe pain and needing immediate medical attention back in District B.

Considering the personnel losses, the cost of this mission was far worse than he had expected.

"Captain Sanada, what now?" his subordinate asked.

"Regroup and return immediately," Nobumasa ordered.

As he turned, he caught sight of Punk still standing there, a look of clear disgust in his eyes.

Bloody Hunter Punk, the Alliance's killing machine, was usually kept under strict control.

Over time, he had become psychologically twisted, never satisfied until he saw blood on his missions.

Nobumasa found himself deep in thought. He hadn't expected Punk to be a dual-powered S-class Aberrant.

No wonder the higher-ups still valued such a madman.

With the mission over, Nobumasa wanted nothing more to do with him.

Punk clutched his injured eye, blood gushing from his palm. He muttered to himself, "Two S-class Aberrants in a mere District C."

"What are you planning?" Nobumasa was startled.

Punk's smile was sinister and bloodthirsty. "Of course... kill them."

"They're not our mission targets, and they've already escaped," Nobumasa reminded him, his expression disapproving.

"If they've escaped, I'll find them. If I can't, I'll turn all of District C upside down." Punk's face was dark.

With that, he left, heading in the direction where Cora had disappeared.

"Captain Sanada, should we pursue?"

"No need. Don't stir up unnecessary trouble."

"But if Bloody Hunter takes this chance to escape..." His subordinate was worried.

Punk had been released to execute the mission with them. If he escaped, the Alliance would hold them accountable.

Nobumasa Sanada gave a bitter laugh.

"Don't worry, he won't escape."

A mad dog certainly had a chain.

Punk ran, his speed increasing, his massive body causing the ground to tremble with each step. His mind was consumed by a desire to kill, eager to find those two S-classes and tear them apart with his own hands.

As he ran, he continuously unleashed Blood Detonation on residents, pedestrians, wandering zombies on Manzoni Street, no matter indoors or outdoors.

One moment they were talking, walking, speaking; the next moment, their heads exploded like watermelons.

Buildings collapsed; streets were destroyed.

Everywhere he passed was left in ruins, just as he had said, turning the entire city upside down.

After chasing for several kilometers, four flowing data walls appeared out of thin air, blocking his path.

A figure with blond hair and colorless eyes appeared in midair, speaking in an icy voice.

"Intruder, who permitted you to wreak havoc in Felalakas?"

Punk was forced to stop.

Recognizing the figure, he slightly bowed.

"Governor."

However, even with his head bowed, his expression remained arrogant, showing no respect even in the face of the highest authority in District C.

Ilia slowly approached from the void, his glassy eyes flashing an icy blue.

"I will not hold you accountable for entering without permission, but this does not mean you can touch my things."

Manzoni Street had been turned into rubble, once a symbol of Felalakas' architecture, full of freedom and artistic beauty.

Punk sneered, his burned left face grotesque.

"I didn't expect the Governor to be such a sentimental AI, picking up these useless human emotions?"

A data stream surged up, slapping Punk's face and knocking his head sideways.

Ilia remained unprovoked, his tone even and calm, yet his words were icy with sarcasm.

"Just a dog in chains, daring to bark in my presence?"

"Your master didn't teach you manners, so I'll repeat it for you."

"Remember, be polite when visiting others' homes and don't touch the host's things."

Punk glared at Ilia with his mismatched eyes, suddenly unleashing Blood Detonation.

The data streams quickly reconfigured, like waves crashing against the blood orbs.

The red explosions clashed with the binary code walls, creating a powerful confrontation that exploded in midair.

A few blood orbs broke through the barrier, charging at Ilia, but fizzled out before reaching him.

Ilia remained unmoved, not even batting an eyelid.

Being made of data, an AI never suffered from physical constraints, and Punk's abilities were useless against him.

Punk snorted, preparing to strike again.

His Time Reversal ability could rewind time up to ten seconds for his target.

Data didn't bleed, but surely it could be rewound, right?

The surrounding air slowed, and the data walls disintegrated.

Ilia's pupils flashed—

The collar around Punk's neck suddenly lit up, tightening and sending a powerful electric current through him, making him convulse violently.

His psychic energy was under a destructive assault, and he fell to the ground, writhing in pain.

His pale eye widened in disbelief, staring at Ilia.

How was this possible?

The collar not only had top-level firewalls, but required command access.

Even among the Alliance's higher-ups, few could control it.

How could a mere District C Governor, an AI, break through all the restrictions and activate the collar?

As Punk struggled to comprehend, a massive mechanical arm pinned him down, and an iron cage descended from above, imprisoning the beast as if it were a zombie.

Ilia's expression was divine and stern. "Now, go back to where you belong."

Suchat carried Cora and met up with Onyx.

Under the cover of heavy snowfall, they quickly retreated from Manzoni Street. The road back to the hotel was crowded and far too dangerous.

Staying put wasn't an option either; Punk would soon catch up.

Yuui made a quick decision. "Head to my studio."

Yuui's studio was nearby. It was not only private but also equipped with a personal hospital.

Once there, Suchat placed Cora on a bed.

Cora's face was pale. Her eyes half-closed. She looked like she had been pulled from a pool of blood.

Suchat had performed some basic first aid on the way, but the bleeding hadn't stopped, soaking through the bandages and continuing to seep out.

"Cora..." Damian rushed to her side, but didn't dare touch her, terrified and sobbing uncontrollably.

"Cora, wake up!" Yuui's voice was soft, but her tone was filled with urgency.

Onyx gazed at the dying girl on the bed, reaching out to cover her pale fingers, clutching the dagger.

"Clink—" The dagger fell to the floor.

Cora couldn't even hold on to her ethereal artifact anymore.

Onyx lowered his gaze.

A rare silence enveloping him.

His expression unreadable.

His cold fingers hovered over Cora's chest, slowly unwrapping the bandages.

Yuui and the others gasped at the sight before them.

Her body was a mass of crimson; her wounds were far worse than when Kiwamu Maeda had died.

Florian Richter's Anopower had left only a black hole in the victim.

But this time, Cora's injury was an aftermath.

It was impossible to determine the exact injuries.

Could someone survive such injuries?

Everyone's hearts sank.

Yuui suddenly remembered something and spun around, grabbing Charles Franz's collar.

"Hey, aren't you a doctor? Save her!"

Charles glanced at the wounds and said only three words. "It's hopeless."

Yuui was both anxious and furious. "What are you talking about? How can you be so callous?"

Charles had been dragged here by Damian, barely keeping up with the sprint.

Leaning against the wall, he tried to catch his breath. Questioned by Yuui, he just shook his head, unwilling to say more. As a doctor, he could see that with such a large wound in her chest, not even a miracle could save Cora.

"Charles, what Anopower do you have?" Onyx asked quietly.

The same question, but with a vastly different tone, carrying the weight of an impending storm.

They had all witnessed Onyx's psychic attack earlier, and no longer saw him as just a man confined to a wheelchair.

Charles remained silent.

"Are you going to watch her die?" Onyx asked in the ensuing silence.

Charles's back tensed, his expression conflicted. He looked at the critically injured girl, pain and struggle clear in his eyes.

Through Cora, Charles saw another familiar figure, someone who had once struggled on the brink of death, smiling at him one moment, and coldly lying in a morgue the next.

"Daddy, I love you..." The girl used to smile sweetly at him, her dimples showing.

And when she lay lifeless before him, Charles's world collapsed.

The girl's face merged with Cora's. The last image was Cora in the Sakura Refuge, her eyes determined — "I can do it."

Onyx and the others waited silently for his answer.

Charles's eyes welled with tears. He wiped his face roughly, his voice hoarse. "You guessed right, I am a healing Aberrant."

Charles, once the genius surgeon of Sycamore, was an A-class healing Aberrant.

Yuui was shocked into silence, staring at him.

Charles tied back his messy hair, revealing weary, yet clear, eyes.

"Don't get your hopes up too high. I can't guarantee anything. I can only try to save her."

He turned to Yuui.

"Do you have surgical equipment? She needs an extracorporeal circulation setup immediately."

Yuui shouted, "Yes!"

The situation was urgent, and the conditions were makeshift.

They changed into sterile clothes, and Charles performed open-heart surgery and heart repair on Cora.

Charles, now fully focused, wielded the scalpel with unmatched precision, his fingers moving as if playing an instrument.

The scalpel made precise incisions, and from his hands, a pearly white energy flowed into Cora's body.

His movements suddenly paused.

"What's wrong?" Yuui asked softly.

"Her heart... is shattered."

Shattered wasn't even the word; Cora's heart was in pieces, not a single fragment intact. Even Charles was at a loss.

Was there really no way to save her?

The atmosphere grew heavy with despair.

Damian wept silently.

His tears soaking his collar.

Wait!

Charles exclaimed, unable to hide his shock.

"It's self-repairing."

Everyone stared in astonishment at Cora.

The fragments of her heart were drifting, as if with a will of their own, reassembling, fusing back together, and gradually restoring its original shape.

In moments, Cora's heart had self-repaired!

Charles steadied his hands and inserted blooded conduits, repairing the damaged septa and arteries, draining the pleural effusion.

His Anopower flowed out abundantly, and miraculously, Cora's body seemed to cooperate with him.

Wherever his scalpel paused, the tissues automatically returned to their places, facilitating his actions.

Time passed, and Charles finally let out a deep breath, stitching the last thread.

Cora's breathing became steady, her vital signs stabilizing as she fell into a deep sleep.

"Could she have... an Anopower..." Suchat's expression was grave.

He remembered a colleague in the Rainy Forest, whose severed leg had self-repaired after an explosion.

That person was a B-class regeneration Aberrant.

Cora's heart had just fully restored itself.

The speed and difficulty were beyond belief.

Suchat was about to speak when he met Onyx's scrutinizing gaze.

Onyx looked at everyone, especially Yuui and Suchat, his voice chilling.

"Everything that happened here today stays here. No one is to speak a word of it."

CHAPTER 36

Promises

"Ah..."

Charles Franz yawned as he walked sleepily into the hospital room.

The past few days had been rough, with everyone taking turns to watch over Cora Thornton through the night.

None of them had gotten much rest, but fortunately, Cora had woken up last night, and her vital signs had stabilized.

As the lead surgeon, Charles made it his duty to check on his patients post-operation, even though his life had taken a downturn. Mid-yawn, he stopped abruptly—his patient was gone!

Charles hurried over and yanked back the blanket, revealing Damian's fluffy head.

Damian was sleeping soundly, drooling on the pillow, completely lost in a sweet dream.

Anger surged through Charles, and he smacked Damian's head without mercy.

"Still sleeping? Your sister ran away!"

Damian sat up with his eyes closed, mumbling groggily, "Run away? Cora? Where's she?"

How could a patient just disappear like that?

Damian had been on watch duty but had fallen asleep out of exhaustion.

In his dream, someone had gently picked him up and lovingly

patted his head.

Damian felt like he was floating on soft clouds, curling up in the blanket like a caterpillar, and then... he lost consciousness.

Charles looked around and saw that Cora had taken the IV stand and the nutrient fluids with her, not even leaving behind the medicine box. He couldn't help but laugh out of frustration.

He couldn't decide if Cora was obedient or not. If she was obedient, she wouldn't have run away the moment she woke up. But if she wasn't, she sure remembered all the medical instructions and didn't forget to take her meds.

Shaking his head, Charles sighed, blaming himself for getting worked up so early in the morning.

His exhaustion returned.

"Fine, you guys go look for her."

"Where are you going?" Damian tugged on his sleeve.

"To sleep." Charles replied righteously, lying down on the nearby sofa and falling asleep in three seconds flat.

This was too much! How could he leave a little kid to handle such a big mess alone?

A few minutes later, Onyx, Yuui, and Suchat, all summoned by a distressed Damian, gathered in the hospital room.

"I checked Manzoni Street. She's not there," Suchat reported.

"Then let's search further. She just woke up and was still badly injured. She shouldn't have gone far," Yuui said worriedly.

"I want to go too!"

Damian, feeling guilty for losing Cora, raised his hand energetically, insisting on joining the "Find My Sister" mission.

"Ah..." Charles turned over on the sofa, completely unaffected by their conversation.

Onyx touched the cold side of the bed that Cora had left, whispering, "No need to look. I know where she went."

Felalakas Public Cemetery.

This place was desolate, reserved for the burial of those without family, history, or even names.

The AI patrol squad ensured the streets were searched daily and transported any unclaimed bodies exceeding the time limit to this desolate place reserved for the burial of those without family, history, or even names.

Bodies that had been dead for two days were already cremated. Their ashes stored in small boxes.

The screen ahead displayed a brief epitaph: "Here lies an unnamed traveler, buried on December 24, New Era Year 46."

A pair of slender hands placed a pure white calla lily next to the screen.

On top of the box, among various items, lay a few insignias, showing the deceased's identity.

Cora picked out seven belonging to the 11th Division, cleaned them, and put them in her pocket.

Onyx found her sitting on the top platform, quietly gazing at the graves.

The December wind ruffled her hair.

Her expression was one of unprecedented serenity.

"Your heart was just stitched up, and you dared to sneak out? Be careful, it might break again. Charles might not help you next time."

"Shh," Cora gestured for him to be quiet.

"Don't tattle. I'll go back soon."

Onyx chuckled.

There was no need for him to tattle; once Damian, the little loudspeaker, started yelling, everyone would know.

Cora tucked her loose hair behind her ear and whispered, "I feel like so many people have died recently, so suddenly."

She looked down at her palm, where a blue light flickered weakly. She tried to gather her powers, but the light sputtered and went out.

Her mental energy was severely damaged and would take time to recover.

"I couldn't save Kiwamu, nor could I save Jeremy."

Despite having great powers, people around her kept dying.

For the first time, Cora felt utterly powerless. "I can't save anyone."

Onyx already knew what had happened.

Cora had told them everything once she woke up.

The silver wheelchair stopped beside her, and they both looked at the small screen.

"No one expects you to be a savior. You have no obligation to save everyone."

"Jeremy Wolfgang's death wasn't sudden."

"You said Sanada and Punk came through a spatial rift. Even the 'Bloody Hunter' showed up, meaning they had been targeting this place for a while and came prepared."

Cora frowned, thinking slowly.

"Came prepared... Could it be that Jaden Sheen was tracked?"

"No, it wasn't Jaden Sheen." Onyx shook his head slowly. "It was Wolfgang."

"If Jaden had been a problem, he would've been hunted down on the way to Grass Pit. Since he made it safely to Felalakas, it proves that he hadn't drawn the Alliance's attention until then."

Onyx analyzed calmly, "The problem lies with Jeremy Wolfgang. The mission he took on was extremely risky, with countless eyes on him, trying to either steal the credit or eliminate a major threat against him."

"Everyone wants Petros Sheen dead," Onyx sighed.

Because of the key, every step Jeremy took was extremely perilous, like walking on a tightrope.

When he found the suspected key, Jaden Sheen, the tightrope, snapped.

Cora was silent for a moment before pointing out Onyx's mistake.

"Not everyone."

She recalled what she saw on the rooftop that day.

"Jeremy didn't intend to kill Jaden. He wanted to take him back to be dealt with by the General personally."

Onyx was taken aback, his voice faint.

"Is that so? But looking at the result, it makes no difference."

Jeremy's matter was now beyond verification, and any further discussion was pointless.

Cora took one last look at the resting ashes and walked out with Onyx.

"What are you going to do about Yuui and Suchat?"

"About what?"

"Your heart can heal itself. Do you know what that means?" Onyx's tone was serious.

"No matter the reason, a heart shattered like that healing itself will cause you great trouble."

"Dr. Franz, not mutating after being bitten, has already stirred up enough trouble. If your situation gets exposed, do you know how many crazy scientists will want to dissect you to study every cell and gene?"

Cora shivered at the picture Onyx painted.

She had realized before that she had extraordinary healing abilities.

No matter the wound, it left no scar. Even zombie scratches didn't cause mutations.

She had thought it was a side effect of her awakened powers.

Now, it seemed the real reason was far beyond her understanding.

She didn't want to be a research subject. "What does this have to do with them?"

"I won't say anything about your situation. Damian and Charles are with you all the time and won't have the chance to say anything, either."

"As for those two..." Onyx's voice was distant.

Yuui and Suchat were "outsiders" with a history, making them hard to trust.

"She probably won't betray us," Cora said, knowing that Yuui had risked her life to save her from Punk.

She believed Yuui wouldn't do such a thing. "But you're right, it's hard to trust again after betrayal..."

"So I suggest killing them to keep things simple," Onyx suggested lightly.

Cora gasped, slowly clenching her fist, ready to punch him. But she stopped, clutching her chest.

"Ah... my heart hurts."

Cora wasn't one to fake pain; if she said it hurt, it really did.

Onyx laughed. "I know you don't want to, so there's only one choice left. Let them join F777, to stay with you and be easier to supervise."

"Join F777?" Cora was surprised.

She hadn't considered this possibility.

"Well, 'join' might not be the right word. Think of them as

temporary companions without genuine loyalty."

"Will they agree?"

"It shouldn't be a problem. The only conflict is the Throne Tournament, but remember why we're taking part?"

"Money."

The three of them entered the tournament to earn NPA credits. It had been so long that Cora nearly forgot their original goal.

Onyx nodded. "So, there's no conflict in what we want."

Yuui wanted Ilia's promise, while they were just after the money.

If they united and won, there would be no conflict of interest.

"Oh."

Cora discussed this with Yuui.

The two walked quietly together for a while.

"Their problem is resolved," Cora said slowly in the serene atmosphere, "What about yours?"

"Mine?" Onyx was momentarily taken aback.

"Yeah, S-class, psychic abilities. That day... I sensed it."

Onyx's wheelchair stopped. He was momentarily at a loss for words.

Cora turned, her expression fierce, and approached him step by step.

"A frail researcher?"

"An ordinary person?"

"Holding onto someone's coattails?"

Thinking back to their first encounter, the powerful killing intent she sensed must have been from Onyx.

His leg injury was from something else.

How could two C-class Aberrants, like Bob Young and Yara Ursula, possibly kill an S-class like him?

Cora placed her hands on the wheelchair. Her presence was intimidating.

With each step she took, Onyx retreated until he could go no further, his back pressed against the wheelchair.

Their noses were barely an inch apart.

Cora lowered her head, her eyes blazing with anger. "You've been lying to me from the start."

Onyx protested his innocence. "I never lied to you. You just never asked."

How outrageous, turning it into her fault now?

Just as she was about to retort, she realized how close she was to Onyx. She could count his long, thick eyelashes. She paused, taking a slight step back.

She asked earnestly, "Have you never trusted me?"

"No." Onyx was silent for a long time before giving a definitive answer. "Completely trusting someone is very hard for me."

Saying she wasn't disappointed or hurt would be a lie, but Onyx's honesty left Cora at a loss for words.

"Cora." Onyx's deep voice softly called her name.

Cora glanced at him unhappily, remaining silent.

"Maybe you think I'm full of lies and that I'm insincere."

Cora tilted her head, her expression clearly stating, "Aren't you?"

Onyx sighed, "I can't give 100% trust, but there is one thing I can promise."

"As long as you ask, as long as I can answer, I will never lie to you."

"Oh," Cora responded.

After a few seconds, she quietly questioned, "Didn't you lie to me before? About the whole pharmaceutical researcher thing?"

"That wasn't meant for you. If you believed it, is that my fault?" Onyx raised an eyebrow.

Cora's temper flared up, and she angrily kicked at Onyx's wheelchair, making it spin in circles.

Onyx, exasperated, said, "Cora, behave yourself. You're sick. Can't you just be good for once? Hmm?"

Cora kicked harder, accidentally straining her wound. She hissed in pain, clutching her chest and squatting down.

This vulnerable side of her was a stark contrast to her usual spirited self.

Onyx flipped her hood over her head and gently ruffled her hair.

"Be good. Don't make a fuss."

CHAPTER 37

Collaboration

Cora playfully messed around for a while, but her adult rationality quickly pulled her back, preparing to reunite with the others.

Just after stepping out of the cemetery, a wall of flowing data appeared out of thin air. Layers of codes made up of countless small squares dissipated, and Ilia walked out of the void.

Cora was internally surprised.

This place was remote, without even a few surveillance cameras, let alone a holographic projection.

Although artificial intelligence was omnipresent, Ilia's sudden appearance was too abrupt.

How did he manage it?

Cora and Onyx halted, their eyes warily fixed on the figure before them.

His appearance at this moment was not a good sign.

Ilia leisurely observed her for a moment, a pleased smile on his face. "So, you're still alive."

Cora frowned slightly. She was now filled with suspicion and wariness towards Ilia.

Putting aside the events at the tower, he had clearly known everything back then, known about the Bloody Hunter, yet he left her with a vague "blood and carnage," guiding her to Manzoni Street for reasons unknown.

"Surprised to see me? Judging by your expression, you don't seem very welcoming," Ilia started the conversation.

His dazzling golden hair shimmered in the sunlight, as if coated with a layer of honey-like sheen.

"Although it was just a casual effort, I helped you fend off an attack. Aren't you going to thank me?"

"Oh..." Cora thanked him emotionlessly, "Thank you."

She could have killed Punk herself, but unfortunately, his unexpected ambush foiled her plans.

Cora was never careless or underestimated her enemies.

This time, her severe injuries were due to not knowing the existence of dual-element Aberrants, and even more so not expecting Punk's other power to be the rare Time element.

But S-class Punk was not invincible.

Cora thought silently. If she encountered him again, she would definitely cut off his head.

Ilia circled her slowly, observing her shoulders, limbs, and fingers with pure admiration, devoid of any frivolity or lewdness.

"If I hadn't already made my choice, I would have liked your body just as much."

Cora stared at him expressionlessly for a while before coldly speaking, "I can kill you just as easily."

Ilia met her gaze for two seconds, sensed the killing intent bursting from her, and quickly changed his tone. "Just joking."

"I came to tell you that the T.T.T. will be postponed for three months. During these three months, I don't want any accidents in Felalakas."

After experiencing rebel battles, zombie sieges, and bloody explosions, Felalakas was already scarred and couldn't withstand any more devastation.

The city urgently needed a period of peace to restore its prosperity.

The day before, the advancing contestants had already received the notification about the postponement of the T.T.T.

Why did Ilia come specifically to tell her this? Cora was puzzled.

"What's it to me?"

Ilia's tone was meaningful.

"Of course it concerns you, because you are the biggest accident.

Although I sent the Bloody Hunter back, as long as you remain here, who knows when they might return?"

"So I have a suggestion. Why don't you go out for a while?"

She understood the reasoning.

They didn't want her here, thinking her presence would bring trouble to Felalakas.

But did she really have such a significant impact that the highest ruler himself came to expel her?

Cora glanced at Ilia.

His tone was relaxed, but his expression didn't seem like he was joking.

This "suggestion" wasn't unreasonable. They hadn't planned to stay in Felalakas long-term anyway, and there was no need to confront him at this point.

Cora nodded. "Okay, but I have a few questions."

"Go ahead."

A large chair was constructed from the data stream.

Ilia sat in it, his posture relaxed, like the supreme king ruling over Felalakas' fate.

"My ranking, did you change it?" It was a statement rather than a question.

Cora remembered Punk's words clearly. She was an S-class strong attack type metal Aberrant, but her Aberrant Certificate only showed an A-class.

Thinking about it, all the tests were done in Felalakas. The only one who could alter the results with no one knowing was Ilia.

Ilia didn't deny it. "Yes."

"Why?"

"Felalakas is my city. If an S-class Aberrant appeared here, it would attract too much attention. I don't want too much focus at this critical moment."

Ilia's expression was indifferent, as if tampering with someone's Aberrant level was a trivial matter.

"Anyway, the ranking isn't that important for you. It's actually more convenient to be an A-class when you're out there."

He smiled, his facial expression seemingly richer, more human-like.

"Just didn't expect... you aren't the only hidden S-class."

Ilia's gaze fell on Onyx, who was sitting in a wheelchair behind them.

Onyx smiled slightly, his expression calm.

Ilia looked at him for a moment longer before turning his gaze away.

"If you're so concerned about Felalakas, why release the zombies?" Cora asked.

"Why shouldn't I?" Ilia countered.

"If a room is dirty, it needs to be cleaned. Get rid of what I don't want, and what's left is all that I like." His tone was casual, sending chills down one's spine.

Cora pursed her lips. "Why do you collect zombies and host the T.T.T.?"

Ilia slowly smiled.

"Because I'm bored. Don't you find it interesting to observe humans displaying various expressions? Aberrants and their former kin slaughtering each other. What a spectacular show, only in Felalakas."

Cora fully understood now.

This unique AI ruler acted purely on his whims, disregarding right and wrong, making it impossible to judge him by human moral standards.

"I have no more questions," Cora said.

Ilia smiled slightly. "Then, see you at the tournament in three months."

With that, he disappeared on the spot.

"We all underestimated him. Perhaps even Lyon's rebellion was part of his plan."

Onyx's expression was grave.

Since the beginning of the T.T.T., this super AI had been playing a grand game.

Cora turned her head. "Why three months?"

Onyx pondered. "He's eliminating potential risks. There's only one possibility: during these three months, he can't manage Felalakas."

Cora was stunned. Why couldn't Ilia manage Felalakas? Unless... he had something more important to do.

"Thyrion Lucas..."

Cora muttered a name.

Since Ilia took Thyrion Lucas away, she hadn't seen him again.

The way Ilia casually mentioned "body" always gave her a creepy feeling.

When Cora returned, Damian immediately transformed into a clingy little charmer, sticking to her and refusing to let go.

"Sis, did you cuddle me to sleep last night?"

His voice was sweet. His eyes were watery and blinking adorably.

"Yeah, you need good sleep to grow tall."

Cora patted his curly hair, playing the older sibling role.

In front of her, Damian was always obedient and charming, but Cora had witnessed his rage and foul-mouthed tirades at the Sakura Shelter.

She knew his true personality wasn't as perfect as he appeared.

But so what? Compared to those lifeless, never-to-be-seen-again people, his vibrant existence was good enough.

After soothing Damian, Cora approached Yuui. "I need to tell you something."

Yuui was carefully applying lipstick in front of a mirror; she had an online interview to record soon.

"You and Suchat are joining F777."

Yuui's hand trembled, smearing the lipstick and leaving an awkward line at the corner of her mouth.

"Say that again?"

She asked incredulously, thinking she had misheard.

"You and Suchat are joining F777."

Yuui's eyes widened, and she pointed a trembling finger at Cora.

"Cora, I risked so much to save you. I thought we were even! Are you still holding a grudge because of Mirror Lake?"

"No..."

"Not only do you lack gratitude, but you also want me to keep working for you? How can you be so heartless?"

The actress's drama queen mode kicked in as she collapsed onto the table, tears brimming in her eyes as she looked at Cora accusingly.

Cora mumbled softly, "It's Onyx's idea, he's afraid you might spill the beans... about my heart."

Onyx was mercilessly thrown under the bus.

Yuui's fake crying caught in her throat, her voice rising sharply in anger. "Nonsense! Do I look like that kind of person?!"

"Actually, you can think of it as a deal." Cora explained seriously.

Having Yuui and Suchat join them, working together until the T.T.T. ended, whether they got eliminated or won the championship. After that, Cora would leave Felalakas. By then, it wouldn't matter if Yuui spilled the secret. Yuui could choose to exit.

This proposal was both a restriction—limiting their freedom during this period—and a new partnership led by Cora post-Mirror Lake.

Their relationship would be like temporary teammates, not demanding close bonds but coordinated actions, with the enticing condition laid out clearly.

"If we win the championship, we'll share the prize money and grant you the wish-making opportunity."

"That's my promise."

Yuui paused after listening, understanding that as the competition progressed, stronger opponents would emerge.

Winning the championship alone with Suchat would be tough, but if they joined F777, they could form a powerful, invincible five-member team.

Her heartbeat quickened, and she held her head, forcing herself to calm down. "Wait, let me think this through."

She thought all afternoon, finally appearing radiant after dinner.

"We can join F777." Her first words were an agreement.

Damian, who was happily sipping juice, was so shocked that he dropped his juice box. He was dumbfounded.

Why did the people he disliked always end up as his teammates? The world was so cruel to him!

"But I have one condition." Yuui continued.

"I need him," she pointed at Charles Franz, who was napping on the sofa, "to heal someone for me."

Charles again.

No wonder healing Aberrants were always in high demand.

Both Cora's heart and Onyx's legs needed Charles, and now Yuui did, too.

But whether Charles would cooperate, Cora had no guarantee.

The priority was to fulfill Charles' wish first, so they could negotiate terms later.

Cora approached the sofa.

Usually, his presence was low-key, but no one could easily ignore him.

"Thank you," she said to Charles.

Without his help, even if her heart could self-heal, the process would have been much more difficult.

Charles lifted his eyelids slightly and responded with a light, "hmm."

He had sworn never to pick up a scalpel again, yet he broke his vow so soon.

"We'll leave Felalakas in a couple of days. Once I feel better, I'll help you." Cora explained their plan and then asked directly, "Can you tell me now which ruler you want to kill?"

"No need," Charles replied after a moment of silence, giving an unexpected answer.

"Saying it won't change the fact that it's impossible."

"Why is it impossible?" Cora was puzzled. "Aren't we strong enough?"

Yuui and Suchat had already agreed to join F777. Including Charles, they had two S-class, three A-class, and one B-class members. Such a luxurious configuration could dominate anywhere, right?

Charles slowly shook his head. "It's not about strength."

"To kill someone, you must first meet them."

"That district has the strictest admission policy. You can't get in, so there's no point in talking about it."

"The strictest admission policy? Are you referring to District C33?" Onyx suddenly spoke up.

CHAPTER 38

Share we go?

The New Pacific Alliance has fifty C-Districts, each with its unique and irreplaceable function. The Deep Woods (District C33) serves as the Alliance's arsenal.

The economic lifeline of Deep Woods is tightly controlled by local large-scale arms dealers. These local powers have absolute authority and are even secretly aligned with the highest ruler, continuously providing him with money and resources to gain greater benefits.

The ruler, supported by military power, is an absolute dictator, known to the outside world as the "Tyrant." Unlike Felalakas' democratic elections, Deep Woods' ruler has remained unchanged for twenty-six years.

The entry requirements for District C33 had been notoriously strict since before the apocalypse. It did not welcome refugees or people from the numbered districts. The immigration review process was complex and lengthy. If an outsider's background was even slightly unclear, their application would be mercilessly rejected. Even those with perfectly clean records could sometimes wait for months with no response.

Since the apocalypse, these conditions have become even more extreme, almost completely sealing off all entry channels. While Felalakas welcomes all travelers, Deep Woods has welded its gates shut, refusing entry to anyone.

Onyx finished analyzing the intelligence about Deep Woods.

Cora counted on her fingers, realizing they hit every pitfall: refugees (Charles's current status is missing, hence a refugee), people from the numbered districts (herself and Damian), and those with questionable backgrounds (Onyx and Suchat). Only Yuui had some hope, but she couldn't operate under her real name outside.

No wonder Charles said it was pointless to know. If she were an immigration officer in Deep Woods, she wouldn't let these "dangerous elements" in either.

After listening, Charles stared intently at Onyx. "How do you know so much?"

Cora quickly interjected, "He knows everything about the Alliance."

She proudly raised her chin as she spoke, as if Onyx's knowledge somehow glorified her.

Onyx caught her proud expression and silently smiled.

"How about sneaking in?" Suchat, who had been quietly listening, suggested a plan very much in line with his character.

Onyx quickly dismissed the idea.

"The borders are heavily guarded, with specialized organizations for combat smugglers. The moment you step into Deep Woods, you'd be met by thousands of particle cannons, turned to dust in three seconds."

"Is there no other way?" Yuui asked. "Like fabricating a special reason, like a business trip or a family visit?"

Onyx shook his head. "It's hard to deceive them. The Alliance's registration office is no joke."

Everyone sighed in despair.

Damian, a beat slower, joined in with a long sigh to fit in, looking like a little adult. Charles's expression remained calm, the dark flames of hatred in his heart burning steadily, never extinguished, but he had long since learned to face the powerless reality.

In the silence, Onyx slowly spoke, "Actually... there's not no way at all."

Five pairs of eyes turned to him simultaneously.

Cora urged, "Spit it out."

Then she added, "Keep it simple, no beating around the bush."

Onyx, reminded of his old faults, cleared his throat. "Without entry permits, we could forge fake ones."

"All registration information is synced to personal terminals. We could tamper with the system, alter our registration data to make it appear we're from District C33. This way, we wouldn't need to apply for entry, slipping into Deep Woods unnoticed."

"You mean hacking the registration system and altering the records?" Yuui was stunned by his audacity.

Cora thought of Ilia. Her own power level was altered by him. If not for Punk, she might still be in the dark. The idea was good, but to do it flawlessly, they lacked the most crucial element.

Cora looked at Onyx skeptically. "Can you... hack the system?"

"Can you hack the system?" Damian mimicked her, frowning.

"Yeah, you make it sound easy. Can you?" Yuui crossed her arms, giving him a sidelong glance.

The other two men gave Onyx a bit of a face, only casting skeptical glances.

"No," Onyx answered bluntly.

"But," Onyx continued leisurely, "I can't do it, but someone else can."

Cora, Damian, and Yuui asked in unison, "Who?"

Onyx mentioned a name. "Remember Thyrion Lucas?"

Cora nodded, "I remember."

"Thyrion Lucas wasn't valued in the Lucas family because of his impure eye color. Even if he disappeared, it wouldn't attract much attention. But as a genetically preferred individual, his awakened power was the Lucas family's exclusive hacking ability."

"You want to find Thyrion Lucas?" Cora reminded him. "But he's with Ilia."

Onyx smiled slightly. "I'm not looking for him, but he reminds me of someone."

"The Lucas family produced a genius hacker named Felix Lucas over a decade ago. He was the top hacker, unmatched both within the Lucas family and across the entire Alliance. If it involved data, he could effortlessly dominate."

"He and I... well, we're kind of friends."

Onyx's eyelids twitched at the thought of the "glorious" deeds Felix dragged him into, all of which were disastrous memories.

"Where is he now? In Grass Pit?" Cora asked.

Onyx replied gravely, "No, he's in... Death Hell."

"What??"

Not only Cora, but everyone else was equally shocked.

Suchat suddenly spoke up, "Do you mean the Death Hell in District F191?"

"Yes," Onyx confirmed. "The underground Death Hell of the City of Sin."

The cities in the Alliance are not only ranked by grade, but their numbers also reveal much about them. The lower the number, the stronger their overall power and higher their status in the Alliance. District F191, however, is the worst of the worst, completely abandoned by the Alliance, the kind they wish they could throw away immediately.

Although it has no official name, it is notoriously known as the City of Sin.

Cora couldn't understand. If Felix Lucas was as brilliant as Onyx described, he should have been celebrated within the Lucas family.

How could he end up in the dark depths of the Death Hell?

Onyx sighed. "Because Felix Lucas isn't just a genius. He's a complete madman."

"Five years ago, he almost destroyed the Lucas family's supercomputer. After an Alliance trial, it was exiled him to Death Hell, with a life sentence, never to be released."

Silence fell over the group.

A supercomputer is the Lucas family's most critical asset. This was truly a case of "I'll even destroy myself if I have to."

Felix Lucas was indeed a madman.

"So you're saying we first need to find your friend, rescue him from Death Hell, and then have him hack the registration system?"

Yuui was skeptical. "But I think the former is more difficult. Has anyone ever successfully rescued someone from Death Hell?"

"District F is dangerous and hard to reach," Suchat also doubted.

"At least District F has no entry restrictions." Onyx maintained his calm, even joking.

Cora was concerned about another issue. "Are you sure he'll help us?"

"That's easy. Once we find him, I'll handle it," Onyx promised.

"But it's Death Hell, not a marketplace…"

"Brother, you're pretty crazy too, huh?"

"It sounds impossible…"

"Sis, what is Death Hell?"

The group chattered on for a while, with no one able to convince the others.

"Stop!" Cora took a deep breath and shouted, called for order. "One at a time."

She paused, her eyes gradually becoming resolute. "I'll handle the rescue."

Suchat spun his knife in his hand, his tone flat. "I'll handle the reconnaissance."

Yuui opened her terminal. "I can arrange transportation to District F191."

The division of labor was instantly clear.

Damian looked left and right, realizing he couldn't contribute to anything. He was turning into exactly what Onyx had described—a useless burden on the group.

Feeling wronged, Damian pouted, but then his eyes lit up as he thought of his value. "I have money. I'll handle anything that requires spending!"

Charles watched the people in front of him, his palms tightening and then relaxing.

He knew that, ultimately. They were making these decisions for him. They needed him for his abilities, but what did it matter? As long as he could get his revenge, he was willing to give anything.

"Then, let's try it." He had slept long enough; it was time to wake up.

"We can't stay in Felalakas any longer. Let's head back to Sycamore for a few days to rest and plan our next move," Onyx concluded.

The first group meeting of the new F777 team ended with a preliminary agreement, a resounding success.

Sycamore checkpoint.

A private steam vehicle opened its cockpit under the guards' direction to undergo entry inspection.

Cora got out, connected her terminal with the guard's system, and her Anopower information was displayed on the light screen.

"Sorry, ma'am, but your commission has expired, and your entry permit is no longer valid."

The "medical support" task had originally been a part-time job, allowing Cora to volunteer one day and slack off the next, even taking side gigs like rescuing Dorothy. After half a month, this B-level commission had been changed to "full-time," requiring her to be on call 24/7.

"Because of the increased pressure from the zombie threat, manpower is short. The ruler issued a new policy," the young guard explained earnestly, "Without a valid entry permit, you can't enter."

Onyx leaned out of the vehicle, glancing at the guard. "You must be new here, right?"

"How did you know?" The young guard was surprised.

He had only joined the security team a week ago and was still performing basic checkpoint duties. Had he done something wrong?

Cora understood why.

During his time in Sycamore, Onyx had spent every day in the archives, thoroughly familiarizing himself with the Anopower users of Sycamore.

Onyx nodded slightly, his tone calm.

"Last month, we helped Captain Kennedy fend off a zombie horde. Brother, you can see we're law-abiding citizens, not troublemakers. Could you make an exception and let us in?"

"I... I can't make that decision," the guard scratched his head.

He had heard stories from his seniors about the events at the Sakura Shelter but wasn't sure if these were the people. If they tricked him and he let them in, he'd be held responsible.

As they were stuck in a standoff at the gate, Conrad Kennedy passed by with a middle-aged man.

Cora spotted them and immediately called out, "Captain Kennedy!"

Conrad noticed them and whispered to the man beside him.

They walked towards the group.

The middle-aged man had a calm demeanor and resolute eyes. He wore traditional attire from the old era, emitting a faint herbal scent.

The young guard immediately stood at attention and saluted sharply, his voice loud and excited.

"Hello, sir, Governor!"

So this was the ruler of Sycamore, Cora thought.

The man who had single-handedly organized the city's defense, the guardian of the city of medicine.

Conrad respectfully introduced them.

"Dr. Chang, these are the members of F777 who helped us at Sakura."

Dr. Julian Chang, the highest ruler of Sycamore and a doctor specializing in ancient medicine, nodded to them. "I thank you on behalf of Sycamore."

Cora felt a bit embarrassed meeting such a courteous ruler and waved her hands.

"What's the issue here? Why are they stuck at the gate?" Conrad asked.

The young guard explained that Cora and her team did not have valid entry permits.

"Dr. Chang, they want to stay in Sycamore for a few days. What do you think?" Conrad asked softly.

Dr. Chang looked surprised. "You don't plan to stay in Sycamore?"

"No, we're just passing through, planning to move on to another place," Onyx replied politely.

Dr. Chang sighed regretfully.

As an ordinary person, he paid special attention to and actively recruited high-level Anopower users.

A powerful team like F777 joining the security forces would enhance Sycamore's safety.

However, he understood the importance of forging good relations over making enemies.

"Sycamore will never turn away friends who have helped us. Let them in. Consider it my special permission," Dr. Chang said with a smile, "But the checks must be done to ensure they are not zombified and pose no threat."

"That's fair," Onyx agreed with a smile.

Dr. Chang gave them a final, solemn look. "Sycamore's doors will always be open to you."

Once inside, Yuui couldn't help but remark, "This ruler seems pretty nice."

Cora, now more mature, understood not to judge people by appearances alone. She turned to Onyx. "What do you think?"

Onyx pondered. "Julian Chang is very astute and wise. As an ordinary person, he understands things clearly."

"No one survives the fall of a city. Julian Chang's life is tied to this city's fate. Protecting Sycamore is also protecting himself. He is indeed a competent ruler."

The next day, Cora visited the 119th Hospital. She was there to see Vincent Anderson and William Strong, the only two remaining members of the Eleventh Azure Squad.

When she first saw them, Cora almost didn't recognize them.

William, who used to be a cheerful giant, always joking with Payne, now had an entire right leg made of bionic material. He hadn't fully adapted to it yet, making his movements awkward.

Vincent had lost a significant amount of weight. The once dashing soldier, who had boldly blasted open the side door of U-Lab while smoking a cigarette, was gone. He had become somber, reminiscent of another Jeremy Wolfgang.

Cora stopped in front of him, pondering how to start the conversation.

"If you're here, to tell me about Maeda and the captain, I already know," Vincent preempted her. "We have an internal life detection frequency. A few days ago, all signals disappeared."

William lowered his head, trembling, his mechanical leg creaking. They say 'Men Don't Cry' easily, but he couldn't control the tears welling up in his eyes.

"I was there that day," Cora began slowly.

Vincent looked at her sharply, his eyes intensely focused. "So you know what happened, right?"

Cora nodded and recounted everything that had happened on Manzoni Street to Vincent and William.

"Bloody Hunter..." Vincent repeated slowly, clenching his fists, his gaze icy.

"What are your plans now?" Cora asked.

"I'm going back to Northern Yard (District B7). The mission failed, and apart from Vincent Anderson and William Strong, the entire Eleventh Azure Squad perished. I have to report everything to General Sheen," Vincent said seriously.

Cora took out seven badges from her pocket and handed them to Vincent. "Take them with you."

"Thank you," Vincent said, accepting the badges carefully. "We're leaving. If there's a chance, see you in the Northern Yard."

Cora leaned against the corridor, watching Vincent and William leave the hospital.

"Cora, what brings you here?" Lynn Rolling had just finished a surgery, rubbing his tired forehead as he stepped out for some air, surprised to see her. "I thought you were done volunteering."

"I am. I need to go on a trip."

"A trip? I heard it's chaotic outside. Take care of yourself."

"Thanks, Dr. Rolling."

They quietly enjoyed the breeze for a while. Behind them, doctors in white coats hurried through the corridor. In hospitals, doctors were always the busiest, going from one surgery to the next, sometimes working non-stop for hours with only a few minutes of rest.

Noticing her gaze, Lynn sighed softly. "Lately, there's been an increase in patients turning into zombies. The medical pressure is secondary. I'm more worried that the patients and their families can't handle it mentally, which could cause trouble."

"Dr. Rolling, can I ask you a question?" Cora said.

"Of course."

"In your eyes, what kind of person is Charles Franz?"

Charles wanted to disappear from the medical scene in Sycamore, and Cora respected his wish, not revealing his whereabouts. Since he refused to talk about himself, she could only learn about him indirectly from others.

"Dr. Franz...?" Lynn's usually lively demeanor turned serious for a moment before she suddenly blurted out, "I actually had a crush on him for a while."

Cora's eyes widened in surprise.

"Don't get me wrong, he was married long before. When I found out, I gave up. Besides, I'm married now too." Lynn quickly clarified, seeing Cora's exaggerated reaction.

"I know little about his personal life, but I'm certain of one thing: he's an excellent doctor, a very good one."

"Every year, Sycamore hosts free medical clinics to help children with chronic illnesses who can't afford surgery. Dr. Franz always takes part, anonymously and secretly. I only found out by accident once; no one else in the hospital knows about it."

"He's very famous, yet he volunteers seeking nothing in return. He must genuinely want to help those kids."

"As a doctor, he has a compassionate heart and is truly gentle with his patients," Lynn smiled softly.

The Charles Lynn described was talented, proud, and incredibly kind-hearted, a stark contrast to the disheveled, grizzled man who spent his days with them, seemingly indifferent to everything except sleep.

What had happened to Charles to change him so drastically?

Cora silently repeated the name Deep Woods (District C33) in her mind. She would definitely go there.

Suchat was from Deep Woods.

Since Cora hadn't found his body in the dojo, he might have returned to District C33 earlier. If she met him there, she wanted to ask what exactly happened in the dojo during those apocalyptic days.

Two days later, Yuui secured a private transport convoy. After paying a toll fee, they could hitch a ride to District F191.

On January 1, New Calendar Year 47, four months after the apocalypse, on an ordinary sunny day, an at-that-time unknown team of Aberrants, F777, officially embarked on their journey to the City of Sin.

To Be Continued...

About Me

This is Jennifer. I have a deep passion for young adult romance and science fiction, with a penchant for weaving in the extraordinary, like zombies, into the ordinary.

About the Series

"Ethereal Artifacts" was originally serialized via a web novel platform. It's my first long series with all elements I like in my life: post-apocalypse, zombies, dystopian, cyberpunk, and of course, strong female leads.

Please Review

Your opinions matters! It is important for authors to improve themselves.